Savaged Devotion

SAVAGED ILLUSIONS TRILOGY • BOOK THREE

JENNIFER LYON

Savaged Devotion
Copyright © 2020 Jennifer Apodaca
All rights reserved.

Cover and Savaged Illusions Logo Designs:
Jaycee DeLorenzo of Sweet 'N Spicy Designs
Editor: Sashaknighteditor.com
Copy Editor: www.kimberlycannoneditor.com/
Formatted by: Author E.M.S.

Published by JenniferLyonBooks
www.jenniferlyonbooks.com

ISBN: 978-0-9984595-5-4

Savaged Devotion

Chapter 1

LIZA CADE SAT IN THE LIMO as they passed throngs of screaming rock fans and media held back by security outside the cemetery. For five long months, she'd avoided the media—and her husband—as much as possible. She wanted no part of that life anymore. Not the fame, the pressure, or the reminders of what she'd lost.

Stop it. Today wasn't about her, it was about the man they were gathering to say goodbye too. Her heart ached at the loss of Drake Vaughn. He'd saved so many boys no one else cared about through his mentoring program. But he couldn't save himself from cancer.

As the car slid to a stop at the drop-off site by the graveside service, Liza steeled herself. *Do it. Get out of the car.* Drake had done so much for her, so she'd damn well do this for him—show up and say goodbye with dignity.

The security detail hired for the funeral opened the car door, and Liza forced herself out of the gloom into the bright sunshine of San Diego, California. The air was heavy with the scent of flowers, grass and earth.

A few yards away, a huge awning had been erected. Beneath it, some mourners were seated in the rows of chairs, while others stood and talked in small clumps.

When she got closer, she spotted the gleaming, dark casket covered in a spray of white flowers, with more floral arrangements spreading out on both sides.

Drake was in there.

Her vision blurred, and pain pierced the shroud of numbness around her heart. Hot sorrow rose like a monster wave threatening to drown her. Not just for Drake, but also for her baby, and her marriage. For the family she'd so desperately wanted, the one she'd dared to think she deserved.

What a fool she'd been to believe that.

"Ma'am," the bodyguard on her left said. "Are you all right?"

She'd frozen in the grass like a statue. People were beginning to turn and notice her. Crap. Her goal was to slip in quietly, not draw attention. "Yes, thanks. I—" Her words stuck in her throat.

A thick group of men parted, and her husband strode out. The sunlight caught the natural blond highlights in his untamed brown hair and the raw determination in his eyes. His face was leaner, the bones more pronounced as if the claws of grief had sharpened them. The scar through his eyebrow was a stark reminder of the night their daughter had died, when Justice had left Liza asleep in the hospital and tried to kill Gene Hayes.

His blue dress shirt open at the collar, the sleeves rolled up and tucked into slim black pants. Damned if he didn't look more tortured and sexier than ever. Seeing him yanked at too many raw, festering places. She backed up a step, desperate to keep the distance between them.

He stopped at her retreat, leaving a few feet hovering between them. "Beth, come sit up front with us."

She ignored the nostalgia of hearing the nickname he always called her. The mourners were settling into seats. In the first row were Sloane and his girlfriend, Kat, along with John Moreno and his wife, Sherry. Seated behind them were the other four members of Justice's band, Lynx, Gray, Simon, and River.

Her stomach clenched. Memories poked and prodded.

"No. I'm here for Drake." Liza made a wide circle around Justice and headed for the last row of seats. She could hear security scrambling after her. Out in the open like this, Liza was a target.

She'd always be a target as long as Gene Hayes was out there, instead of rotting in a cell. She'd rather risk her life than her heart. She'd been down that road, and it led to shattering emotional devastation.

Never again.

She sat in a chair on the end of the row, hoping he'd pass her by to the front row.

He stopped by her shoulder. "Beth, I don't want you back here alone. Please—"

His words were cut off when a smooth voice announced, "Ladies and gentlemen, thank you all for coming out today. If everyone will take their seats, we will begin the service to commemorate the life of Drake Vaughn."

Liza stared at the minister to avoid her husband.

After a few seconds, he sighed. "We'll talk later." Justice walked away stiffly as if he had to push his muscles to obey.

Guilt nagged at the ice around her heart. She should have told him how sorry she was that he'd lost Drake, the man who'd helped change Justice's life after he got out of juvenile hall. But how could she get the words out when she couldn't look at Justice without the terrible, clawing grief threatening to crack through her numbness? If that happened, she'd break and shatter.

Better to keep her distance and stay in her emotional safe zone by not thinking about the past. Instead, she concentrated on the funeral, especially Sloane's powerful eulogy that burned her eyes with tears she didn't want to shed. Lowering her head, she whispered her goodbye to Drake and wished him the peace he deserved. The ceremony closed with final prayers, and guests were invited to file by the casket to pay their respect.

Liza rose with the others but held back. She couldn't go up there.

Drake's casket conjured the memory of another coffin, this one heartbreakingly small, white and edged in wings and roses. Icy sweat pricked her skin. She hurried across the grass, aiming for the line of limos to escape.

"Liza, wait."

The familiar voice surprised her enough that she turned before she thought about it.

Simon Bender, the lead guitarist for Savaged Illusions, and the man who'd labeled her the band's Yoko, jogged up to her.

Why had he stopped her? "What? I'm leaving."

The scar on Simon's cheek whitened, and tension practically twanged off the tall, lean man. "You have every right to hate me."

Why would he say that now? He hadn't cared about her feelings when he'd convinced the band to ban her from the tour. It hadn't mattered that she was Justice's wife or pregnant with his child. She'd been the girl who'd ruined one rock star, and Simon hadn't wanted her ruining their band too. None of them had.

"I'm sorry, Liza," Simon said. "So goddamned sorry. I've wanted to tell you, but you wouldn't see me or take my calls. I was wrong. We all were. We should never have banned you, or signed that contract with World Rock Stage once we realized Gene Hayes was part owner."

She internally recoiled at the name. Hayes had drugged and raped her when she was fourteen years old. Then, during the trial, he'd fled the country and been convicted in absentia. Liza felt like she was the one who'd been branded and judged.

Lynx jogged up, his tats gleaming in the sun. The drummer wore an MMA T-shirt with an old picture of Drake sweaty, shirtless and holding a UFC championship belt over his head in triumph. "I had to catch you. I'm sorry. We fucked up."

She started to answer when River's long stride ate up the distance as he closed in on her too. "We blamed you for the things Hayes did. You were the victim, and we made it worse. I regret that every damned day."

Before she could fully grasp that they were apologizing, Lynx jumped in. "Justice loves you, Liza. I've never seen him like this before. He's wrecked over the baby, and you."

Gray slid up beside Simon. The pianist wore a perfectly tailored navy suit that set off his blue eyes and blond hair. "Not one of us stood up for you when we should have. We lost sight of right and wrong and were protecting our careers over our friend's wife."

She couldn't handle this. "You didn't want me there. Didn't want me in his life or..." What was she doing? No. Just no. She didn't want to hear it, and she sure as hell wasn't up to absolving them when she couldn't even face herself in the mirror. Instead, she told them the truth. "You were right. I was too big a liability to Justice and the band." She couldn't even protect her baby. She didn't deserve to be a mother or have a family.

She spun and headed to the car. Her driver got out and stood by the rear door. When she heard footsteps behind her, she snapped, "Go away, Simon."

"Beth, it's me."

Keep going. Don't turn. Tremors skittered along Liza's spine, a recognition that was soul deep. She turned, the pull of the man she'd once loved stronger than her need to stay in the shadows.

"I have to go." It came out more of a plea than a statement. How did he still have this power over her?

Torment swam in his eyes. "To what? Go back to your condo and sit alone?" He grimaced. "Please, Beth, I need to know that you're okay. Come to Sloane's house. We're gathering over there, eating some barbeque and hanging out on the beach. It was Drake's favorite place." He held out his hand. "You don't have to be by yourself. Drake was your friend too."

Longing traveling through her to that weak and desperate girl inside her. She'd given in to that girl once, and that had led to utter devastation.

Liza shook her head, drawing away from him and into herself. When he touched her, she remembered their love, and it unleashed a torrent of aching for him. Until she recalled the hours in the hospital, people she didn't know telling her the baby was dead, and urging her to push. Her beautiful baby girl born silent and still.

All because Liza had done exactly what her aunt had told her not to, made bad decisions by falling in love with a rock star, and having a child with him. Never again. "My aunt was right. I took a stupid risk by falling in love with, and trusting, a rock star. Our baby paid the price. We did that..." It hurt so damned much. "We didn't protect our baby. I understand why you chose your career over me...you were doing it all along. But you risked her too." Hot tears tracked down her face, and she hated him for making her feel this.

Liza hated herself more.

"Beth." He fisted his hands, his face contorting in torment. "I can't stand when you cry alone. Let me hold you."

"No!" She spun away from him. She'd break if he touched her. All the anguish inside her would rush up, swelling so big her skin would stretch like a rubber band. Blood would rush in her ears and crank up and up to a piercing pitch, until all she could think about was escaping.

By cutting.

"Fuck."

The word came out a low snarl of pain and compelled her to turn. Lines of regret fanned out around the edges of Justice's eyes.

"I screwed up and hate myself for signing that contract. I told myself I was protecting you, but it was a lie. I was protecting myself by not telling you because I was scared of losing you. I own that, and I'm trying to be better, to be worthy of you. I'm doing everything I can think of. I bought the safest condo I could find for you when you refused to come home. I've told every media outlet I can that you're a smart and strong survivor of that sick child predator, Gene Hayes. And that I had known the baby was mine from the moment I learned you were pregnant. I always trusted you, never doubted that. Not once." He rocked slightly, as if so much need pulsed inside him he couldn't stay still. "What else can I do? Tell me, I'll do it."

She closed her eyes, trying to escape his desperation. She didn't want to relive this. "It doesn't matter anymore. Our daughter is dead, and I'm done."

"Done?" His head snapped up. "You've filed for divorce?"

She flinched and shook her head.

"Why?"

He wouldn't give her a break. Liza reached for the limo door, her fingers closed around the edge, needing something to hold on to. "I..." What? She just wasn't ready to think about that step. Couldn't. He was her baby's father, and the man she'd loved more than anything—except her child. Damn it, this was why she didn't want to near Justice. He made her think. Feel. Remember.

"Don't file, Beth."

Facing him, it was her turn to ask, "Why?"

"Wait a year. Give me a chance to prove my love and earn your forgiveness. We can see each other, reconnect and heal. I'm traveling for concerts, and you can come with us. It'll be good for you to get away."

A harsh, ugly laugh escaped her. "Did you ask them?" She nodded toward the four other men in his band standing a half dozen feet away. Yeah, they'd apologized, but the hurt ran too deep for her to fully believe it. "Last time you were on tour, I was banned. Told to stay home and keep quiet." She and Justice had had a few beautiful moments and so much ugliness. "You let them." Those words slipped out, tearing open more wounds.

"That won't happen again. I swear it, you'll be with me, and no one will tear us apart. No one."

Fatigue and grief a thick blanket weighed her down. There was no going back. "They already did."

His jaw clenched, and he rocked back as if she'd slapped him. "I can't bring our daughter back, and that's a guilt I'll live with every single day." Each word was low and rough with heartbreak.

He lifted his head, his eyes nearly animalistic with determination. "I will show her that her dad loves her mom. You, Beth. It's been you since the day we met. Before that day, I thought music was my everything. Then I met you and discovered the truth that *you're my everything*."

It was too much. She couldn't bear this. "Justice—"

"One year to show you that you can trust me, that our love is strong enough to survive this. If you need space, I'll back off for a while. I won't call or show up at work or your condo. I'll limit my contact to an occasional text until you're ready for more."

The plea was a demand wrapped up in a love so powerful it terrified her. She didn't deserve this love, didn't want it nor did she understand. "Why? I thought when I left you in Paris, you'd hate me like you hate your mother. So why?"

He leaned into her. "Because you're not my mother. She abandoned her child. Me. She never wanted me. You wanted our child. From the day you realized you were pregnant, you fought for Savanna Rose."

Liza flinched at the name. The one they'd chosen with such love and hope, and the one she hadn't been able to say since she'd returned from Paris.

Justice went on, "I'm not your family who abandoned you. I love you, Beth. I will always love you. I want you back."

The anger buried deep within the fog of her sorrow shot up her throat, and she blurted out, "I want Gene Hayes to pay. I want him publicly ruined and exposed for what he is. I want him to feel what it's like to lose the thing he loves the most." Damn it, hot tears of frustration stung her nose and slid down her face. "We don't always get what we want. Hayes keeps winning."

"Beth—" He reached for her again, his arms opening, his chest as familiar and comforting as anything she'd ever known, beckoning her. She could feel the icy numbness cracking, the utter devastation reaching to swamp her. She'd drown in it.

She turned to escape into the gloom of the limo, but stopped, unable to leave him hanging. She had to give him an answer. "One year. No contact unless we both agree. Then you file for divorce."

"I'd like to text you once in a while."

She dropped her head at his soft request. What difference did it make if he texted? She didn't have to answer or even have to read it. She could delete and forget.

"Fine." She climbed inside the limo. The door closed, locking her in the cavernous car, all the empty seats mocking her loneliness. It was better this way. Safer.

As the car pulled away, she couldn't resist looking back. Justice stood there, his shoulders tensed as if carrying more weight than he could bear, his face grim. His band stood behind him, but not with him.

Justice appeared as alone as she felt.

Chapter 2

DEAR JUSTICE,

I know your heart is heavy, and my dying right now was bad timing. I want to tell you that I'm proud of you. You have a gift, Justice. Many people in life have talent that they squander. You respected your voice and worked damn hard. You formed a band with an extraordinary group of men, and you have done your best for them in every way.

I'm proud of you for taking care of your grandmother and doing all you can for your father in his battle with PTSD. And I'm proud of how very much you love your wife and the daughter you both tragically lost.

That last night in Paris, when you got back to the room to find Liza had gone, leaving behind her rings and a goodbye letter, I saw you at a breaking point. That could have been your knockout punch. First you'd lost your daughter, then in the rage of your grief, lost your temper and tried to kill Hayes, landing your ass in a jail cell. And when you finally got out—your wife had left you.

Many men would have folded, crumbled or blamed the world.

But you stood there, holding Liza's wedding rings, and accepted the truth—you'd made a mistake that broke her trust in you. You vowed to win her back.

I believe in you, Justice. I have since the day I met you, and I will continue to believe in you when I'm gone from the earth. Find a way to show Liza you've grown and learned, and that she can trust in you to be her husband—the man who will put her first above all else.

I hope that I will see your grandmother again, and get a chance to hold your daughter. I will give them both your love.

Your friend,
Drake

Justice gathered around the fire pit on the deck of Sloane's beach house with Simon, River, Gray and Lynx. Sloane was inside with Kat saying goodbye to the last of the dinner guests who had come over after Drake's funeral. Just yards away, waves crashed in the rhythmic cadence of the sea. The other men's voices ebbed and flowed, but Justice kept thinking about Drake's letter Sloane had given him after the service.

Drake had stepped into Justice's life on the day he'd been released from juvenile hall. He'd been at a critical turning point in his life and could have easily gone down the troubled path. Drake had shown him how to accept responsibility for his past mistakes and how to make better choices. Drake had been proud of him until he'd fucked it all up, betraying his wife and child. And even after that—Drake still believed in him.

"Justice?"

He dragged his gaze from the flames of the fire pit to Lynx. "Yeah?"

"I kind of wondered if your dad would show up today. You know, bring Drake's dog by to say goodbye."

Radar had been a mangy mutt living on the streets and scavenging food when Drake found him and took him in. Just like many of the boys Drake had taken under his wing. "Drake didn't want that. He felt Radar had another journey in his life with my dad."

"Your dad has Drake's dog?" River couldn't seem to get his head around that. "I thought he'd given Radar to one of the boys he'd mentored. That dog was a sneaky little thief who stole my sandwiches and chips, but he was damned good with troubled kids."

Justice swallowed the irony. His dad wanted nothing to do with his son, or most people, but he took care of a dying man's dog. His dad still had a few surprises in him. "The first few times Drake was really sick in the hospital, Radar ran away trying to find him. No one could locate the dog, but somehow my dad realized Radar was missing and tracked him. Radar would only stay with my dad. Drake was so worried when he realized he had a short time left that he tried to slowly rehome Radar, but the dog ran away from every one. If Radar couldn't find Drake, then he'd find my dad. When Drake moved in here with Sloane, Dad ended up with Radar."

"Sounds a bit like Radar chose your dad," Gray pointed out. "Possibly to give Drake the peace of knowing he'd be okay."

"Maybe," Lynx said. "Drake seemed to believe that Noah needed Radar."

"I can't believe Drake's gone," Justice blurted.

How could a man who'd shaped and changed so many lives for the better not be here anymore?

"Cancer's a ruthless bitch." River drained his glass of scotch and poured another, then handed the bottle to Justice.

What the hell, he wasn't driving tonight. Why break the pattern now? He'd been drinking himself stupid three or four nights out of the week to keep himself from becoming a stalker who sat outside his estranged wife's condo desperately texting her to please open the door and talk to him.

The ache in his chest grew to a vicious throb, and he dumped out a few fingers of the amber liquor. He set the bottle down as Sloane walked out from the house. His eyes were red-rimmed with fatigue and sorrow. Focusing on him, Justice asked, "Where's Kat?"

"She went upstairs. I coaxed her into taking a pain pill and getting into bed to watch TV. It's been a long-ass day, and she hasn't slept much."

Sloane and Kat had been through a shitastic month between Kat nearly being killed, taking care of Drake, and finally losing him. Drake had been the closest thing Sloane had to a father.

"I saw you talking to Liza today." Sloane sat across from Justice, the fire pit between them. "All of you."

Before Justice could respond, Lynx jumped in. "That was brutal. We all tried to apologize, but Liza hates us, and she avoids Justice, as if being near him hurts."

"Why should she forgive us?" River demanded, his eyes dark and troubled. "I can't forgive us."

"I can't either." Lynx tapped a beat on his thigh. "It's worse after seeing her so haunted and sad today."

Gray stared down into his glass. "I'll never forget that image of her in the hospital bed, holding the tiny bundle. Her face crumpled in gut-wrenching grief. I could hear her sobs out in the hallway and... Jesus."

Justice clamped his jaw against the wave of agony at the reminder. And the memory of her earlier today, so pained and alone. It dug into his need to protect her, hold her, and comfort her. He couldn't touch her, not without her permission.

"Beth gave me a year."

"For what?" Sloane asked.

"To win her back. To show her that this time, I won't let her down. After the year, I'm supposed to file for divorce and let her go."

"Maybe it'd be better if you let her go now." Sloane's voice was brutally soft. "You're a rock star. 'Expired Hero' hit number one on the charts after your World Rock Stage performance. You can go live that life and let Liza sink back into obscurity. She'd be safer."

Justice narrowed his eyes, a thread of heat running in his veins. Beth's family had forced her to choose between him and them, and cut all ties when Beth chose him. Even after losing their baby, her aunt had released a statement that she had no contact with her niece. Then they'd sold the house in Santa Barbara and moved out of state.

Beth was alone, except for her mom in prison, her friends, and him. He wouldn't forsake her, wouldn't give up on her. "I'm not leaving my wife."

"She left you," Sloane pointed out.

Like he'd forget that? "Yeah, she did. It'll have to be her choice to come back. Right now she's afraid." She'd withdrawn and was in hiding. Just like she used to hide in a locked bathroom at night after her rape and her mom's arrest.

And possibly cutting. He gripped his glass, fighting

the bone-deep urge to jump in his car and get to Beth. When they'd been together, he'd helped her fight that compulsion. It happened when she let her fear build up and didn't talk. Now she was shutting everyone out. Including him.

"Afraid of Gene Hayes?" Sloane asked.

That name sliced right through his worry, igniting his rage and driving him to his feet. He stalked to the railing, gripping the polished wood. Slivers of moonlight danced on the surface of the ocean, as bright and caustic as his fury. "Partly. I wish I'd killed that bastard when I had the chance. Because I failed, that coward is back in his hole, harassing Beth through his Bring Gene Hayes Home gang of psycho believers. Those groupies worship Hayes like a cult leader." He turned, facing the men, and thought of what Beth had told him at the cemetery earlier. "She's afraid of Hayes, yes. But she also wants him to pay. Wants him to feel the pain of losing the thing he loves the most. Hayes keeps doing this shit and getting away with it." He confessed the flat, ugly truth. "She's afraid to trust me again."

Sloane studied him. "You think she still loves you?"

Justice didn't need to think about that. "Yes. If she didn't, if there was nothing left, she'd have filed for divorce." Instead of cutting all ties to him, she'd agreed to give him a year. Yeah, she loved him, but would it be enough?

"I don't know, man," Simon said. "Liza's so broken."

"She does seem fragile," River added.

Sloane snorted. "Fragile, my ass. She's hurting and retreated emotionally, but she can stand up to pissed-off MMA fighters, intimidating CEO's, and me. She's had to deal with a lot of that while I was here, taking care of Drake. So fragile? No. She needs time and space to heal."

A dose of pride surprised Justice. Beth was Sloane's executive assistant, and despite her grief and need to hide, she still worked her ass off and earned Sloane's respect. "That's my Beth," he said. "She's not broken, she's grieving and blaming herself. Beth isn't weak. She's survived before, and she'll do it again."

"So you think she'll forgive you?" River asked.

"Yes." He had to believe that. He needed her. Beth was his song, the only woman he'd ever loved aside from his grandmother. He thought of Drake's letter, the faith the man had in him, and in Beth. In them. "When I earn it back."

"It won't be easy," Sloane pointed out. "Liza is a smart woman who learns from her mistakes. It's going to take real time to show her you've changed, and she can trust you."

He closed his eyes, hearing the waves rise and crash beyond the deck, feeling the vast emptiness in his chest without Beth. His guilt, regret and self-hatred. For a year, she'd believed in him even when he'd let her down. All those months on the road when she'd been at home, working and taking care of everything. They'd banned her from the tour, and Justice hadn't shown up for the ultrasound or doctor appointments because there'd always been another show, another interview. Yet she hadn't given up on him. He wouldn't give up on her now. "I'll wait for her as long as it takes."

"What now? How do we help?" Simon asked.

That answer was easy. "We work on Liza's goals. She supported ours of becoming rock stars, now we use that power to publicly destroy Gene Hayes."

"I have an idea," Sloane put in.

Interested, Justice returned to the seat he'd vacated earlier. "What?"

"World Rock Stage forced Hayes out. They announced it last month."

"Yes." He tried to see where Sloane was going with this. "It took them four months. I'm guessing they had to pay him off since he was a silent owner." Or Hayes would have sued their asses.

Sloane nodded. "No doubt they did, which is infuriating, but that's the real world. That likely reduced World Rock Stage's net worth, and there's now an opening for another band to buy in." He leaned forward. "Make World Rock Stage an offer to buy in as a public owner. Let the world know you, Savaged Illusions, took his seat at the ownership table. Then use it to ruin Hayes on the international front."

Buying into World Rock Stage had never occurred to Justice. A fission of excitement danced down his spine. It'd be awesome for the band if they could do it, but more importantly, they could use the power to really fight Hayes. It would enrage the man, maybe enough that he'd try to come after Justice.

Lynx whistled. "You're talking millions of dollars. I'm not an accountant, but even I know we don't have that kind of capital."

"No, we don't," Simon said. "It'd be a huge risk, and we could lose everything we've worked for if we got into a deal and couldn't pay up."

Justice flinched and whipped his head around to his lead guitarist. "Like we could have if I hadn't signed the Indie Breakout Band contract with World Rock Stage?"

"Exactly."

Justice measured the other man. "So what are you saying?"

The band had rallied behind him after Paris. They'd had his back in firing their backstabbing band manager Christine, and in going public with their support of Liza. With everything. Until now, when shit got real and the risk could truly hurt them.

Simon smiled. "Let's do it. We owe it to you, Liza and your daughter. It's time we stop protecting ourselves and go after Gene Hayes. We'll get the money, if you're willing to work, Justice. We need to cut our second album, arrange promotion, do gigs, and sell merchandise." Simon leveled a sharp stare on Lynx. "Are you sober enough to vote if you're on board with going after Hayes's seat on World Rock Stage?"

Lynx snorted. "Don't need to be sober to know I'm one hundred fucking percent in on helping Liza and Justice while destroying that bastard Hayes."

Simon shifted to Gray. "And you, piano man?"

"I'm in."

"It's unanimous," River announced.

"I'll help where I can," Sloane added.

With Sloane's assistance, he and his band would stand up and fight the man who'd raped and tortured his wife. Before they went any further, he said, "If we do this, I will tell Beth. I'm not keeping secrets from her." Never again. Although since he'd promised to limit contact, he'd have to text highlights to her. Would she read it? Delete it?

Simon asked, "Do you have a song good enough to go to the top of the charts? Something we can build a tour from, get endorsements, sell merchandise. Capitalize on our brand."

He twisted his wedding band, the one he'd taken off while touring. He'd known it hurt Beth, yet he'd done it. She'd seen photos of him with his arm around various woman, no ring on his finger.

Today it'd been her ring finger that had been bare.

He'd let his quest for fame savage his vows to his

wife. That was his truth, the one he'd write into a song. "I do." It was the one that had been playing in his head like a tune just out of reach.

Until tonight when he'd touched the ring on his finger and heard it loud and clear.

"The song is 'Savaged Vows.' It's the truth about what it's like to be torn between love and fame and make the wrong choice."

He could sing the fuck out of the song, he was sure of it. With his band, they'd have another hit, and millions would love them all over again. They could buy into World Rock Stage and attain enough power and backing to reduce Gene Hayes to a party clown.

But none of that would matter if he couldn't win back his wife.

Chapter 3

LIZA FOLLOWED THE ATTENDANT TO the beautiful table on the private deck overlooking the Pacific Ocean. The cool, damp breeze ruffled the hem of her thick terrycloth robe as she sat in the cushioned chair beneath the thatched roof canopy. Potted palms swayed leisurely, while the waves rose and fell in a timeless tune.

Emily sank into the other chair, wearing a matching spa robe and slippers, her long blonde hair twisted neatly on top of her head. "I'm nearly boneless after all those treatments. How about you?"

Liza pushed a rogue frizzy curl away from her face. She should be relaxed too after the sea-mud facial and mani-pedi, followed by the Hawaiian massage, but a dull fatigue headache refused to leave. She'd drifted off to sleep once or twice last night, but had woken in bone-chilling, sweat-popping terror.

Before she could think of a suitable reply, a server appeared at their table and set down their salads and a basket of fragrant bread. After inquiring if they'd like anything else, she vanished.

Liza eyed the fresh, crisp greens mixed with pecans

and tropical fruits. The scent of bread made her stomach growl, and yet the thought of eating nauseated her.

It was a little like being pregnant.

No, God, don't think about being pregnant.

Instead, she dipped her knife into one of the healthy, plant-based spreads and layered a thin smear on her bread. "The massage helped my sore neck." An honest assessment that should reassure her friend. Trying for a casual tone, she inquired, "Any more treatments after this?"

Em took a bite of her bread and swallowed. "Impatient to be done?"

Guilt jabbed at her. "Sorry, I don't mean to sound ungrateful. I appreciate you sharing your gift certificate package with me." One of the organizations Em had arranged a conference for sent it to her as a thank you. Being an event coordinator for Opulence Hotel had some serious perks. "It's just that I have to go into the office."

"It's Sunday, and you can take the day off. I knew yesterday would be rough with saying goodbye to Drake and seeing Justice at the funeral," Em said gently. "I wanted to do something to help you relax."

"It helps. You've done nothing but help me for months, and I love you for it." She meant every word. Em had shown up at her condo this morning and all but dragged Liza with her. "Work helps me too, and I need the money. I'm hiring lawyers and consultants to direct us in putting together my mom's parole release plan that will satisfy the board, and file the paperwork to request her parole supervision be moved from Los Angeles to here in San Diego."

Em frowned. "What happens if they refuse to let your mom live here?"

"I'd have to move there and find another job." Leave her job, her friends...her baby's resting place. The idea overwhelmed her. "I can't let anything go wrong that will delay her release in May. It'll be nine years this summer. She's served enough." Her mom wouldn't have gone to prison at all if Liza'd listened to her and stayed home that night. Instead, she'd believed her loser dad that Gene Hayes wanted her in his music video. Of course it'd been a lie. Her dad had sold his fourteen-year-old daughter to Hayes for a chance to be in his rock band.

"More than enough," Em agreed, and eyed her with concern. "That's a lot for you to take on."

"There's no one else. I'm all my mom has." Her aunt and grandmother were gone and wanted nothing to do with Amber or Liza.

"I'll help anywhere I can. I have to ask, would your mom want you working brutal hours and never relaxing?"

"I'm relaxing now."

"No, you're tolerating it to humor me. You're tense, exhausted and grieving." Em softened her tone. "And that's okay, Liza. What's not okay is killing yourself at work, barely eating, or getting sleep."

She chose her words carefully. "Work keeps me sane. Sloane needs me," she pointed out. "I feel useful and good at something, rather than lost and sad." Her boss had taken care of Drake in his last months, and during that time, SLAM had been hit with a steroid scandal involving one of their up-and-coming fighters, Ethan Hunt. Worse, Ethan was a kid Sloane had taken in off the streets and cared about like a brother. While Sloane handled Drake and Ethan, Liza had stepped up and created a steroid responsibility, education and transparency campaign for SLAM to help the company navigate through the bad press.

"You sure you're not using work to hide from your grief?"

Was she hiding? God, yes. Guilt, remorse and self-hatred clawed at her every day. The nightmares were worse. But she was also—

Liza's phone dinged. She reached into her robe pocket to see who the text was from: Justice. The part she could view on her home screen read, *Beth, I want to talk to you. The band and I have a plan to...* She'd have to open the text to read more. A fist squeezed brutally in her chest, threatening to crack the ice around her heart and force her to feel. Every one of her muscles tensed, and part of her mind retreated.

"What's wrong?" Em's voice grew sharp. "Who texted you?"

Her friend was too damned observant. Quickly, she hit a button to get rid of the message unread, and put her phone away. "Justice. I deleted the text." She tried to shift topics. "How did the fifty-year anniversary celebration you planned turn out?" Em had offered to get someone to fill in for her so she could go to Drake's funeral with her, but Liza refused to let her. She'd taken enough time off work to help Liza in those first dark days after returning from Paris.

"Eat and I'll tell you. Otherwise I'll nag you about Justice. You choose."

She picked up her fork and made a show of piercing a piece of fruit and eating it.

Em waited until she took a second bite, then said, "It was lovely. They didn't do a vow renewal because, and I'm quoting, 'Our vows and our love don't have an expiration date.'" She went on to describe the video put together by the family, the grandkids all singing the couple's favorite song for them to dance to, and other highlights.

When Em paused to take a bite of her lunch, Liza asked, "Did you run into any snafus?"

"There was a mix-up with the salad course that was easily fixed. The bigger issue was when one of their granddaughters spilled something on her dress before the performance. She was nearly inconsolable."

"What did you do?"

"Called the owner of SunGlam. She gave me permission to take her and her mom into the closed shop and find her a new dress."

Opulence Hotel had several high-end shops on the first floor. "Quick thinking."

Em shrugged. "They were nice people. I enjoyed working with them to make the evening special. Unlike some of these events that test my rule about spilling blood in the workplace."

"Like that Living Organic group you had last summer?" Liza had listened to Em vent about those bullies about three times a day and once more in the middle of the night during that conference. They harangued her about food, drinks, the air conditioning, what kind of carpet cleaners did they use? What about dishwashing soap? And the soap in the bathrooms? The list went on and on. Worse, they harassed employees, trying to push their products on them. They made a server cry with relentless suggestions of ways to treat her acne and another embarrassed a guest into tears over her weight.

"I was seriously tempted to fill their cars, sitting in the sun all day, with dead fish and ask them if that was organic enough for them."

Liza narrowed her gaze. "You didn't do it, did you?"

"Nah. They aren't worth killing fish for. But I did eat processed food like bags of chips and moon pies in front of them."

Liza snorted an almost laugh. "This from the woman who loves going to the farmers' market and buying cruelty-free products when possible."

"I could fill Justice's car with dead fish if he upset you yesterday."

Liza raised her eyebrows. "Thought if I ate, you weren't going to talk about Justice."

"You're not eating now, so reprieve is over. Did you talk to him?"

No point in trying to avoid it, Em had her nag-to-death badge in the best friend club. "Just long enough for him to convince me to hold off for a year on filing for divorce. He thinks he can win me back."

"What do you think?"

That her dream of Justice and a family had died with her baby. She opened her mouth to answer when their server walked out, carrying an elegant gift bag with the familiar SunGlam logo on it.

"This was sent over for you." She set it down in front of Em.

Em thanked the server and immediately started digging through the delicate tissue layers while practically bouncing with excitement. She pulled out a thick cream-colored envelope and dropped it on the table.

"Aren't you going to read the card?" Liza picked it up and read the writing. *Emily Manchester, Opulence Hotel Event Coordinator.*

"You open it. I want to see the gift! I'm sure it's from the owner of SunGlam, probably thanking me for the sale to replace the girl's dress last night."

Liza opened the flap of the envelope and slid the card out. While Emily continued peeling back layers of gold tissue, she quickly scanned the handwriting:

It's not safe to be friends with a baby killer. You

could end up hurt or even dead like her baby. Tell Lyin' Liza to do the world a favor and kill herself like she killed her daughter.

Dropping the card, she blurted out, "Stop!"

Too late, Em plunged her hand into the bag, then jerked it out. "What the hell?" She held up fingers coated in blood.

"Oh my God!" Liza jumped to her feet and wrapped her napkin around her friend's hand. "What happened? Did something cut you?" Nothing made any sense. She looked into the bag.

A dead baby covered in blood stared back at her.

Involuntarily, she opened her mouth to scream, but her throat closed as horror and terror collided to form a tight fist lodged in her windpipe.

A day later, and Liza still couldn't erase the mental image of a bloody baby. It'd taken several horror-soaked seconds for her brain to comprehend that it was a doll covered in ketchup, not a real baby.

Liza's head throbbed, probably because she'd had another sleepless night. She'd gotten to work by six, and hadn't stopped since she'd arrived and it was only noon. Mondays were always busy, but this one was a coked-up version, mostly due to Sloane not having returned to the office yet after Drake's death. In his place, Liza ran the staff meeting. She handled a few calls, videoed a steroid scandal update that would go on their website, and along with John Moreno, dealt with an injury at one of their gyms.

Now she was in her office tackling piles of emails. There was one from Opulence security, letting her know they were taking the whole incident at their spa seriously, while trying to respect her wishes and keep it out of the media. She rubbed her temples, but it didn't scrub away her memory.

Focus on your job, she told herself. She and Em had quietly filed the police report with the hotel's help, and there wasn't anything else she could do. Work was something she could control, so she read three more emails, including one from Keith of the extremely successful Indie Rock Broadcast that began as a blog and branched out into a TV show. He had a popular segment on the show called *Rock Wives*. He mentioned that he saw she'd attended a funeral over the weekend and sent his condolences. The message was quick and kind, and he didn't push for her to respond. He'd been checking in with her every month or two since she'd cancelled her appearance on *Rock Wives*. She appreciated knowing there were good people out there, even in the most cutthroat industries.

She deleted a third email asking for a comment on a picture of her and Justice talking at Drake's funeral. Liza didn't want to see the picture and moved onto the next email.

The subject line stopped her cold.

Amber Ranger, Injured in Prison Fight.

What? A rush of adrenaline buzzed through her, slamming her heart against her ribs. Was her mom hurt? Frantic, she opened the email and read the body.

It will happen if you don't tell the truth, Lyin' Liza. Your mom, your friend...we can get to anyone. Leave a suicide note confessing your sins on Bring Gene Hayes Home.

Another threat from the trolls. They were ramping up their game. Dizzy, she dug her fingernails into her palms. A quick check of the sender showed a string of numbers and letters that meant the IP address had been stripped to hide the identity of whoever wrote the email. Standard operating procedure for the cultlike assholes cyberstalking her. She forwarded it to the police to add to her file, and copied SLAM Security. Done with that, she texted one of the prison guards Liza'd grown friendly with over the years. She had to be sure her mom was okay.

Once she'd received confirmation that Amber was fine, she returned to getting through her emails. She'd just opened the next one when her office phone rang. Her display told her it was the receptionist at the lobby desk. Picking it up, she said, "This is Liza."

"Emily Manchester to see you," Sophie announced. "She said to tell you that she brought lunch."

Damn it. She'd fought with Emily about this very thing yesterday after the disastrous end to their spa day. Liza had made it clear it wasn't safe to be around her. Did Em listen? "Tell her I'm in a meeting."

She heard Em's loud answer. "Tell Liza I'll call Sloane at home and make sure he knows about the threat yesterday. Then I'll make sure Justice knows. I have my phone out right now."

Crap. Liza hadn't told Sloane or Justice. Sloane had other things on his mind. Justice was supposed to be back in L.A. for something or other. She didn't want to think about him. "Fine, send her up." She slammed the phone down.

Two minutes later, Em barged into her office, dropped a plastic bag and two bottled drinks on her desk, and glared at her. "You are really pissing me off." She stalked to the door, shut it, and then sat in one of the chairs.

Liza ignored the smell of chicken and spices to focus on the crazy woman staring at her. "I'm pissing you off? You're being stubborn and foolish. I know you graduated college, so you can read. Like that one line from the note yesterday. *You could end up hurt or even dead like her baby.* That's a threat. Do you want to end up stabbed like I was? Do you remember that?"

Emily stood and smacked her hands on the desk. "You know what I remember? The time my first college boyfriend got drunk and tried to force me to get in his car with him driving; you told him to stop and he shoved you. Did you back down?"

"That's not the same situation. No way in hell was I letting you get in the car with a drunk." Or with any man she didn't want to go with.

"You snatched his keys from him, while I dived into your car. You got in, locked the doors and called 911. While he stood there banging on the window and screaming threats. Then you gave the report and his car keys to the officers. I was scared, shocked and confused because I hadn't seen this side of him before, but you took control."

So? She'd taken her mom's keys away from her probably a dozen times while growing up. "He was a drunk jerk, Em."

"Yeah, but I'm not. You didn't abandon me, and I'm not abandoning you. It's one thing for you to cut off Justice. He deserves it. I don't. Am I clear?"

Liza gritted her teeth in utter frustration. "He could kill you."

Em drew her head back slightly. "Gene Hayes?"

"Yes, him or one of his psycho minions." So many people had believed the rich rock star over Liza. After all, she'd just been the fourteen-year-old daughter of a hard-partying groupie. It hadn't mattered that Hayes had been convicted in a trial, or that he'd fled the country, making him a fugitive. They rabidly defended him. "He won't stop until I'm dead. If he can't get to me, he'll go after those I care about, like you." Or her mom. "He's amassed a small army."

Em sank into the chair, her shoulders softening in the geometric dress. "I know, and it's maddening. They post lies and smears like true disciples. Since the note yesterday called you *Lyin' Liza* like Hayes and his creepers do, it's a pretty safe bet someone from the website orchestrated delivering that lifelike bloody doll and the note to me."

"Yes, and they had your name, your work title, and knew exactly where we were."

Em nodded. "It was on social media. People took cell phone shots of us walking through the hotel and into the spa. They tagged your name, making it easier for people to find us."

Liza grabbed the soda Em had brought, opened it and took the hit of caffeine. "This is my life, Em. Aside from that blasted website, I get nasty comments all the time, sometimes in public from people who think they know me. Sometimes on SLAM social media. Once, I had groceries delivered, and *Baby Killing Liar* was written on a Post-it Note dropped into the bag. Another time, I found a dead rat in my desk drawer." Video had shown it was one of the cleaning crew, and they were fired. Undoubtedly sent by trolls on the website, but the police hadn't been able to find that connection.

An unbearable weight of fatigue rolled through her. She didn't get to feel sorry for herself since she was the one who set all this in motion. Her aunt Mari had warned her over and over, *Stay quiet, Liza. Don't talk about it.* She had cautioned her not to trust friends from school—they could be plotting to sell her out. Just like her former friend Nikki had when she sold Liza out to Hayes.

She straightened her back. "I can't be the friend I used to be to you. It's too dangerous. In Paris, Hayes swore he'd kill me. I saw the violent obsessive hate in his eyes, felt it in every syllable of his words." It was what had driven her into the wild flight that had resulted in her falling down those stairs and losing her baby. "Right now, I'm trying to stay alive long enough to get my mom out of prison and make sure she's physically and financially secure."

Em grabbed her soda and gulped it. Done, she slapped it on the desk. "I hear you, that asshole won't stop until he kills you or he's caught."

Finally. She opened her mouth, but Em cut her off.

"Now it's your turn to listen. I'm not letting fear of a rapist asshole and his moron brigade of butt-licking losers choose my friends. I get that you're scared, grieving and angry, and God knows you have every right to be." Rising, she pulled a box out and set it on the desk, then picked up the bag. "What you don't have a right to do think I'd let you go through this alone. Also, this weekend, my brothers are picking up that old kitchen table you were procrastinating buying and will bring it to your condo. I negotiated a good price, and I'll send you the bill with the cost of lunch added because you're really ticking me off. Oh, and pick out a color, we'll start refinishing it. I have to get back to the office but I'll call you later."

Liza didn't even get her mouth open before Em was gone.

How had she started her day intending to distance herself from Em and keep her head down while remaining alone, yet by the end of lunch she had a plan to have the table delivered and begin refinishing it together?

Chapter 4

AT THREE IN THE MORNING, Liza stood in the bathroom, snapping a rubber band on her wrist as she tried to banish the images of the blood-covered baby doll. Kids had left it on her doorstep last night, Halloween, and one of the adults saw it and called security. It'd been nearly a month since the doll had been delivered to Em at the spa.

Her gaze slid to the razor in her shower. "Don't do it," she whispered. If she started cutting, she feared she wouldn't stop until all the pain was gone. No more horrible dreams, no more waking drenched with sweaty fear and a scream of terror locked in her throat.

Her mom's desperate voice echoed from a long-ago memory. *Don't leave me, Beth. I can bear living in here. I can bear anything but losing you. Please, baby, don't leave me.*

Liza jerked her left wrist up, eying the jagged white scars there. At fifteen, she'd jammed a broken piece of glass in there to stop the screams of haters out on the street calling her a whore, a liar, and other vile names. When her mom spotted the healing cuts, she'd been devastated.

She wouldn't leave her mom. Determined to get control, she scooped her phone off the counter to pull up the picture of her and her mom from one of her visits. An unread text from Justice caught her attention.

Beth, I need an answer from you. Just a yes or no. It's about our plans to make an offer to buy into World Rock Stage now that they've forced Hayes out.

Liza sat on the closed toilet of her large master bath and read the rest of the message about how they were putting together the numbers, and their plans for their next album they'd need to pay for it. They'd have to do a tour too, but he'd keep it short because he wanted to be available to her. The key here, Justice reiterated, was that if he was part of World Rock Stage, he'd have more power to block Hayes and his efforts to reestablish himself in the music world, especially internationally.

Plus it would really piss Hayes off. Make him insane that Liza's husband took the spot Hayes had been forced out of, and as a public owner, not a silent one like Hayes had been.

Justice had reassured her if she resented the idea of him being involved with World Rock Stage because of what happened there, he wouldn't do it.

Liza read and reread the message, her mind tumbling between flinching every time she read Hayes's name and impotent rage that he was still free. He never suffered for the misery he caused.

She wanted him stopped. Liza typed her reply. *Do it.*

Seconds later, her phone vibrated. *Can't sleep?*

Justice had texted back in the middle of the night. Had he been awake? He was in L.A., maybe they had a gig? Or were working on the new songs?

Don't answer. She'd said what she had to. But part

of her craved the connection, the distraction from her roiling pain and sadness and the constant fear that Gene Hayes would pop out of some dark corner. She typed out, *No. You?* She only debated a second and hit send.

Not now, when I know you're awake and alone. Do you still write to cope with the terrors? I miss your book.

She sucked in a breath, refusing to remember those days and nights. The way he'd begged to become a part of her secret world, the one she'd escaped to after the rape. *No. That was another life.* She hit send, needing to shut that down.

Done with Justice, she went to the kitchen, flipping on every light, and grabbed a small water from the fridge. It was pitch black outside, but she had security lights that even a small rodent would trigger. Plus the 24/7 guards who patrolled the complex and her excellent security system. They were watching her house closer tonight after the baby doll prank.

Her phone vibrated in her hand. Before she could stop herself, she lifted the device and checked the screen.

I read your book some nights when the loneliness, grief and regret haunt me. Those pages reflect the most fierce and courageous part of your soul, and I hold on to them with all that I have. I see in there you discovering the power of your voice—the one that so many have tried and failed to silence. That book is part of you.

She squeezed her eyes shut, trying to block out Justice's ability to remind her of the woman she'd so desperately wanted to be; good and strong enough to deserve love and a family, friends and a full life where she didn't have to hide.

She went to her table, sat and typed out, *It was fiction, not real. I deleted it all. That's not who I am now. Maybe once I stupidly believed in romance novels, but that led to more disaster exactly as my aunt said it would. Never again. I won't live it, and I won't write it.*

He'd wanted to talk to her, begged her to at least text. Okay, then he could have the truth. She hit send, but couldn't shake the memory of how writing that book had fueled her hope that she could live a normal life as something other than the girl who'd ruined a rock star. Telling that story had made her feel powerful, and in control.

It had been lies.

That dream had died with all her other ones. She wasn't going to have love, a family or use her voice as an author to touch other lives.

Clearly, she'd irritated Justice since he'd stopped texting.

Liza got up and started the coffee brewing. She'd get a list organized for today, and tackle some work before she had to jump in the shower and dress for the office.

Going to her freshly refinished table, she woke up her laptop. The rattle of her phone dragged her attention from the machine. Futilely, she told herself not to look. But she reached for the device, confirmed it was from Justice, and opened the message.

No one said your story had to be a romance. It's your voice and your world. You have the power to shape the story into whatever you want it to be.

Frustrated, she tapped out, *I told you I deleted the book.*

I told you I kept it. Check your email. It's yours to do what you want with, Beth. Your book, your world, your rules. You can even delete it again, and I'll keep it for you until you're ready.

"Damn it, Justice." She couldn't get drawn back into his world. Liza had her own goals. *My rules, right? What if I told you to delete the book?* She punched send, then eyed her computer. If she opened the email program, she could delete the message and get to work.

Her phone alerted her with a response seconds later. *I'd do most anything for you, except that. I will never try to erase any part of who you are, and that book is a very important part of you.*

"Crap." She tried to work back up to mad, but the thick nostalgia for the times he embraced all of her, even the sections her aunt tried to eliminate, rushed at her in vivid color. Another sharp reminder of the family she'd never have.

She turned to the email from Justice and opened it. There was the attachment of a Word doc. She assumed it was the last version of her book they'd passed back and forth when they'd still been together.

Liza dropped her hands in her lap and fisted her fingers as the memories of being in love, pregnant with the child she desperately wanted, and the passion to find her voice as a writer building inside her. A shrill whiny static ignited in her ears, like the feedback from a speaker or microphone. Sweat popped out on the back of her neck beneath her hair.

She didn't even want to think about the past. Liza moved her curser to the delete button, but instead she hit the attachment. It began downloading immediately.

Her heart thumped. What was she doing?

Once the download completed, Liza opened the file and scrolled down to read the first line.

Molly Gillibrand just wanted to be loved. So how

had she ended up branded the most hated girl in rock?

Stupid. She and Molly were both so damned stupid. Anger nudged red-hot spikes against the icy lockdown Liza worked to keep around her heart. God, that girl! Surging up, she got out a cup and thumped it on her counter. Dumped in some coffee, followed by a splash of cream. She dunked in a spoon and stirred hard enough to splash the hot liquid on the counter.

She wiped it up, grabbed her mug and stalked back to the table.

Those first two lines sat there on her computer screen daring her to read more.

Nope, she was not getting pulled back into that world of rock stars and silly girls with dangerous dreams.

But it wouldn't hurt to read a little more before she deleted the book.

Chapter 5

LIZA HAD ALWAYS LOVED CHRISTMAS, and it'd become all the more special one year ago today when Justice had proposed to her under the tree they'd decorated together. In that moment, she'd had it all.

This year, she'd gone full Grinch with no tree, decorations or so much as a Christmas card in sight. Other than talking to her mom on the phone, she ignored the holiday memories by losing herself in writing. In the last two months, the book had gotten her through some terrible nights, and in the process, she'd begun to feel a new sense of power in Molly.

The girl rebuffed every attempt Liza made to change the storyline. No matter what Liza did, Molly kept turning up pregnant until Liza threw up her hands in exasperation. How many times had Liza highlighted that entire file then been unable to push delete? Ten? Twenty?

She couldn't do it. She had to find out what happened next in the story, even if the potential disaster looming over Molly and her baby scared her.

Her doorbell rang.

Liza jumped and swiveled her head to the door on the other side of the living room. Her heart rate surged. She wasn't expecting anyone, and a fresh wave of apprehension flared. Had one of Hayes's groupies gotten inside the gates despite all the guards in the high-security condominium complex? They continued to harass her with things like the Christmas card sent to her at the office that read, *Why are you alive after you murdered your baby?* with a picture of the newborn-like doll covered in blood at the base of some stairs. The line below that read, *Give the world a Christmas gift and kill yourself.*

Grabbing her phone off the table, she pulled up the camera view of her front porch. Despite it being dark outside, she could see perfectly from her excellent lighting. No one hovered or crouched ready to spring out at her, but there was something resting on her welcome mat. She zoomed in on a white bag with a fast food logo. Should she call the guards and have them check it out? Was it a prank? Or a threat from the same lunatics who sent her bloody baby dolls?

Or had someone really left her fast food? Who would do that?

Quickly, Liza accessed the stored feed captured on her system, and going a few minutes back, she spotted a man with a dog at his left side as they approached her door. The man had on a jacket Liza recognized instantly, and her heart thumped in shock. *Noah!* Justice's dad, and the dog with him was Radar.

She fumbled with the lock, finally getting the door open, and called out, "Noah?"

Silence.

"If you're there, you and Radar can come in." She scanned the cars, the trees, and any spot that Noah might hide behind.

"Please, Noah?" Hearing that pleading pitch to her voice, she reined herself in. She didn't need the neighbors thinking she was losing her mind. If Noah wanted to see her, or come inside, he would have.

The scent of French fries wafted up, drawing her attention to the bag on her porch. A renewed sense of caution kicked in. She was sure she saw Noah on her feed, but what if she was wrong? Carefully, she knelt and eased open the bag. Inside was a frosty drink, a carton of fries, a chicken sandwich and napkins.

One of the white napkins had black ink scrawled on it. Tugging it free, she read the words, *Thought you might need a chocolate shake and French fries. Merry Christmas from me and Radar. Will you tell Justice Merry Christmas too? N.*

Hot tears filled her eyes instantly, and Liza scooped up the bag, hugging it to her. "Oh, Noah." She'd told him once that everyone knew you needed a chocolate shake and fries when you got out of the hospital. After he'd broken his arm, she brought him shakes and fries daily.

Now he'd brought it to her on Christmas Day. Even managing to get through the complex security that had prevented so many others in their attempts.

She couldn't stop her tears of both gratitude and disappointment that he hadn't stayed. Returning inside, she shut the door and rearmed her security system. Then she scrolled her phone to find Noah's number, opened a message and typed out, *Thank you. Merry Christmas, Noah. You and Radar are always welcome here.*

Hitting send, she wished all over again her father-in-law had stayed. Having seen him on the video, it hit her how much she missed him. Unfortunately, Noah had his own struggles with PTSD. He blamed himself for the deaths of the men he'd been trying to save back when he was a Marine on tour in Afghanistan. A bomb had gone off, severely injuring him and killing two of the men.

She wanted desperately to hug the man that she understood better now. Sometimes, no matter how hard you tried, you couldn't save someone.

Noah couldn't save those men.

Liza hadn't been able to save her child.

There was one thing she could do for her father-in-law. Going to the table, she took out her food and the frosty shake and snapped a picture. Then she got a close-up of the napkin with the words. Done with that, she sent a text message with the pictures to Justice:

Your dad rang my bell and left this on my porch. He'd already vanished by the time I checked my surveillance camera. I didn't see Noah's face, but I recognized the jacket your dad wears, and the dog, Radar. When I opened the door, they were both gone. I called his name, but he wouldn't show himself. From what I could see on the camera, he and Radar looked okay.

Should she ask about the bid his band had submitted for part ownership in World Rock Stage? She'd picked up the phone a dozen times, wanting to ask Justice, but she'd resisted. Where was Justice? What was he doing? Having Christmas dinner with his friends? Was he lonely?

With a woman?

She rejected that instantly. He'd been too distressed and honest at Drake's funeral when he dragged out of Liza a promise of a year before they filed for divorce. He wasn't with other women. Not yet.

Crap, this was exactly why she avoided texting Justice. Just typing the text pulled her right to the edge of an emotional hurricane. Deciding against adding the question about the World Rock Stage seat, she hit send and slapped the phone down as if he might burn her.

Grabbing a fry, she bit into the crisp greasy potato covered in salt and sin. Her stomach growled in hearty approval. She took a sip of the chocolate shake, surprised that it tasted better than anything had in months.

Her phone vibrated, the screen lighting up with an incoming text. Justice. Once she'd called him Rock Rooster on her phone, but she'd changed that. They weren't together anymore, so she didn't have cute nicknames. Sliding her finger over the screen, she read the message.

Thank you, Beth. It's the best damn gift I could have had. At least I know he's alive, Radar is with him, and they're here in town. I wish he'd come inside with you, then neither of you'd be alone on Christmas.

Her entire body tightened. She gritted her teeth and reached for another fry to fill the empty yearning in her.

A second text popped up.

Justice: *Can you tell Dad I'm not at the house, and he can go there? I have food and stuff for the dog too. He knows the code to the gate and security system.*

Liza read that last line twice while eating another crispy potato. It still didn't make sense, so she asked, *What gate?*

Justice: *The eight-foot wrought-iron security fence around the property. I had it installed when I thought you might come home. I wanted you safe, I still do. I worry about you every hour of every day.*

He'd done that? She hadn't been able to go home. Not to Justice, or the house, or to face her baby's empty room that Justice had painted a warm shade of yellow.

She drank some of the shake to wash down that hard lump in her throat. Part of her wanted to retreat from the pain, but she owed this to Noah.

She typed out, *I'll tell him you're in L.A., so he and Radar can get warm and have the house to themselves.* Justice was staying in L.A. working on music for the new album.

After another sip of the shake, she typed the text to Noah to let him know what Justice said about the house. She'd barely hit send and began typing out her question to Justice about World Rock Stage when her phone vibrated a new message.

Justice: *Busted, baby. If you know I'm in L.A., that means you've been reading my texts.*

Damn him, her lips twitched with amusement and the need to answer his challenge. To sink into the banter they used to enjoy, the silliness that kept them connected even when thousands of miles separated them.

No, she had to stop this. It was the holiday making her too needy. Liza set her phone down.

She couldn't settle. It was too much. Seeing Noah hurt. This growing need to write Molly's story really pissed her off. Texting with Justice distracted her more. She really wanted to know what happened to that seat Hayes had lost. God. She grabbed the phone and hit his number.

"Beth," Justice answered. "Are you okay?"

Hearing him shocked something deep inside her, intensifying the ache for her child, and longing for a family made worse by the holiday. What was she doing calling him?

She gripped the phone tighter. "I can't bear it being Christmas without her here. You're the only other person who held her, who loved her." She hadn't meant to say that, but Justice was the only one who could really understand. They'd had a few precious moments with their baby in the hospital, and Liza had seen his love for their daughter.

He just hadn't loved them as much as he'd wanted fame.

"I miss her too. I hate myself for not protecting her every damned day. It's worse this time of year, when I see the kids with their parents...it fucking hurts. It has to be worse for you. You're her mother."

Sorrow and heavy regret clung to every syllable, but that last sentence, that had been uttered with such love and respect, it shattered her defenses. "I can't say her name. I...my throat locks. I can think her name, but when I try to say it..."

Don't talk about it, Liza. Her aunt's voice played the endless loop in her mind. Mari had meant don't talk about the rape, about Gene Hayes, her mom or anything before she'd come to live with her aunt and uncle.

The lesson stuck, and she couldn't say her own daughter's name.

She finished with, "...it's like a silent scream." All pain with no sound.

"That sounds like your night terrors. Are you cutting to cope?"

It was easier to talk about this than their child. "No, well the first few months I struggled with the urge."

"And now?"

She looked at the computer monitor. "I write."

"Really?" His voice pitched up. "You're writing again?"

"Don't get excited. I'm not penning the great America novel, it's a way to pass the time in the middle of the night." And keep from losing her mind, which

45

made her soften a little. "Thanks for sending the book to me."

"You're welcome. I thought you'd delete it."

"I tried," she admitted, and stopped herself from saying more by changing the subject. "I've wanted to ask you something."

"Anything."

"Have you heard back about buying the seat Hayes was forced out of?" She pressed her ear against the phone, hoping to hear that Hayes not only lost his seat but her husband's band bought it.

"Not yet, but we're following up."

Disappointment slumped her in the chair. "Oh, okay. Well thanks. I should—"

"Beth, we're fighting for it, I swear. The whole band is ready to stomp Hayes's balls. I want this as badly as you do, that bastard is going down."

She believed that he and his band would do everything they could to ruin him professionally. "I appreciate it."

"When I get an answer, can I call and let you know?"

Liza hesitated. She'd crossed a line today by calling him. But she really wanted to know. "Yes."

"Beth, do you want to help us? Be involved on some level once we get the seat?"

Be a part of finally getting revenge on Hayes and making him pay? Half of her leapt at the chance, the other half cowered in the corner. Logic kicked in, "I can't. I have my job, and I can't risk my mom. It wouldn't be that hard for Hayes to send someone after her in prison." That secret anonymous email Liza'd had a few months ago threatened Amber being injured in a prison fight. "I have to get her home and safe. She's all the family I have left." She missed her mom more than ever, and wanted to get to know her again.

"You're right about keeping your mom safe, but you're wrong about family. You also have me, and you have my dad. He came by your condo today, Beth. That's huge for him and shows he cares about you. We're all your family, and you have your friends; Emily, Sloane, Tess and more. You're not alone, sweetheart."

Her throat tightened. This wasn't her plan. Not when Hayes had vowed to kill her, and would hurt anyone who got in his way. "I need to go."

"Okay, I'll call you as soon as I get an answer."

"Thanks." They hung up.

Before she put her phone down, a text message popped up from Justice.

You didn't tell me about Molly. Send me pages?

She thought of the two month battle she'd had with Molly as she tried to write out her pregnancy or end it in an early miscarriage. She'd failed, and gotten drawn into the story of a young mother willing to do anything to protect her child.

Liza told herself to put the phone down without answering, but the phone felt like a lifeline as she endured a sad, lonely Christmas. Liza could almost feel Justice on the other end, holding the fragile line and refusing to let her sink in a pit of lonely despair. Shit. She typed out, *Get that seat on World Rock Stage and I'll think about it.*

Should she send or delete? First Justice wrangled a pledge not to divorce him for a year, and had somehow gotten her to call him. Emily refused to be smart and unfriend Liza. Tess and Sophie at work had taken over Liza's beloved SLAM Heroes program of matching victims with a MMA fighter hero to protect them at court dates and whatever else they needed, and then somehow refused to let Liza step aside. She still had no idea how that had happened. Noah had popped back into her life, and she'd been wrangled into the role of delivering messages between him and Justice. Now Molly dragged Liza back into her writing.

No matter how hard she tried to cut herself off, she kept getting drawn back in. Definitely delete.

She hit send.

Chapter 6

JUSTICE CHECKED HIS PHONE FOR the millionth time as the limo navigated Las Vegas Boulevard to the Mandarin Oriental Hotel. The second he'd gotten off the stage at the New Year's Eve concert, he'd texted Beth, *Happy New Year. Did you hear from my dad?*

Nothing. No response. She hadn't talked to him since Christmas, yet Justice could almost feel her on the other end of the phone.

"She could be asleep."

He glanced up at Simon. Lynx and River sat on his left, doing their best to drain the well-stocked bar on the ten minute drive. Gray was next to Simon, doing his weird paranoia thing of checking out the back window and fidgeting. He'd ducked out of the preshow interviews too. The dude was off his meds again or something, but he was a fucking genius at his piano and keyboard rig onstage and never missed a performance.

Justice focused on Simon. "Maybe." He didn't think she slept much, but she'd said writing helped and that made him happy.

His phone screen lit up.

Beth. *Happy New Year, and no.*

The five words from her thrilled him more than the entire crowd on their feet, clapping and screaming after their concert tonight. *Are you spending New Year's with Molly?*

He'd been stunned when she called him Christmas Day. Then she shocked him more by sharing how much she missed their baby. Since then, it'd been a herculean effort to not text. He fidgeted with his phone, willing her to answer.

Finally the screen lit up. *I'm spending it in New York doing my job.*

You're in New York? Was she safe?

Huge New Year's Eve fight in Madison Square Garden. I'm here on my last trip as Sloane's assistant and media consultant. I'm in my room now, which I'm sharing with my bodyguard, Whitney. I need to get some sleep. Night.

At least she had a bodyguard with her, but what did she mean her last day? *What's going on, did you turn in your notice? Get another job?* That could be dangerous. SLAM had security that watched out for Beth.

Promotion to Director of Communications. Seriously, I'm turning my phone off.

Wow. Pride spread in his chest at Beth's accomplishments. She'd begun as a college intern and made her way to the executive team in, what, two years? Amazing. He had to fight the urge to call her and find out more. She'd said he could call her when he had news, and he would. If he forewarned her now, she might tell him to text.

He told her goodnight and put his phone away.

Two more minutes ticked by as the limo turned into a parking lot and slid to a stop. Hank, head of their personal security, opened the door.

"Let's roll," Simon said, and headed out the door. They walked through the lobby.

"Justice! Oh my God, it's Justice Cade!" a girl squealed.

People rushed in, begging for autographs and pictures. It was the same scene everywhere they went whether it was two in the morning or afternoon. Aside from his limited contact with Beth, getting on the stage and singing his truth for his fans to hear was the only real solace he had.

Even now, surrounded by people screaming his name, begging for his touch, he truly ached for one woman—his wife.

They stopped to take some pictures before moving to the private elevator of one of the large suites. The door opened before they could knock, and Justice smelled food the second he walked in the door. A variety of catering trays were overseen by a chef and two servers.

"Justice, glad you made it." Slade, the legendary lead singer of Seventh Ring and founder of World Rock Stage, strode up.

"Hey man." Justice firmly shook Slade's hand. "We got caught up in a signing after the show."

"Justice, lovely to see you." Monique wore a bright, silky dress that fell to her ankles. Her dark hair flowed around her face. The former model was a knockout. "We had our chef get some late supper ready. Grilled tuna, deep fried shrimp, rice, vegetables."

River draped an arm around Monique's shoulders. "I'm in love with you."

She threw her head back and laughed. "You love every woman."

"True." He kissed her head, and rushed for the food.

"We figured you hadn't had time to eat." Slade closed the door, an amused smile tugging at his pierced lip.

They piled around the long white table, and everyone dug in while telling stories and catching up. Once the table was cleared, they moved to the living area with deep, white couches and chairs around a dark wood coffee table.

Monique sat next to Justice. "How's Liza?"

He drained off half his beer. "She's hanging in there. Mostly by texts in the last couple months, but we're beginning to talk more."

She settled her hand on his arm. "She's not talking to me or Althea, other than polite responses. Not that I blame her." She cast a glare at her husband.

"My wife's still pissed at me." Slade sat on the opposite couch, next to Simon. Gray and River had taken the chairs, and Lynx was on Justice's left. "I never told her Hayes was a silent partner of World Rock Stage."

Surprised, Justice asked, "Why not?"

Slade set down the glass. "Because I wasn't proud of it. World Rock Stage went through a cash-strapped phase during the recession. Hayes came in with the right offer. I was against letting that fucker in, but I was outvoted and furious. Hayes did it by having his connections do side deals with Forticulture and Cellular Evolution, two of the four band owners. We kept it a silent-partner deal. Hayes had an executive loge, but he'd told us it was for his friends. For years, he stuck to that agreement. When he sent the name and information for security clearance, it was the false name he used in France, a supposed industry professional." Slade paused, then added, "I swear I didn't know he was there that night. When I saw him later on the security cameras, I was shocked." He leaned back. "The only good thing about the whole nightmare of that night is that I was able to boot his ass out."

Justice nodded and caught Simon's eye. They'd agreed they'd let Slade lead the discussion of their offer to buy into World Rock Stage, but his nerves were strung tight waiting. He needed this chance to wield power over Hayes and give Beth some satisfaction.

"Did anyone fight you on that?" Simon asked.

Slade's face tightened. "I went into that meeting furious. Shit got broken, and it was a fucking miracle it was only glass and not someone's face. My drummer, Damon, in fact my whole band, were just as pissed. World Rock Stage is our dream, we built that organization from the ground up. It's about rock music, and now..." He shook his head. "We're smeared, and we deserve it. We let a monster into our organization, and he got to your wife because I didn't fight hard enough to keep him out. I compromised, and you, your wife, and your baby got hurt." He ground his teeth. "I don't fucking compromise."

The fury in the other man was as real as his music and love for his wife.

"Nor do you lie to me," Monique added.

He met her gaze. "Yeah, that too."

Yet Monique forgave him, Justice noticed. While his wife... *Monique didn't lose a baby. Or been raped and terrorized by Hayes. So yeah, not the same thing.* He focused on why they were there. "Hayes is out now."

Slade dropped his hand from his lip and inclined his head. "He is, but it cost us a hell of a lot of money to do it. We had to pay him off, or he'd have sued and tied us up in court battles for years. Which brings me to your buy-in offer."

About damn time. Justice forced himself to stay relaxed. It'd taken a month to get their offer together, and another month to receive a response. He'd expected it to come through their lawyers, but Slade wanted to meet with them. A backroom deal. That was how the world worked, and they all knew it.

"We've had multiple offers, but World Rock Stage can't afford another mistake. One issue is that the four current bands in the group have been in the business for over a decade and we're widely considered legends."

"We're not," Simon said flatly.

"No," Slade went on. "That's not all bad. We may be legends, but we're also considered old school, or whatever the current jargon is. WRS needs younger blood whose songs capture the passions of the thirty-five-and-under demographic."

Justice leaned forward, struggling to contain his urgency. "We hit number one with our album and single."

"Yes, but you're still a rock baby who hasn't proven your longevity in the business yet. We're not jumping into this decision. Instead we've chosen the top three bands from the newer rock generation to compete in a contest for the ownership spot. We have a set of criteria, including U.S. and international sales, other streams of revenue like merchandise, licensing agreements, and so on. Fan engagement is also critical, and we will require a world tour. We want to see who has the chops and staying power to eventually become a true legend. If you're selected, the price is one and a half times what you offered. You have less than a year and a half to do all that and secure potential financing, with a down payment going into an escrow account. We will select the winner a year from April in place of the cancelled Indie Breakout Band."

"Shit," Lynx muttered.

"That buy-in figure is a hell of a lot higher than our team's market eval." Simon's voice was measured.

"Your team was wrong," Slade answered. "Your offer was the lowest of the top three."

Justice reared back, too many thoughts competing for attention in his head. "Who beat us out?"

"Fury Run was number two. They're young, dynamic, have a new album dropping in spring, and as an all-girl band, they bring some positive female optics to the table."

Justice opened his mouth in shock, but snapped it closed. It hadn't even crossed his mind that Wendy and her crew would throw their hat in the ring, but it should have. They were a fierce band and competed hard. Savaged Illusions and Fury Run had been in a friendly rivalry ever since they'd been on the *Court of Rock* reality show together.

"No way are we letting those girls beat us again," Lynx said.

River drained his glass and reached for the bottle as a small smile touched his mouth. "Sounds like a good chance to kick their butts on the world stage as a little payback."

He wasn't the only one still bitter about second place on *Court of Rock*. But Justice had to point out, "They won't be easy to beat." He was laser focused on his goal of securing the seat Hayes was forced out of, then using their power to systematically destroy him. However Fury Run wasn't the only competition. "Who was the highest offer?"

Slade slapped his glass on the coffee table, his jaw tensing. "Jagged Sin."

For a second, Justice went blank. "Jagged Sin? How would they get that kind of money? Their last album did get into the top ten, but they never hit number one.

They lost the Indie Rock Band." Savaged Illusions had won.

"Pull your head out of your ass," Simon snarled. "How do you think they're doing it?"

Hot anger flashed through Justice's cells like an electric shock, driving him to his feet. "Gene Hayes." He paced to the floor-to-ceiling windows overlooking the city of Vegas. Dawn was only a couple hours away, but partiers were still out celebrating the New Year, while his mood turned dark and ugly. "That bastard is behind their offer, he'll stake them, and then control their decisions. Jagged Sin is a band of puppets with Hayes pulling their strings."

"Probably, but two of our bands, Forticulture and Cellular Evolution, disagreed. Jagged Sin has a new, independent producer for their next album, and they licensed their single to an online streaming service for a new series."

"You're shitting me," Lynx said. "Those butt plugs sold the licensing rights to one of their songs?"

"Hard to believe," Slade answered. "They aren't bad when they're not strung out on drugs and actually show up to work. But I don't trust them, and I'm not letting another degenerate into World Rock Stage. That's why I need your band to win and Jagged Sin to lose."

"What about Fury Run?" Gray asked. "You already said they bring a lot to the table."

"Fury Run is a solid band, and for damn sure I'll take them over Jagged Sin," Slade answered. "When it comes down to it, though, I trust you guys not to be in Hayes's pocket. I don't know Fury Run and can't be a hundred percent certain he won't get to them somehow. I don't want even a fraction of a chance of Hayes getting a foothold back into World Rock Stage."

River snorted. "You think Wendy would cut a deal with Hayes?"

"You did when you signed the contract with Gene Hayes's name on it." Slade shifted his attention around the room. "You all did, but now you want to destroy Hayes, and between us, I'm on board with that."

Justice didn't let himself flinch at the hard truth that they'd sold out to Hayes once. That was exactly what they'd done. He could list a million excuses, but it didn't change the fact. "We have to win and get that seat."

Slade got up, grabbed a fresh beer, popped the top and handed it to Justice. "I have a plan. You have a new album coming out. I'm assuming it's good."

"Best fucking cuts yet," Lynx said.

Justice took a drink of the beer. "So, what then, a tour like we did for 'Expired Hero'?"

Slade leaned a shoulder against the window. "Bigger. A year-long world tour that keeps you guys right in the face of rock music. Promotion, merch, endorsements and licensing agreements."

"That kind of tour takes time to set up." Simon said. "We don't even have a business manager. We used a company to set up a three-month tour."

Gray set down his drink. "The album releases in March. You're asking the impossible."

"I can make it happen," Slade answered. "I have a manager ready to work for you today. He's the best."

"Who?" River asked.

"Gavin Ward."

Justice jerked with another jolt of surprise. "Your manager? I thought he retired to sail around the world or something."

"He got bored. He's ready to come back on as your manager. He knows the stakes, and he has the experience, skill and connections to get this done."

Justice turned to study the city again. "A world tour." He'd be back on the road, with the relentless demands on his time and energy. He'd be away from Beth for a goddamned year. He'd only wrangled her agreement not to file for divorce until October, but Slade was talking about a tour well past that into the following March.

"I have to talk to Beth before I agree to anything."

Really, what choice did he have? If he didn't do it, there was a chance Gene Hayes would maneuver his way back into World Rock Stage.

Chapter 7

LIZA FINISHED UP HER BUSINESS at the front desk with the hotel manager, wanting to make sure he knew how much his staff had helped during their trip. This had been a huge MMA fight, scheduled on an incredibly busy New Year's Eve, and they'd assisted in every way. Including the afterparty celebrating their fighter's win and helping build SLAM's brand in New York.

Liza joined Sloane at the top of a humming escalator leading down to the street-level exit where the car waited. Their luggage had been loaded. Since Sloane was on a call, Liza studied the elegant hotel. It was done in soft pinks and creams, trimmed in rich gold. It wasn't her favorite color palette, but it created a quiet, sophisticated atmosphere. Crystal chandeliers, rare paintings, and pastel-colored flowers rising from exquisite vases all added to the experience. Even her sensible heels sounded muted on the slick floors.

Sloane ended his call. "Is the plane ready?"

His impatience radiated in the deep timbre of his voice. She checked the latest updates on her phone. "It will be by the time we get there."

"Let's go." He stepped onto the escalator to the ground floor exit.

"Mrs. Cade! Your coffee!"

Liza turned, but before she could respond, Whitney, one of SLAM's security who'd traveled with them, cut off the middle-aged man striding toward her.

"It's okay, Whitney," Liza called out as she recognized the hotel manager she'd just been talking to. "He's right, I set it down and forgot."

Whitney relaxed and held out her hand. "I'll take that for her, thanks."

Liza pivoted back toward the escalator when something slammed into her back. She stumbled forward, pitching right for the long, moving risers with the spiked edges. She grabbed the gold-trimmed wall behind handrail, she stopped herself from falling.

"Let me go," a woman screeched. "That bitch ruined my life."

Liza craned her head. On the floor a couple feet away, Whitney had a woman pinned facedown, hands wrenched behind her back. She couldn't move her body, but her voice worked. "Get off me! She's a liar! Lyin' Liza! Baby killer! Let her die by falling down the stairs! She should die!"

"Christ." Sloane snarled next to her.

Liza jerked, surprised. "I didn't see you."

"I was more than half way down, and ran back up when I heard you yelp. You caught yourself before I could get to you, but that lunatic was ready to shove you again when Whitney subdued her."

Holy shit. The woman had tried to kill her. If it hadn't been for Whitney reacting, she'd be lying at the bottom of the escalator. Probably dead.

Her mom would be alone.

Hayes would consider that a win.

More people ran up, including hotel security. They got the woman on her feet.

Furious, Liza stalked up to her. Sloane tried to stop her, but she shrugged him off, too ticked off to let anyone deter her. Two feet away, she halted. Her attacker was lean, taller than Liza, with a long, athletic body. Lines dug into her forehead, around her eyes, and between her nose and lips. She wore a black sweater and leggings.

"You're like all the whores Hayes screwed," the woman spat at her. "You were nothing!"

Liza found her voice. "Who exactly are you?"

"I'm a dancer! I danced in Hayes's videos. I was going to be a star, not a whore like you! You ruined my life, all our lives."

Was she serious? Liza ruined her life? What about the life of that fourteen-year-old girl who Hayes drugged and raped? "So your life sucks and you think going to prison for murdering me will make it better?"

She struggled against the security guards holding her. "It's not just me. All of us on Bring Hayes Home want you dead. We watch you, post your whereabouts, that's how I knew you were in New York. You'll die, Lyin' Liza. You'll die."

Liza let a cold smile curve her lips. "Is everyone on that site as dumb and clumsy as you?"

The woman lunged, nearly ripping her arms out of their sockets.

Liza walked to her boss, hot fury breaking through the shock. "It's not going to end."

"What isn't?" he asked.

"The attacks. The attempts to kill me."

"Nope." He glanced at security helping Whitney deal with the crazed woman. "The question is, what are you going to do about it?"

That was the question, wasn't it? She thought of Justice working his ass off to fight Hayes professionally. Even Molly, her fictional character, was fighting hard to keep her baby.

Wasn't it time Liza took some action?

She tilted her chin up with determination. "I'm not going to die, that's for damn sure. I'd like to hire Whitney away from SLAM, and I want to take self-defense. Can you get me someone good? I'll pay for it, but I need to be safe."

She was done being anyone's victim. If another attacker got through her excellent bodyguard, then Liza would kick their ass.

The dark SUV stopped at the transitional center's guard gate, and Liza handed over her license to her driver, Whitney, to collect her waiting visitor pass. It was there exactly as Justice had texted her it would be.

Whitney steered the car around to the front of the building, jumped out and opened Liza's door before she'd gotten the badge clipped on and gathered her purse.

Sliding out, Liza paused. Although it was dark, lights illuminated the familiar landscape of flowers and shrubs lining a walkway. To the right was a grassy area bracketed by palm trees around a few benches. Straight ahead was the beige and glass building that rose several stories and sprawled out in multiple directions.

Was Justice here yet? More to the point, why had she agreed to meet him instead of insisting he fill her in about World Rock Stage's counter offer over the phone?

Because it mattered too much. Liza wanted Hayes to pay. That part was simple.

Justice was the dangerous complication drawing her back into a world that wasn't safe and wouldn't be until the prison door slammed shut on Hayes. Was she ready to see him? Could she handle it?

"Liza?" Whitney asked. "Have you changed your mind? Do you want to leave?"

She jolted, realizing she stood in the way of closing the door. "I'm fine, I just haven't been here in a while."

Whitney's gaze tracked around the grounds, then returned to her. "I'll make sure you're safe. Then I'll park the car and wait until you're ready to go. Text me before you come outside, and I'll meet you in this spot."

"Thanks." Liza headed into the lobby and stopped. A sculpture of a soldier standing watch presided in one corner. Carved into the stone base was:

Transitioning Warriors Recovery Center

The toughest battles are the ones fought in the dark tunnels of our mind.

The words made her ache for Noah. Yeah, Liza had her own issues, but she hadn't endured anything like her father-in-law had. He'd suffered an explosion, had his body torn apart and burned by an IUD while he listened to young men he cared about scream and die. When he'd agreed to come here a little over a year ago, she'd so hoped he would find some help and peace. It hadn't worked out, and Noah had gone back to the streets.

"Beth."

She whirled around, and winced at her sore muscles from her first two classes. Justice stood a couple feet away. Her heart thumped, and her pulse jumped. At six feet, Justice took up a lot of space, but it wasn't only his height that commanded attention. It was his energy, the living electricity in him that lit up when he was on stage. And when he sang...

She shivered as memories stretched and writhed, trying to break free. She'd been his biggest fan once, now she couldn't bear to hear his songs.

"Thanks for meeting me," he said softly. "I wasn't sure if you'd come."

He looked good. Much better than the last time she'd seen him. The cut through his eyebrow had healed to a jagged scar, adding more ruggedness to his face. He didn't appear as gaunt and haunted. He'd trimmed his beard down to the neat scruff she'd always liked. Justice had on a black T-shirt and jeans resting low on his hips. Behind him, two women at the counter watched him. Of course they noticed him. He captured the whole hot, sexy, and tortured rock-star vibe.

She was suddenly conscious of her own appearance in her conservative black dress. "You can be persuasive, especially by dangling an issue with your dad. That was clever." And likely intentional since he knew how much she cared about Noah.

"I wanted to see you. Needed to. You're beautiful, but you always were. Now there's something even more compelling about you, a layer of…"

She resisted the urge to lean closer. "What?"

He tilted his head. "A don't-fuck-with-me confidence. One that says I deal with idiots like you before breakfast and without breaking a sweat. You've grown up into a powerful woman. Director of Communications for a billion dollar company."

"Yet you're not intimidated."

He grinned. "I find it sexy and tempting."

Liza rolled her eyes. See what happened when she let herself get drawn in with him? "Knock it off. I'm not a reporter you need to dazzle with your charm so I don't ask the hard questions."

"Not charm, baby. Truth. You're amazing, and I'm so damned proud of you."

His sincerity robbed her of complaints, or even her don't-fuck-with-me armor. Justice had the same ability as Em to see past her defenses to the real person. He'd seen past her plain clothes and cardigan the first day they met. Liza changed the subject. "Thanks for the mug." He'd sent a coffee cup with a chicken on it, and the phrase, *Why did the chicken cross the road? To get the promotion!* Liza loved it. If he'd sent her an expensive or showy gift, she'd have been annoyed or sent it back. He'd known that, so he found something silly and fun that reminded her of the kitchen decorated with chickens in his grandmother's house.

"You're welcome. Let's go to the private visiting room I reserved, and I'll fill you in." He walked at her side through the halls. "You're moving a little stiff. Are you sore from that woman pushing you?"

"Nope. I didn't have a scratch from that."

"Have you found out if they're going to charge her?"

Liza tensed. "They'll send it to the D.A. as attempted murder, but it'll be pleaded out to something less serious." She hadn't actually been hurt, and intent was tough to prove.

"So if you weren't hurt from that shove, why do you seem stiff?"

It was disconcerting that he could tell. "Sherry Moreno is teaching me self-defense. It's nothing like the tame little classes I took in college." They went into a room painted a soft mauve. A couch and two chairs faced off over a coffee table. A big window spilled in the fading light of dusk over a children's play area with a brightly colored table, two chairs and toys. The other side had a small fridge and a coffeemaker.

The center had a couple of these small private rooms that could be reserved for special, sensitive or difficult discussions.

"Self-defense, huh? Thought you hired Whitney as a bodyguard."

Vivid awareness of Justice looming a few feet behind skittered along her skin. She sat in a chair and noticed the large manila envelope on the coffee table. "I did, but I'm damned tired of being a victim. Some lunatic gets through my protection, I'll handle it."

He grabbed a couple waters from a small fridge. When he held out one for her, the sleeve of his T-shirt pulled up, revealing the guitar and music note tat wrapped in a crown of thorns and the single drop of blood. Her fingers itched to trace it as she once had when they lay in bed. Needing a distraction, she said, "No comment about me training with Sherry?"

He sat across from her. "Trying to get passed the pissed."

Not quite what she'd expected. "At?"

"Myself. Hayes. All the asshole groupies who'd kill for a child rapist. Take your pick of the reasons you don't feel safe." He chugged a gulp of water. "Your determination to kick ass, that's another layer of sexy."

Liza opened her bottle, and let the cool exterior dampen the confusing mix of desire, curiosity, anger and the sad regret that lined her world no matter what she did. A few minutes in his company destroyed the emotional distance she'd used at work, nearly stripping her back to the girl who'd taken the foolish chance of falling in love with a rock star and gotten burned. Hadn't she learned? Regaining control of this meeting, she gestured to the table. "What's in the envelope?"

"I've made arrangements here at the center to hold

a room and/or outpatient care for Dad if he decides to return for treatment."

Ah, that's why he'd suggested meeting here. "You think Noah might? Come back here, I mean?"

"Maybe. I had a meeting with the counselor who worked with Dad when he was here before. He feels Dad leaving you the food and a note on Christmas Day was a big step. Like he's trying to reconnect after no contact for months." Justice's face softened. "Dad always watched out for you, and he knew Christmas would be hard. Which, the counselor pointed out, means Dad is thinking about you."

"And you. He wanted me to tell you Merry Christmas." She set her water down. "I get that Noah was being kind to me, but I think he's also trying to talk to you the only way he's able to." It was hard for Noah to be in the same space as Justice let alone have a conversation with him.

"Through you. That's what the counselor said too. He reiterated that I need to accept that the dad I knew is gone. I have to decide if I want a relationship with the man he is today." He fisted hands in his lap. "I'm trying, Beth."

His real pain sliced into her. How could she not feel empathy for Justice? While her dad had been an asshole who traded his daughter like she was nothing more than a shiny toy, Justice had a hero for a father. A man he'd admired for most of his childhood, and that man left him. It didn't matter that it was illogical, that Noah had been severely injured and dealing with PTSD, for Justice it was abandonment. After all, his mom had flat out abandoned him when he was arrested as a teenager. Later, his grandmother died, and Liza had left him after they'd lost their daughter. Then Drake died.

Justice was hanging on to his dad.

She didn't know what to say to him exactly, so she asked, "What do you need from me?"

Justice slid the envelope across the table to her. "In there is the house key, security codes, and various information. If you're willing, I'm listing you first on all the contact lists for the transitional center, and the management and security companies for the house."

The house she'd lived in with Justice, made their child together and been happy until it all fell apart. "Why for the house if you have a management company? I assume you notify them when you're not there?" He'd been living most of his time in Los Angeles while the band recorded their second album.

"Yes, but you know what Dad needs more than some management company," Justice answered. "I was hoping you could make sure the house is stocked with things like a warm coat, first aid, cash, canned food or frozen food, and anything he needs for Radar."

Go in the house? She'd refused to step foot in there after Paris, unable to face the memories. Could she do it now? *It's for Noah*, she reminded herself.

"It's still the same, everything except the security fence." He slid the enveloped closer to her.

Justice appeared relaxed, but his right knee bounced, giving away his tension. Was he thinking about the baby's room that he'd painted the perfect shade of yellow as a surprise for her? Liza had the room all planned to the last detail, and intended to buy the crib and other necessities after they returned.

Her palms got slick with sweat, and her fingers tingled. *Don't think about her room.* She picked up the envelope, slid out the papers, and efficiently skimmed the pages until she came to a bank statement. Frowning, she honed in on her and Justice's name.

"Our joint account? I'd forgotten about that." Scanning down, she gasped. "That's a lot of money. Are you sure you want to trust me with access to it?"

"There's no one I trust more. With the money or my dad."

"Tell me what's going on. This"—she gestured to the bank statement—"is way too much money to be a short-term emergency fund."

His jaw clenched, creating more hollows beneath his cheekbones. "World Rock Stage didn't accept our offer. Instead they've chosen the bands of the top three offers to compete for it. They are setting up tough conditions, including requiring us to do a year-long international tour."

Obviously Savaged Illusions was one of the bands chosen. "You'll be gone a year? I guess that explains wanting me to look out for Noah." It unsettled her to think of Justice being away so long. Loneliness closed in, darkening her world a little more. Of course she wasn't going back to him, but this was so...final. Had he changed his mind about them? "Do you want me to file for divorce?"

His head snapped back as if she'd hit him. "No! You promised, Beth. I have until October."

"You're leaving in March," she pointed out. "You won't even be here in October."

Shooting to his feet, Justice paced the small room, his anxiety so vivid, it made her skin prickle.

"I can't say no. I'd rather stay here with you, and for my dad. I... Fuck." He spun around, the muscles in his back cording beneath his shirt.

"You want to perform more." Liza rose, went to the window, and looked out into the falling night. "You want another number-one song and to get that seat on World Rock Stage. It's who you are, who you always were." It stung deep in her chest, like multiple burning points sizzling against the ice of her heart. She'd loved him so much and been so damned desperate for him to love her.

"You're wrong."

He was right behind her. So close, his breath feathered over her hair. Too close. Yet she didn't move away, the weight of their past anchoring her there.

"I'd turn it down," he said softly. "But there's a problem."

She ignored the urge to escape, run to the safety of her condo and not face whatever was coming. "What problem?"

"The other two bands? One is Fury Run."

A chill went down her spine. Not at Fury Run, they were an excellent band and solid women. They weren't the problem Justice mentioned. "Who's the third group?"

"Jagged Sin."

Oh God. Savaged Illusions had been in a battle with Jagged Sin twice before, and the last time Hayes had been involved, pulling strings behind the scene. Savaged Illusions had won, but Hayes used the situation to get to Liza, and that confrontation had resulted in her losing their child.

Wait, Jagged Sin wasn't in the same league of success as Savaged Illusion or Fury Run, so how were they getting the financing for this contest? The answer slapped her in the face. "Gene Hayes." Tiny nuggets of hot anger and outrage erupted, like bursting popcorn kernels. "Hayes is backing them."

Tension radiated in the harsh line of his jaw beneath the trimmed scruff. "He has to be. He'll stake them, and they'll be his puppets." He rocked on the balls of his feet. "I can't let them win, but I don't want to leave you for a year."

Despair billowed up, dampening her entire being. It was never going to end. Hayes was out there, scheming and bullying. Being forced out of World Rock Stage had diminished his power some and smacked down his ego, but he was plotting to get it back. "I want him destroyed. Go on the tour, I'll watch out for your dad, and the house. Please, stop him."

Justice ground his jaw. After a moment, he said, "I will. But you gave me a year. I'm not letting anything come between us again. Not Hayes or Jagged Sin, not my band members, and not a world tour. Nothing. As long as you're willing to give me the chance, I'll do everything in my power to earn back your trust."

Liza couldn't move as her heart tried to lean into him, while her brain warned her to pull back. Her mouth dried, and the woman in her nearly begged him to touch and kiss her. She'd had no idea how much she'd missed him until this moment. It was huge and terrifying. "I didn't think that was possible when we talked at Drake's funeral."

"And now?"

She couldn't break this connection sizzling between them, yet fear snaked up her spine. Not the same kind of fear as when that woman tried to push her down the escalator in New York. That had been a physical response that had propelled her into action. Taking the chance of having her heart crushed again sparked an emotional terror that made her want to hide.

"I don't know." She pulled herself from him, gathered the papers and key back in the envelope and went to the door. "Thank you for going after Hayes professionally." She headed down the hall.

He walked at her side. "Can I see you again? Before I go? I'll be here at the center a couple more times."

It'd be safer to say no. She felt the weight of the

papers in her hand holding that key to the house. In the reception area, she stopped. "Why? If I'm handling all this, why do you need to be here?"

A grin teased his mouth. "Meet me again and I'll tell you."

He was trying to lighten the moment, and draw her back to him. "I'll call you."

"When?"

Liza spotted her car pulling up outside. "When I want to know why you're coming back to the center." She strode out the door and into the car.

She'd won that skirmish, but the battle loomed big and scary. Should she see him again?

Chapter 8

JUSTICE LEFT HIS APPOINTMENT AND hurried through the maze of hallways at the transitional center. He spotted Beth walking with her head down away from him. He jogged, catching up to her. "Hi."

She whipped her head up from her phone. "Justice, you startled me."

More like scared her. "You're the one who called me to meet you here." Well, she'd asked if he wanted to see the upgraded room that allowed dogs she'd gotten his dad next time he was in town. Justice hadn't thought of that, but Beth had.

"So I did, which means you have to pay up. Why do you need to come here if not for your dad?"

"You held out for nearly a month, did it drive you crazy wanting to know?" It sure did him. He kept in contact with her mostly through texts, discussing the upcoming contest and tour, or her book. She still wouldn't send him pages, but she talked about her battles with her character, Molly.

She slid her phone into her purse and stopped at the end of a hallway in front of a door. "I barely thought about it."

Liar. "Then I guess you can wait until dinner to get an answer."

She frowned. "I didn't agree to go out, or to eat with you."

Which was why he hadn't asked. "I ordered food for us and had it delivered to the room."

"Deal or date?"

He leaned closer. "I don't give a shit what we call it, all I care about is spending time with you. If I thought you'd agree, I'd have whisked you away to a private island, or yacht, or any secret location where we could share a romantic meal. I don't think you're ready for that, so we'll start here in the room you thoughtfully secured for my dad. You can leave anytime." She'd take another piece of his heart with her if she did, but it was her choice.

She stabbed the keypad. "Dinner better be worth falling for your charm." Pushing open the door, she flicked on the lights and strode between the living space on the right, with a slider that led to a balcony, and the bedroom area on the left.

Beth headed to the small square table where the white food containers waited with sealed bottles of water. She opened one. "Caprice chicken!"

"I ordered it from Stilts, that restaurant that just opened on the pier. I thought you'd like it." Sliding out a chair for her, he added, "Will you eat with me?"

"You make it hard to say no." She sat, picked up her fork and sampled her dinner. "Delicious. Okay, I'm eating, start talking. What are you doing at the center?"

Justice took a drink of his water. "They offer counseling services here to family members of the center's patients. My first appointment was last month when you met me here. Tonight was my second. I'm working on becoming the son my dad needs and finding a way for us to communicate."

Surprise pushed her back against the chair. "You're in therapy. That's huge." She touched his arm. "You're doing this for Noah. That's awesome, Justice. Even more amazing that you're making time now as you're gearing up for your album release and tour."

That single touch from Beth sent echoes of longing through Justice. Desire, yes, but it was so much more. It'd taken a conscious effort not to take hold of her hand just to feel the physical link to her. "I want a relationship with my dad, and it takes work. I can't run off on tour and expect the people I love to just wait. That's partly what 'Savaged Vows' is about." He told her about the song, how he came to write it and Lynx adding the death scream.

"I listened to the cut you sent me. It's a great song, starting powerful then ending on rage. That death scream gave me chills."

"I thought you'd delete it without listening."

She toyed with a piece of olive. "My delete button appears to be broken around you."

He laughed and changed the subject. "How's your new position going?"

Beth cleared her throat. "Well, I've only had the job for a month and a half, but I like it. It's a challenge running the marketing and publicity department. Thankfully, I was able to hire my assistant, and she's been awesome. You remember Sophie, from the front desk in SLAM's lobby?"

He nodded, easily recalling the bubbly blonde.

Beth smiled. "She's my right hand. We're developing a vodka brand, Slam Vodka, which is exciting."

She'd always been good at publicity and had worked her ass off at SLAM. "That's impressive."

"It keeps me sane, and it's helping me pay for my mom's lawyers to make sure things stay on track for her release and build up a fund to take care of her once she's out of prison."

Justice fought the urge to tell her he'd help, that she or her mom would never need anything. Beth would resist that. Which was ridiculous, given how much she did for his dad. "How is Amber? Everything set for her parole?"

"So far, yeah. Her official date is May 12th, and we got approval to move her supervision to San Diego. The lawyers warned me not to be photographed or videoed with you, or with anyone in the rock world. If the parole board thinks living with me is unsuitable, at the very least they'd move her supervision back to L.A., or they could revoke her parole altogether." Liza fidgeted for a moment. "They encouraged me to start divorce proceedings, but I told them we had an agreement to wait until October."

Thank God.

Before he could respond, she went on, "Mom told me something. Did you try to get her an early release? After Paris, I mean. I don't think she'd lie, but...did you?"

He studied her, wondering if he should have told her. "I had my lawyers approach the governor's office, pleading that Amber's only daughter had lost a child and was virtually alone. They wouldn't even consider it." He was still pissed about that. They'd taken Beth's mom away at the worst moment in Beth's young life, putting her mom in prison for killing a man who deserved it to protect her daughter. Then, years later, Beth needed her again, and they wouldn't do it. How was that justice when it seemed like the victim didn't matter?

"You never said anything."

"You wouldn't see or talk to me." She did everything she could to avoid him—except disappear like his mom had. Beth had access to money in their joint accounts and credit cards. She could have gone far away from him, but she hadn't. Which meant he could have informed her by text or email. "I didn't want to tell you when it was a long shot." Had he been right? "I was desperate to help you. You were so alone, grieving with no family around. I thought you needed your mom."

She looked down, and he could almost feel her struggle to keep her emotions under wrap. "Thank you for that. I didn't know."

He didn't like her avoiding his gaze, so he shifted the subject back to more comfortable territory. "Why did you think your mom might lie?" He was curious.

Her mouth tilted up in a wry expression. "Don't let it go to your head, but she's one of your biggest fans. Deep down, Mom is still a rock-band groupie at heart."

That ripped out a wry laugh. "She told me that if she were free, she'd cut off my balls for hurting you, and for not protecting you and her grandbaby. She said I'd better damn well prove my love for you and take care of her baby. That's you," he added, in case she was confused. "Or find a good place to hide when she gets out."

Beth's fork froze halfway to her mouth. "Seriously? Wait, you saw her? In person?"

"I visited her once, and it was a huge ordeal. The prison helped me do it quietly as we didn't want media to show up and create more frenzy. I told her you needed her, and would she talk to my lawyers so they could try to get an early release, or parole or whatever. She agreed."

Her lips shot up into a grin. "Then she threatened you."

Justice could still feel Amber's hard stare when she said it. "I don't think it was a threat. She meant it. Given she killed your dad for you, I may have to buy a remote island in shark-infested waters."

Beth snorted. "You weren't too afraid if you went ahead with the effort to get her released."

"Because I love you and will prove to you and your mom that I grew the fuck up and will put you first." Yeah, it was blunt, but she knew he wanted her back.

Beth sat back in her chair, fingering the edge of the food container, her faint grin shifting down and up in a show of conflicting emotions. The smile won out. "There's that ego, Rock Star. So sure of yourself, but I'm not one of your groupies."

Hearing her nickname for him, and her teasing, went straight to his heart. "No, but I'm still yours. How's your book going? I miss seeing you get lost in writing."

"You used to get jealous and bug me for pages." She tilted her head. "Now you hound me by text."

"Guilty." And not a bit remorseful about it.

"Molly keeps me company, and we're figuring it out together."

"Yeah?" He hoped she'd keep talking.

"Sometimes I hate her for being pregnant. Other times, I admire her." Fiddling with the label on her water bottle, she added, "She's putting her baby first. I don't know if it'll end in disaster or she'll win."

"Don't you want to find out?"

She set her fork down. "If she fails this baby, I will kill her. I really will."

The fierce anger told him Molly was hitting nerves, digging around in the painful areas of Beth's heart. "It's your book."

Beth pushed her container back. "I wanted to ask

you, with all that is going on with Jagged Sin and Hayes, have you heard any mention of Nikki?"

The bitch's name pissed him off. Beth had completely trusted Nikki as a friend, and the woman had sold information about her and their baby to Gene Hayes. "No." Worry hit him hard. "Have you?"

She shook her head. "The smart thing for her to do is get far away from the mess she made here. She escaped charges because the D.A. couldn't find evidence that linked her to Hayes. They never found the cell phone she used to contact Hayes, and her extra income was through selling designer items on eBay or Etsy. It appeared legit. It was all there on the website, and the money through PayPal. She even had her shipping receipts." She grimaced. "My guess is Hayes found a way to get those items to her, and she sold them, creating the facade of a legitimate income."

Justice frowned. "If the smart thing to do is leave, why do you think she'd hang around Jagged Sin?"

"Because she wanted to be a rock star's wife. It was a like a drug to her. She must have kicked the habit and headed to greener pastures." Liza set her napkin on the table. "I need to go. Thanks for dinner." She stood.

Since she was determined to leave, Justice followed her to the door, and once there, he reached past her to open it.

At the same moment, she turned, and they were face-to-face, her mouth just inches from his, her scent filling him. "Beth."

"What?" Her voice was breathless, her pupils dilating.

"I've missed you so damned much, and it's killing me not to touch you." He wouldn't until she let him. "Do you miss me?"

The pulse in her throat quickened. She compressed her mouth, but her gaze remained on his.

The air vibrated around them. Would she answer? Or tell him to back off? She had the power here, and she knew it or she'd have panicked the second he crowded her against the door.

"Do you?" he pressed.

"Yes." The word seemed to surprise her. "I don't want to miss you, and I don't want to feel this."

"Feel what? Our chemistry? Desire? The way it felt when I kissed you? Or the way it felt when we talked and laughed?" He clenched his hands with the effort of keeping them at his sides. "Or when I held you."

"All of it." Her jaw worked. "I hate that you can make me want you, want us and what he had together, again."

"Yeah, well, I hate that I can't fucking breathe without you. I hate that you can strip me back to this animalistic creature that will do anything to win his mate back." Slowly, he reached up to set his hand on the door close to her head. A lock of hair that had escaped her pins brushed his skin. He almost groaned at the sensation of her hair gliding over his hand. "And I hate that I have to let you go home to your condo tonight. Alone."

She inhaled sharply, turning her head enough bring her mouth tantalizing close. He curled his fingers into the door, fighting for control.

Her eyes glittered like emeralds. "You're not moving."

"Before you go, I need to know one thing. Do you want me to kiss you?" Desperation pounded in his skull, while his body throbbed to feel her again, her lips against his, their tongues mingling, and her warmth in his arms. He craved it like a man dying of thirst.

How could Liza answer him? Captivated by the intense raw heat of him surrounding her, she could hear a layer of ice around her heart cracking. She'd missed this easy intimacy tinged with sizzling sexual need and the sweet ache of love. On top of that, Justice had been trying. He'd defended her at every turn, attempted to get her mom out of prison to be with her, and risked his newfound wealth and fame to ruin Hayes. He was even getting therapy.

Did she want him to kiss her? "Part of me does," she admitted.

He moved his hand from the door to cup her cheek. "And the other part?"

The warmth of his palm and fingers sank in, and Liza closed her eyes. How long had it been since someone touched her with this tenderness?

She lifted her lids. "Is afraid."

"Of?"

Of what he could make her feel. Of how badly she'd wanted him to love her enough. He'd shattered her once, yet she pressed her face against his hand, trying to soak it up. "Of us. Of what happens outside."

He traced his thumb along her bottom lip. "I love you more than anything outside this room, Beth. Tell me if you feel that from me."

The slow sweep of his thumb ignited the softest of tingles. They traveled over the skin of her throat to her nipples. She shivered, surprised. Other than an occasional dream, she hadn't felt this since...

No. For this moment, she didn't want to slide into the dark, icy pool of grief. Justice's touch had pulled her above it, making her feel alive. They were alone, no one had to know. She reached up, threading her fingers into his hair. The thick locks gliding against her flesh gave her another tiny jolt.

"I feel it." As long as they kept everything else on the other side of the door behind her, she was almost normal.

The blue in his eyes sizzled. "And?"

"Kiss me."

He wrapped his other arm around her and tugged her to his warm, hard chest. He brushed a stray piece of her hair back and lowered his mouth to hers.

She caught her breath as his lips covered hers. He took his time, lingering as if her mouth were a pleasure to be savored. Teasing, tantalizing then retreating.

She gripped his hair tightly and parted her mouth.

A half laugh, half groan rumbled between them, and he deepened the kiss. Her world fuzzed at the edges, melting as he touched her everywhere. One hand on her face, his thumb caressing her jaw, his arm banding her to his length, his tongue sliding and dueling with hers. For the first time in months, all her nerve endings came alive. She wanted this, craved—

A sharp noise jangled.

Breaking the kiss, the cool air sent a wave of *What the hell am I doing kissing Justice?* through her. Yet she hadn't wanted to stop.

"That your phone?"

Liza reached for her cell. "Probably, Whitney." She read the text.

"Everything okay?" Justice's voice vibrated with low frustration.

Okay? She'd been kissing him. Losing more control with every heartbeat. Feeling alive and sexy, while their daughter, their baby...

Fury raced through her. Oh no, she was not doing this. Not while that bastard walked free. "I have to go. Whitney is waiting." Turning, she reached for the door.

"Can I see you again? Take you out? We can go on dates, anywhere you want."

She stilled, unable to leave yet, and looked over her shoulder. His jaw was rock hard, his hands tense at his sides.

"No, not now. I need to focus on getting my mom paroled and safe. To do that, I can't be in your world right now. You need to concentrate on the tour."

His jaw tightened. "Is this what you're going to do, Beth? Keep running from me, until the year you gave me expires and you can file for divorce?"

She spun. "I'm not running. If I want a divorce, you'll be the first to know. I'm not ready for more with you, and I won't be pushed into anything until I am. If you can't handle it, then you file for the damned divorce yourself."

He folded his arms. "No chance, baby. You're mine until the day you stop loving me."

It really irritated her that she was relieved to hear it. "Who said I still love you?"

"That kiss."

"I have to go." She narrowed her eyes. "Don't you dare accuse me of running." Yanking the door open, she stalked out.

He kept an easy pace by her side. "You're in a rush. Big plans later? A date with someone else?"

She was tempted to throw her elbow into his solar plexus like Sherry had taught her. Instead she amused herself with a verbal jab. "Yep."

He stumbled. "What? Who? When?"

Liza smiled. "Molly. She's a lot less annoying than you."

Molly didn't have the power to hurt Liza the way Justice did.

Chapter 9

"GOTTA RUN." SHERRY MORENO WAVED at the door of a private room of SLAM's gym. She looked cute wearing black cropped yoga pants and a powder-blue tank top. Sherry held a black belt in Tae Kwon Do and taught several classes a week. "See you Thursday."

"Thanks, Sherry." Liza lifted a hand, pleased that her arm still worked despite feeling like a wet noodle.

Once the door closed, a groan came from the floor. *Thanks, Sherry*," Emily mimicked in a whiney voice. "That monster almost killed your best friend and you're thanking her?"

Emily slumped against the mirrored wall. Her blonde hair was matted to her skull, her face splotchy, and her yoga tank drenched. "You're the one who insisted on coming to my self-defense class."

Liza was pretty damned proud that she could at least stand. She'd been taking the classes for a month, and her body was adjusting to the torturous rigors disguised as basic martial arts, plus strength and endurance training with horrors like pushups and running on a treadmill.

"I'm being supportive." With agonizing slowness,

Em pulled her cell out of her bag and groaned her way up to standing. "You owe me for this. You're buying dinner from Wylie's. I'll call in an order, and we'll pick it up on the way back to your place."

Liza zipped her gym bag. "Seriously? You want Mexican food after that?" She shook her head. "Besides, I have work to do tonight."

With the phone to her ear, Em raised her eyebrows. "Phone's ringing. Pick something or I'm ordering your usual tequila ribs."

Liza sighed and gave in. "Salad." Em flat out refused to do the smart thing and stay away from Liza, even though she could be hurt or killed.

The thought made Liza nauseous.

Em ended her call. "Get that expression off your face. I'm not hiding from that asshole. I'm here taking self-defense with you to learn to protect myself, and I'm careful. Also, I ordered you the Tex Mex Bowl. It has vegetables in it, so it's like a salad. And a side of their handmade tortillas."

"Let's not forget the Sugar Dancer brownies you brought for dessert." Em had shown up at her door with them before the class.

"Those are to make you talk."

Liza studied Em. "Using innocent brownies as bribery?"

"My backup plan is to get you drunk. Cooperate and you won't have to endure a hangover. Up to you." Slapping a hand on her hip, she added, "Did you think I'd let you get away without telling me everything about your little dinner date with Justice?"

Liza tightened her mouth. "It wasn't a date. We met there to look at Noah's room. I had no idea he'd have dinner delivered and waiting for us." Liza left out the part about Justice getting counseling at the center.

"So you've said."

Her stomach tightened as she gathered her things and sent a quick text to Whitney to pick her and Em up. She was in the gym somewhere, so it'd take her a few minutes. Liza strode to the door. "I texted Whitney, let's go."

Her friend's gaze softened. "Wait. Let me say this before we get in the car with your driver and you figure out a way to deflect me."

"Right, and while I'm performing miracles, I'll sprout wings and fly," Liza muttered to the closed door.

"Ha-ha. Are you going to listen, or will you spend the night watching me eat all four brownies myself?"

Turning, she faced her friend. "Hurry and spit it out."

"I was pissed at Justice for what he did to you."

"Hello? Not a newsflash. You haven't hidden your feelings." Em had been her rock right after Paris, often staying with her at the Opulence Hotel and handling everything that Liza couldn't, including Justice. More than once, she heard Em on the phone, telling him Liza didn't want to see him and that he didn't deserve her, in colorful ways. She'd stood guard between Liza and the world those first awful days and weeks.

Em smiled. "It's part of my charm and why you love me. It's also why I'm going to tell you this."

Curiosity kept her pinned in place. "What?"

She crossed the several feet separating them and touched Liza's arm. "I saw that picture of you and Justice on social media."

"You and the entire world." Some kid visiting their dad at the center had seen her and Justice walking down the hallway together and posted a picture on social media.

"It was written all over your face, you still have feelings for him, and that's okay."

Her mouth tingled with the reminder of the kiss, of what it felt like to be held by him. To feel Justice, his passion and love tugging at the part of her that had gone cold. Then came the confusion and guilt.

"We kissed." The words tumbled out.

Em touched her arm. "And?"

That single touch spilled out her feelings before she could catch hold of them. "I wanted him. Us. It's been so long since I've felt that part of myself. Then I remembered our baby, and I had to stop and leave. He asked me to meet him again, and I refused to commit."

"Do you want to?"

"It's tempting, but at the same time, scary." That was as honest as she knew how to be. She pulled open the door.

In the hallway, music blared, weights clanked, and voices echoed. The scent of disinfectant, rubber, and sweaty energy filled her nostrils as she stalked down the hall, through the main room to the navy-colored chairs ringing the lobby desk. Taking a seat, she kept an eye out the windows for Whitney.

Em dropped her bag on the floor and fell like a stone into the chair next to her. "It's okay to live again, Liza. To let yourself feel. And it's okay to pull back when you need space. No one else can tell you how to grieve and heal."

Liza took her friend's hand. "Thank you, Em. For everything you've done. I wouldn't have made it through without you."

"You'd do it for me. Besides, remember when Ben and I took the train to Disneyland?"

Liza shuddered. By the time they hopped the shuttle into the park, they were both queasy and assumed they needed to eat. "How did Ben not realize you two had a stomach bug?"

Em shrugged. "Doctors make the worst patients."

Liza had driven out there, gathered the two invalids from the park first aide center, and managed to get them to a nearby hotel. Her name had power—she'd gotten a suite and spent two long days caring for her ill charges. She'd been able to work remotely, and by the time she got them back to their condo, Liza barely made it home before she'd started vomiting. "I hated you the day I got home."

Em half smiled. "I got that from your text when you wrote it all in caps."

"Next time I rescue your sorry butts and nurse you guys back from the brink of death, send chocolate, not the plague." Grabbing her water, she took a sip and spotted the black SUV stopping in front of the gym. "Whitney's pulling up."

Em groaned as she rose. "Someone is stabbing a voodoo doll of me with an ice pick."

Liza laughed as they headed outside to the vehicle. "Wait until you try to get out of bed in the morning." She reached for the back door.

"Liza!" a male voice shouted. "Mrs. Cade!"

"Hey!" Em bellowed. "Get away from her!"

Liza whirled around to a microphone thrust into her face. "Ross Jackson from..."

Reporter. She didn't catch the media outlet and didn't care. More people crowded toward her, flashes of light exploding. She squinted through her glasses, but the glare pierced her vision. Where was Em? Was she okay?

"Get in the car!" Whitney ordered somewhere from her left.

"What kind of accident did your mom have? Or was

it a fight?" the man directly in front of her demanded.

"What?" Liza yelled, her entire body jerking with shock. *Mom is hurt? Is she alive?* Heart thundering, she plunged her hand in her gym bag, searching for her phone.

"Liza, get in the damned car." Whitney shoved a man with a camera and shoulder-rammed the guy with the microphone. "Now."

Another woman rushed up, and a brilliant strobe of light flashed on. "Liza! Was it a prison fight? Will this affect your mom's upcoming parole next month?"

Liza couldn't make sense of the words. Her mom... oh God what was going on? Real panic rose in a boiling wave to drown her.

Whitney broke through the throng, shoved her into the car and slammed the door. Liza gripped the edge of the leather seats and fought to calm down so she could think. What happened to her mom? Where was she?

More chaos erupted outside the car. Men poured out of the gym, a few she recognized as SLAM fighters. She caught sight of Em's blonde head among them and realized she must have run back inside to get help. The car door opened again, and Em climbed in, her face red with fury.

A second later, the driver's door opened, and Whitney slid in. "Seat belts, now." The automatic locks clicked, and the car started.

Liza snapped her seat belt in place, dimly aware that the gym staff and clients were physically blocking reporters so Whitney could drive out. Her biggest thought was her mom. "I don't know what's happening."

Em had her phone out. "I'm seeing headlines saying various things like, *Amber Ranger at Hospital after Prison Incident.* There's a grainy picture." She held up her phone.

Liza peered at the long-distance, blurred image of a woman sitting on a gurney in a hallway, her wrist handcuffed to the gurney railing and a grim-faced guard at her side. Gauze was wrapped around her head, and there appeared to be a dark spot on above her right temple. Her face was pale, thin and twisted in pain. The shot was clearly a quick cell phone snap from someone in the hospital, but Liza recognized her.

"It's...oh God, that's my mom." *Calm down, Mom is hurt but alive in the picture.*

Em laid her hand on Liza's arm. "Check your phone. Maybe the prison left you a message."

Grabbing her phone, she unlocked the screen to find dozens of texts and missed calls. Some were from Justice, a few from her assistant, Sophie, and many were from the media. Wait, there was a text from the guard she knew. She opened the text and read it aloud so Emily can hear it.

"I have permission to inform you that your mom fell down some stairs this morning. She has a concussion, bruised kidney and three broken fingers. She will be moved to the prison infirmary where she'll be monitored and under guard. If you have any questions, you will need to go through official contacts."

"He won't answer questions?" Em said.

She shook her head while typing out, *Thank you.* "No, he could get into trouble for contact with inmate family members outside the approved channels. It could give the impression he's passing messages for an inmate. He said he got permission to tell me as much as he did."

"You can't talk to her? Call and ask?"

"They won't let me until they resolve this. If the prison suspects a fight, she'll lose privileges."

Another text flashed on her screen. *Beth, I see the*

media is surrounding you at the gym on news sites. Please call me and tell me you're okay. If I don't hear from you in the next five minutes, I'm getting on a plane back to San Diego.

She told Em, "It's Justice. He's in New York for the announcement of the World Rock Stage Battle of the Bands for the owner's seat. He's threatening to fly home, I have to call him." She quickly pulled up his number and put the phone on speaker.

"Where are you?" he answered. "It looks like you were mobbed leaving the gym."

"I was, but I'm okay now. We're safe in the SUV on the way to my condo. Whitney is driving, Em is with me, and you're on speaker."

"What the hell is going on? Amber's hurt? I saw the picture online."

He sounded as shocked, worried and bewildered as Liza felt. "I'm still putting it together, but I got a text from a guard I've known a long time that said my mom fell down some stairs and is in the infirmary with a concussion, bruised kidney and broken fingers."

"Damn." His voice calmed a degree or two. "So it wasn't a fight but an accident?"

"This wasn't an accident." Rage burned in her chest. "It was a hit by that bastard. Hayes and his minions have threatened my mom before."

"When?" Justice asked.

She told him about the email she'd received months ago with the headline, *Amber Ranger Injured in Prison Fight.*

"Christ, Beth, did you report that?" Justice demanded.

"I report everything to the authorities, but it all comes from hidden email addresses."

"Fuck, why didn't you tell me?"

"First I heard of it," Em added.

Liza sighed. "Stuff happens all the time. Notes dropped in groceries calling me a baby killer, bloody baby dolls left at SLAM, sometimes people get my number and scream at me. It's nothing new, and it doesn't matter. What I'm wondering is why attack my mom now? I got that threat months ago in October. Is it because my mom's closer to parole? Or a warning to me."

"Warning for?" Justice asked.

She gripped the edge of the seat. "To stay out of your world, which Hayes believes he owns. Especially since that picture of you and I surfaced from the transitional center." Fear tightened her throat, while anger churned in her stomach. "You guys have your security team with you, right?"

"You're worried about us?"

"Yes."

"Our security is with us, we're well protected." He paused a second. "It's you I'm worried about. Beth, do you want me to come home?"

She had a second of temptation before she stiffened her spine. "Stay there and safe. As long as the prison officials believe my mom fell down the stairs, then her parole shouldn't be affected. I'm okay."

A few beats passed, and he finally said, "Can I call you later tonight?"

She thought of the night hours stretching out before her. "I'll probably be up late with Molly." And her fears, but she was getting better. Stronger.

"Yeah? Well tell Molly she's going to have to share tonight. I'll call you, baby." They said bye and ended the call.

Em said, "I saw your face when he asked if you wanted him to come home. You thought about it for a second."

Liza sighed as the weight pressed down on her. "Hayes got to my mom. He could get to Justice."

Who else would he try to hurt? What did she have to do to make him stop?

Chapter 10

JUSTICE PACED BACKSTAGE AT CLUB Nosh in Los Angeles, downing water to prep for a physically demanding show. Security had cleared the area. It was just him, Lynx, Simon, River and Gray, and a few others, including Screech, who would make a special appearance at the end of the show. The crew checked earpieces and various details. Their photographer and videographer were getting footage to post on social media.

Justice ignored them, the crazy energy pounding in his head, snapping and twitching his muscles. It was impossible to stand still. Ever since Drake's funeral, he'd worked nonstop getting ready.

This was the moment. He lifted his hands up in front of him.

Shaking.

Like a junkie needing a fix. His drug was getting on that stage. He looked up at the monitors showing the crowds packing the venue. The stage was a rectangle facing the pit backed up by the general audience seating, and a balcony with VIP seating, adding up to about twenty-five hundred fans. It was a smaller setting than some of their concerts, but Club Nosh was a legend in the industry, and they loved performing here. Every seat was filled. "Sold out."

"Damn right," Simon said. "This album will be bigger than our first."

Hell yeah. "Savaged Vows" had already outsold "Expired Hero" in presales. The buzz was growing hourly. *Thump Beat* called it "The raw truth about the price of fame." *Indie Rock Broadcast* proclaimed it "The tearing of a man's soul in true rock style." Justice even had women sending him videos proclaiming their love, wanting to heal him.

While he was happy with the seemingly instant success, pressure mounted on him. Everything was riding on this album and tour. If they didn't get enough revenue, media attention, and social media interaction, they'd lose.

They had to win. Had to. The stakes were too high, and on top of what he owed his band and all the employees and others who relied on him, his vow to Beth drove him relentlessly. "We have to start strong. We can't fail."

Simon's eyes darkened. "Not happening. I'll sell a kidney and both my nuts before I let Jagged Sin win. So would you."

He'd give anything to go back in time and right his wrong to Beth and their baby. If he couldn't have that, then he wanted to wrap his hands around Gene Hayes's neck, and this time, make damn sure he killed him for the pain he'd caused his wife.

And for Savanna Rose. This was all he had to give his daughter now, to right the wrong he'd done, and give her mom, his beloved Beth, peace. That meant driving Hayes to either come after Justice so he could kill him, or to publicly self-destruct and land his ass in a prison cell or casket.

His phone vibrated in his pocket. Pulling it out, he checked the screen.

Beth: *Just got a text from your dad that said,* Check your porch. *He left fries and a chocolate shake with a note that said,* Tell Justice Good Luck. *So good luck from your dad.*

She'd pulled back after the kiss they'd shared, and her mom's push down the stairs. Beth had talked to Amber on the phone, and her mom had carefully confirmed that she'd been jumped and pushed.

Then out of the blue, his dad once more nudged Beth to talk to him.

"Lose the phone, dude. We're going on in four minutes," Simon said.

He had a million things he wanted to say to Beth, but he typed out, *What about you? Any advice? Last-minute corny jokes to calm my preshow jitters?*

She shot back, *If you're good enough tonight, and if 'Savaged Vows' cracks into the top ten, I'll send you pages from my book. Be good enough, Justice.*

Stunned, he reread the message. This was huge. Beth was inviting him deeper into her world.

Deal. No going back now. Get the pages ready, baby. They'd better be as good as my performance. He sent it, locked his phone and handed it off before Simon's head exploded.

Would Beth actually watch any of the live streaming? See the music video?

Global Magic, the band Savaged Illusions had signed to their S.I. Records label, and had hired as their opening act, came offstage, glowing with their performance.

"Holy shit, do you hear that?" Gray said.

All of them stopped, and Lynx pulled off his headphones. Clapping for the opening act gave way to shouts and calls.

"Sav-a-ges! Sav-a-ges!" Interspersed with, "Justice! Jus-tice!"

The monitors showed the crowd growing more restless and demanding.

The announcer began the intro.

Justice turned to his guys. "This is it."

Lynx held out his fist. "Let's do this."

They bumped fists as the lights shifted and the crowd roared. They hit the stage, the routine familiar and exciting. Simon on his right, River in the center, with Lynx and Gray on raised platforms in the rear.

The applause poured over them, and Justice scooped up his waiting guitar, holding on to the neck as he spread his arms and shouted into his mic, "Hello, L.A.! The Savages are in the house and ready to rock!"

The jumbo screens lit up with supersized images of them so everyone in the club had a good view. The best part was the audience's shouts and clapping. They were engaged and ready to jam.

The house lights dimmed, and the colored lights swept back and forth over the stage, creating a strobe effect. Justice slid on his guitar.

Quiet fell over the crowd, the only sound Lynx tapping his sticks together in the four count to take them into the song.

Justice picked out the opening melody, the light landing on him. Leaning into the silver mic, he launched into the first verse about the girl who became his song, the tune in his head that wouldn't stop playing on repeat. But fame was his flame, pulling him away. Which direction did he go?

Justice powered into the chorus, turning to Simon as they played the rage, the regret, the love.

She's the song so powerful
It drives me to my knees
Broken hearts and savaged vows
Won't stop the words.
She is my song.

By the time he finished the song with the vocal-destroying death growl, he poured sweat, and his muscles burned from the energy he'd expended. When the audience erupted in screams and applause, adrenaline flooded back in.

Justice soaked in the moment. He told the truth—that he'd had it all in Beth, until he savaged their vows.

"Thank you," he shouted. "Next up is a song written by Simon, the monster over here on guitar." He gestured to the man. "It's called 'Words on Her Skin.'"

The rest of the show kicked ass, and two hours later, they were all riding high on the wave of music. "For our last song, we've asked a friend to join us. Give an L.A. welcome to Screech Rizzo from the Hellblades!"

The band's lights went dark, the spotlight going to Screech sitting at the piano on the far left of the stage that had previously been darkened.

Quietly, Justice set down his guitar and picked up his hand mic. This song was another stark reminder of Beth, and Justice hadn't sung it publicly since they'd lost their baby. With Screech's permission, they'd recorded it on the *Savaged Vows* album.

A hush rolled across the crowd.

Screech played the haunting opening. A few beats later, he sang the first verse of the song.

A second piano joined Screech's, and the light snapped on Gray as he added his playing to capture the agony of a parent fighting for their child's life against a reaper.

Savanna Rose filled his head, along with the knowledge he hadn't had a chance to fight at all. His baby girl had been gone before he'd gotten to the hospital. The raw pain gripped him, and the pressure swelled in him. It took all he had to hold back and wait.

When Screech reached the chorus, the rest of the band joined in, amping up the passion.

Once the chorus faded, Justice's spotlight snapped on, and he opened his mouth, spilling all his energy and grief into the second verse as he strode across the stage to Screech's piano.

He was swept up in the fierce battle to rip a child from the arms of a reaper. The seconds of false hope soaring and then the crashing defeat in the song's crescendo.

The reaper wins.

In the pounding rage of the moment, Justice ripped off his shirt, revealing his yellow rose tattoo for his baby girl wrapped in the blue wings of his grandmother. His grief drove him to his knees as he sang the final notes.

The spotlights snapped off, leaving only Screech and Gray illuminated as they played out the song.

A pause hung there in a powerfully charged moment. A softer light clicked on over Justice on his knees. This wasn't planned, but he was unable to breathe or move beneath the potency of his grief that he'd shared with every person in the club. He'd ripped the scab off his heart in his singing tonight, communicating his heartache and rage to the world.

And his love for the woman who was his song.

The first clap came from directly in front of him, a twenty-something girl. Then a few more morphed into a thunderous roar.

Rising slowly, Justice laid a hand to his heart covered in ink and dipped his head. Screams of twenty-five hundred fans nearly split his eardrums, robbing him of words. All he could do was feel the wave of admiration and energy pouring over them. Him, his band, and Screech at his piano, looking as gobsmacked as Justice.

Finally, the deafening screams faded, and Justice waived his arm to acknowledge the man who was the genius behind the song. "Ladies and gentlemen, Screech Rizzo!"

Screech stood and bowed as the audience hooted their appreciation.

"And the heart and soul of the Savaged Illusions band: Grayson Price, Lynx Steele, River Donovan and Simon Bender!"

As they exited the stage and the applause and adulation faded, loneliness crept in.

On the stage he was alive.

Off it?

Without Beth, he was empty.

As the band left the stage on the live feed link Justice had sent her, Liza wiped her tears as longing bled through the cracks of her heart. Memories of his first opening night, the power of his voice sparking her pride and joy in her husband. Justice was so insanely talented.

This was more, so much more. Justice had surprised her by performing "Reaper's Child." He'd sung it with a love powerful enough to transcend the bounds of earth and reach the heavens. He'd been fearless in his honest tribute to his baby girl. He'd exposed his heart, his grief and his regret on the stage before thousands of fans, and millions who would view the video.

She touched his tattoo where she'd frozen it on the screen, compelled and enchanted by the magnificent yet ethereal beauty. The idea of her baby wrapped in the wings of Justice's grandmother brought her a sense of comfort.

Leaving the screenshot on her computer, she picked up her phone. It was too soon for the ranking on "Reaper's Child" to move since he'd just sung it. The song they'd pushed was their album title song they'd opened the show with and the single release, "Savaged Vows." She pulled up the song's ranking.

Number eight.

She squealed in excitement. He was doing it. The whole band was going to kick Jagged Sin's and their evil puppetmaster Gene Hayes's asses. Savaged Illusions had released the music video for "Savaged Vows" last night, and that was already trending too.

Justice was doing exactly as she'd asked—using his fame to keep Gene Hayes out of World Rock Stage. What was she doing? Working, taking self-defense lessons and writing a book she showed no one. All while trying to work up the courage to go to Justice's house.

It was time she show a little bit of guts. She couldn't go public, not while her mom was a sitting duck behind bars.

She could do one small thing. On her computer, she pulled up her book, cut and pasted the two chapters into a new file, and sent them to Justice.

Done. She'd invited Justice back into her secret world.

Chapter 11

SUNDAY AFTERNOON, LIZA DROVE THROUGH the security gate of Justice's house and shut the car off. Scooping her phone out of the cupholder, she pulled up Noah's message.

Grease fire in kitchen last night. Put it out. I'm ok. Cupboard by the stove is singed, pan ruined. Had to leave. Sorry.

Liza had texted him back, asked if he was really okay.

Radar and I are both okay. Tell Justice sorry.

She could almost feel his anxiety coming through the phone, and she quickly reassured him. *Justice only cares about you and Radar. Don't worry. I'll take a look and have anything fixed that needs it.*

That was it. Nothing else from Noah. It killed her that he was upset. Noah had serious burns from a bomb in Afghanistan, so she could imagine a fire had triggered his PTSD. Yet he'd evidently managed to put out the flames.

This was the first time she'd come to check the house. Shame curled her insides, but she pushed past it and got her butt out of the car. The lawn was cared for, the rosebushes beginning to bloom. Someone had fed them, likely the gardeners. The house itself surprised her. It had a fresh coat of paint, a cream with a slate-blue trim. Not bad.

Had the inside changed? What about their baby's room?

Stop it and go inside. She opened the door and stepped into her past.

A stale, acrid scent of cooking oil and smoke made her eyes water. Liza slid open the front window. There was an old couch and loveseat in the living room, and a plush tan dog bed with a blanket. Past that, the dining room remained the same with the dark oval table and matching hutch filled with Justice's grandmother's flowered dishes.

Her gaze darted to the hallway on the right. The first room was—had been—Savanna's. It was literally one wall away. Was the door closed? The urge to leave climbed up her spine. Instead, she headed into the kitchen. The smell of burnt plastic and oil stained the air and left the old faded green cupboards around the stove coated in smears of greasy grime. Much of the stove and pan were covered in white powder matted with soot.

A glance at the opposite side of the kitchen showed an empty baking soda box sitting on the cracked tile of the counter. Liza picked up the tongs sitting by the stove and investigated the pan with the plastic handle now burnt and twisted. Poking through the layers of singed baking soda in the pan, she found two pork chops floating in a congealed lake of grease.

Noah had obviously been cooking dinner. Got distracted or let the oil get too hot, and boom—grease fire.

The pan was toast. Liza tossed it in the trash. Next,

she'd air out the house. She headed over the ancient carpet to the hallway. A few feet from the closed door to her daughter's bedroom, her heart rate boosted into a hammer of harsh dread.

She went into the bathroom. Several used towels were spread out over the shower rod and towel rack. Had Noah been coming by to take a shower most days? After opening the window, Liza picked up a bottle on the side of the tub. Dog wash. Noah had been bringing Radar here and giving him a bath too.

Noah clearly loved that dog. Did having Radar with him compel him to seek out the warmth and comfort of the house? Would they come back after the fire? Had it triggered Noah's PTSD, so he wouldn't be able to return?

She kept moving, opening the window in Noah's room and then into the master. On the bed was the plain comforter piled with all the pillows Liza had added. She was swept back to the hours she'd spent in that bed with Justice—making love, talking, the two of them working and eating candy.

Or the times she'd been alone while Justice had been on tour, and they'd talk endlessly on the phone, often about her book.

Memories trailed her like a shadow as she crossed the room, opened the window and retraced her steps then stopped in front of the door to the third bedroom. She steeled herself.

Once this room had been her safe space. Like the bathroom at her aunt's house she'd locked herself in when the night terrors had come after her rape. Now if felt like a barrier.

Come on, turn the knob and step across the threshold. She scraped her damp palms on her jeans. Dread raced up her spine, and buzzing roared through her head. Sweat prickled her armpits.

Liza pivoted, rushed out of the hallway to the backyard and sucked in fresh air. Her erratic heartbeat slowed as she surveyed the freshly cut grass, trimmed bushes and empty flowers beds. Her hydrangea plants must have died. They'd been so beautiful when they'd bloomed.

You're avoiding thinking about why you can't go in her room.

She clamped her jaw. Maybe she could put some hydrangeas on her back patio in her condo? She'd always loved them, and she had some planters that might work.

A knock came from the front of the house. Relieved at the distraction, she figured it was Em since Liza had asked her to come over and help. Going to the door, she opened it and confusion flooded her. It was indeed Em, but she was flanked by Tess, Sophie, Kat and Sherry.

Liza tried to mentally adjust. "What's going on?" Why were two of her coworkers, her boss's girlfriend and the woman who taught her self-defense here too?

"I stopped by Sugar Dancer Bakery to get us some snacks, and..." Em walked past Liza then waved at the others with her. "Word spread that you're cleaning up the house after a small fire."

Sloane's pretty girlfriend, Kat, held up a bakery box. "I brought cookies, brownies, cinnamon pecan rolls and some macadamia coconut bars." She walked in smelling like cinnamon rolls and chocolate. She had her long brown hair with the trademark lavender streaks in a ponytail.

Liza focused on her. "Didn't you work all day?" Kat opened her bakery early and woke up long before roosters even thought to crow. Noting the slight limp from her bad leg, Liza assumed she had to be tired.

"My assistant opened today, so I was only there a couple hours doing admin work." She headed to the table and put the box down.

"I brought some sparkling waters and flavored teas." Sherry barreled in, full of her usual energy.

"I have cleaners, buckets and mops." Tess pushed past Liza, with Sophie right behind her carrying more supplies.

Sophie set everything down. "So this is the house the famous Justice Cade grew up in?"

Vividly aware of the house's aged shabbiness, the carpet and couches that were probably older than her, Liza tried to swallow down her defensiveness. Closing the door, she answered, "Yep, he spent most of his childhood here when his dad was on tours of duty as a Marine. You all came to help?"

"Kat bribed us with all the cookies we could eat," Sophie said.

"Don't sugarcoat it," Sherry announced. "This is your first time in the house and we're here to make sure you can handle it."

Liza whipped around and glared at Em. "You told them that?"

Em folded her arms. "You asked me for help, and I brought it. You got a problem with that?"

Liza opened her mouth, but what could she say to that? Did she have a problem with her friends dropping whatever they were doing on a Sunday afternoon to help her clean? "No, I don't. Thank you for coming. I'm grateful for all the help I can get."

Shock blazed over Em's face, then vanished. "Well, okay then. Let's go."

Liza led them into the kitchen and instantly lost control as Tess took over, issuing orders. Liza's job was scrubbing the cupboards, and she got to work while

Tess and Sophie tackled the floor. Em and Kat were sent to strip beds.

"I have a cleaning service—"

"We're here, we'll do this right. All the linens washed and beds remade. Smoke gets into everything. All surfaces cleaned. Carpet should be shampooed too, but we'll settle for vacuuming."

Several sweaty hours and two pizzas later, Liza made a pot of coffee while Em got cups down. The others were in the dining room, scarfing down the treats Kat had brought. Liza had figured the least she could do was feed her friends after they'd shown up ready to clean.

"How are you doing? Was it hard to come into the house?" Em asked.

Liza eyed the chicken decorations on the walls that she'd carefully washed. She loved this kitchen, loved that it had a history of family. "It wasn't bad."

Em laid her hand on Liza's arm. "What about Savanna's room?"

Dread flickered along her nerve endings. She didn't want to talk about it. "No."

Em opened her mouth.

Liza changed the subject. "I finished my book. Or at least, I think I did."

Drawing back her hand, Em squealed. "No way! I've only read half of it, so you've been holding out! I think about the chapters you let me read all the damned time. You really finished it? Okay, what happens? No! Don't tell me. I want to find out when I read it. Are you going to publish?"

Liza blinked at the onslaught. "Are you going to breathe?"

"Not when you just did this freaking amazing thing! You finished writing a book!"

"Liza wrote a book?" Kat walked into the kitchen. "Wow, I had no idea."

Freezing where she stood at the coffeemaker between the table and counter, Liza struggled to come up with an answer. She'd told Em and let her read some of it. Then blurted it out to Tess and Sophie one day when they were eating lunch because Liza was so distracted thinking about her book. She hadn't let them read it yet because—

"You better not let Kat read it before me." Sophie walked in. "Are you guarding the coffee like you guard your book? Or will you share?"

Liza filled a cup for Sophie. "Kat, would you like some coffee too?"

"Sure." She accepted the mug. "Is your book a secret? It must not be published if Sophie can't read it. I'm sorry if I overstepped."

Liza didn't want the other woman to feel bad. "You didn't. Not at all."

"Do you want to tell me what it's about?"

"What am I missing out on?" Sherry walked in. "I'm getting Tess coffee."

Liza considered the women gathered in Justice's kitchen. The one that now sparkled after a deep scrubbing, the scent of orange cleaning spray mixing with fresh coffee. Why shouldn't she tell these ladies about her book? She couldn't exclude Tess, so she filled more cups with coffee and turned off the coffeemaker. "Kat was asking me what the book I'm writing is about. Let's go back to the food, and I'll tell you all at once."

Liza took a seat at the end of the table. "You guys are amazing. Thank you for helping me today. I sent the video and pictures to Noah." She really hoped it reassured him that everything was fine, and he'd feel safe to return to the house. In any case, she was deeply grateful her friends had shown up.

"Yeah, yeah, we're awesome." Sherry scooped up a pecan bar. "Now I want to hear about this book. I had no idea you wrote."

Liza snagged a brownie roughly the size of a brick and gathered her thoughts.

"Not many people do," Liza began. She explained how she wrote before Paris, then stopped after losing the baby, and Justice sending it back to her. "It's not the same kind of book as it was before."

"How's it changed?" Kat asked.

"I guess..." She struggled articulate it. "In the beginning, Molly is a rock band groupie and she thinks if a band member falls in love with her, it'll make her somebody. She makes a bad choice and finds herself pregnant. Things get worse quickly when the band breaks up and Molly is blamed. This is when it all changes. Molly discovers that her love for her baby is more powerful than anything she's ever known." Liza took a sip of her coffee, her brain whirling as she searched for the way to convey the heart of the story. "I guess a clearer way to sum her up is: How does the woman who's become the most hated girl in the world transform herself into the best mother? Is it possible, or does her child have to pay a horrible price for her sins? Or will the love of a mother save her child?"

All the women stared at her, cookies and treats forgotten.

Liza dropped her attention to her dark brownie gleaming with shiny chocolate chunks sitting on the stark-white paper plate. This was one of the reasons she didn't tell anyone—it was too scary. What if they hated it? This book meant so much to her, the words on those pages telling the story of a woman braver and smarter than Liza. A woman who wouldn't fail her child. "Molly isn't me. I mean I know there are similarities, but she puts her baby first." Not her own pathetic need to be loved.

Kat put a hand on her arm. "Your book sounds incredibly powerful, and so brave, Liza. I'd read it in a heartbeat if I saw it in a bookstore."

"Me too," Sherry said.

"It's so damned good," Em added. "At least as much as I've read is, since Liza is holding out on giving me the second half of the book. Trust me, it's a *just one more chapter* kind of book that you end up inhaling then have to read a second time in case you read so fast the first time you missed something."

Liza blinked back tears at the utter sincerity and support. Why had she guarded her secret so zealously? But she knew—her aunt had told her over and over to stay quiet. It wasn't until Justice had pushed her in her fiction writing that she found real freedom to explore her voice. Speaking of voice, she needed to say something. "Thanks."

These ladies weren't her aunt. They weren't Nikki, the woman who'd sold her and her baby out to Gene Hayes. These women were all her friends, her real friends. "I appreciate all the support more than you can know. When the book is ready for readers, you guys will be the ones I ask first."

"I'm looking forward to it," Kat said. "So Justice kept your book even after you left him, and then sent it back to you. Not all men would have done that."

Liza opened her mouth to say that was the kind of man Justice was when she felt a vibration in the front pocket of her jeans. She shifted enough to pull out her phone to see who it was.

"Justice." Of course it was. He had uncanny timing

like that. She accepted the call and put the phone to her ear. "Hi. I thought you'd be getting ready to go on stage." The band was in Texas and had an early concert tonight.

"I'm at the venue. I got your text about the house. Is everything okay? Can you find a cleaning crew?"

Liza laughed, cutting him off. "The cleaning crew is here right now. Me, Emily, Kat, Sherry, Tess and Sophie."

"You guys are all at the house?"

The incredulity in his voice matched how she'd felt when she opened the door. "Yep. It was all superficial damage that cleaned up. I'll send you pics."

"You didn't have to clean it yourself. I'd pay for a crew."

"I know." Liza got up and slipped out to the backyard for privacy. The sun was sliding lower in the sky as the afternoon dissolved into dusk. "I promised you I'd take care of your dad, and I am. Plus it was time for me to come into the house." Face at least some of her ghosts.

"You sound like you're okay."

"I am, actually. Em brought all the others with her, and we worked together. I even told them about my book, and that I've finished the first draft." She held her breath, hoping he wouldn't ask about their daughter's room.

"A lot has happened while I'm on this tour." The sadness in his words slithered through her anxiety.

"Are you okay?" Or was it her book? Liza had sent him her ending. Did he hate it? Or was something else dogging him? Tours were exhausting, and the guys ended up fighting due to being on top of each other. Her nerves yanked so tight she could barely stand still.

"I'm fine, I just miss you. I read your pages on the plane earlier today. I can't talk long now, but I was wondering...can we meet?"

Her mouth dried, and her brain turned into a parrot. "Meet?"

"To talk about your book. I have tomorrow night off, and you'll be in Los Angeles, right? I can fly there tomorrow, and we could have dinner. Anywhere you want."

"I..." She trailed off, struggling to form a response. Yes, she was going to L.A. in the morning with Sophie and John to oversee shooting a commercial for SLAM gyms. She stared at the long shadows stretching across the backyard in the fading sun. Shadows made her uneasy, as if they hid a monster like Hayes.

"Beth?" Justice said gently. "I'd very much like to see you. I really miss you, even more since being on the road. Reading your work is... God I just miss you. If you say no, I'll respect it. We can talk about your book after the concert tonight if you're still up."

Should she say no? Did she want to see him? One thing she was certain of, she desperately wanted to know what he thought about the ending of her book. What could one dinner hurt?

"Okay. Dinner, but not in public." It felt like Hayes and his crazies were always watching her, and she feared her mom would be attacked again. Amber had managed to convince prison officials it had been an accident, not a fight. She didn't want to do anything that could trigger another attack.

"We can have dinner in my room at the Four Seasons." In her room? Had she lost her mind? "Seven or so?"

"Done. I'll be there. Text me your room number when you get it. Gotta run, so—"

"Justice?"

"What?"

"Give me a hint, did you like the ending of my book?"

In the background, she heard a deep voice call, "Justice, come on, move your ass."

He laughed with much more cheer than when he'd first called. "Gotta go. I'll tell you all about it tomorrow night. Bye." He disconnected.

She yanked the phone away and glared at it. Then she typed out a message. *You suck, and you better bring dessert as an apology for making me wait.*

"So you have a date with Justice."

Liza turned to Em standing a couple feet behind her. "Eavesdropping is rude."

"So is giving your estranged husband the whole book when you only gave your best friend half."

The corners of Liza's mouth twitched up. Yeah, she figured Em would gripe about that. "Then we're even."

"Nope." Em grinned. "Not until you come back and tell me if you slept with him or not. Then we'll be even."

Liza rolled her eyes.

Em squeezed her shoulder. "You're allowed to be happy, Liza. If you want to let go and sleep with him, do it."

Was she ready now?

Chapter 12

LIZA BARELY HAD TIME TO brush her teeth and swipe on lip gloss before a knock sounded at her door of her hotel room. Her stomach bounced with anticipation. Did she look all right for the secret rendezvous with her husband?

No time to worry about that now. Besides, this date was to discuss her finished book not seduction.

Tomorrow Justice had to fly out to Kansas, and Liza had meetings here in L.A., but they had the rest of the evening.

Enough time for books *and* seduction.

Liza squared her shoulders, checked the peephole and opened the door.

Justice grinned beneath the light beard scruff. A wine-colored T-shirt strained to cover his shoulders and made her hands itch to touch him.

"Beth." His gaze traveled over her and back up. "You're beautiful." A husky tinge rumbled through each syllable. "You must have had men hitting on you constantly at the shoot."

"Me? I'm not the rock star that drives girls to strip naked and hide in our hotel room." Yep, that had happened on the night of his first concert on his last tour, and it still stung. Arching an eyebrow, she added, "Has that happened yet on this tour?"

"No. They've tried it, but our security team is the best." A grin teased the corners of his mouth. "If you're jealous or worried, come on the rest of the tour with us. I could use the protection of my badass wife."

Once, she'd longed to hear him beg her to go on tour with him. "You probably shouldn't stand in the hall, someone might recognize you. Everyone has a camera these days, and it'll be all over the internet within an hour like that picture at the transitional center was."

Justice bent and picked up a big brown box, then walked past her into the room.

She caught a whiff of his scent, wood and cedar like a freshly oiled guitar. Suddenly, she was back in his old house, sitting on their bed typing on her book, while Justice fiddled with a song on his guitar. He'd go silent, and she'd feel the weight of his regard. Then he'd tug her laptop away from her...lay his mouth on hers...

Liza let the door shut in her hotel room and on her memories. Justice prowled the room, then set the box down on the small round dining table. "What did you bring?"

"Come sit down."

Liza walked over to the table, where Justice laid out thick white plates topped with creamy napkins wrapped around silverware. Two bottles of sparkling water appeared next, followed by a pair of crystal wine glasses, and a chilled bottle. "Champagne?"

"We're celebrating, Beth. You did an incredible thing. I know it's fiction, but you unleashed something powerful from your soul into that book, an elemental truth about what love is and how it can change us for the better or worse, depending on our choices. I know how hard it was to write, how many times you had to climb a mountain, and at the very top, walk barefoot over broken glass to find the right words. It took the bravery of trusting your voice when you couldn't trust yourself. You wrote an emotional, beautiful story. So you're damn right I brought champagne." He peeled off the paper and pulled the cork. A slight white foam spilled down the side. "Will you have some? If not, we'll celebrate with sparkling water."

She flushed with pleasure and pride. Justice understood what her book meant to her. On top of that, he'd made sure to open the bottle in front of her. She had a fear of alcoholic drinks that she hadn't seen opened or mixed herself. Justice's thoughtfulness chased out some of her anxiety over seeing him. She nodded to the foaming bottle. "Yes, thank you."

He smiled and poured the golden liquid. Liza took her glass, holding it up to see the hundreds of fragile bubbles shooting to the surface. Pretty and so very delicate.

Raising his glass, Justice said, "Congratulations, baby, you're an author."

His words flowed into her chest, swelling her pride and sense of identity. After touching her glass to his, she sipped to his toast. The liquid flowed with a tart sweetness, but the wine paled next to the praise of her husband. Joy and fear twined, fighting like the fragile bubbles in the champagne to reach the surface.

Setting her glass down, she resisted the temptation to ask him a thousand questions. Did he really like the book? Was the ending okay? Did the middle sag? Instead, she kept quiet as he pulled out two black plastic containers, opened one, and began filling her plate with salad, tender steak morsels in a burgundy mushroom sauce, and sautéed baby potatoes. He grabbed a bag, pulled out a warm, fragrant roll, and added it to her plate.

"This looks and smells wonderful. It's all warm still." She sampled the steak, savoring the layered flavors of wine, seasoning, mushrooms and meat.

"I asked the chef from one of the restaurants here to put together a dinner for us. Eat. Let's enjoy our meal, then we can talk more about your book."

"You're living dangerously, Rock Star. First, you made me wait all day yesterday and today, and now you're still stalling?" She was mostly teasing. Yeah, she wanted to know what he thought, but what could it hurt to wait a little longer? Plus she'd tasted the fresh spinach salad boasting apples, candied pecans, and dried cranberries dressed with a white wine vinaigrette, and she was suddenly starving.

"Tell you what, sweetheart, you be a good girl through dinner, then we can discuss your book over dessert."

Liza glanced in the box Justice had moved to the floor, but all she saw was an unmarked bag.

"No cheating. You'll find out dessert if you behave."

Liza shrugged and ate more salad, as if curiosity wasn't killing her. What was in there? Ice cream? But it'd likely melt. Cake? Her attention shifted back to the man across the small, two-seater table. Fatigue darkened the skin beneath his eyes, and while he didn't appear thinner per se, he appeared leaner. Knowing him, he'd ramped up his cardio to deal with the physical demands of traveling and had honed more wiry muscle. He dug into the steak and reached into the bag between them for another roll.

He caught her studying him and rolled out a slow and sexy smile.

Busted. Talking to him on the phone or video chat didn't compare to sitting here with his energy sizzling between them and making her skin tingle. A pulse of need woke deep in her belly—something more primal than hunger.

The yearning to be touched and...God. Liza grabbed her water, cracked the seal and took a drink. She set the bottle down, all the while feeling his intense scrutiny. Desperate to break the rising tension of unspoken desire, she forked a morsel of steak. "Thanks for dinner. It's delicious, and I was starved."

His smile shifted from sexy to wicked. "I want to satisfy all your hungers." He leaned in, his voice down-shifting into a promising growl. "Every single one."

She was in trouble here.

Justice still couldn't believe he was sitting here with Beth. As much as he loved singing and performing, he didn't want to be on the road without her. He felt the calendar turning the pages, shoving him ever closer to the deadline seven months away when he'd agreed he give her a divorce if she still wanted one.

While he was touring the States before going overseas, Beth was moving on. She'd finished her book, at least the first draft, and that was fucking amazing. She'd gone into his house for the first time since Savanna died, and she'd told her group of her friends about her book. All of those were big steps for Beth.

His wife was healing, gaining strength and rebuilding her life while Justice was trapped on the road, using his fame to stop Hayes and Jagged Sin.

He couldn't tear his gaze from her wide green eyes framed by dark glasses, hair tumbling around her, and the demure cream-colored top with the long necklace bouncing around her breasts as she moved. Polished, with an edge honed by tragedy and experience. She'd grown into a stunning woman, and yet...this was still his Beth. The woman he loved so damned much he'd barely slept in his desperation to get here.

His gut ached with the need to touch and kiss her again. Stunningly sexy girls surrounded him all the time, but none of them ever affected him like this woman.

"You're staring."

"Yep. You're perfect. Beautiful. I'm trying to absorb as much of you as I can before I have to leave again. I have to keep reminding myself not to touch you unless you tell me I can."

A slight flush darkened her cheeks. "How's the tour going?"

She was feeling it too. Deciding to take mercy on her, he launched into telling her about the hilarious shit that happened on the road, the frustration of travel delays and equipment malfunction. The crazy requests of fans and demands of other stars who wanted to meet them.

"Look how famous you're getting. Now you have big stars wanting to meet you. You've attained the status you dreamed of."

"I'd give it all up to change the past, but I can't. All I can do now is use that fame to right the wrongs I let happen. We've sold out the concerts and are hitting all our numbers. We're going to win this contest."

"I don't want you to give up your dream, I never wanted that. I just wanted to be a part of it." She went on before he could say anything. "I want you to know that I appreciate all you're doing to keep Jagged Sin, and Hayes, from winning."

She'd never asked him to give up his dream. She'd fallen in love with all of him. He was the one who'd pushed her to the side to chase the fame he so desperately craved. "It's not just me. The entire band and crew are working our asses off." He finished his steak, and said, "Jagged Sin isn't releasing their song or going on tour until June. They're already behind."

Liza pushed the last of her potatoes around on the plate. "How can they do that? Didn't you all sign contracts to do the year tour?"

"Yes, but there was some latitude. This whole contest is a win-win for World Rock Stage. They have three well-known bands going on a huge tour on most every continent promoting their brand. They have a kickass female band in the mix, bringing in more demographics. They have us, who are appealing to a blend of classic and independent rock fans, and Jagged Sin, the outcasts with a vague public connection to the infamous Gene Hayes. To top it off, we have a well-known rock feud with Jagged Sin."

Beth twisted her mouth. "And a competitive one with Fury Run. Essentially, World Rock Stage are the winners here. Unless Jagged Sin somehow wins." She paused and added, "It seems stupid for them to let you and Fury Run gain momentum."

He and the guys had wondered that too. "Gavin, our manager, heard that their title song of the album was so bad they trashed it. They've gone into seclusion, releasing a bunch of cloak-and-dagger media, running all kinds of contests and creating social media fire by trashing us and Fury Run with rumors. They send protesters to our concerts saying things like *Truth Won't Be Silenced! Jagged Sin Drops Truth Bombs!* with the release date stamped on the sign. Media has been picking it up, anticipation is building."

He set his fork down, the buzz of worry tightening his neck. "They're plotting something. They've all been too quiet. Too..." He couldn't put his finger on it.

"Hayes is always plotting." Beth grabbed her champagne and took a drink.

"Like the plot to lure you up to his suite in Paris."

She set the glass down. "For tonight, can we keep all that outside the room? All of it. Hayes, his crazy groupies, the constant threats, can they stay out there?" She waved across the room toward the door.

Part of him resisted, knowing it was the *Don't talk about it* bullshit her aunt had pounded into her head. In his better moments, he'd urged and sometimes bullied her into verbalizing her feelings so the internal pain didn't build up into the need to cut to mask the hurt. He had to earn back her trust for her to confide in him her deepest fears and sorrows, so he gave her the space she asked for. They'd leave it outside this room for tonight.

"And us in here," he added. "Celebrating your book."

She relaxed her shoulders, some tension draining out of her. "And your success with 'Savaged Vows.' You always did love performing, Rooster."

The old nickname made him laugh. "It's the way I express myself to the world, but I wrote that song for an audience of one—you. You're still my song, Beth."

Her cheeks flushed a warm rosy peach. "Charming me, Rock Star?"

"Telling the truth. Every time I sing 'Savage Vows,' it's to you."

"Hmm." She ran her finger around the rim of her glass.

That had sounded underwhelming. "You told me it was a powerful song when I saw you last time. The death scream gave you chills."

"Did I bruise your ego?"

"Hell yeah. I bled to write that song. Nights, Beth. When I couldn't sleep, I knew searching for my dad was pointless and you avoided me, I poured my rage, my grief and helplessness into it. I wrote and rewrote like a demon. I couldn't stop— Why are you smiling?"

"Because you're describing me with Molly." Her eyes widened. "That's how you knew I'd get hooked into the book. Why you sent it to me."

"Partly, yes, and because writing is your voice." It was more than that, Beth had been hiding from her emotions, and he'd worried she was cutting herself to avoid the agony. With Molly, she could process some of her emotion in her safe, fictional world. He believed her assurance to him she wasn't cutting now that she had the book.

"Thank you for saving the book for me."

He leaned back in his chair, folding his arms. "If you want to thank me, you should admit 'Savaged Vows' is brilliant."

"You wish, Rock Star, but I'm not one of your groupies feeding your insatiable ego. 'Savaged Vows' is amazing, but the song I love..." She trailed off and shook her head. "Nope. I think we've established that your ego is too fragile to handle the truth."

A flash of amusement rippled into his annoyance, and yeah, he was annoyed. He'd written that song to tell the world the love he and Beth had together meant more than anything, including fame. Now she was teasing him by picking at his ego. "Playing games, little author?" He grabbed his glass of champagne, scooped up the bag on the floor next to his chair and went to the couch. "If you want dessert, you'll have to tell me what song of mine you love."

Beth rose with her glass. She'd gained back some of

the weight she'd lost, filling out the curves he'd always appreciated. He didn't care about her weight, but he cared that she was happy and not starving herself in a pit of loss and despair.

Beth skirted the small coffee table and sank onto the couch next to him. "What's in there? I have to make sure the prize is worth it."

They'd played this game once before, the first time she'd come to his house to interview him. That was the night he'd learned one of her weaknesses. Reaching into the bag, he pulled out his triumph.

She sprang up straighter. "Peanut butter cups! I haven't had those in forever."

Oh yeah, he had her now. "Spill your truth...unless you're chicken?"

"You want to know? Here it is. My favorite song you've ever sung is 'Reaper's Child.'" She held out her palm. "Pay up."

Well shit, he'd asked. He should have known. Beth had loved that song from childhood. "That's not one of our songs. It's Screech's." He tugged the candy back.

"It's on your album, so it counts." She snagged the bag out of his hands.

"Hey!" He tried to snatch it back. "That's mine!"

Beth sprang up and raced around the table, dug into the bag and yanked out several pieces. She opened one and popped it in her mouth, then closed her eyes, as if soaking in the pleasure of chocolate and peanut butter.

He rose, half stunned at her quickness. Her self-defense classes had given her a new agility that added another layer to her sexiness. His mouth dried as he watched her savor the candy in a totally unguarded moment of pleasure. "That's cheating, sweetheart."

Her eyes popped open, and her brows shot up. "I don't cheat, I create my own opportunities."

Pride glowed in her self-satisfied smirk. Beth was having fun. So was he. "You're pretty bold when you know I can't touch you. But you haven't thought this all the way through."

She tilted her head, clearly considering that. "You can't touch me?"

"Not the way I want to until you give me permission. Even if I can't wrench that bag away from you, I still have leverage. You sure you want to play this game?" Because he did.

Holding the bag to her, she let out a scoff. "I have possession of the prize, so it's mine. Don't think your golden voice is going to seduce it from me."

"Is that a challenge? You want me to verbally seduce you?" Oh yeah, he liked this game. He stepped an inch closer, until he could inhale the scent of candy and peanut butter along with the lighter peach scent of Beth. "Should I tell you what I'd do if you consented? How the first thing I'd do is toss that bag out of my way and capture your hand in mine? I've missed holding hands with you, baby."

"That's all you got?" She dug into the bag, opened another candy and popped it into her mouth.

"While I held one of your hands, I'd use my other to trace softly along your cheek to feel your skin, then glide my fingers over your jaw and throat before I sank my fingers into your hair and slowly lowered my lips to yours. I'd kiss you with the days of longing and nights of need until you forgot about the taste of chocolate and craved me. All of me. Then, Beth, after hours of kissing, I'd peel your clothes off and caress every inch, lavishing all my passion on the woman who isn't just my wife, friend, partner or damned North Star. You're my song, the one that plays in my heart every moment of every day."

Her skin flushed to a ripe peach, and her breath hitched. She swallowed, and his attention drifted to the fluttering pulse at the base of her throat. Excitement. Desire. Need. He could almost feel it swelling the air between them.

She inhaled quickly, and her chin went up. Determination practically poured from her. "Nice, but not chocolate worthy."

That was his girl. At her core she was a fighter. "If you let me touch you, I'll prove you desire me over the candy. Since I won't do that without your agreement, I have something else to trade for the dessert I brought."

One side of her mouth dented with skepticism. "What's that?"

He pulled his phone out of his front pocket. Opening the note app, he turned the screen toward her. "These are all my thoughts and suggestions that I wanted to remember to discuss with you to make your book stronger. The story is damned good and compelling, and I couldn't stop thinking about its potential to be extraordinary. So I made all these notes while reading, and refined them on the plane here because I can't get Molly and her journey out of my head."

She fast-scanned, trying to read all his notes.

Snatching the device back, he chided, "No, you don't. If you want to hear them and have a copy sent to your phone, give me back my candy."

She scrunched up her face in clear frustration.

"All it costs you to hear and see my notes is giving me back my candy."

And her love.

Chapter 13

LIZA STOOD AT A FORK in the road. If she traded the candy for those notes, she'd take another step on the trail twining her and Justice's lives together. If she rejected them, she'd travel the safer path.

Those damn notes called to her curiosity, and something much deeper. The knowledge that Justice loved her enough to be so invested in her book. She stalled with, "How many pages of comments did you make?"

His grin unzipped over his face. "One way to find out."

She made a sound low in her chest and snapped out her hand holding the bag.

Justice took his prize, wearing a smirk.

Liza moved around him, grabbed up her glass and finished the champagne. He'd said he'd brought the bottle to celebrate, but she used it to fortify her twanging nerves. How bad could his supposed notes be? Setting her glass down, she strode to the couch and sat. "Pay up. Your notes better be worth giving up my chocolate."

Rounding the table, he sank down next to her.

"My first note is on making the villain clearer and more desperate. Differentiate between the two men Molly thought she was falling for: the lead singer and the bassist. The lead singer is the real villain and needs to be developed more. Molly was another chick to screw, use, and discard to him until he saw that the bassist really liked her and she was falling for him. That didn't just annoy the lead singer, he set out to destroy their relationship by engineering this threesome with alcohol, drugs and lies. Why was it even worth all the effort to him? At some point in the book, we need to understand what's driving him."

Liza had forced herself to listen, then blurted out, "He's a narcissist and believes he's entitled. That's obvious." Wasn't it?

"You show Molly to us. We see her need for love and attention because we know she grew up with a cold and borderline-cruel stepmom and an important dad who couldn't be bothered to notice his daughter. His work and new wife came before Molly. We get how she internalized that to mean if she did something amazing like snag a rock star, then she'd be important enough to notice. You use enough of her backstory for us to understand what motivates Molly, but what drives the villain?"

"Oh." That made sense. "Okay, I'll grant you that point."

Justice's mouth twitched, then he pulled out a chocolate and unwrapped it. "My reward." He popped it into his mouth.

Annoyed, she snapped, "Can you focus, Rock Star?"

"Right, focus. Moving on to the bassist, he needs to have a *come to Jesus* moment. He was falling for Molly, then let himself and Molly get suckered into this threesome. He knew Molly had very little experience, and he didn't want to share her but let himself be convinced. Each of them had different reasons, but it turned out bad. Molly got pregnant, the two men got in a brutal fight, ending with both of them being arrested, things spiraled from there. The band was dissolved, and the world blamed Molly. The bassist at first blames it on the lead singer, but he's the one who let the shit happen while riding the train to fame, so he has some blame too. He has to take ownership and change. He can do that by finding Molly and telling her this. Have the whole possibility of fatherhood have him re-evaluating his life, and recognize that he actively participated in bringing Molly so much grief. He should confess he'd known what a degenerate the lead singer was, but he'd ignored and excused it for a chance at stardom."

"Wait, this is Molly's book, not the bassist's." How could she do all that?

"As written now, Molly cuts him out, and he disappears from the story as if nothing more than a plot point. What if he gets back into Molly's life, creating more drama and conflict? He tells her his truth, and that includes demanding a paternity test after the child is born. Then if the kid is his, he wants a relationship. That's going to push her more. Is he really on the level, a true friend? Or is this some game? You then have the two men who could be fathers: the lead singer who doesn't feel anything but contempt for the child and Molly, and is trying to destroy them. And the bassist, who appears to desperately want a relationship with the child, and that might cause Molly concern too—will he take her baby away?"

She began to see it. "She's afraid to let him in, but she needs a friend."

"Think of her child, wouldn't she want the baby to

have a father who loved him? That's more internal conflict. Molly's fighting for what's best for her baby."

Excitement buzzed, and Liza touched his hand resting between them. "You put a lot of thought into this."

"Not as much as I've thought about you." He nodded toward her fingers on his hand. "Is this permission?"

"What?" Her thoughts were so tangled in her plot and Justice, she couldn't grasp his meaning.

"To touch you." He flipped his palm to press against hers and laced their fingers together. "Hold your hand."

The fizzing in her stomach made her think of the champagne she'd consumed. "I only drank one glass."

He smiled. "Feeling intoxicated?"

What she felt was a vivid, sexy pull of want throbbing low in her belly. Damn, she needed a distraction. "I...do you have more?"

"Champagne?"

She shook her head, determined to get back on track. "To tell me about the book."

"Yes. In the climax." He squeezed her fingers gently. "Not our climax because those were perfect, and the ones we have together again will be even better."

She shivered, his words drawing her deeper into this moment with him. The thick and desperate longing bubbling along her nerve endings scared her. "There's that ego again."

He raised an eyebrow. "You want to talk about our climaxes or the books?"

Before she could respond to that, he went on while keeping her hand encased in his, the warmth like an anchor. "When the villain launches his attack,

Molly is hugely pregnant and desperate to save the unborn baby. What if you went farther and the baby was already born? Let the readers see, smell and feel that baby, and Molly's bond with him. Bring him to life for the readers. Up to that point, we know Molly loves the baby inside her, but to see the child would make the scene even more vivid. Then when the villain arrives, Molly now has to protect the child outside her body—outside of herself. You could add more in with the bassist there too—maybe he's visiting the baby for the first time. Amp up the drama with even more at stake."

Liza's fingers ached, and she realized she was squeezing Justice's hand. "I don't know. I mean...Molly protects her baby before he's born."

"It's your story, your choice. It's something to think about." His voice was so reasonable, so gentle.

"I don't know if I can write that." It would hurt too much, and she didn't want to think about it right now. Not here, not tonight.

"I'll send you my notes, and you can delete them if they don't work for your vision of Molly's story. You really wrote an incredible, compelling novel, Beth. I'm so damned proud of you."

"Thank you." The slight panic at the idea of trying to write scenes of Molly having her child, holding and loving him, faded. "For the compliment and for coming here tonight, bringing dinner, reading my book and writing the notes. I appreciate it."

"Enough to kiss me?"

The air between them crackled with familiar need. Liza wanted his touch, his hand holding hers, fingers caressing her, lips tasting her. All the things he'd promised.

"Do you want me to stop touching you?"

He gave her so much power. Tonight, she reveled in it. "Keep touching me."

"Like this?"

The pad of his thumb stroked sensually, sending ribbons of pleasure up her arms. Heat unfurled in her belly. Her nipples tightened. "More."

He laid his other hand on her cheek. "I want to kiss you." His voice throttled low as he cradled her face in his warm palms.

The hairs on her arms stood up with a static reaction. Her heart thumped with desire. "Yes."

She lowered her gaze to his full lips. The mouth that could bring thousands of screaming fans to their knees. That teased and cajoled her, pushed her, talked rough and dirty to her until she squirmed with need.

He slid his hand to cup the back of her head and tug her to his mouth.

Her breasts ached and belly knotted with hunger. Only he could satisfy her. His lips were everything she remembered, she wanted more and dug her fingers into his hair. The thick strands wrapped around her hand created a sensation that rippled through her belly, and lower. She pushed her tongue into his mouth, eager to taste and feel all of him.

Justice's growl of approval drove her to a lava-hot desire tinged with the frantic need to get closer to him.

Lifting his head, he said, "Christ, you taste so damned good."

She swallowed. "Then don't stop."

He scooped her up and tugged her to his lap. Beth opened her mouth in surprise at his strength.

He kissed her again, one hand sliding beneath her shirt to brand her lower back. He tasted like rich chocolate and Justice. His groan rippled down her belly, and his thick arousal pressing against her thigh.

Justice broke the kiss, his chest heaving, and eyes half-lidded with desire as he stroked her face. "I want you so damned much, but if this isn't what you want, or you're not ready, we should stop."

"No one's touched me like this, not since you kissed me at the transitional center." Her voice sounded husky and desperate to her own ears. "I didn't know how badly I craved it until now." He was dragging truths out of her that she'd barely acknowledged herself.

"What do you want, Beth? We can end the night with kisses, or I can stay and feed your need for touch, for us together."

Us. Them. It was too scary to think about their future. Instead, she focused on the moment. "I want a night with you. Just one night with everything else locked outside that door. I'm on birth control so I'm safe. Please. One night with no promises." To distract him from asking for commitments beyond the night, she reached down and tugged her silky shirt off.

Heat flared in Justice's eyes.

Emboldened, she slid off her bra. Between the icy hotel air and the burn of Justice's heated attention, her nipples tightened unbearably.

"One night." She'd deal with consequences tomorrow.

The skin over his cheekbones flushed with heat. "You'll never be just one night to me. You're my forever." He didn't give her a chance to answer before he lowered his head and teased one nipple with his mouth, then another. Fiery steaks of pleasure arrowed from her nipples to her clit, making her writhe and undulate. She rocked against the hard ridge of his cock beneath her spread thighs, trying to alleviate the ache.

He groaned, lifting his head, and pushed her to her

back on the couch. Justice gave her a tight smile and drew a single finger between her ribs to the waistband of her pants. He removed her pants and underwear, tossed them aside, then trailed his gaze slowly down her bared body draped across the small couch.

Her flesh pebbled in response to his obvious lust, and was that love? Possession? Before she could figure it out, he stripped off his shirt, revealing his lean, rippling body and tats.

The ethereal blue wings over his heart cradled a perfect yellow rose. She absorbed the beauty shimmering in the ink, another layer of who this man was. He wore his feelings on his skin, rather than hiding them in his soul.

Justice recaptured her attention by releasing the clasp of his pants and shoving them and his boxers down to kick them off. He returned to pick up her legs and settle between her thighs on the couch. He eased the foot of one of her legs to the floor and braced the other on the back of the couch, leaving her open, exposed. Urgent desperation to feel his touch tingled through her nerve endings until she nearly burned with the demand. She wanted to feel all of him.

He lowered his head to stare between her spread thighs. His mouth parted, and his nostrils flared.

Her clit ached in response to the need carved into his face. Pleading words rose in her throat, but they caught on a sob when he lowered his head to drag his wet, slightly rough tongue over her clit.

She bowed, her stomach tightening as a furnace blasted in her belly. She sank her hands into his hair to hold on as she rode his mouth, her desire rocketing into near insanity as he kissed, tongued and then suckled. She was nearly there when he stopped.

"Justice!"

He lifted his head, the full impact of his sizzling desire and love slamming into her. This was more than sex, it had always been more than physical between them. Now, it throbbed with an added significance and intimacy, as if their battered hearts needed one another more.

Appreciated each other more.

Justice rose over her. Settling his hips between her legs, he held himself on one rippling arm, his other catching her hand and linking their fingers. "You'll come with me inside you. I'm going to feel you let go, Beth. Trust me to give you pleasure." His cockhead pressed against her and then pushed inside. "And to feel mine. It's yours. I'm yours."

Each inch he burrowed with agonizing slowness made her body clench and pull, trying to draw him deeper. "Not enough," she begged. "More." Her entire being screamed for the fullness only he could give her.

"Oh yeah." He surged, buying himself to the hilt. "I'll always give you more." He pulled out and thrust again. "Every damn part of me."

She jerked up to meet him as he hit her very center.

His face shifted into a mask of agonizing need. "Not just for one night."

And again. "But for all the nights."

She bucked beneath him, losing herself in the moment with Justice. Everything tightened as he pushed her higher and higher. Not enough, she had to get closer, feel more. Liza dug in her feet, raising her hips and taking every inch of Justice.

He drove into her and growled, "You're my forever."

Liza crashed, her control shattering into a million stars of glittering pleasure pulses. She panted beneath the onslaught, only aware of the breath-stealing bliss and Justice pumping into her twice more before erupting with a feral groan as he came apart with her.

It wasn't until later, after he picked her up from the couch, laid her on the cool sheets and cradled her to his body that she admitted the truth to herself.

She'd never stopped loving Justice. Tonight, she was falling even more in love with her husband. The thought utterly terrified her.

How was she going to walk away tomorrow?

Chapter 14

JUSTICE SURFACED TO SEMICONSCIOUSNESS AT the sound of an annoying tapping. He frowned and tugged Beth closer, refusing to acknowledge the nagging noise. For the first time in almost a year, he had his wife curled up in his arms, and her hair spread out on his chest. When she moved her thigh against his groin, his dick snapped awake. It didn't matter how many times they'd made love in the night, he hadn't been able to get enough of her to quench his desperate thirst. Not with the fear of losing her again driving him with some primal need to mark her to her soul.

"Is that knocking?" Beth asked sleepily.

Justice sat up. Crap, he'd ordered breakfast for them last night.

"Breakfast," he told Beth, then called out, "Coming!" Surging out of bed, he grabbed his pants, yanked them on and rushed to the door.

Beth ducked into the bathroom.

A quick check out the peephole showed him room service with a cart. Opening the door, he waited while the woman set up, signed everything to his card, then she left. He called out to Beth, "Room service is gone, come eat."

Beth strolled out wearing her glasses and his shirt from the night before.

"Now that's sexy, and damned unfair. I was being incredibly thoughtful by ordering breakfast with coffee last night. Now I'm going to toss you on the bed and make you beg for tempting me this way."

Her smile spread. "Is that right?"

He leaned closer to steal a morning kiss.

Beth ducked beneath his arm and sprinted away, flashing her bare ass beneath the shirt. "Not before coffee!"

Her laughter hit his heart with a blast of fierce love. He couldn't leave her. Not when Beth was relaxing and opening up, letting him closer, emotionally and physically, than she had in a long time. Their relationship was too fragile, and needed time to strengthen and cement then into a recommitted couple. More than anything, he wanted to put her rings back on her finger.

"Coffee?" she asked.

I just have to convince her to see me again. "Sure." He limited himself to one cup to protect his vocal cords. After she poured the brew, they made their breakfast tacos from the array of fluffy scrambled eggs, sliced avocados, leafy spinach, whole wheat wraps and assorted other veggies and salsas.

"I love breakfast tacos." Beth sat across from him and bit into hers with gusto.

A memory flooded back of her in the kitchen making eggs for his dad when she'd suddenly paled. Morning sickness. She'd been pregnant and so happy. That was when he told his dad about the baby. Noah had gone into therapy wanting to get well enough to be a part of the baby's life.

Justice had it all that day and hadn't even realized it.

"Aren't you going to eat?"

He cleared the cobwebs of the past, and focused on this moment with his wife. "I'd better before you steal my breakfast like you did my candy." He took a bite, enjoying the heat of the salsa against the creaminess of the avocado. Once he'd swallowed, he asked, "How's your mom? Are you all set for her release?" It was next month.

"So far she's fine. I'm as ready as I can be. It's going to be weird having her there, and, well, I'm kind of nervous." She forked up a piece of honeydew. "I haven't lived with her in nearly a decade. Much of the time I did live with her she was a partier. It was only the last two years she'd stopped drinking, doing drugs and living the groupie life. Then we fought. I mean, before that, I often took care of her. Then she was trying to parent me and..." Beth lifted one shoulder beneath his shirt. "I didn't like it."

Yeah, and that had led to her dad being able to manipulate her, but Justice didn't want to talk about that, or Gene Hayes. He wanted to stay in their bubble. "Do you have a job for her?"

"We got a reprieve on that condition from the parole board due to safety concerns. Instead, I have my mom in regular counseling and related classes like art therapy and anger management. It's not enough to fill her days, but maybe she'll make friends." Beth finished her first breakfast taco and sipped her coffee. "We'll figure it out. I just need to get her home and safe."

"Are you going to take time off when she comes home?"

"I'm trying to take a week, or at least work from home, to help ease my mom's transition." She shrugged. "I can't abandon my job. I'm building a nest egg for my mom."

He frowned, unsure what that meant. "Nest egg for what?"

Her attention shifted to her fruit. "Anything. I'm all she has."

"And me."

"What?" Her eyes snapped up.

"I'll help your mom, Beth. Anything either of you needs. I want to be there for you."

Surprise froze her hand holding the coffee cup midair. "I appreciate that. But you bought us the condo, and you're taking care of your dad." She set her cup down. "Speaking of Noah, Have you talked to him?"

He let her redirect the conversation. "No. I mean I send texts." A smidge of jealousy spilled out. "He doesn't bring me milkshakes."

Her face softened. "He did that twice, on Christmas and your opening night, with messages for you, Justice. I forwarded his latest one about the grease fire to you."

Yep, that text had sparked his urge to fly home and search the streets for his dad, the desperation riding him to tell Noah it didn't matter. He could burn the house down, and Justice wouldn't care as long as Noah and Radar were okay. He hadn't been able to of course, and as usual, it'd been Beth who took care of it. "I appreciate everything you're doing for him."

"I wanted to, and as far as the house goes, I had help."

Ah yes, Emily, Kat, Sherry, Tess and Sophie had shown up to help clean. "You didn't mention if you went in Savanna's room."

Beth studied her plate. "No, the girls showed up and we got busy." She lifted her head. "Did I tell you we sent your dad a video of the kitchen all cleaned up?"

The diversion bothered him, and the fact that she still never said Savanna's name aloud, but he didn't want to ruin the short time they had together before he left. "Yep." He switched to a safer subject. "How'd it feel telling everyone about your book?"

She relaxed, and her smile spread like warm butter. "Pretty good. They were so genuinely interested that I felt silly for being so worried about sharing my dream to write. All these years I haven't confided in anyone but you. I've told my mom I'm writing, then there was that time Em and Nikki found out..." She trailed off and tensed for a second, then Beth shrugged it off with a renewed determination. "The women who helped me clean after that fire are real friends who won't sell me out."

He ordered himself not to let the memory of Nikki's betrayal steal any space in his time with Beth. "Have you shared with your mom about your book?"

"I haven't told her a lot about Molly."

He reached across the table, taking her hand. "Your book is amazing and powerful. Don't hide it from your mom." The smile that lit up her face turned her from pretty into stunning.

She glanced at their joined hands then up at him. "I'll tell her when she's home. In the meantime, I can revise."

He lifted an eyebrow, pride edging in. "With my suggestions."

"Your ideas on developing the two men more and giving the bassist a bigger storyline popped into my brain a couple time during the night."

"Huh. If that's true, then I didn't do my job. You should have been so satisfied that you didn't have the energy to think about my brilliant notes."

Beth tugged her hand away, scooped up her water

and took a sip. "I can multitask. You know, have sex a few times and mentally review your ideas."

He unfolded from his chair, loving that her stare went to the wing and rose tattoo first, then roaming like a lover's caress over his inked arms and down his belly. Moving around the table, he recaptured her hand and tugged her up against his body. The feel of his shirt covering all her skin irritated him. He wanted nothing between them.

"What are you doing?"

"I'm going to drive every thought but how damn good I make you feel out of your head. Kiss and touch you until there's no space left between us."

Her full lips parted.

He lowered his head an inch. "Just us." He settled his mouth over hers, tasting coffee, avocado, salsa and Beth when his phone on the nightstand started to vibrate.

No way was he stopping now. He only had an hour until he had to leave. One hour. Cupping the back of her head, he deepened the kiss.

Buzz, buzz, buzz.

He slid a hand over the curve of her hip to her bare thigh. Warm, silky flesh over muscles more defined than he remembered from all her self-defense classes. He trailed up as he tangled his tongue with hers. His cock ached with the need to bury inside her, feel the hot, welcoming...

Buzz, buzz, buzz.

Beth pulled back. "You'd better check it."

Hell. Reluctantly letting her go, he grabbed his phone off the nightstand and glared at the screen. "Missed call from Simon." He scrolled. "Three of them. Two from Gavin. I—"

The phone buzzed in his hand. "It's Simon again."

His stomach clenched. A sense of dread spread in his gut. He didn't want to answer the call, didn't want to let the outside world in.

Beth's mouth flatlined, and she wrapped her arms around herself. "Answer it."

He accepted the call. "You're on speaker, Simon. What's so important?"

"Jagged Sin just made a huge announcement," Simon said.

Irritation prickled his skin. "You're interrupting my last hour with my wife to talk about the Jagged Assholes?" He resisted the urge to hang up on the lead guitarist.

Beth laid her hand on his arm, her touch soothing.

"Pay attention, J," Simon snapped. "This is bad. The title of their album is *Witch Hunt*. Guess who is featured on the title song with them?"

Dread hardened into a lump of hot lead. "No fucking way." It couldn't happen.

"Gene Hayes," Simon's icy voice snarled. "He's doing the title song with them."

Adrenaline flooded through him while Beth's fingers dug into his forearm. "They can't do that! The contract with World Rock Stage is for Jagged Sin. They'll be disqualified. I'm calling Slade." The lead singer of Seventh Ring would have to know about this. He'd put a stop to it.

"It's a fucking loophole. Our lawyers are checking, but they're pretty sure there was nothing in the contract that said we couldn't feature another singer. Like we had Screech sing with us on our opening night. Hayes got the drop on us."

"Shit." Justice ripped his fingers through his hair. Mentally, he went back through the contract, but he wasn't a lawyer. He'd never have looked for something like that.

"Get on the plane and get your ass here. We have to figure this out. Plan to deal with it. It's going to create a shitload of media and hype for Ace and his crew."

"And Hayes." Justice turned from Beth and stalked to the window. "He can't perform in the States, he can't travel with them, or he'll be arrested. It's their big single."

"I don't know, just get your ass back here. We have to get our shit together and issue a statement."

"My flight leaves at noon. Later." He hung up. Beth had vanished. A minute later, he heard the shower go on.

What the hell? Going to the door, he turned the knob.

Locked. Frustration boiled beneath everything else. They'd had a great night and morning. Beth had been more open with him, shared her book, and made love with him. It'd been a perfect date, and a solid start to rebuilding their marriage.

Then Gene Hayes managed to fuck it up.

Killing anger curled his fingers as if he once again had the bastard's neck in his hands. This time, he'd get the job done.

Liza took a quick shower, trying to calm the sick rage and icy fear brewing into an emotional cat-5 hurricane. Gene Hayes featured on Jagged Sin's lead song, getting what he wanted all along, while her baby—

No. God. Liza got out of the shower and kept moving. Dry, dress in black pants and pale shirt. Smooth on minimal makeup. Twist up hair. Move, move, move. Settling her cool composure around her, she walked out of the bathroom to the sound of Justice's voice.

"I want a full boycott. If any venue books Hayes, we'll pull out. We can't stop them from contracting with Jagged Sin, but Hayes is a wanted felon and rapist. We—"

He cut off, and Liza could feel the weight of his attention on her.

"We're agreed on this, right?" A pause, then Justice said, "Good. I'll call again once I'm in the car, but right now, I'm out."

Liza focused on packing her clothes and toiletries. She traveled light, so it was quick. "Here's your shirt." She laid the folded garment on the edge of the bed then zipped her suitcase and set it on the floor. After slipping her feet into her heels, she pulled on her blazer.

"I take it you're leaving."

Liza flinched and turned. He was two feet from her shoulder. Damn, he moved quiet when he chose. "I have a lunch meeting. We aren't coming back to the hotel. You have a plane to catch."

"I called the pilot. They'll wait. You're more important."

Her stomach pitched, and she took a slow breath to calm herself. "Don't, Justice. It was one night. We both knew it."

"Bullshit." Passion glittered in his eyes. "You're not just one night to me. You're my life. I know you're upset, but we can fight Hayes together."

"No, we can't. Hayes will come after me, and it's up to me to be ready, and to make sure he doesn't get to me before I have my mom safe and secure. I owe her that after she spent a decade in prison for trying to save me."

Justice jerked his head back. "Hayes isn't going to get to you or your mom. We won't let him. We'll keep you and her protected."

Sadness filled her. "You swore that before, and you know what? You lied. That's on me for being naïve and foolish."

"Damn it, I screwed up, but I didn't know Hayes would be there in Paris, I didn't think he'd really go after you."

A furnace of fury blew up from her deepest recesses. It shook her, until her hands trembled and her vision narrowed. "I knew he would if he ever had the chance. He was always coming after me. I testified in court, I destroyed his life, me"—she tapped the flat of her palm on her chest—"a worthless girl. I told you that. I thought you believed me. I trusted you."

Two spots of crimson blotched his cheeks and carved sharper grooves into the angles of his face. He reached out a hand but stopped short of touching her. "You can still trust me. I won't make the same mistake twice. If Hayes gets anywhere near you or anywhere accessible to me, I'll kill him."

"No!" Her guts churned now with acid fear. "You were nearly killed once, and how was I supposed to live with that? Huh, Justice? I got my dad killed, my mom shoved into a prison cell and our daughter...and then I was supposed to live with either you getting beaten to death or succeeding in murdering Hayes and going to prison? I'd have destroyed your life too." She couldn't bear anyone else getting hurt. "This isn't happening. I have to go." She grabbed her purse, her rolling suitcase and strode to the door.

"At least I'm willing to fight. All you're doing is running. Hiding. I screwed up, yeah, and I hurt you badly. But I'm all in, Beth. I fight for the people I love. I don't walk out on them. Not even when they make a mistake."

His words were like slaps to her back, each one

vibrating deeper. Reaching the door, she turned and faced him across the short hall. "I'm not running. I'm going to self-defense, I'm trying to be strong enough. I'm taking care of my mom, I'm not running out on her."

His lips twisted grimly. "Just on me, then."

His pain was so raw, so thick, it graveled his voice and ripped another hole in her heart. What could she do? "I'm sorry. I wish we could go back in time and change things. We can't."

"Hayes wins every time you run and hide. Every damn time. It'd be different if you no longer loved me, but you do. The problem isn't whether you love me or not, it's that loving me scares you."

Tears threatened and her throat closed. In his arms last night, she'd felt like she was home again after being away on a long, painful journey. Hell yeah she was scared. Terrified. The memory of holding her precious baby, looking into that beautiful face and knowing she'd never take a breath, hurt like a punch to her solar plexus. Then waking that night and finding herself alone after she'd agreed to take pain meds? "You weren't supposed to leave me that night." Crap that came out thin and broken.

The blade-sharp anger on Justice's face softened, and he dropped his folded arms, taking a step toward her. "I know. I wasn't thinking, Beth. I was insane with grief and rage. I'd never make that choice now, I swear it."

He wasn't wrong about her loving him, she did. She couldn't risk loving so much—her husband, her child—and losing them again. "I can't."

She opened the door and walked out.

Chapter 15

LIZA LEANED BACK IN THE leather chair, studying each of the label mockups for SLAM Vodka flashing on the PowerPoint presentation. Once it was finished, she shook her head. They were targeting men, and worse, they were being lazy about it. "That's not what I asked for. SLAM Vodka is bold, in your face, and our customers, both men and women," she emphasized, "don't tap out. A curvaceous woman on the label is insulting. We have one female fighter on our roster and she's fierce. This label"—she gestured to the mockup frozen on the screen—"looks like a trucker mud flap. SLAM Vodka isn't about a gender, it's a state of mind. Mental toughness."

"Exactly." Sloane pushed off the wall where he'd stood after quietly slipping into the room a few minutes ago.

Liza waited to see if he'd say more. She'd been handling this part of the SLAM Vodka project, although she'd run the first couple sets of designs by Sloane and John.

He nodded at her, leaving her in control.

She rose from her chair. "Thank you for your efforts,

but we'll be going another way that won't require your services designing the SLAM Vodka label. Your job is done as of today."

Jeremy Carson, owner and CEO of the graphics arts company, glared down his nose at her. "You're firing us? You can't do that."

"Actually, I can." Liza firmed her tone to match her unyielding posture. "It's in our contract with Back Hills Distillery that SLAM has final say. I asked you twice to redo the mockups, and you've failed with each effort."

Jeremy turned to Sloane. "Mr. Michaels, Liza is not being clear on your vision and doesn't understand the market for vodka. My company has two decades of experience and a sterling reputation to bring to the table. While, frankly, Liza's reputation is questionable at best, and a huge distraction with all the media about her mom getting out of prison for murder. Perhaps she's under too much stress, and that's why her actions here have been less than rational and professional. If we work with you directly, Mr. Michaels, things will go smoother."

Sloane leveled his gaze on the man. "I thought she was very clear in firing you. If you feel you need more clarification, I'm sure she'd be more than happy to call security to escort you out." He turned and left.

Liza kept the satisfied smirk off her face at her boss's reaction to that ugly rant and crossed the room to stand at the door. "We're finished here."

Jeremy got up and stormed by her, muttering, "Bitch. I'm going to destroy you."

"Good luck. Have a nice day." She added enough sweetness to her voice to give him diabetes. She'd been called much worse and survived. As threats went, that one was just plain lazy like their designs.

Now a baby doll covered in ketchup took real effort and imagination.

Liza kept her smile as the three assistants meekly followed their fired boss out the door.

Sophie moved up beside her. "That was such a nice fuck you."

"The art of subtle communication is an invaluable tool when dealing with a sexist asshole who thinks he can call women names and make stupid threats."

Her assistant laughed softly. "Pretty sure he's calling you names all the way out to the car and beyond. He was definitely trying to undermine you with Sloane."

She shrugged. There were days when she questioned why Sloane put up with the hassle that followed her around like a desperate puppy. Most days, Liza knew damn well it was because she'd proved herself valuable, hard-working, capable, and loyal. "I don't let it get to me. Jeremy lacked the vision we need. Mixed Martial Arts is a male-dominated field, but we're also diving into the female viewership and consumerism. We will do the same with SLAM Vodka. We need to create our own fresh, strong branding to reflect the wider market."

"Go bold and don't tap out," Sophie said.

"You got it." Once she was sure the group had left the executive floor, Liza headed into the hallway with Sophie at her side. They stopped in front of her office. "We'll design the SLAM Vodka labels in house. Set up a meeting with the graphics department."

Sophie nodded. "I've got all my notes and the mockups. I'll go down there to give them copies, set up the meeting, and answer any questions they have. Anything else?"

"No, thanks."

"How are you doing? I mean your mom is coming home in a week, the media's been brutal, plus all the rising hype about Jagged Sin's new song with Hayes." She touched Liza's arm. "You look a little tired."

Because she wasn't sleeping. "I'm writing a lot at night. I have to finish the revision, but the ending is giving me trouble." It was like trying to go through the door into Savanna's room—the barrier was too much. Too frightening. "I have to though. I sent the first half of the book and a synopsis with the revised ending to my agent. She loves it and believes she can sell it." Actually her agent had said it'd likely go to auction.

A squeal pierced her thoughts, and Sophie hugged her. "Liza! That's amazing. You're getting so close to finishing the rewrite and selling your book! I can't wait to read it!"

She laughed, trying to disentangle herself. "Thanks. But it's all preliminary. I have to be able to write the revised ending."

Sophie sobered. "When we were at Justice's house cleaning up after the oil fire, Emily mentioned that Justice was the one who sent the book back to you, and you sent him pages and you guys talked about it. Have you tried running this by him?"

Crap. Liza hadn't told anyone but Emily what had happened between her and Justice. Emily had been predictably outraged at Gene Hayes being featured on Jagged Sin, and supportive of Liza.

Sophie peered closer. "Liza? Is something wrong? Did you and Justice stop talking?"

"Not exactly." More like she was only responding to discussions about Noah. She didn't answer when Justice called. Didn't send him her revisions. *Hayes wins every time you run and hide.*

She wasn't hiding. More like...avoiding.

Feeling her assistant's waiting stare, she added, "We're both busy, and I don't really want to talk to him about this." Liar. She'd picked up her cell a few times. More than a few.

Sophie said, "Well if you need anyone to read it, I'll be first in line. Or if you want to talk about it. In the meantime, I need to get downstairs and do some work." She left.

Guilt had walked out of that room with her, and nagged her like an itch between her shoulder blades. Was she hiding and not willing to fight as Justice had said? Or protecting herself and everyone around her? The danger was real, and it'd ramp up the moment her mom was released. If she got a contract on her book and created a media splash, that kind of attention would infuriate Hayes and trigger his need to destroy her.

She went into her office and settled behind her cream-colored antique desk. One step at a time. She had work to do. She'd talk to Sloane in a few minutes, but she was sure he'd be fine with having the vodka labels done in house with their excellent marketing department. They'd only agreed to the outside firm because this was so new to SLAM, but in retrospect, that had been a mistake.

Her phone dinged a text, and a mixture of excitement and dread danced around her belly. Was it Justice? Even though she'd barely answered him, he'd been sending her constant encouragement about revising her book, telling her things like, *It's your book, Beth. Molly's your creation, follow both your hearts*. He kept her updated on their plans to fight Hayes from appearing anywhere. They sent out social media blasts, and warned all venues they wouldn't do an interview with someone who interviewed Hayes with Jagged Sin about their upcoming album.

They'd gotten Fury Run to do the same thing.

Maybe he had a new update? She scooped her phone up off her desk.

Not Justice. It was Noah. *Can you meet me at the emergency veterinary clinic? I need a credit card and don't have one.*

Oh God, had something happened to Radar? *I'll be right there. I just need to know where exactly to go.* She grabbed her purse out of the desk drawer.

The reply came back in seconds. *Fur Friends Small Animal Emergency Clinic. Pls hurry. Radar's hurt, and they don't believe I can pay.*

What happened to the dog? she started to ask, then realized it didn't matter. *Leaving work now. Be there ASAP.*

Fifteen minutes later she pulled into the clinic, parked and rushed to the door.

"Liza."

Spinning around, she spotted the older man limping toward her, carrying a whimpering bundle wrapped in one of the jackets she'd bought Noah over a year ago. His hair was almost all gray, but his ragged beard still had streaks of brown. The web of twisted scars on the left side of his face were the same as she remembered.

"Noah, what happened?" He was thinner and his limp worse. When he was close enough to see the reddish brown stains on his sleeves, alarm spread through her. "Is that blood on you?"

"Radar's blood, not mine. Do you have a credit card?"

"Yes, but I have to make sure you're okay."

"He's hurt. Leg broken, bad lacerations and who knows what else." His voice dipped to vibrant anger. "They wouldn't take him. I told them you or Justice would pay." He looked away. "They wouldn't believe me that Justice is my son."

The cries coming from the animal wrenched her heart. Liza stepped closer, peeling back the edge of the jacket.

The dog's elegant Doberman-like face was covered in blood and cuts. One of his ears was nearly torn off. The dog let out a wail, burying his head against Noah's chest. His whole body trembled. The front right leg— she closed her eyes.

Breathe. Don't faint. That leg was badly broken with bones exposed. Her mouth watered, and her stomach pitched. They had to get him help now. "Come with me."

He shook his head and held out the bundle. "They don't want me in there."

A flush of heat ballooned up from deep in her gut. She almost said, *Excuse me?* That was stupid. She understood him perfectly well. If she took the dog inside, Noah might disappear. "I don't want to hurt him any more than he's already suffering. You carry him." Moving slowly, she touched Noah's arm. "He trusts you."

Noah met her gaze. "I promised Drake I'd take care of him. I tried. They hurt him, and I couldn't do shit."

His words were rough and furious, conveying his torment.

Something horrific had happened, and Liza feared what he'd do if he left. "You're taking care of him now. Hear me? Radar needs you, and Drake needs you to do this. Okay?"

Was she saying the right thing? Sick fear for both the beloved dog and this man who meant so much to her, and even more to Justice, filled her.

He stared back her, one beat, then two, before he finally inclined his head in agreement.

She pulled open the door, and while holding it for Noah, she saw he didn't have his battered backpack. Just keep moving, she told herself. In the waiting room, vinyl-covered benches lined two walls, and a reception desk stood at one end.

Striding up to the window, she leaned in. "This dog is seriously injured and needs emergency treatment." She slid her credit card from her purse.

The girl glanced at Noah, then said, "I told him we don't treat..." She trailed off and her brown eyes widened with recognition. "You're Liza Cade."

For once, Liza was more than happy to be recognized. "I am. Here's my credit card. The dog is suffering with a broken leg so badly I can see the bone. He has deep lacerations and other injuries. I'm asking you to treat him immediately before he goes into shock and dies due to your refusal to do your job."

"Of course." She scrambled up, zoomed around and opened the door. "We'll get you in a room. I didn't realize, I mean..."

Nothing like being the wife—estranged or not—of a rock star to get things done. "Let me clear up your confusion. Anything this dog needs, or Justice's father wants, I or Justice, will pay for. Are we clear?"

Two red spots appeared over the cheeks of the girl's chalky face. "Yes."

"Good." Liza laid her hand on Noah's arm, and the two of them followed the woman into a small exam room.

"The doctor will be right in," she said and scurried out.

"Leave the door open, please," Liza asked, vividly aware of Noah's claustrophobia.

The girl nodded and vanished. Hushed conversations rose in the hallway, but Liza focused on Noah. He'd paled once inside, and a sheen of sweat coated his face. He hated hospitals, and this was close enough to make him uneasy. Maybe she shouldn't have forced him to come in.

She opened her mouth but was cut off when a woman wearing a white coat knocked on the open door. "Hello, I'm Dr. Kim, and this is Tracy." She motioned to a girl with her—not, thankfully, the same person from the front desk. She moved straight to the table, smiled at Liza then addressed Noah. "I understand your dog is injured. Can you tell me what happened while you put him on the table?"

Noah moved slowly to the exam table opposite the doctor. "I was in the public bathroom, and Radar waited outside. Some men were already in there and started pushing me around. Radar rushed in and attacked the one nearest me. The guy pulled a knife, cutting my dog's ear. I managed to get up off the ground and attempted to stop them, but two of them held me back while the third taunted my dog, slashing at him with the knife. When Radar lunged again, he kicked him in the side, then stomped on his leg."

Noah clamped his mouth shut, his scars whitening further with rage. Yet he was exceedingly gentle as he laid down the dog wrapped in his jacket.

Radar let out a shrill cry, trying to clamber back to Noah. The vet tech quickly and carefully restrained the dog, and the doctor examined him. She eased aside the coat covering Radar's front leg.

Liza covered her mouth, struggling not to cry at the sight of the blood and bones poking through torn skin. She couldn't image what kind of monsters would do this. The dog was in horrible pain, and terrified. His eyes rolled to Noah, desperate pleading in them.

Noah closed his fingers around one of the dog's uninjured paws. "Easy, buddy. The doc will help you."

Liza settled her hand on Noah's arm. "Are you okay? Do you need a doctor?"

He shook his head. "I didn't break free fast enough. They laughed. I can still hear them laughing. Radar was trying to protect me, and they laughed like he was nothing."

Disgusted fury shivered down her spine, but she had to ask the right questions. Noah knew how to kill. "What did you do?" She had to find out if he was going to be arrested. Get him a lawyer, or get him away. She wouldn't let him go to prison like her mom.

The light in his eyes dimmed. "Nothing. Some car backfired outside, they panicked, grabbed my backpack and ran away. I couldn't go after them, had to take care of Radar. It wasn't until I got here I remembered I had my phone on the inside of my jacket I was carrying Radar in, not my backpack they stole."

Which explained why he didn't call her for help sooner.

"Okay, let's get Radar taken care of." She was concerned Noah was hurt, but he wasn't going to cooperate while he was frantic about the dog.

The next few minutes passed in a blur as they got the pup's vitals, the vet felt for other injuries, listened to his heart and lungs, then started an IV.

"Okay," the doctor said. "I've given him some pain meds. Mr. Cade, Radar responds to you. If you could try to calm him, the meds will help him faster. Let's get him comfortable then discuss a treatment plan."

Noah went to the dog, gently stroking behind his good ear.

The dog whimpered and nosed Noah's hand. The older man carefully stroked Radar's head and neck, soothing him until Radar closed his eyes and relaxed.

"Good," Dr. Kim said. "The next step is X-rays to see the full extent of the damage, but from my initial exam, I believe this break will require surgical repair. We also need to do an ultrasound to check for internal injuries since Mr. Cade said he was kicked. He's also going to need all the wounds cleaned and a few stitched, and I don't think we can save much of that ear. I'm going to start him on antibiotics too."

Liza dug her fingers into her palms. Poor Radar, he'd just been trying to protect Noah. Beneath all that, a tiny voice in her head said, *This is Drake's dog.* Justice, the guys in his band, Sloane, everyone was going to be upset Radar was hurt, and it'd be worse if he didn't make it.

She glanced at his leg covered by sterile gauze. "You can save the leg, right?"

"No guarantees, but if you okay it, we have an excellent staff including an orthopedic specialist. I have to caution you that it's going to be a financial investment."

Liza waved that off. "We'll cover it." Justice would pay for it, and if for some reason she couldn't access all the money she needed, Sloane would do it. "Please, we want the best care and treatment for Radar."

Dr. Kim nodded and turned to Noah. "Mr. Cade, I've been told you were refused treatment. That's not something we do here. I'm very sorry. I'll handle the situation with our staff."

Noah stared at the dog and barely nodded.

"All right. I'll get the forms I'll need you to sign and make sure we have your contact information. I will personally call you to let you know how Radar is doing, and the treatment plan with itemized costs." She slipped out the door.

"Thank you." Noah's voice was rough and tired.

Liza moved up beside him and stroked Radar's neck. His fur was matted with blood and grime, but his glazed brown eyes opened to look at Noah with a profound trust that nearly broke her heart. The love between dog and man was as evident as Radar's wounds and Noah's scars. "Anytime. You aren't going back to the streets and leaving me alone with this dog. I don't know the first thing about taking care of him. He needs you."

"He was protecting me. I told him to stand down, but he wouldn't."

Liza could almost feel his internal battle. She'd bet her book that he wanted to go after the worthless thugs who did this to Radar. "Will you let me take you to the house? You'll stay there while we get Radar through this?"

He finally looked at her. "I don't leave a man behind. So yes."

Justice got offstage in Virginia and stormed toward the greenroom, ignoring their crew and people with backstage passes. His head throbbed, and blood welled through the shirt wrapped around his upper arm.

Their manager rushed after him. "Justice," Gavin called. "Hang on a second."

"Get out of my face." Goddamn it, he just needed five minutes, a chance to shower off the sweat and blood, and slap a bandage on his arm. He'd finished the show on pure adrenaline. They'd been on the road for two months with only minor issues.

Until tonight—the first of a three-night run in the biggest venue in Virginia. One of the high-tech moving spotlights had exploded, firing jagged pieces of treated glass and metal at him in the last few minutes of the show.

Gray jogged up. "Justice, listen, dude, your arm looks bad, and you have some welts on your face and neck, probably burns. We need to get you treatment."

"Back off. All I need is a few butterfly bandages." And a drink. He limited his alcohol intake to stay fit enough to perform. Now that was some ass-biting irony—when that light had blown, the sudden pain had turned his death growl into a pussy squeal. Forget protecting his voice, he needed the drink to drown the memory of that squeal.

Spotting the greenroom door, he barreled inside.

The room had the usual couches, a couple chairs, TV and a refreshment table. Justice stumbled into the bathroom and slammed the door. Finally. He dropped the hand of his uninjured arm on the counter and stared into the mirror.

Hell. Gray was right. A few angry welts stood out on his cheek and neck. River's black T-shirt tied around his biceps was soaked. More blood dripped down his arm. "Double fuck," he muttered.

The door to his left eased open, and Lynx stuck his head in. "You alive?"

Did it seem like he was in the mood for jokes? "Where's the damned first aid kit?"

Lynx strode in carrying a bottle of water and another of juice. Setting those on the counter, he said, "Water first. Drink it." He quickly unwrapped the shirt and tossed it onto the floor. "Slashed right through your skull tat and deep enough to earn you a trip to the hospital."

Justice looked down at the five-inch wound and thought of bloody meat. "Get a doctor or someone. Not going to the hospital." He'd be there for hours. It was a sure bet that news would hit the media and turn into a big deal. Shit like a light blowing out could get twisted into something to scare fans away from their concerts.

Lynx pressed a clean towel to the wound. "Gavin's been trying, but he can't get anyone here within an hour. Faster to have the limo drive you to the hospital."

Justice set his jaw.

"You're going, J. It's deep enough you could have nerve damage. Gavin's getting a specialist called into the hospital. Ethan's got the car ready at the door. You can walk, or River will fireman carry your ass and Gray will video it."

Justice would have shoved Lynx into the wall for that threat...if he'd had the strength.

The other man's eyes narrowed. "You're dehydrated. Too much blood loss on top of what you normally sweat off in a show." Grabbing the water, he shoved it in Justice's good hand.

"What are you now, my nanny?" He took the damned water and drank it.

"Manny, asshole. Have some respect. A man is a manny. If you die from sheer dumbassery, that will be my next career move. Go." Lynx pushed Justice to the door while holding the towel on his arm. In the greenroom, Lynx spoke to Hank, their head of security. "Let's go before he passes out."

"Fuck you. I don't pass out." To prove it, he strode to the door, ignoring the waves of dizziness and pain.

"Reverse psyched you into moving your ass. I'd make an excellent manny," Lynx crowed.

Justice climbed into the limo and leaned his head back. "Better have good drugs there."

Managing to keep the towel on Justice's arm, the drummer slid in next to him. "Dude, you don't touch drugs."

He opened one eye. "For you. To shut you up."

Justice didn't do recreational drugs since he'd gotten out of juvie, but he was totally on board with painkillers when needed. Like deep, burning cuts or Lynx riding his very last nerve.

"Now that you're in the car, there's another reason we're heading out instead of calling in a doctor," Lynx said. "Our lighting crew told Gavin and security that the light had been tampered with. It was sabotage. Hank and his team are handling it now, and they're going to have to check out all our crew."

"Goddammit." It came out weak, his throat raw from his squeal and anger. "One of our guys." They had so many people on their payroll, someone could have slipped through. Cold fury kicked back his exhaustion. "Hayes is behind this."

"Or Jagged Sin," Simon said.

"They're on the same team of dirty assholes," River added. "The image of you getting hit by glass and butchering the death scream hit the Bring Gene Hayes Home and Jagged Sin social media sites damn near instantly. The video is shot from the front rows of the concert, so obviously they sent a troll to capture the moment the light blew."

"They're hoping we have to cancel a couple concerts." Gray shifted his gaze to the bloody cloth over Justice's arm. "Or more depending on how much damage was done to your arm."

His mood blackened like a charred hillside. "We're not cancelling."

Not a chance. He didn't care if he had to crawl onto that stage.

Chapter 16

JUSTICE FINALLY GOT BACK TO his room closing in on four a.m. when he spotted his phone sitting on his bed.

Gavin must have dropped it off. Justice snatched it up, passcoded in, and then swore. He'd missed a message from Beth. Had she heard about the light exploding on stage?

He sat on the bed, leaned against the pillows, and opened her text.

Hi, bad news. Some men attacked your dad with a knife—Noah is okay, but Radar was hurt. He's at the vet's. They cleaned and stitched cuts today, and if he's strong enough tomorrow, they'll surgically repair a badly broken leg. I put it on my credit card, and I'll move the money to cover it later. Your dad is at the house, he agreed to stay there while we get Radar through this.

Oh Christ. He reread the line reassuring him his dad was all right. Radar, Drake's dog, was injured. Who did that?

What time was it in California? Almost one a.m. by his calculations. *Just got in my room, any chance you're awake?*

His phone rang with a video call from Beth, and he accepted it.

Beth appeared on the screen, her hair pulled back, eyes magnified by glasses. "Hey Beth." He shifted the phone to his other hand, so he could shove a pillow under his arm.

"What happened to you? Your face." Her gaze traveled down. "Your arm!"

Well, shit, he hadn't thought about the burn marks on his face, the blood he hadn't washed off yet, or his bandaged biceps. Shifting the phone around had probably given her a good view of his injuries. "I'm okay. We had an incident on stage." He quickly told her about it.

"Hayes got to someone on your crew?"

"Don't know. It's possible, or it was someone working in the venue that got access. Our security is damn good, so they'll find where our weakness is and plug it. I can tell you this much, assuming Hayes and/or Jagged Sin was behind this, their plan won't work. We aren't cancelling any concerts."

"Are you sure you can, or should, perform? You're traveling out of the country in, what, two days? What did the doctor say?"

The concern in her voice touched him. "I can't play guitar for a few days, but I can sing and I'm fine to travel too. Gavin's arranging for ongoing medical care while we're out of the country. I'm more worried about things on your end. Your message said my dad was attacked and Radar is hurt? What's going on?"

His guts twisted as she described some assholes jumping his dad, then cutting Radar, and stomping on his leg. He'd had to swallow down a surprising wave of nausea. What a dumpster fire of a night. "Is Radar going to be okay?"

"He will. They ended up doing surgery this evening, put some hardware in to hold it, and they had to remove most of the injured ear. The vet said Radar was in good shape before the attack, with a resilient spirit, and if nothing else goes wrong, he should be home in a few days."

That was a piece of good news. "What about dad?"

"Older, tired, and his hip is worse, I think from being thrown to the ground by the thugs, and he walked miles to the emergency clinic carrying Radar. He was so upset, Justice."

His head pounded, and his vision blurred with pulsing anger and frustration. "Does Dad need a doctor?"

"He wouldn't go when I suggested it. I don't think he's cut anywhere, just sore. I had to go back to work, but I took dinner over last night. Noah ate some, I got him to take one of the pain pills left over from his broken arm and offered to stay overnight with him. Noah shook his head. He wasn't talking much, and I, well, I don't think he could handle having anyone around. Without Radar, I mean." She took a breath, then blurted out, "He kept reaching his left hand out, as if expecting the dog to slide under his palm. It broke my heart."

He dropped his head back against the wall, feeling the weight of his dad's pain. Back when his dad had been in treatment at the transitional center, his counselor and others who worked with him had been troubled that Noah hadn't made a connection with anyone on their staff or the patients. They felt like no one was really reaching through the barriers he'd put up from the extreme hyperawareness that came with his PTSD. They couldn't help Noah if they couldn't get him to lower his guard enough to let them in.

From what Beth was telling him, Radar had done that. Noah'd made that critical connection with the dog, and some fuckers hurt the poor animal. "Dad must trust Radar." It made sense. Weren't dogs known to be man's best friend?

"Apparently, with good reason," Beth responded. "Noah said the dog wouldn't back down until his leg was broken and he couldn't get up anymore."

"Unbelievable." He brushed his hair back and tried not to wince. Damn arm hurt, and the burns too.

Beth went on, "Noah's bond with Radar might keep him off the streets and at the house. Or he'll go to the transitional center since he can take the dog. As bad as all this is, maybe there's a silver lining, you know?"

There she was, his strong, determined wife, who believed Noah could live a better life. Her ability to see the best parts of his dad, and to hope, had helped Justice to understand the father he once knew wasn't coming back and that it was okay. He could build a different relationship with the father Noah was today— if he accepted him. Adjusting his arm on the pillows, he started to speak.

She cut him off. "You need a pain pill and sleep."

"Later. Talking to you is better than anything else. How are you holding up? It's been a tough day." She was handling all this by herself. He ran his thumb over her face on the screen, the longing for Beth overwhelming him. He wanted to smooth the tired lines from around her eyes and hold her.

She shrugged. "I'm okay, and very glad Noah called me. Going in the house was easier this time."

But not Savanna's room, he guessed. He didn't want her to withdraw, so he said, "I'm glad you were there too. Radar isn't the only one my dad trusts."

"He was absolutely sure you'd pay for Radar's care. He'd told the admissions clerk, but she wouldn't believe you're his son. Noah seemed really sad about that. The way he said it was like he wanted the world to know. He's proud of you."

Proud? "Of my music?"

She shook her head. "It's more than your music. The first time I talked to your dad back before you were this famous, he told me you'd never leave a man behind—he meant your bandmates. He'd been proud of that character trait in you. So while I'm sure he respects your music too, it's you he's proud of."

He wasn't sure what to say. "Thanks for telling me, Beth." She'd been so damned upset, scared and withdrawing the last time he'd seen her. "Do you want to talk about your book? I've missed hearing about Molly. You said you were revising, how's that going?"

She tightened her mouth. "It was going great until the end. It's all your fault."

He raised his eyebrows and resisted the urge to stretch his shoulder. "Mine? What did I do now?"

"You put the idea in my head about revising the ending to include Molly's baby. My agent—"

He half sat up. "You signed with the agent?"

"Yes. Do you want to hear this or not?"

A half-dozen worries popped into his brain. Was the agent good enough? Did she know how to protect Beth's rights? He had to stay focused and listen. "Sorry, go on."

"After I revised most of the book, I sent about half to my agent. She read and loved it, and wanted a synopsis. I sort of panicked and used the ideas you had in your notes to change the ending. She loved that too and now wants to shop the book. Which means I have to write the revised ending."

Justice may have smirked. "So my ideas were good."

"Why did I even bother telling you? I can't write the scenes. I try, but I can't."

His amusement died. "Yes, you can. It'll be hard, Beth and it'll hurt. But you can do it. Use your voice. Tell Molly's story about the mother who loves her child so much she battled with everything she had to save him. You'd have done that for our baby if you could have. I didn't come up with the ideas I suggested because I'm some kind of genius, but because Molly dreamed of the day she'd hold her baby. It's what kept her going, kept her fighting. It's the payoff for Molly and your readers. It was right there in what you wrote, but you didn't follow through."

"Dang." She drifted off, clearly thinking, before her forehead wrinkled. "How'd you get this good?"

He shrugged. "I listen to audiobooks on the road when I'm not listening to music or writing songs. I may have listened to a few on story structure too."

"Why?"

"Drake left me a letter. I read it after his funeral, and many times after that." He still missed his friend and mentor, and through all the waiting and hoping on Beth, he'd hung on to Drake's belief in him that he could win Beth back. "Drake told me to be the partner you needed. So I decided I'd learn more about one of your passions—writing. At the time it was romances, but story structure is basically the same for most fiction, so I got a few books and took online courses, hoping I could help you."

Her mouth softened. "I'm touched. I...wow."

"Are you really that surprised? I've grown up, Beth. I understand that love is about choices and actions, and doing all I can to be the partner you need. I recognize now that that's what you were doing for me, and I was too fucking blinded by ambition to fully appreciate it."

"I believe you," she said in a quiet tone. "Now I need to tell you something. I'm sorry for running out on you in L.A." She ground her jaw. "I knew I was wrong even as I walked out the door."

Her raw honesty hit him hard, and he squeezed the phone. "I can handle you losing your temper and telling me your feelings about how I fucked up. It's the walking out that rips me apart."

"I know. It was one thing for me to do it in Paris because I believed that was the right choice. But L.A..." she trailed off then gathered herself. "You didn't deserve that and I regret treating you that way. I couldn't make myself go back and talk to you." She closed her eyes. "I was too damned scared."

This was huge for her, and Justice grabbed onto the moment. "What scares you the most? What is it that you keep hiding from?"

She opened her eyes, and the sheer vulnerability in them sucked out his breath.

Beth put a hand to her throat. "A lot things. You were right that loving you scares me, and...I don't want to lose another child. I tried to go in her room when I went to your house. I couldn't."

He leaned forward, wishing to God he could touch her. There was something here, though. Going in Savanna's room was tied to Beth's fears that were blocking her. "Why, baby? Talk to me. Please." His face, shoulder and arm ached, but the agony of waiting for her choice to answer or not was worse than the physical discomfort.

She swallowed, and looked away.

Don't hang up, he mentally begged her. Desperate, he held up his hand. "See this ring? I put it on when you left and never took it off. It's my symbol to be the man you can run to, not from." He was asking her from a huge leap of trust, but her apology told him Beth was trying. "What scares you about Savanna's room?"

She stared at his hand, her throat working convulsively for a few seconds. Then she swallowed. "Going in and finding out she's not there." Her words rushed out in a hoarse whisper. "That she's just gone. Or worse, feeling her anger and hatred for failing her. I loved her so much."

Her voice thickened with all the tears she hadn't cried. It broke his heart how much Beth had held in. "Oh Beth—"

"That's why I can't write a scene with Molly's baby. How can I when I can't face my own daughter? And why I keep running from you when it gets too scary." She yanked off her glasses, rubbed at the bridge of her nose and put them back on. "I won't do this."

Panic clawed at him. "Won't do what? Us?" Was she bailing on him again?

A tiny flicker of amusement twinkled in a myriad of grief, anger and regrets. "There's that ego again, Rock Star. Believe it or not, this isn't about you, it's me. I need to face this. For our baby, for myself so I can live full on, and for us."

His heart leapt. "Us?"

"Us," she confirmed.

Despite the burns, he smiled. "I have your rings Beth. I've kept them for you."

Joy lit up her face and his hope soared.

Then she said, "Hold on to them. Next time I put them on, I won't take them off again. I will be the wife who gets in your face and demands you run to me, not from me, when things get tough. Now I'd better go. Night, Rooster."

God he loved this woman. That fire in her was breaking free and it was fucking sexy, and scary since the more Beth put herself out there, the bigger the risk to her.

He had to trust in her to figure things out, stay safe and come back to him so he could put the rings on her finger and never let her go again.

Chapter 17

A FEW DAYS LATER, LIZA was still reeling from the conversation with her husband the night Radar was hurt as she stood in the kitchen of Justice's house.

"Did you hear me?" Noah asked.

She jerked, realizing she'd been deep in her own thoughts. Liza had picked Radar up after work tonight, and Noah studied the instructions from the vet while carefully examining bottles of antibiotics and pain meds.

"When do I give him his first dose?"

"Um, the antibiotic with his dinner tonight, and the pain meds before bed. They said he's doing pretty well, and his pain is improving, but Dr. Kim suggested we give him the pain meds at bedtime for a few nights to help him rest and regain strength. In the day, use only if needed."

"That's stupid. How will I know he needs it?"

Liza opened her mouth, then shut it, and they all looked at the dog sitting on the new orthopedic dog bed.

"Maybe he'll cry?" Em suggested from where she sat next to Radar.

Noah huffed, clearly not happy with that answer. He carefully lined up the medicines. "Radar doesn't cry. He's a tough warrior."

Liza smiled at Noah's outrage and agreed he was a tough and very special dog. If Liza had endured the things Radar had, she'd have cried a hell of a lot more than the dog had.

"I'm going to research these meds." Noah headed toward the dining room, then turned back and waited as Radar slowly got to his feet to follow. He nodded toward Em. "I made stew for dinner. You staying? Plenty there."

"I'm in," Em said.

Noah and Radar left the kitchen.

"Hey," Liza called after him. "Radar is supposed to wear the cone." She'd brought him home with the plastic cone fastened around his neck so he couldn't bother the bandages on his leg or the stitches on what remained of his torn ear and a couple other lacerations. The first thing Noah had done was take it off with an annoyed grunt.

Silence floated back to her.

"You're going to lose that battle." Em helped herself to a water in the fridge. "So, Noah risked using the stove again? Guess the fire didn't freak him out too much."

Liza shook her head, but even she had to admit that cone looked extremely uncomfortable for the dog. "I'm staying here tonight to help with Radar, I'll try to get Noah to put the cone on at bedtime. During the day, we can give the dog a break as long as someone is watching him. As for Noah cooking..." She eyed the simmering pot of meat and vegetables, "...I'm a little surprised, but the stew sure smells good."

Em shrugged. "Maybe he was just happy Radar was

coming home. God, Liza, that poor dog. I hope the men who did that to Radar are bit by rattlers and die slowly in the hot sun with no one to hear their cries for help."

Liza put a mug of water in the microwave to heat for tea. "Radar's a hero."

After the microwave dinged, Liza pulled out her cup, dropped in the tea bag and took a seat at the table. "How are you doing?"

Em sighed. "Today sucked at work. One of my brides cancelled her wedding, and that's a freaking nightmare. Most of the deposits aren't refundable at this point, but I'm doing what I can."

"Why'd she cancel the wedding?"

"Her fiancé was arrested in connection with a dog-fighting thing. He was caught on camera dumping a dog in a dumpster behind a restaurant, then he tried to set the dumpster on fire. Couple homeless guys happened to be there rummaging for food, chased him off, got the dog out and called the police.

"Jesus." Liza couldn't even imagine the horror. "What is wrong with people? Will the dog live?"

"The dog didn't survive. I just...the story made me sick. My poor bride is utterly devastated that the man she was going to marry turned out to be so awful. It ruined my day. So being able to see Radar and buy a few things for him, I know it sounds silly, but it made me feel better."

Liza took Em's hand. "It's not silly." Not even a little bit. She thought of Em sitting on the floor in the kitchen, petting Radar as he rested on one of the orthopedic beds Em had bought him. "I'm sorry for your bride, her family, and for you. Is there anything I can do to help?"

"Maybe. I'll let you know." Em shook her head.

"It feels good to just get it off my chest. I had to be so professional today when all I really wanted to do was offer to help her kidnap her ex and toss his ass in a pen with fighting dogs, then throw his bleeding carcass in a dumpster."

Liza squeezed her fingers. "In a place where there are no cameras or witnesses. Then we'd donate any money of his to a rescue that helps dogs." Rising, she turned to the pantry behind her and pulled out a bakery box. "I stopped at Sugar Dancer on the way home. I got your favorite."

Em perked up. "Brownies?"

"Do I look like an amateur? Of course." Getting out a knife, she cut one in half. "If you swear you'll eat your dinner, you can have this now." Liza slid half the brownie over to her friend.

"Damn, this is better than sex." Em dove in. "Well, not always, but right now? It's heaven." She ate a couple bites before frowning at Liza. "Why aren't you eating any?"

"I ate two chocolate chunk cookies on the way here."

Em sat back. "Are you anxious about your mom coming home?"

Liza sipped her tea, then answered honestly. "Very. It's also the uncertainty. She's not technically paroled until May, but they swear they're releasing her sometime in the next few days. I'm waiting to know when to go pick her up, and hoping like hell no one dangerous finds out." She pressed her hand to her stomach.

"That's one cookie, what was the second one for?"

It'd been several days since that conversation with Justice, and she hadn't gone into the room despite being in and out of the house helping Noah. She took a sip of her tea, and answered, "Courage."

That night, Liza helped Noah give Radar his pain meds before they went to bed. Once they were finished, Noah leaned back against the counter in the kitchen. "You tell Justice that Radar is home?"

"Not yet." The band had left yesterday for the Northern European leg of the tour. Liza raised an eyebrow. "You could tell him."

"Could, but that wouldn't help you two work out your problems." He headed to the doorway.

Suspicion bloomed and she called out, "Was that kitchen fire an accident?"

He turned at the doorway, the light catching the scars on one side of his face. "It started off an accident."

She should be shocked, but she wasn't. "And then?"

He lifted one shoulder. "I let it get a bit farther than necessary."

"Why? What were you doing?"

"Helping my son the only way I know how by keeping you two talking. He'd do anything for you, he loves you. Face your memories, Liza, and move on. Don't be me and lose out on having Justice in your life."

Surprise vibrated through her, and before she thought it out, she blurted, "I had to leave him." What was she doing? She didn't have to explain herself. She'd needed to find her own strength.

"So did I, but he never left us. He screws up, I'm not denying that. But he never left us." Noah shuffled away with Radar following him.

Liza shook her head. The battle-hardened, emotionally-scarred former Marine had been playing matchmaker. "You haven't lost out, Noah," she called out.

"Justice won't let you go." Hadn't she found that out? Softly, she added, "He won't let either of us go."

From down the hallway, she heard a slight shuffle, and then the click of a door closing.

Noah found a way to take the steps to facing his ghosts.

Now it was time to face hers.

She turned off the kitchen light, and she stopped in front of the door to the third bedroom.

She put her hand on the doorknob. Hot dread coiled her muscles. Buzzing filled her head. Run. Get away.

"No." She wasn't doing this, hiding from her daughter, or worse, shoving her memory in this room and shutting the door like she could cut her out of her life. She pushed open the door.

Behind her light flooded in, revealing shapes. Her heart jumped. What was in here?

She flipped the switch on the wall and lit up the room. Hot tears stung her eyes. Baby furniture, the white crib, the sweet bassinet, changing table and dresser she'd wanted, along with the gray chair that rocked and reclined. There was a lamp on the table next to the chair with a soft yellow shade. On the floor, resting by the chair, was a flat rectangular present wrapped in pale-yellow paper and tied with a soft peach ribbon. A small square envelope on the top right corner had Beth penned in familiar handwriting—Justice's.

Going into the room, Liza sat. The last of her walls crumbled to dust, leaving her heart exposed. Leaning over, she tugged the envelope off the box and pulled out the card.

In memory of our beloved daughter. She was blessed with a mother who loves her beyond any and all boundaries. Love, Justice.

She peeled back the layers of paper to reveal a painting. Her entire chest swelled with pain and love so massive, she couldn't breathe. It was a picture of Justice holding Liza while she cradled their baby, painted in soft strokes. Liza's eyes shimmered love and pain so profound, she could almost feel that tiny body nestled tightly against her. And remember the bottomless sense of loss combined with a powerful and deeply tender devotion for this child.

Justice looked over her shoulder at the child, his gaze filled with deep wonder and overpowering sadness. His long index finger gently caressed the baby's cheek.

It was the most wrenchingly beautiful painting she'd even seen. More emotion welled in her, a storm rising from her soul. Liza set the picture back against the wall and considered the room. The baby furniture must have been Justice's surprise for her when they returned from Paris. She expected pain, and yeah, it hurt, but there was also the love and joy she'd felt during the months her baby had been growing inside her. Hours of dreaming, and laughing when the baby kicked. The way she'd always reacted to Justice's voice.

Happiness.

This tiny baby who'd never taken a breath had been a huge part of Liza's life for a very short time, and she'd given Liza tremendous love and joy.

"Thank you," she whispered. "Did you know both your daddy and I picked your name?" She paused, waiting to see if the fist formed in her throat. "Savanna was my choice, and Rose was his. Savanna Rose," she repeated softly.

Warm chills spread slowly over her skin like a hug. Grateful tears spilled down her cheeks as Liza rocked in the chair. For the first time since Paris, a feeling of peace tinged with determination rolled through her. Savanna Rose was a beautiful name for a beautiful soul that had touched their lives all too briefly.

Did she want her daughter's legacy to be that losing her had destroyed her mother, and shattered her parent's marriage? Or did Liza want to show her daughter the courage of a mother's love?

Justice woke up tired. Where was he? Right, Finland. Then Sweden, Norway, and after that, Ireland. The constant travel and grueling pace were a bitch, but it'd be worth it if they could drive "Savaged Vows" to the top of the international charts. Couple more weeks, and he'd get the first real break. Rolling out of bed, he started his single cup of coffee, when his phone vibrated. Scooping it off the nightstand, he checked the screen.

Beth. He hadn't talked to her in days. He quickly answered with, "Hi, Beth, everything okay? Were you able to bring Radar home?"

"I'm in her room."

Her voice was thick, clogged with tears that wrenched his heart. "Savanna's room?"

"You did this. The furniture I'd picked out. You bought it all, and had the portrait done. It hurts to look at, but I love it so much. When did you have that painted?"

"I had it started after Drake's funeral. The artist worked from the pictures the nurses took. I sent Em the card I wrote out, and she was the one who waited at the house for the delivery and put it in the room for you. My dad knew too. I texted him so he wouldn't happen to be there and surprised by Em or the delivery. You love it?"

A wet sniffle filled the next few seconds before she got out, "Yes. It's more precious than anything. Those were our only moments with her. I...thank you."

Hearing the love and pain rushing in her words caused him to blink away the wet in his eyes. "You're welcome."

"You kept her room like this for a year," she said, her voice still thick but laced with curiosity. "Why? You could have sent it back that first week."

"I didn't want to send it back, that would be like erasing her. We didn't get to bring her home, but she was still real and ours."

"You always kept your dad's room ready for him too."

This was the Beth he loved so much, the one who saw past Justice's fame and failings to the man he was, or at least the man he strove to be. "I knew she wasn't coming back, but wherever she is, I just..." With anyone else, he'd feel stupid saying this. "I want her to know that she has a room, a place she belongs here on Earth and in my heart. Our hearts."

"Yes she does." She paused, then added, "There's so many things I'd like to tell you."

"I want to hear them all." He hated being on another continent where he couldn't pull her into his arms.

"Okay, can you tell me when the picture was delivered? Was it before I saw you in L.A.?"

"Yes, why?"

"Because tonight your dad admitted that he let that fire in the kitchen get far enough along to do some damage."

Justice frowned, deep, familiar worry flooding his gut. "Was it another suicide attempt?"

"Oh, I didn't think of that. No, Justice, that's not it,

I swear. I asked him exactly what he was doing, and his answer was that he was helping you, so we'd keep talking to work out our problems. He also told me to face my memories so I wouldn't end up like him and lose out on having you in my life."

Justice took in the words, soaked in their message. "He really said that?"

"Yes, and he defended you more as we talked. My point is, Noah told me to face my memories, knowing the picture was in the room. He did it for you, Justice. He wanted me to see us as a family, to understand that even though she's gone, we're still a family."

A profound truth swelled inside him. Noah wasn't the dad he'd known as a kid, but he was the dad Justice needed now. The feeling was incredible and freeing in that it was time to let go of his old expectations and embrace what he had in his dad now.

"You know what's weird? He can't really talk to me, I mean not face-to-face, but he's a strong presence in my life. Some part of me has been relying on him to help both of us. Even as far back as before you got pregnant, he saved your life the night you were stabbed." He hadn't lost his entire family after Savanna died and Beth had left him.

His dad had been there, quietly supporting him from a distance.

He squeezed his eyes closed, taking in the gift of his father. "I didn't even realize it, but I guess my subconscious knew he was there in his own way." Helping him, and the woman he loved.

"Isn't that what dads are for? Like this room you made for our daughter and kept so she'd know she had a home even if she can't be here?"

He swallowed, unable to speak. His wife was breaking him with her ability to see through the paint and wood of the furniture to the heart of what it meant. He'd desperately wanted to be a good father. All he could manage was a thick, "Yes."

"When I look at this picture you had painted, I can see the scope of our love and pain, and more."

"Like what?"

"I see our daughter, Savanna Rose Cade."

"Beth, my God, you said her name."

"Because I'm finally forgiving myself. Savanna wasn't locked in this room, she's been with me this whole time as I write Molly's story. The drive kept me going, the reason I couldn't delete the book, or end Molly's pregnancy, but had to fight through to the end of her story. I believe that was her, Justice. Savanna was showing me how to stop hating myself, and to release the guilt that kept me from being able to write the scenes of Molly with her baby. Yet I couldn't not write it because I know she was pushing me to face my grief, forgive myself and..."

Her words came so fast, then trailed off with an echo of pain. He leaned his forehead against the wall, not wanting to ask, but knowing he had to. "And what?"

She drew in a shaky breath. "Accept that she's not here, and let her go into the part of my heart that will hold her as my beloved firstborn child. Or I'll be stuck in the place I was when I stood on the other side of the door to her room—afraid to risk loving anyone again. I'm still afraid."

"But?" His body tensed, waiting to hear what she'd say.

"You were right, I'm letting Hayes win by being afraid. I don't know what the future holds for our love. Can we really survive losing a child? The demands of your career? My life as the woman who destroyed a rock star? I don't know, but I want to commit to finding out. I want to see you and work on our future."

The air rushed out of his chest. With it, a flood of hope took its place. For the first time in eleven months now, he was able to take a full breath. "I'm flying back to the States in a couple weeks, we can meet anywhere."

She laughed. "You're moving fast, and this time, it doesn't scare me."

Ten minutes later, after Justice had reassured her that his arm was healing well, they said goodbye.

He sat on the bed, trying to process it all.

This was his second chance with the woman he loved more than his life. He wasn't going to fuck up and lose her again.

Chapter 18

LIZA HAD SPENT THE LAST two weeks working every moment she could on her book. She'd barely slept between the drive to get those scenes right and excitement about seeing Justice.

Now she was in Paso Robles, a small town in central California known for its wineries and olive groves, located about halfway between Los Angeles and San Francisco. Her eagerness kept her from really noticing the landscape as she sat in the dark-colored SUV with the bodyguard from the private protection company Justice's security team worked with. Finally, the driver guided the car through a security gate, past mossy grass, huge trees and endless views of the hillsides, to a sprawling house. It had a mountain feel, with rich dark wood, gorgeous arched windows, and two stone chimneys rising out of the sloping roofline.

Before she could thank the driver, the passenger side door opened. Liza jerked her head around, and instantly recognized Justice. The late-afternoon sunshine illuminated his blond-streaked brown hair and a fatigue around his eyes that tugged at her heart. He'd been on tour for about two months, and she knew how damned hard Justice worked. He had on a white T-shirt, revealing his tatted arms. He held out his hand. "Beth."

She took it, slid out then pushed up his sleeve and bared his skull and clock tat to study the fresh scar of newly healed skin.

"It really doesn't hurt?" She ran her finger lightly over the mark slashing through the skull ink.

"Not the injury. But your touch is scorching." He pulled her into his arms.

God, the heat and strength of him was so familiar and fed a need that had grown hungrier and hungrier since their night of passion in L.A. It wasn't just for sex, it was for this—the feeling of being held and valued.

Liza sank her fingers into his hair and kissed him deeper, needing to get closer and feel more of him.

A voice interrupted with, "Would you like me to take this in the house?"

Justice broke the kiss and said to the bodyguard, "I've got it." After taking her overnight and laptop bags, he added, "Thank you and your team for getting her here safely."

The man nodded. "We're available anytime you need us. If you choose to drive yourselves somewhere, we'd appreciate if you'd give us your itinerary." He said goodbye, and left.

"Let's go inside."

She followed him up the steps and through the front door. Inside the great room, the dominant features were the beamed cathedral ceilings that matched the dark wood floors covered in thick rugs, high arched windows, and the stone fireplace surrounded by bookcases filled with tomes and framed pictures. Liza did a three-sixty, taking in the heavy leather furniture with purple pillows piled up and a purple afghan thrown over the back of the couch.

They crossed to a dining room with a thick, natural-cut table made of oak, and over that hung an iron wagon wheel chandelier. This room flowed into a spacious area with a TV and more couches on the left and a sprawling upscale country kitchen on the right. The showstoppers were the most enormous windows revealing a deck and more greenery covering the hills.

"This place really is charming. I was surprised when you said Slade had a retreat here."

"Why?"

"I guess I'd have expected a Malibu beach house or New York penthouse. Not this. It's rustic and—" She cut herself off when she noticed the kitchen. "Oh!" The cupboards were a gray wash with counters that were a gorgeous thick granite on a huge island. A red pitcher vases filled with dried flowers, and cobalt-blue canisters painted with white flowers that matched the mugs hanging on iron hooks, added bold touches of color. A red bowl sat in the middle of the island brimming with fresh citrus, bananas, tomatoes and avocados.

Whoa, there was a sliding barn door. She rushed past the huge stainless-steel fridge to the big wall, and grinned. The exposed side was a glass-fronted wine fridge, but when she slid the door, a walk-in pantry was revealed. "Cool."

"So this is what excites you? A barn door?" Justice teased her.

"This kitchen! It's not the same as everyone else's. I mean, yeah, granite and stuff. But it has color and it feels like a home." She smiled at him. "I refinished the table in my condo, did I ever tell you that? It's teal and beechwood. I love it. I hung a pounded metal picture of a coffee cup with steam rising in the shape of a heart.

It spoke to me because my heart felt cold, dark and dead, in contrast to the warm, steamy feeling from the picture." Heat flushed her face. "Sorry, I'm babbling."

"Not even close. I want to hear more. Everything." He recaptured her hand. "Come on, I'll show you the rooms so you can get settled and we'll eat." He led her past a couple rooms to double doors at the end of the hall. "I think you'll like this one."

Liza went inside, and gawked. One long wall was comprised of huge arched windows overlooking the sloping hillsides, and another had a stone fireplace. A massive king-sized bed was draped in a thick pale-aqua comforter and pillows and placed diagonally to take in both the view and the hearth. The room was painted a soft hue of green, creating the feeling of walking into a forest. An open door showed her an attached bath, but the tranquility of the landscape drew Liza to the windows. The sun sank low, casting long shadows. "It's lovely, so peaceful."

"If you'd like to stay in your own room, I'll move my stuff to the other one." After placing her suitcase on the bed, he wrapped an arm around her waist and pulled her back to his front. There was no mistaking his erection. He dropped his mouth to her ear. "I want you, Beth. So badly that I ache. We can make love as long and hard as you're up for, and I'll go sleep in the other room if you need space. Or we can wait, just spend time together until you're ready."

She leaned into him and let his golden voice caress her. Feeling the acceptance of this man. "I want us to sleep together."

He groaned and released her. "You're too tempting. I'm going to go cool down and put something together for dinner while you unpack and get comfortable."

She followed the lines of his in T-shirt outlining his

shoulders, pecs and flat belly, to the bulge in his pants. Desire and power swept through her, along with the familiar twinge of worry. It wasn't like him to back off when she gave him an opening. He'd pursued her relentlessly, but maybe the hurt she'd caused him went deeper than he'd realized? "Now who's running?"

"I'm not running, I'm being strategic. Because once I get you in that bed, I'm not letting you out until I can take a breath without the gut-wrenching fear that I'll lose you again. That I'll go back to missing you so damned much, not even singing in front of a crowd of diehard fans can fill the gaping hole in my heart. Only you."

Now she got it, he worried that she'd leave him again. Liza closed the space between them. It was time to get it all on the table. "I'm done running. I'm here because life is full of choices. I've tried fear, and running and hiding didn't do shit to protect me or those I love. So now I'm going full bore, one hundred percent choosing love. Choosing you, and us. And when I say I'll fight, I mean it. You don't get to lie to me, evade or worry that I'm too weak to handle the truth."

"I never said you were weak."

She snorted. "You blew up our lives with a lie because you thought I was too weak to handle it."

"Or I was a coward who didn't want to be forced into a choice I didn't want to make—like picking you and financially destroying my band and all our employees, or choosing them and losing you. So you're right, choices do matter."

She shook her head. "You could have told me all that, but instead you tried to carry that burden alone." She touched his arm. "We're in this together, or we're not. I'm here because I've chosen together. That means that I won't run out again like I did in L.A. when we learned Hayes is featured on Jagged Sin's newest release. That's my choice. What have you chosen?" Dropping her hand, she crossed to her bag and pulled out her toiletry kit. "I'm going to take a shower. I'll be out soon to help with dinner."

Liza went into the bathroom, having meant every word. They both had to rebuild trust in order to have a marriage that would survive the challenges of their lives.

The huge bathroom had a free-standing tub in front of a picture window that tempted her, but she was too wound up for a leisurely soak. After running the water in the shower, she stripped out of the shirt and dark pants she'd worn all day, through meetings, and budget reviews, a tense lunch with a pushy sponsor who had an endorsement deal with one of their fighters, and the trip here.

The water washed all that away, leaving her in the moment. The warmth penetrated her skin and eased what felt like a year of stress.

"This, Beth."

On the other side of the half glass, Justice yanked off his shirt, pulled off his pants, and skimmed out of his boxers.

"This what?" she asked.

"Is what I want. You, in my face, fighting for me, and us. I've never had that. Never. Not from a woman who loved me enough to forgive me. Fight for me. Or on the flip side of that, cared enough to fight for what you want instead of just leaving."

Liza stood there, holding the bottle of soap, as Justice filled the large stall. His body gleamed in the lights, and water droplets clung to his skin, creating rivulets over his inked shoulders and biceps, down the flat plane of his stomach to his engorged cock. A shiver of hot desire spiked through her, riding a wave of pure female power.

He advanced on her, taking the bottle from her hand. He poured some in his palm and began lathering her skin. Her shoulders and arms, her throat and breasts, every stroke of his calloused fingers and slick soap raising gooseflesh and tingling straight through her center.

His grin spread slow and wicked. "Nothing to say? You've spent nearly a year bringing me to my knees."

She snatched the bottle from him, squeezing a dollop out and gliding her hands over his shoulders and biceps. "I didn't bring you to your knees." She trailed her fingers down the center line of his belly.

"Are you asking me to get on my knees, baby?" His voice rolled low and teasing.

"No. I'm telling you that I got off mine. I won't accept being pushed to the edges of your life again." She slid her hand around his cock, feeling the hard shaft jump in her easy grip. Leaning closer to his face, she added, "I'm demanding to be a part of all of it."

He thrust deeper into her palm. "Same here. You don't get to hide either, Beth. For every moment of the rest of our lives, you will know I'm on your side. No matter what." He glided his hands over her back, down her thighs, and lifted her back to the wall of the shower. "You are first in my world." He took her mouth with a confident possessiveness she hadn't felt in a long year. His tongue not asking, but demanding, his grip holding her in place as his cockhead pressed against her.

Liza arched, desperate now to be filled not just with his body, but with the truth of his words. As he entered her, chasing out every lingering doubt until all she could see, feel, and hear was the love that burned between them, she clutched onto Justice tighter.

She didn't want to be alone anymore. Didn't want to be scared.

They'd been torn apart by lies and fears, could they now come together in honesty and trust?

Justice woke alone, a shaft of panic jerking him up and out of the bed. His heart hammered, and thoughts bumped around in the dark room. Where was he?

No, wait, where was Beth?

Had she left him again?

He grabbed his boxers and yanked them on. Adjusting to the moonlight flowing in through the huge windows, he fought to calm his racing heart. He headed first to the bathroom, but that was empty. Doubling back, he left the room with the fear prickling the bare skin of his neck and back. It was like the nights he'd woken after his father left, and he'd been compelled to search the streets of San Diego.

He headed down the hall, heard soft music, and smelled...cookies? Confused, Justice rounded a corner, coming into the big family, dining and kitchen area. The sounds of piano music hit him first.

Beth wearing a tank top, long hair wild around her face, swaying to the music behind the bar. She was using a rubber spatula to move freshly baked cookies from a pan to a dark blue plate and finished as Pink began singing "Just Give Me A Reason."

Beth raised the spatula like a microphone and launched into the song about a relationship breaking down as both partners try to hold on. She closed her eyes, singing with a restrained quiet that told him she probably worried about waking him. Justice leaned against the wall, drinking in Beth performing into her pretend microphone. She hadn't left, hadn't run. She'd simply woken and come into the kitchen, probably because she'd been hungry.

They hadn't eaten, at least not dinner, he mentally clarified. He'd most definitely feasted on his sexy wife.

As Beth segued into the song's chorus, he raised an eyebrow, surprised she hit some of the more powerful notes here and there. Her voice was decent enough for karaoke, but she flat out didn't have the passion for anything more.

She tilted her head back as she finished the chorus.

Justice pushed off the wall, pulled to her and the song with an irresistible force. He opened his mouth, hoping he'd remember all the words to the second stanza sung by Nate Ruess, since Beth loved Pink and had listened to her music all the time when they were together. The lyrics came as he launched into the male part, and unlike Beth, he didn't restrain his vocals.

She jerked her head and nearly dropped the spatula. He rounded the kitchen counter, daring her to back down now. Keeping her stare, he let loose with the section about all of it being in her mind.

Her gaze sparked behind her glasses as she raised her spatula to her mouth and hit him back with the reply reaffirming they were growing apart.

His skin tightened at the confidence brimming in her rendition, and in the way she owned her moment of singing with a kitchen tool in the middle of the night like she was a rock star. She was doing exactly what they'd talked about earlier, standing up to him in a song by Pink and Nate.

Justice couldn't have held back now if he had a punctured lung, and he poured more passion into the verse. Singing was his way of communicating, of having a voice in the world after being a kid whose parents didn't want him, and then thrown into juvie as if he'd been human garbage to be tossed in a dumpster. Later, it'd been all he'd had left after losing their daughter and Beth leaving him.

Beth stayed right there with him in the moment, belting out her part and not the least bit cowed by his powerful vocals, nor did she stumble when she couldn't hit the amazing notes that Pink could. Nope, here in this kitchen alone with him, she sang like she wrote—all in with no censor. When she wound her voice with his in the chorus, his entire body twanged with a wild joy that was damn near orgasmic.

Just as he'd worked so hard to find a path into her secret world of writing, tonight Beth had found her path into his world of singing.

As the song ended, he reached out, taking her spatula and pulling her against him. Tilting her face up, he said, "You trying to steal my limelight, baby?"

She grinned. "I don't think you or Pink need to worry."

He laughed. "I'm sure Pink will be relieved, but you're not bad. You can sing. Not as good as me, of course."

She rolled her eyes. "Did your fat ego fall off the bed and wake you up?"

He couldn't help but grin. "Nope, I missed my wife. What woke you? Hunger or a nightmare?"

"Hungry. I came out here to get something healthy, but then I found chocolate chip cookie dough. Want one?" She gestured to the plate on the counter.

He leaned down and kissed her, tasting warm cookie. He wanted her. Again. They'd made love in the shower, and in bed. Still not enough. He also wanted this, sharing cookies in the middle of the night. Lifting his mouth from hers, he asked, "Yes, and how many have you had?"

"One, and I'll eat as many as I want. I'm not one of your skinny groupies." She pulled away and hopped up to sit on the counter. Giving him an evil smile, she took a cookie and bit into it. "Of course, you're probably on a special rock god diet."

He glared at her. "I was born hot. I don't a diet." Actually, he had a fairly rigid diet to keep him strong enough to handle the rigors of multiple shows, travel, and all the endless promo for the tour. Mimicking Beth, he easily jumped up and sat on the counter, the plate of cookies between them. After biting into one, he said, "Not bad. You really love this kitchen, huh?"

She tilted her head. "Yeah, I do. I'd probably change a few things."

"We could build a house in San Diego, you can design the kitchen any way you like, and an office to write in. You can work at SLAM if you want, or write, or whatever you want to do."

Beth reached for a bottle of water. "You been thinking about building a house?"

"Or buying one. I search online sometimes." He took another cookie. "What would you want in a home?"

She studied him, then held out her water. "A big kitchen with a bar. A backyard where I could have lots of plants and an herb garden. Something with color." She turned, bringing up one leg to fold under her as she eyed the barstools at the counter.

"How about a dog?"

"Huh, a dog? I've never had one."

"Me either. I haven't really ever had a home."

"You had your grandmother's house."

"That was for my dad. I've promised not to go back there. I rented a condo in L.A. but let that go when I went on this tour. I want a home, with you. I know I'm moving fast, but we're just talking, not signing escrow papers."

Her face softened. "We can look for a home. If we find something soon before you're off tour, I can work on any renovations while living in my condo with my mom."

Surprised, he said, "You're willing to start searching soon?"

Her attention went back to the barstools.

He nodded toward the barstools. "What are you looking at?"

"The future." She turned to him. "I hope to have more children that will sit on barstools like those one day. Not now. We're just putting our relationship back together and figuring out our future, you're on tour, and the biggest reason in my mind, Hayes. He's a threat to anyone I love."

Justice swallowed down a shot of anger that Hayes ruined everything, even a middle-of-the-night conversation about where to live. "You want more kids?"

"Yes, and a home with you. I want something else too."

"What?"

"To publish my book as Liza Cade. I'm not holding back anymore. It'll be complicated, make things harder for your band as you fight to win the World Rock Stage seat."

He grinned. "Bring it on, baby. Let's complicate the shit out of things. I don't care as long as you're mine."

Two days later, Liza was in a helicopter with Justice, their pilot and the same bodyguard who'd picked her up at the airport. They flew over the central coastline and then back to Paso Robles to get a beautiful view of the fields and vineyards. Their pilot pointed out areas of interest through their headsets and Liza soaked it all in. She even took pictures, but she didn't think it was possible to capture the beauty of the experience through the window.

After a couple hours, they set down at a mountaintop winery with rows of grapevines spread out around them. One their bodyguards had checked the area, Liza stepped down in the cool breeze and sweeping vista. While Justice talked to the pilot, she took some photos, capturing the landscape, and her husband.

She kept snapping pics as he walked to her.

His grin widened. "You don't need pictures, you have me."

She tilted her head back. The sunlight framed him and the wind tousled his hair. "I've never flown in a helicopter. It's so cool."

He took her hand. "Yeah? I asked Sloane, and he said he hadn't used a helo with you, so I took a shot." He led her over a dirt path. "Time for lunch. The winery is closed, but I rented the outdoor space and got catering in the deal."

She stopped. "Seriously? You've already done so much." They'd gone on walks, cooked together, talked and watched movies. Last night, he'd taken her to a private dinner in some wine caves, and then surprised her more when they ended up at a skating rink he'd rented for the night. The two of them skated and danced, then raided the snack bar—all while she wore a sexy, tight-fitting dress. She shivered at the memory of him barely getting her back to the house before he ripped off her panties.

"I want to take you on dates, and spoil you. We can't go to restaurants or anything really public, so I improvised. To give credit where due, the security company arranged most of this. I'm not taking any chances with you. They ran checks on everyone involved, and made sure there won't be any leaks." He tugged her arm. "Come on."

Liza gasped when they reached the end of the row of vines. A gazebo trimmed with netting flowing in the breeze and garlands of dried flowers sat in a field, with two cushioned chairs waiting in the center. Three different sized wine barrels were topped with covered dishes, along with plates, cutlery, napkins, glasses and several bottles of wine. "Wow!"

"Pretty impressive, right?" He broke into a jog, and Liza rushed after him. "Where's the staff?"

"They set it up and left. They'll be back in an hour and a half." Justice opened the wine and poured out two glasses. Handing her one, he said, "To a lifetime of dates together."

She clicked his glass and sampled the wine. Light and crisp.

Justice uncovered cheese plates, assorted olives and marinated vegetables, a baguette with brie, cranberry and walnut chutney that made her mouth water.

"Let's eat."

She smiled up at him. "Thank you for this, for everything." The warm sun softened the cool breeze. "For not giving up on us."

"Never."

They filled their plates and sat side by side, indulging in wine, olives, cheeses, the amazingly delicious baguette with the Brie en Croute.

Rising, she topped off her wine, and held the bottle up to Justice.

He unfolded his long body, strolled to her and set the bottle and the glass aside. He lowered his head, kissing her. "I've wanted to do that since we left this morning."

"Me too, but security is close by." Close enough to keep them in view without hearing every word they said.

"Damn right. Not taking chances."

He'd heard her when she told him that she wasn't safe, and wouldn't be until Hayes was caught. "This is stunning. I love it. The surprise helicopter ride, sightseeing, lunch and most of all, you."

"Yeah?"

"It feels like I'm alive more than I have been for a while." She turned to look at the view. When Justice put his arms around her, she leaned back against him to savor the moment. "I don't want this trip to end." The idea of being separated again loomed bigger than she'd through it would. She had to be strong. One of the things she'd learned over the last year was that no one else could fix her life.

She made her own choices.

"I fucking hate leaving you. I'll get back to San Diego to spend time with you and your mom as soon as possible."

"I think she'd like that. I'll come see you as soon as my mom is okay to leave." Would her mom have a hard time adjusting after prison?

"In the meantime, I have something for you."

"A present? After all this?" What more could he give her?

When he released her, she turned.

Justice fished a square velvet box out of his pocket.

Her throat grew thick and her heart leapt. "My rings." She hadn't seen them since that night in Paris when she'd taken them off.

"When I found these in our hotel room, what remained of my world imploded, and I held on to these rings in my fist. When I opened my fingers, speckles of blood shimmered on the diamonds. Our love is like the rings. We've both bled a little, but what we feel for each other is strong enough to withstand the sorrow." He opened the box. "I love you, Beth. I've never stopped, and I never will. The first night here, you said you're choosing me, our love, and us. I'm choosing you, our love, and us. If you're ready to wear your rings, I'll vow to never again give you a reason to remove them." He took the rings out of the box. "Are you ready?"

She stared at the simple design of his grandmother's diamonds in the setting Justice had done for her. It had been all he could afford at the time, and Beth had loved them. She reached out a finger, tracing the beautiful stones, picturing the moment he'd described of gripping them so hard he cut his hand. She'd caused him so much pain, yet he'd never stopped believing in their love.

"I can get you new rings if you want."

She jerked her head up. "No! I love these rings. They're mine. I've missed them." It wasn't that she hadn't felt whole without them, it's that with them, she had a partner. Someone who knew their intimate joys and heart-wrenching sorrows. "I want these." Summing all her courage, she lifted her left hand. "Please."

He slid them onto her finger. "I swear it, Beth. If I make a mistake, I'll own it. But I won't knowingly betray you."

Her eyes filled. "I vow to stand together and fight for us, Justice. I love you." She rose on her toes.

He kissed her with the fire of a love that had survived. In the darkest corner of her mind, she worried. She had her husband back, and after long years in prison, her mom was coming home. On top of that, Noah was living in the house Justice had kept for him, taking care of Radar and pretty stable.

Liza had her family.

Could she lose them all again?

Chapter 19

IT TOOK ANOTHER WEEK, BUT at midnight Friday, Liza's mom walked out of the prison gates a free woman. Wearing a button-down shirt, jeans and boots, Amber carried a paper bag and hurried toward Liza waiting next to the SUV.

Unable to restrain herself, Liza rushed the last few steps and hugged her mom. "You're free. Finally."

Her mom pulled back, the prison lights revealing deep lines around her eyes and mouth. "It doesn't seem real yet."

"It will. Let's go home." She took the bag of belongings and gestured to the tall woman standing close by. "This is Whitney. She's my driver and bodyguard."

Whitney stopped scanning their surroundings long enough to hold out her hand. "Mrs. Ranger."

"Call me Amber." Her mom shook Whitney's hand.

"In the car. I want to get out of here before anyone realizes Amber is out." She shooed them into the backseat.

Once inside, Liza turned to her mom and suddenly had no idea what to say. It just felt...weird. After another beat or two, she said, "I have your room ready, but once you're settled in, you can change it. Fix it up any way you want. If there's any food, or anything else you'd like, we'll order it for you. Clothes too. Anything you need."

"Thanks." Her mom touched her hand. "You're wearing your wedding rings. You and Justice back together?"

Liza's stomach tightened, worried Amber might think Liza was abandoning her to be with Justice. "Yes, but I'm going to be living in San Diego with you while he's on tour."

"What changed your mind?"

She tried to figure out what to tell her. "Time, healing, and...well...I wrote a book. I mean I finished the book I mentioned to you, and in that process, I got to a place of forgiving both of us."

During the entire drive home, her mom asked a million questions about her book, Justice, and all their plans.

Once home, Liza led her mom into the condo.

Amber walked the space slowly as if unsure what to do. Liza showed her around the living area, the formal dining room that she'd turned into a home office, and the eat-in kitchen. Finally she took her mom into the hallway, her bathroom, and her room.

Her mom eyed the bed, side table, dresser and chair in the corner. Liza had chosen a bird and bloom comforter set with pink tropical flowers and bright contrasting birds in blue. The bed itself was piled with fluffy pillows. She had a pretty rug that matched a blanket thrown over the chair. On the walls were lush tropical prints.

Amber walked to the dresser and touched one of the fresh flowers in the vase, then over to the chair with the small ottoman in the corner and rubbed the soft blanket, followed by stroking her fingers along the outside of the slim laptop.

Liza shifted on her feet, tension creeping in. "We can change anything you want to. Redo the whole room in your taste. I got a few clothes in the closet, but we'll get you more."

Amber turned.

Liza hissed in a breath at her mom's red eyes. "Mom, what's wrong?" She rushed in a few steps, and froze, uncertain. Should she hug her mom? Or give her space?

"Remember all the rundown, shitty places we lived in? You'd try so hard to fix them up, bringing home flowers you picked or some trinket you managed to buy with what little money you had." Her mom looked around. "I never gave you this kind of room. Instead I was off partying and..."

Surprise slowed down her reaction, and it took her a few seconds to figure out of how to respond. "You gave me something else, though."

"What's that?"

She held out her left arm. "The will to survive."

Her mom touched the old scars bisecting her wrists. "I was so scared for you, and so damned helpless in prison. I tried to reach your aunt, but she wouldn't accept the calls."

"Mom, you begged me to live. I saw so clearly how much you loved me. I mattered to you, and so I lived and endured. If I hadn't learned how to do that then..." She considered how to make her point. "I need to show you something else."

"What?"

She led her mom across the hall to her room, where she'd hung the painting of Liza holding their baby while they were both cradled in Justice's arms.

Her mom drew in a sharp breath. "That's her? That's Savanna?" She got up on the bed, knee-walking to the center to touch the painting. "She's beautiful. Oh God, Beth." Tears spilled down her face. "I don't know how you survived losing her."

"That's what I'm telling you, Mom." Her gaze went back to her lost child. "I couldn't have done it if you hadn't made me strong. So all that in your room..." she waved toward the hallway, "...it's just things. Your love was there for me when I needed it the most." It was truer than she'd ever realized.

Her mom got off the bed and wrapped her in a hug. "We're going to be okay, you and me. I'll make you proud this time, Beth. I swear it."

Liza hugged her mom back, releasing some of the anxiety she'd been holding since she'd learned of her mom's parole. "I'm so glad you're home."

Almost a month later, Liza was in her office, trying to focus on her job, but all she could think about were the updates from her agent. They'd had four amazing offers on her book and been in negotiations for two long days.

Enough. She got busy reviewing the budget numbers for her department. She'd just finished when her cell phone vibrated. Her heart jumped, and she scooped it up.

Nope, not her agent, but a text from Em. *Any news?*

No. Dying here waiting for the last publisher, Mertz Publishing Group, to counter our offer before we decide. That was the publisher Liza wanted. They were huge, well-connected, and the one they believed would give her the most promotion.

No dying! This is my big moment! I'm going to be the beautiful and fabulous best friend of a bestselling author. Don't ruin my moment by dying.

She grinned at Em's ridiculousness, exactly as her friend had intended. *I wouldn't dream of putting a damper on your moment in the sun.* She'd just hit send when her phone rang. It was her agent, Natasha.

Her stomach flipped as she stabbed the accept button. "Liza Cade."

"They came in with the offer. Everything we wanted!"

No way. She knew how negotiations worked. "Everything we asked for?"

Her agent gave a wry snort. "No. We asked for twenty things and got the eleven we truly wanted. This is it, Liza. Check your email. I sent you the deal memo. If you approve this, the deal is done, and they'll go to contract. Which takes a while, sometimes months to complete."

She pulled up the email and downloaded the deal memo. She and her agent spent a few minutes covering everything, then Liza said, "I'll look it over, and I'll give you my answer in the morning."

"Sounds good."

After thanking her, Liza hung up. A deal memo. For her book. With the best publisher. The advance had more zeros than she'd have thought possible.

She glanced at her watch. It was almost four here, which made it nearly seven p.m. in Quebec, Canada. Justice was going onstage at ten, she thought. She might catch him.

She'd seen him several more times since Paso, including his trip to San Diego to get to know her mom better. They'd managed to avoid the media, and she hadn't seen his band yet, although she'd talked to them a few times when she video chatted with Justice. They knew about her book, and Lynx texted her for updates every few days.

When Justice's voicemail answered, she hung up, rose, and paced. She really needed to send the end-of-the-month budget numbers to accounting, but...

Her phone bobbled on the desk. Scooping it up, she opened the video chat from Justice. "Hi."

He looked tired. "Hey, Beth. Sorry, we were in a meeting with our web people and P.R. team. I stepped out to take your call. Did you hear back on the last counteroffer?"

"Yes! They met our conditions. Well, we asked for more, but got the key things. I have the deal memo right here." She read it off to him.

"That's incredible! Congratulations! Did you agree?"

"I told her I'd let her know for sure in the morning. I'm too excited." And scared. "It's a big leap."

He leaned into the camera. "Are you going to hold back now? After all that work you did writing a brilliant book?" He hesitated, then added, "Or are you going to show the world what Savanna's mother is made of?"

She straightened her spine, and a warm glow spread over her heart. Her daughter was telling her to be brave and live again. "I guess it's time to find out if I'm any good as a writer, or just another hack with a dream."

"That's my girl! When you come visit, we're going to celebrate. Hey, I need to get back to the meeting. Can I call you tonight after the concert?"

A tingle of worry pierced her exhilaration at the tightness around Justice's eyes and the whiteness in the scar slashing his eyebrow. Oh, he was genuinely happy for her, but he had something on his mind. "First, tell me what's wrong."

He let out a sigh of frustration. "This is your moment. I want to celebrate with you, not bring you down."

She appreciated that, but they had a deal. "Tough shit. Spill."

He nodded and rubbed his temples. "Our website was hacked with a big promo for Jagged Sin's song featuring Gene Hayes. 'Witch Hunt.'"

Liza called up their website, and Justice surrounded by the band appeared on the homepage. "It looks fine."

He dropped his hand. "Our team got it down pretty quickly, but Jagged Sin got some presales off it. They had a link up, and we're all furious. They did it to Fury Run's site too. So I'm pissed about that, but right now, I'm so damned proud of you. Tell me you aren't going to let this latest crap change anything?"

She hated that he had to ask her, but how could she blame him after the way she'd acted when they found out Hayes was going to be featured on Jagged Sin's album? To reassure him, she raised her left hand into camera view. "I chose our love when you put these rings on my finger. I'm not running. Not from you and not from my chance at publishing."

And not from Gene Hayes.

Liza grabbed her phone as it buzzed on her bedside. The screen was a blur, so she put on her glasses. A text from Noah. *I fell and my hurt my hip.*

Shit! Throwing off the covers, she called him.

He answered in a pained whisper. "What?"

"How bad, Noah? Do you need an ambulance?"

"No. Maybe...emergency room."

Damn, he must be hurting to say that. "Okay, hang on, I'll be there." She raced into the bathroom, peed, splashed water on her face, and rushed out to yank on some yoga pants and a T-shirt. What else?

"Beth?" Her mom stood in her doorway. "What's going on?"

"Noah's hurt. I have to go. Set the alarm when I leave."

"Go? It's midnight! I'm going with you."

She opened her mouth to argue, but her mom had vanished. She heard her moving around in her room and reconsidered—she might need help with Noah.

By the time she put on her shoes and got her purse, her mom reappeared dressed in loose-fitting leggings and a flowing shirt. Her hair tumbled around her face in a freshly cut layered style but her eyes, yeah, they still looked tired and haunted. Adjusting to life outside prison, while mostly trapped inside a condo complex and saddled with a list of parole restrictions, wasn't easy.

"Let's go." After getting in her car, they rushed to the house. Liza hurried up the sidewalk, unlocked the door, and pushed it open to fierce barking and deep growls.

Liza blocked the doorway with her body, keeping her mom behind her. Instinct had her keep still. "Radar."

The dog skidded to a stop and sniffed a couple feet from her. His stiff posture relaxed, and his barks disintegrated into a whine.

"It's okay." She walked in and gently stroked the clearly upset dog. "Mom."

Amber moved in slowly and crouched a couple feet back. "Hi, Radar. I'm here to help Noah too."

The dog leaned forward, neck outstretched, and

sniffed her. Then he whined, turned, and trotted around the couch and down the hall.

"Noah?" Liza called.

"Bedroom."

Liza broke into a jog and found Noah lying on the bed, jaw clenched, and the web of burn scars whiter than usual. "Got up to turn out the light and caught my foot in a blanket. Twisted my bad hip."

Liza walked up to his side and lightly touched his shoulder. "Two choices: you let me take you to the emergency room or I call an ambulance."

He closed his eyes.

"Ben's going to meet us at the hospital." Liza had called Emily's doctor-boyfriend on the drive to the house. He specialized in anesthesiology, but he also worked with veterans and understood PTSD.

"Radar can't go?" Noah asked.

"Not to the emergency room. If at all possible, I'll bring you back here, okay? I'll stay with you as much as I can."

He swallowed. "Give me a hand to the car."

"You sure? I could call an ambulance. Ben will still meet you there, and I'll get there as soon as possible."

Noah pushed upright and carefully got his feet on the floor. "Let's go."

"Let me help." Her mom walked in, got on the other side of Noah. "I'm Amber, Liza's mom. Cool dog. His ear makes him look badass."

Noah's lips tilted in a slight smile.

Together, Liza and her mom lifted him to his feet and helped him down the hallway. The biggest problem was keeping Radar in the house. The dog was stubbornly determined to go with Noah. When they finally shut the door, the dog cried.

Noah hesitated.

"He'll be okay," Liza assured him. "I can ask Sloane to come stay with him."

"I'll stay," her mom volunteered.

Noah hesitated a second longer, then nodded.

Once they had him in the passenger seat, Liza shut the door. "Mom, are you sure?" She should be safe with the gate and security system, but could she handled it?

"Yes. Go and be careful. I'll stay with the dog and sleep on the couch with my phone by me."

"I will. Forget the couch, and sleep in the other bedroom. It's going to be a couple hours or more."

Amber nodded. Liza waited for her to go inside and lock the door, then she left.

Three hours later, they returned home. Amber rushed out to help her get Noah inside. Despite the pain and muscle relaxer shots, he was clearly agitated, sweaty, and twitching his hands. The second Radar darted outside and slid his head beneath Noah's palm, he calmed.

Liza met her mom's startled gaze as they helped Noah into the room and bed. Radar wasted no time, gently settling at Noah's side, and shoving his head back under Noah's hand.

"Amazing," Amber said when they were in the hallway.

"I know. Noah's tried all kinds of treatments, but that dog is doing more for him than anything else." With fatigue settling in Liza's bones, she added, "I don't want to leave him alone, so we need to spend the night. They didn't find a break, but Ben said Noah strained some muscles and ligaments in his hip area, creating muscle spasms. Go back to sleep. I'll stay on the couch."

Her mom's hand settled on her arm. "I saw

Savanna's room when I was exploring which room I should lay down in. Are you okay? You must have done it up before Paris."

The concern in her mom's touch radiated warmth through her. "Justice had the furniture delivered as a surprise while we were in Paris. I didn't know that until I just recently went in there." She glanced toward the door her mom had obviously reclosed. "I'm okay. He had the painting in there, did I tell you that? Kept it in there for me until I was ready."

Her mom smiled. "He loves you. He better not hurt you, or I'll put his balls in the air fryer, but he does love you."

"I love him. I planned to go see him this weekend, but now I think I'd better stay here for Noah. He needs a hip replacement, and tonight he told me he doesn't want to leave Radar to have it done. Anyway..." she rubbed her head, "...I'll work remote from here tomorrow."

"Go to work. I'll stay here with Noah. If he does okay with me for the day, then you can go visit Justice."

Half of her leapt at the idea, and the other half resisted. Could Noah handle having her mom around? What if there was an emergency?

"It'll give me something to do," her mom added. "Can you trust me, Beth?"

She knew how bored her mom was, but at the same time, she occasionally got overwhelmed with too many decisions or choices that she wasn't used to making in prison. "If Noah doesn't object, I'll go to work, and you stay here."

"Fair enough. Now let's both sleep in the bed. That way at least one of us should hear Noah if he needs us."

That seemed reasonable. Liza surprised herself by

actually falling asleep until her phone alarm woke her.

In the morning, she helped Noah up, got him to eat and take pain pills while her mom took Radar outside to stretch and potty.

"Do you mind if my mom stays with you while I go to work? If you call or text, I'll come right home."

Noah ate some of his toast and shifted the bag of frozen peas he was using to ice his hip.

Liza sipped some coffee and restrained her impatience.

"Don't need a babysitter."

He sounded like a petulant toddler. One look out the window to the backyard gave her inspiration. Amber played a vigorous game of tug-of-war with the mostly healed Radar, making the dog nearly bounce with joy. "Not for you, for Radar. What if he needs to go outside suddenly and you can't get to the door?"

Noah set the last of his toast down and stretched up to see outside. "Fine." His answer was gruff, but his mouth softened, and his lips tilted up. Then he turned to Liza. "You bringing me a chocolate milkshake tonight?"

Liza lowered her coffee. "For a strained hip and terminal stubbornness about getting the surgery? You think that's milkshake worthy?"

Noah lifted his cup. "I'm going to need the milkshake energy to read your book."

That was a twist on their game she didn't expect. "Are you preloading energy? My book won't be published for months or even a year."

"I'm hurt now. I need something to read. Besides..." triumph gleamed in his eyes, "...if I read it, I might have something to talk to Justice about over text."

She slapped down her mug. "That's emotional blackmail."

"Is it?" He pushed himself up, slowly and painfully limped toward the doorway, then braced his hand on the counter to support himself. "Or is it a broken old man's attempt to talk to his son? You decide." He shuffled off.

Decide? Ha. The first thing she'd do when she got to her computer was send that file.

First, she had to go hug the dog with the big, brave heart giving them all hope that Noah was finding a way to live with his PTSD.

And talk to his son.

Liza hugged the man at the airport. "Ethan! It's great to see you."

The six-foot-five former MMA fighter turned bodyguard awkwardly patted her back. "Let's move."

He took her rolling case and ushered her out the door and into a waiting SUV at the curb. Ethan quickly stowed her bag and then climbed into the backseat next to her. "Go," he told the driver.

As the car pulled away from the airport, Liza focused on the man next to her. His blond hair was cut shorter than she remembered, the angles of his face a little sharper. "What's it like providing protection for the band?"

"Like herding cranky, feral cats."

She laughed. "I worked with them for a while. They can be a handful. So do you like it?"

He shrugged. "For now. I'm good at it, and I have debts to pay."

She touched his arm but didn't say anything. Ethan was still working to put his past behind him, and God knows, she understood that.

"What's it like to be an author?"

A slight flush warmed her face. "Surreal, I guess. I'm still getting used to the idea."

"I'm happy for you, Liza. You deserve good news."

"Thanks, Ethan." They talked a few more minutes, then the SUV circled the massive hotel and stopped at the back entrance.

Ethan got out, his head swiveling as he scanned the area. "Okay, Liza, let's go."

She slid out.

Ethan took her computer bag from her. "Someone will bring your other bag up for you. It'll be safe." They headed inside and caught a private elevator up to the top floor. Liza trotted at his side, damned glad she'd swapped her work heels for flats before getting to the plane.

Finally, he stopped in front of double doors.

"This is our room?"

"It's a suite." Ethan tugged out a keycard and swiped it over the sensor.

"Oh, nice." Did all the guys in the band have suites? She forgot her musings as Ethan opened the door, and she stepped inside.

"Surprise!"

Liza froze. What was happening? Her birthday wasn't until August. This wasn't a suite, but rather, a large lounge with a bar running along one side, a dance floor in the center, big chairs and couches scattered around. Huge TVs were mounted around the room, making Liza think of an upscale sports bar. One end had a long table covered in a white tablecloth and set with a meal. Across one wall hung a huge poster of a mockup book cover featuring her face and the huge words *Congratulations, Liza!*

As the applause waned, she took in the people. All the band members; Lynx, Gray, Simon and River.

The lead singer, Slade, from Seventh Ring, and his wife, Monique. The drummer, Damon, along with his wife, Althea. Oh, and there was Screech from Screech's Nightclub.

She was shocked to see Sloane, Kat, Sherry, Tess and Emily all wearing smug grins. How'd they get to Canada? Well she knew *how*, they flew, but...

"Surprised?" Justice strolled up to her with his easy, rolling gate and beaming smirk.

"Gobsmacked. What is this? I mean...we're in Canada and..." She was still trying to get her head around it.

Justice tugged her into his arms, planting a kiss on her mouth, then shifting to stand at her side. "Everyone came to celebrate your book contract. Come on, let's get you a drink, and you can catch your breath."

She was quickly engulfed in the crowd and hugged more people in the first hour than her entire lifetime. She caught up with the stunningly gorgeous Monique and insanely talented Althea, who had a very chic clothing line.

Kat, Tess and Emily easily bonded with them too, which made Liza supremely happy. When Monique and Althea found out that Em was an event coordinator, the three of them got lost in talking about wedding dresses, bridesmaid clothes, etc.

"Liza."

At Simon's voice she turned. The guitarist stood with all the guys from Savaged Illusions, and a few others.

He raised his glass to her. "I've never been more wrong about a person. I wish you success as an author beyond your wildest dreams, and I will be first in line to buy your book when it's released. Congratulations!"

His words touched her deeply. The two of them had

a lot of history, but Simon had done his part both in apologizing and trying to make amends. Walking to Simon, she hugged him.

He was stiff for one second, then his arm went about her.

Once he released her, Lynx swooped in and hugged her.

She raised her eyebrows. Black hair with a white stripe down the center. "New look?"

He shrugged. "Don't know. Got drunk as fuck, and when I woke the next afternoon, I was rocking this skunk head. Cool, huh?"

"He's an idiot, but my hair is still amazing." River scooped her off her feet and spun her. "Hey, Liza!"

She touched a strand of his long dark hair. "You're the envy of all hair-challenged people."

Gray smiled at her from where he stood just slightly apart from the others. "If I preorder a few books, will you sign them once I get them?"

"That's sounds so weird to think of me signing books." Like she mattered, like her words mattered. "But yes, it'd be my pleasure."

"Beth," Justice cut in. "I'd like to introduce our manager, Gavin."

The tallish, tanned man who looked like he belonged on a tennis court or yacht took her hand. "Nice to meet you, Liza. Congratulations on your book, and I hope you'll be with us on the tour as much as possible." His handshake was quick and businesslike.

"Are you regretting coming out of retirement yet?"

His business façade dissolved in a grin. "These guys are babies compared to the shit Seventh Ring pulled. It's a wonder any of them are alive."

Damon said, "I still have pictures of your ass tattoo, Gav."

Liza nearly choked on her drink. "Ass tattoo? Really?"

"Photoshop," Gavin declared.

Lynx shoulder nudged River. "We could find out."

Gavin glared at Damon. "Why?"

"Because I can."

Liza couldn't help her laughter. She had no idea if the ass tattoo was real or just Damon stirring up trouble, but it was pretty funny.

"Stop thinking about my manager's ass, sweetheart."

Justice stared at her with a hot possessiveness that stirred another kind of trouble in her belly. "Whose ass will I think about?"

Around her, the talk faded, or maybe it stopped because they all listened.

Liza didn't care. Justice had done this for her, arranged this celebration, flew in those of her friends who could make it, and he'd supported her dream to write and publish.

Even when they both knew it could backfire on him and his band.

He wrapped an arm around her, dragging her to his body. "Your eyes, your thoughts, all of you are on me. Always me."

"Says the rock star making women lust after him nightly?" Yep, she had her own possessive streak.

"You see any of those girls here?"

She didn't bother looking. "No."

"Damn right. Because you're my girl. I might sing to them on stage, but it's you I'm singing to in my heart. Every. Single. Time."

He took her breath away and made her heart soar.

Please, this time, don't let our love crash and burn.

Chapter 20

A COUPLE HOURS LATER, THEY'D all eaten and were in full party mode. Beth was more relaxed than Justice had seen her in ages. He enjoyed watching all the girls dancing and laughing together, but his gaze always went back to his wife.

Simon sat down next to him. "Meeting went well today. We're still ahead of Fury Run."

"Barely." Justice didn't underestimate that band for one second. Those women were talented and driven.

"Enough for now, but '*Witch Hunt*' is climbing in presales."

"I was at the meeting, I know the numbers." He sure as fuck didn't want to rehash it all now. This was Beth's night. Yet it hovered there in the back of his mind, the threat of Hayes and Jagged Sin looming like a dark cloud moving in. "Give it a rest, okay?"

Simon opened his mouth then stood. "You know what? You're right. Tonight's about your wife. Enjoy." He strode off.

Did hell freeze over? Because Justice couldn't recall the last time Simon let go of worrying. Before he could check the temperature in hell, Beth came over and dropped onto the couch. "I'm sweatier from dancing than getting my ass kicked by Sherry."

He laughed at her description and put his arm around her.

"Justice! I just said I'm sweaty."

He pulled her close to his body, loving the feel of her. "Don't care."

She sighed. "It's a great night. Thank you. It almost feels real."

"What does?"

"That my book will actually be published. It's been so dreamlike, then your dad fell—"

"He didn't fall," Justice corrected. "The damned blanket tripped him and twisted his hip, but he did not actually fall."

Beth's eyes widened. "You've talked to him."

His grin sprouted with pride. "Text. He's reading your book and texting me. He even gives short answers when I ask him what he thinks of a section."

She sat up. "What has he said? Does he like it? Or hate it? Think it's stupid?"

Justice studied her flushed face. "Have you asked him?"

"Asked him? I tried withholding a chocolate shake to get him to tell me how much he's read or what he thinks. He refuses to discuss it until he's read the whole book." She pursed her lips. "Why is he such a slow reader? I can read a book in two nights. One night if I don't sleep. It's been like three days!"

Outrage blazed in her flushed face, and he fought hard not to laugh. "I'm sure he'll tell you when he's ready."

She lightly smacked his shoulder. "You'll tell me now, if you want sex."

"Are you threatening me?"

"Yes." Then her indignation doubled. "Did he tell you to keep me in suspense?"

He scooped up his furious wife and settled her on his lap. "It wouldn't matter if he did. Not even Dad could get me to withhold a secret from you. He loves the book so far. Honestly, Beth. We've mostly talked about Molly and the foolish choices she makes in the beginning. He's just gotten to the threesome. No, he didn't say not to tell you."

Her outrage melted. "You're really talking to your dad. That's how he got me to give him the book—he said he wanted to have something to talk to you about. Of course, my mom found out, and I had to give it to her too."

She'd told him that on the phone that morning, and he believed it was true his dad was trying. "It's amazing. It started with Dad sending me a pic of Radar, when I asked if the dog was improving. It was sketchy communication, but a start. Then this week, it's been more." He hugged her, dropping his face into her hair. "Thanks to you and Molly, we're talking over text."

She pressed her head against his neck. "It's Radar who's the hero of this story. That dog helps your dad cope." Picking up his left hand, she stroked his ring. "You did keep one secret from me."

Justice looked down. Seeing both of them wearing their rings sent a spark of deep happiness through him. "This party?"

"Yep. I honestly had no idea. Ethan sure didn't let on. I'm happily surprised."

"You can show me how happy when I get you alone in our room. By the way, you're sexy as hell in that dress."

Liza grinned at him, happy she'd worn her black

and white scuba dress that hugged her curves. "You should have seen me in my heels."

He groaned. "If you packed them, you can model the heels for me later, wearing nothing but—"

"Oh my God," Em's voice reverberated over the music.

"Shit," Simon muttered. "Get the remote! Turn it off."

The music stopped at the exact second Beth scrambled off his lap.

"No!" Simon thundered. "Turn off the TVs!"

Justice looked up to one of the half dozen big screens around the room to see Alicia from the talk show, *Late Night with Alicia*. Justice loathed her for playing video of Gene Hayes during a Savaged Illusions interview. He leapt up to find the damned remote himself.

Beth shot to her feet. "That's Nikki."

Justice jerked around to see at the woman who'd betrayed his wife to a monster. What the hell was going on? They hadn't heard a peep from her in over a year since she'd vanished from her condo after Liza lost the baby in Paris and Emily confronted her. Now she'd reemerged on *Late Night with Alicia*?

"We're back from commercial break," Alicia said. "Our guest tonight is Nikki Poole, the woman who Liza Cade accused of conspiring with the once-famous rock star turned fugitive, Gene Hayes. For a year, we've seen nothing of Nikki Poole. Tonight, she's here to share some explosive news."

The camera swung to Nikki, who smiled and said, "Hi, Alicia, thank you for having me on to share this moment with all your viewers."

"What is your news?"

"After a year of living in hiding, of spending long

nights writing and days working with industry professionals, I'm releasing my new book next week." She held up a hardback book with a split screen cover of Nikki on one side and Liza on the other. "*Friends to Enemies: My Year Inside the Life of Liza Cade.*"

Oh fuck, the disaster train just left the station heading right for them.

Shock coursed through Liza at the sight of the woman who'd betrayed her. Nikki had changed her hair from darkish blonde to strawberry and had it cut and styled around her face, giving her a more polished appearance.

A book? Oh Jesus. That's what Nikki had done? Disappeared to write a book about her and get a publishing contract? Clammy prickles burst over Liza's skin. She'd underestimated Nikki. They all had.

Emily stalked over to Liza. "That conniving coward dares to show her face after what she did?"

On the screen, Alicia said, "So, Nikki, Liza Cade has been the most hated women in rock for nearly a decade. This news is going to cause massive waves. Why did you keep it secret?"

"Once you read it, you'll understand," Nikki assured Alicia. "I reveal many secrets that will stun the world. We had to protect our information and sources in order to bring this book to readers with pristine honesty."

"What motivated you to write a story about your experience with Liza?"

"Money," Simon snapped. "What else?"

"Being a narcissistic bitch," Lynx answered him.

On the screen, Nikki explained, "I wanted to set the record straight and get the truth out there. Like so many people, I too had believed Liza was a victim." Nikki shook her head, her sleek hair flowing around her chin.

Alicia smoothly interjected, "And now?"

Nikki's eyes blazed with conviction. "Liza Cade is the architect of her life. I didn't see her ability to lie and manipulate until I found myself one of the unwitting villains in the story she'd created. She told the D.A. I was in contact with Hayes, and that I had sold him information, pictures and videos about her. It was a complete and total lie. I had no contact in any manner with Gene Hayes ever, and the subsequent investigation cleared me. I'd done nothing, yet in moments my life was destroyed. It was hard to grasp what she'd done to me. I mean, even after my band lost on *Court of Rock*, I helped her come up with ways to promote her band. Then she got that job at SLAM, which she wasn't remotely qualified for, but I helped her with her work, teaching her how to set up her boss's calendar and reviewing at the various fighter's social media to help her come up with ways to improve their engagements. I'd done so much for her, and I couldn't believe it when she turned on me." Nikki shook her head, as if the shock still baffled and upset her. "I guess I was a convenient scapegoat and totally expendable to Liza."

Concern stretched Alicia's smooth features into something that might have been a frown pre-Botox. "That had to be awful. What did you do?"

"Well, I didn't have a job—no one was going to hire me after that—all my friends vanished, and people I didn't even know were saying horrible things about me. I was lost." She paused a second, then said, "I retreated to my dad's house in Minnesota and tried to regroup. Eventually, I realized I wasn't the first person

Liza had ruined, and I wouldn't be the last—unless I did something about it. I needed to create a document to inform and warn others. This book is the result of months of painstaking work as I carefully reconstructed everything I witnessed, or that Liza told me. I relied on my calendar, detailed journals, pictures, and some interviews to make sure I am giving the most authentic version of events."

"You kept journals?"

"I did, as well as a lot of pictures. See, I'm from Minnesota, you know? I moved to San Diego after my dad married my stepmother." Nikki gave a rueful twist of her mouth. "I'm afraid I was a pretty stereotypical stepdaughter who resented the new woman coming into our lives. We didn't get along, and I left abruptly, determined to prove I could finish college and support myself on my own. I was struggling big-time, so when I landed the college intern publicist job for one of the top three bands on *Court of Rock*, I was over-the-moon excited. I splurged on a couple fancy notebooks to document every single thing that I did, said, heard...honestly, I was so naïve it's a bit embarrassing now. At the time, I thought it was a big deal and I'd document it all to show my dad that I'd done these remarkable things all on my own."

Liza snorted. She'd fallen for Nikki's lines, the girl with all the terrible first date tales, and the family sob story about the mean stepmother getting her dad to financially cut her off.

"And that's where you met Liza?" Alicia kept the interview on track.

She nodded. "Liza and also Karl, the college publicist for the band Fury Run. We all got along, and despite our bands being in competition, we had fun and even shared advice and tips. Then my band lost."

"Jagged Sin," Alicia put in. "They have a feud with Savaged Illusions?"

"Yes." Nikki detailed the bad blood between the bands.

Alicia said, "Sounds like there was a lot going on behind the scenes during *Court of Rock*."

"There was. Including the budding romance of Justice and Liza." Nikki flattened her mouth. "It was frowned on bigtime, but she didn't care. What she did care about was keeping her past as the girl who ruined Gene Hayes secret. The only one who knew that Liza was really Elizabeth Ranger was Justice. He kept it from his band and caused major problems between the guys."

"Speaking of Gene Hayes," Alicia smoothly pivoted. "You address the rape and court case in the book."

"I told everything I know in these pages, never holding back," Nikki answered carefully.

"Was Liza part of her father's scheme?"

She squeezed her hands together. "I don't want to give my opinion like so many others have done. I'd much rather people live the experience as I did through the year I was Liza's friend, really get to know her, and come to their own conclusions. I feel strongly that rape, and any kind of sexual abuse, is serious. Victims suffer tremendously. So I don't want to give some glib and careless TV sound bite that can be taken out of context. I trust readers to be able to live my experience and decide for themselves what truly happened that night in Gene Hayes's bedroom." She focused on the studio audience.

Liza hissed between her teeth. "A suggestive non-answer, ending on a salacious hook. She's a lot better at marketing than we gave her credit for."

Alicia pivoted to her next subject. "I can't help but

notice you are releasing this book right before Jagged Sin releases their new album. Gene Hayes is featured with them in the song 'Witch Hunt.' Is that by design?"

"The publisher scheduled the book release, not me. I had zero control over it. All I can tell you is I've followed Jagged Sin, and I have to say I'm excited about their new release. I only worked with them a short time on *Court of Rock*, but I could see they had some serious talent, even more than Fury Run or Savaged Illusions. Unfortunately, Jagged Sin's chances were sabotaged by Liza and Savaged Illusions' dirty tricks. Now Jagged Sin is really coming into their own and are amazing. Teaming up with Hayes?" Nikki shrugged. "I guess we'll see what happens, but I'm dying of curiosity like most of the world to hear that. 'Witch Hunt' is an intriguing title."

Gray folded his arms over his chest. "That was some sly promo for 'Witch Hunt.'"

Liza agreed, but she kept her focus on the screen.

Alicia said, "The book title is *Friends to Enemies*. Do you really feel that you are enemies now? Are you in danger?"

Nikki twisted her hands briefly. "Absolutely, but I'm determined to tell the truth."

"Unfortunately, we're running short on time. Is there anything else you'd like to share with us before we go?"

Nikki turned to the camera. "I'm inviting all of you to get to know Liza Cade AKA Elizabeth Ranger as I did. Read about the secrets, lies, schemes, even naked groupies in Justice's hotel rooms that provoked Liza's world-class tantrum, and Liza's obsession with reading and writing sex scenes. Once you complete the book, drop me a line and tell me what you think of the woman who destroyed one rock star, then got pregnant by and married another, and when the heat was on him, she took an inexplicable tumble down the stairs at seven months along." Nikki paused and blinked dramatically, as if trying to stop herself from crying. "Of all the players in this story, that baby is, and always will be, the one truly innocent victim."

Liza jerked upright, her entire body bowing with shock and a raw, sick fury. Her baby. That bitch Nikki was talking about Savanna.

The show wrapped up with Alicia saying *Friends to Enemies* was coming out on Tuesday, and that it was up for presale now.

As the show music played them out, someone muted the TV.

"She did not just do that," Justice growled. "Go on TV and...a book. A goddamned book." He swung around. "Gavin, get the lawyers on this, now."

"Can we stop it?" Lynx asked.

"Not a chance." Gavin strode up to them while thumbing through his phone. "I already spoke to the law office, clued them in. They'll try, but they kept this so secret I doubt we could even get an emergency injunction."

Liza stood in the same place, her shock fading beneath a rising tide of white-hot fury. The internal pressure swelled until her skin felt tight and her heart raced. Part of her wanted to run, get to her room...and what? Hide? While Nikki went public with her smears? "What the hell is Nikki up to with this book?"

Em grabbed her forgotten glass and drained it. "She's getting the money and fame she always wanted. Off you. That double-crossing, conniving bitch wrote a tell-all book filled with salacious, damning lies about you. After we befriended her." She slapped her empty glass on the bar. "She was always jealous of you, she wanted your life. Now she's written a book when that was your dream."

The thought of it stoked her rage hotter. She could almost feel actual flames bursting straight up from her gut.

Em's voice got her attention. "What makes her think she can get away with this?"

Liza stalked to the bar and then spun around to face the room. Justice, his band, Em, Sloane, Kat, Sherry, Slade, Monique, Damon, Althea, Gavin the manager, Hank, the head of security. "Up till now, she's gotten away with every damned thing. Selling me out to Hayes, and who knows what else. She hasn't seen me stop anyone yet."

Justice strode up to her. "That's about to change."

His faith in her strengthened her resolve. "Damn right. I think it's time we told our story publicly. Let's do something big next week." Adrenaline-fueled determination filled her. She wasn't staying quiet any longer. "Nikki's book drops Tuesday, and the album with Hayes and Jagged Sin on Friday night. Let's do Wednesday or Thursday."

"The week is tight," Simon reminded him. "We're doing concerts and events all over."

Justice turned to their manager, who had his head bent over his phone. "Which day is possible for me to fly in and out? Make it happen, Gavin, get us booked on something big. Let Beth and me know, and we'll both be there."

"One minute," his manager said.

She turned to Justice. "There's no way in hell this is a coincidence of timing with this book coming out right before Jagged Sin and Hayes's album."

His jaw clenched, and the scar in his eyebrow whitened. "Think they're working together?"

"Maybe." After all, she got away with it once. There were other possibilities. "Or she's trying to get Hayes's attention again. She's that desperate. Or she could be secretly working with Jagged Sin, but this timing? Not. A. Coincidence." Liza'd been a gullible fool once. Not this time. Nikki had some scheme to benefit herself with bigger rewards than a book. But what?

"Got it," Gavin called out.

Liza and Justice both looked over. "Got what?"

Gavin pulled his phone away. "Miraculous luck that landed you all a booking for Thursday of next week on *Chatterbox*. Even better, they're telling me Nikki Poole tried to get on the show, and they turned her down."

Stunned, Liza blurted, "*Chatterbox?* That's huge. Bigger than *Ellen* or the late-night shows. Probably the biggest audience on TV, plus they stream an AfterChat segment. How did you pull that off?"

Pride spread on his face. "They had one of my other former clients booked, and I got them to trade Savaged Illusions booking there in six weeks."

"Amazing," she said. "Thank you."

Justice added, "Now we have to make sure we get there with no fuckups."

"I'll get you there," Gavin promised. "I'll have to move a couple interviews to other days, compressing your schedules more."

Liza looked around at everyone there. Gavin, the band, a lot of her friends, and they were all jumping in with ideas and support.

This time, they were all fighting together.

Chapter 21

JUSTICE FINALLY GOT BETH IN their room after another hour or two of planning and strategizing. It was a one-bedroom suite with a small kitchen and an open living space with an efficient office nook.

After he double-checked the door was locked, he turned to—

"Oomph!" Beth threw herself into his arms.

His back hit the wall of the small hallway, but he closed his arms around her sweet body. "What—?"

His question was cut off by her kiss. She tasted of chocolate, coffee and pure Beth. Her tongue demanded entrance.

While he mentally scrambled to make sense of this wild, sexy creature, his dick surged with heat. Hot, needy blood pounded in his groin. His heart thudded as the sudden lust hit with the force of a train. He kissed Beth back, and it wasn't enough. Getting a hand on her full ass, he lifted her higher and finally broke the mad kiss.

"You want something, baby?" Christ, her dress had ridden up her thighs, and the feel of her skin burning through his clothes inflamed a primal urge to satisfy the hunger raging in her.

Threading her fingers into his hair, she tugged just enough to sting. Damned if that didn't streak a path to his groin. His cock thickened and swelled in his pants to the point of pain.

"I have what I want. *Who* I want. You. Now." The fiery confidence in her voice shoved him to the edge of crazy.

"You have me." He walked her to the closest room—the living space with the massive sectional couch—and laid her on the chaise. Wasting no time, he shoved the skirt of her pretty dress higher and caught sight of pale panties covering her. No time to admire. He stripped them off her legs. After quickly undoing his pants, he pushed them off. His cock sprang out, thick, hard, and desperate to glide into her tempting body and feed whatever need was driving her. "I'm all yours." Gripping her legs—

"Wait."

He snapped his attention up to her face. To his surprise, she rolled off the couch to her knees.

Holy Christ. She knelt there with her hair streaming in fire-streaked waves, her professional power dress bunched up around her waist, and her thighs spread just enough to show her pussy. And she wanted him to wait?

His cock bobbed and strained, darkening with the blistering demand. He closed his eyes, trying to slow his body down. Think of anything but his gorgeous wife—

Her mouth closed around his cockhead and sucked him into the wet heat.

Justice's mind melted, and he wrapped his hand in her hair. "Beth. God."

Cupping his balls, she stroked her thumb along the sensitive flesh as she worked him into a frenzy so high, he growled with the effort of not coming.

Not yet.

Unable to bear it another second, he broke free and tugged her into his arms. With nothing but ferocious urgency driving him, he swung her around to the side table against a wall, dropped her butt on it, and pressed against her entrance while taking her mouth. Trying to consume her and fill her, he thrust deep inside her.

Beth moaned in his mouth and grabbed his ass to demand more. Harder. Fiercer. Whatever remained of his control snapped, and he pumped into her, riding a rising storm until her entire body bowed into beautiful pleasure.

His orgasm raced down his spine and exploded in flames of bliss. It took long moments before the aftershocks eased.

Panting, he stared at Beth's flushed, damp face. "You're a hell of a surprise."

She leaned back against the wall, as if her muscles were melting. "Because I jumped you like a porn star?"

He couldn't help his satisfied grin. "You can jump me anytime, but I thought you'd be distracted and upset."

"Wanting to hide?"

He studied her flushed face. "Not hide, fight. Your hiding days are over. I thought you'd keep working."

"I'm not letting Nikki or anyone, including Hayes, take this from us again. They got between us once and tore us apart. We won't repeat that mistake. We come first."

He was impressed as hell, and touched by the gift she was giving him. Trust that he'd fight by her side. She'd turned to him, taking what she needed, rather than running away. "We won't let him, Beth. We're in this together."

"I saw that tonight. Not just you, but your band, your manager. Plus a lot of my friends were there, and they aren't Nikki. It took me a while to trust anyone but Emily, Tess and Sloane. Now, there's Sophie, even though she couldn't come this weekend, and Kat and Sherry. I have so much more to fight for."

"I'm so damn proud of you. FYI, having you fling yourself into my arms tonight with that need. Hottest damn thing ever."

Her grin spread slow and tired. "You threw me a surprise party for my book. Even with Nikki reappearing with her bombshell, that meant so much to me. I know you're proud. Just like I'm proud of you, of your success and the way you're using it to fight against the man who destroyed our family once."

"We're all in for each other." He separated from her and scooped her up in his arms because he needed to hold her, feel her. Because he was scared too, terrified of losing her again.

Nikki wasn't the real threat. She was a serious annoyance that would cause them some aggravation. But their real enemy?

That was the reaper—Gene Fucking Hayes. He'd already taken their child. Justice wasn't going to let that bastard get his wife too.

The persistent vibrating noise forced Liza awake. Still wrapped in Justice's arms, she squinted in the darkness. Was it predawn, or had they pulled the blackout drapes? She couldn't remember. It'd been close to two a.m. before her husband had tugged away her computer and pulled her against him, telling her to try to sleep.

Obviously, she'd fallen asleep.

The buzzing persisted. Reality cleared away the lazy remnants of sleep. Her phone! Had something else happened in addition to Nikki's book? Pushing up, she grabbed her glasses.

"Beth?"

"Phone," she muttered. With her glasses on, she eyed her screen, and her stomach clenched. She put it on speaker and swiped accept. "Noah? What's wrong?" A glance at a clock told her it was after nine a.m.

"They're scaring Radar."

Noah's rough voice shot a dose of raw adrenaline through her. Fully awake, Liza spiked upright and swung her legs off the bed. "Who?"

"I...the screams, I can't stop the screams."

The harsh stress riding his words alarmed her. Justice must have heard because he leapt up, grabbing his phone, and she heard him talking rapidly to someone.

Another voice took over the call. "Beth, it's me."

"Mom, what's happening? Is Noah okay?"

"Thank God you answered! Media swarmed the house at daylight. They've even tried climbing the back fence. There's a picture online of me running out in the backyard and screaming at the reporter before Noah let Radar out. That dog was pissed and chased the guy right back over the fence. Listen, Noah's not coping well. He's sweating, pale, and losing track of where he is. He thinks the backyard is the battlefield. He dragged me inside and pushed me down behind the couch."

"Oh no." Liza had seen Noah stressed, but never like that. "Are you hurt?"

"No, he wasn't trying to harm me. I'm not scared *of* him, I'm scared *for* him." She paused a second. "The media got that picture, so they know I'm here at

233

the house. I was going to take the car and get us to the condo, but I called the guard gate to check, and he said the media is swarming there too. They're looking for a response to Nikki's book. Beth, people are screaming that I'm a murderer, you're a baby killer, and Gene Hayes is innocent. What...?"

As her mom trailed off, it hit Liza that Amber was close to crying. She was falling apart, scared, and didn't know what to do. Was Liza there as she'd promised? No, she was out of the country with Justice. Helpless anger flooded her. "Mom, hang in there, okay? I'll figure something out. I swear. I'll get you help."

"Where can we go?" Amber asked.

Desperate, she strove think of a solution. "I'll find a safe place. Maybe Sloane's or—"

"Beth, I've got help coming."

She turned to her husband and held the phone between them since it was on speaker. "Mom, Justice has an answer."

"Amber," Justice said. "The police are on their way." His voice was steady, smooth and in control. "Dad's counselor from the transitional center will meet them there to pick up you, my dad and Radar. You can spend a night or two there, they said, until Beth's home."

Utter relief flooded her, and when Justice put his arm around her, she leaned into him. "We'll stay on the phone until they do. Is Radar with Noah?"

"Right next to his leg," Amber answered. "Every time Noah gets confused, Radar presses against him, licks or paws him. It grounds him and keeps him here in the present."

Justice said, "Amber, can you put the phone on speaker?"

"Yes. One sec...done."

"Dad, it's Justice. The police are coming, and so is Dr. Miller. The doctor will take you, Radar and Amber to the transitional center. You can go right to your room there if you want to. Radar will stay with you the whole time. Okay?"

A pause hung there, then, "Understood." A short inhalation sounded. "Protect Liza."

Justice's eyes widened, but he managed to answer. "Count on it, Dad. I won't mess up again."

After a silence, Amber said. "Beth, the police are pulling up in front of the house now, so we're safe."

"Call me once you're at the veteran's center."

Her mom agreed and disconnected. Liza ignored the alerts and texts lighting up her phone, instead turning to Justice. "Thank you, I didn't know what to do."

He tugged her against him. "All I did was call Dr. Miller. He called the police."

"I'm grateful."

"Hell of a wake-up call, huh?" He ran a thumb along her jaw.

"Yeah, but something pretty damned amazing came out of it—your dad talked to you, even while struggling with a full-blown PTSD episode."

Some of the earlier tension melted from his face, peeling back years to the boy inside him. "He did. Of course, he told me to protect you."

Liza shook her head. "Nope, you don't get to minimize this, Justice. It's big."

"It is, isn't it? We've been texting, but this was a significant step. Also, he called you and is willing to go to the transitional center." Finally, a smile rolled out. "Your mom did okay too. My dad didn't scare her."

Liza pulled away and walked to the dresser to gather her clothes. "She was scared, but not of your dad. She's been struggling with making decisions. Sometimes, just trying to choose what to eat for breakfast can overwhelm her. And she walks for hours a day in the complex, I think as a way of coping with being out of prison." She looked at him over her shoulder. "But she handled it despite being stressed, and she was making decisions. Good ones, like calling the guard gate at the condo before going there."

He walked up behind her and wrapped his arms around her. "Your mom knew about your party, Beth, and she made sure you came. She decided that on her own after my dad hurt his hip."

Liza turned him. "My mom knew?"

"Yes. I told her about it. I knew she couldn't come because of her parole, but I wanted to include her by facetiming her in. She said no, it'd be better if you just enjoyed yourself. She asked if we can have a book release party in San Diego when your book comes out. Which we will, by the way. At that time, I didn't know Dad would hurt his hip and your mom would offer to stay with him. She made those choices."

Tears of love welled in her eyes. Her husband and her mom did this for her. So many of her friends too, flying all the way to Canada. "That party is very special to me, and now you just made it more special by telling me what my mom did. Not even Nikki can ruin the fact I'm getting my family back." Including the precious memories of Savanna stored in their hearts. "Nikki's desperate, cheesy, tell-all swipe won't ruin the experience of finishing and publishing my book."

She wouldn't let leeches like Nikki, or monsters like Hayes, take anything away from her again.

Chapter 22

JUSTICE WAS GOING TO CRACK his jaw if he kept gritting his teeth. His pissed-off meter hit the red zone as the car tried to wade through protestors clogging the streets around the *Chatterbox* studio to get close enough for the guys to get out and not cause a riot.

Many of the protestors held signs that said, *Boycott Savaged Cheaters* and *Arrest Baby Killer Lyin' Liza*. Or *End The Witch Hunt, Bring Gene Hayes Home*.

In the last week Nikki had saturated the media, her book had released, followed by Hayes coming out in support of the book. All the while swearing he'd never met or talked to Nikki, and then accusing Liza of blackmailing World Rock Stage into making sure Justice and his band got the owner's seat.

People actually believed him, including his accusation that the contest was rigged, just a show to appear like it wasn't a backroom deal made with Liza to keep her from suing over Savanna's death.

His head throbbed like a motherfucker from pure rage and clawing frustration. The show was live in less than a half hour, they'd been held up at customs, and now they couldn't get through the streets of fools.

He'd get out and run, but his security team had nixed that, swearing they'd tackle him to the ground, drag his ass right back in the car, and hogtie him if they had to.

No one was in a good mood.

As if the day wasn't shitty enough, their warehouse in L.A had been targeted by protesters, who'd covered it in graffiti. They also broke windows and set one of the merchandise trucks on fire.

Thank Christ no one was hurt.

So yeah, his pissed-off meter rang hard, but worse was the sick feeling of letting Beth down. He had to be there when the show started as he'd promised.

Finally, the car stopped, police and security held back the hoards, and ushered the band inside. They were met by a frantic-looking woman. "Justice, with me. The rest of you can wait in the greenroom. We'll call the band to the stage for the second half."

Before he could say a word, she jogged off.

"Go!" Simon shoved him.

Justice caught up to the woman. "How long?"

"Eight minutes. Liza is ready. She's talking to Wayne and Toby up ahead, waiting for you. The crew will get your equipment, guitars and so on, and when we do a set change for the songs, they'll be there for you. We had a stand-in for sound check, everything was fine, and cross your fingers it stays that way through the live show." She slowed as they approached a group.

"Justice!" Toby spotted him first.

Then Beth swung around. He skidded to a stop and caught her hands. "Wow, baby." Her hair was a mix of straight with a few long curls pulled down over her shoulders. Her bluish gray shirt skimmed the top of sleek pants that glided over her body like a waterfall and ended at her calves. High-heeled shoes embossed with metal and complicated straps around her ankles added height and major cool to her look. Otherwise, Beth wore nothing but a pair of small diamond earrings and her wedding bands. He noted she didn't wear a watch or bracelet to cover the scars on her wrist. "You're stunning."

Her smile lit up her face. "I was so scared I'd have to go on by myself, I was hyperventilating."

"Nah, she was cool and calm." Wayne held out his hand.

Justice shook Wayne's hand, then turned to the other cohost, Toby. "That shit outside is crazy. I damn near got out of the car and ran here."

Wayne waved it off. "You made it, we're good. Every seat is filled, and social media is blowing up. People want to hear Justice and Liza's story. Especially with Gene Hayes's video that claimed he read Nikki's book and fully supported her as another person Liza Cade used and abused."

Furious disgust had Justice flexing and fisting his hands as a team of hair, makeup, and sound engineers swarmed him. "People actually believe him."

Toby took over. "They'll believe anything if it fits their life narrative. Okay, here's the plan." He outlined the show, then asked, "Any questions or problems?"

Justice pulled his shirt down over the mic pack at his back, while the woman clipped on a microphone. "Not as long as Beth is comfortable."

She half laughed. "Does the urge to throw up and run like hell at the same time mean I'm comfortable?"

He squeezed her hand. "Stage fright. It'll calm once you start talking. If you're too nervous, then look at me instead of the audience."

The door opened and someone stuck their head out. "Need you on set. Ninety seconds."

The hair and makeup sorcerers melted away. Justice and Liza followed the cohosts into the wings, where the warmup guy was finishing up. The audience laughed and clapped. As the comedian trotted off the stage, music swelled, and an announcer's voice boomed. "Ladies and gentlemen, welcome to *Chatterbox*, live from New York! Give a hand to our hosts, Toby and Wayne!"

The audience hit their feet applauding, and the two men burst out of the wings, waving, and launched into their opening.

Justice tuned it out and focused on Beth. She stood ramrod straight, her neck tense. "Breathe, Beth. We're telling our truth. Anything you don't want to talk about, we'll...what's the word when you change the subject?"

"Pivot."

"See, you got this."

She squeezed his hand. "We got this."

Toby's voice rose. "Welcome to our stage to break their silence about their wild love, traumatic loss, and triumphant reunion. Ladies and gentlemen, Justice and Liza Cade!"

"Smile and wave," he reminded her, and they walked out.

"Justice! Justice!" the crowd roared. Over that he heard a shout of "Lyin' Liza baby killer."

Practice kept his grin in place as they walked to the hosts and went through the second round of handshakes and air kisses for Beth. More waves at the audience, then Justice and Beth took a seat on the two tall stools positioned at a high table with mugs featuring the show name and logo.

"Are the rumors true, and the two of you have reunited?"

Justice kept Beth's hand and turned in his seat to face her. "Yes. I never stopped loving Beth."

"I wanted to stop loving Justice," Beth said. "I tried. Losing our baby broke something in me, and I was desperately afraid to love anyone that much again. But Justice..." she stared into his eyes, "...he wouldn't let me stop. He fought for our love, and me. I love him more today than when we married."

Justice turned to the audience. "Do you all want to get to know the woman I love so much it ripped my heart out when I lost her and inspired the song, 'Savaged Vows'?"

The audience responded that they did.

"We hear you," Wayne said. "Liza, are you willing to take us back to the night you and your father went to Gene Hayes's house?"

She gathered herself, then gestured to the big screen behind her, and a picture flashed on.

The girl had long brown hair with fiery streaks of reddish gold surrounding a bare face, smattered with freckles. She wore a T-shirt with kittens on it, and a pair of shorts. It had been one thing to hear Beth was fourteen when she was attacked by Hayes, but to see it right there in full color—she'd been a young girl in that awkward stage with thin arms and legs, but starting to develop a woman's curves. If one of his bandmates brought a girl like that around for sex, Justice would kick their ass then have them arrested. In a fucking heartbeat.

"This is me when I was fourteen years old," Beth explained. "Taken on the day my father showed up with his latest scheme. He told me Gene Hayes was filming a music video, and I could be in it. I was insanely excited at the idea. Me! A nobody girl with a groupie mom whom even her own family didn't want around.

I could be important enough to be in a rock star's video."

Liza sat forward. "Believing him was the first step in the terrible night that shattered my childhood, took away my mom, and ultimately made me the most hated woman in rock."

Justice couldn't look away from his wife. She told her story of her dad and Hayes tricking her into drinking the drug-laced strawberry margarita. Panic at feeling herself losing consciousness and calling her mom. Then waking in the hospital dog sick, in pain, and begging for her mom, who had been arrested for murder. She took the audience through living with her aunt, and what it was like to testify at the trial and then Hayes escaping the country.

Beth stood up. "The day I learned Hayes had run rather than face the remainder of the trial and the verdict, I was distraught. What made it worse was that night, protestors were outside my aunt's house where I lived, screaming. The called me a liar, a tramp... terrible names. By then I had turned fifteen, and the amount of hatred broke me." She walked to the edge of the stage and held up her left wrist.

"This is what happens when you're an innocent teenaged girl and hatred infects your soul."

One of the cameras zoomed in on the jagged white lines on her inner wrist.

"I tried to kill myself to escape. That's what rape and hate does to a child. That's what Gene Hayes and his supporters did."

Beth strolled to another part of the stage and faced the crowd. "Those days, they weren't the worst. That came when Justice and I went to Paris, France. Savaged Illusions had won the Indie Rock Band award and would be performing at World Rock Stage.

We went a few days early for a delayed honeymoon. We ate, did some sightseeing, and talked endlessly about our future with our daughter. We even chose a name." She turned to him.

Pain swam in her eyes, and his heart clenched hard.

She returned her gaze to the audience. "We were living the dream. All the way until I came face-to-face with Gene Hayes and ran in terror. I raced into that stairwell and fell."

Justice went to her, wrapping his arm around her shoulders.

Beth leaned into him. "Savanna Rose Cade died before the ambulance got me to the hospital. That was the worst moment of my life."

When they came back from commercial break, Wayne handed over the portable mic to a woman in the audience. She asked, "Liza, why do you think Nikki wrote this book? Is it revenge?"

Before she could say anything, Justice answered, "Jealousy. Nikki latched onto Beth, hoping for a ticket out of her sad life. She imagined being a rock star's wife was all glamour, but she never grasped how hard Beth worked at her job and taking care of our home while I was out on the road touring for our first album and trying to make it." Justice settled a hand on her shoulder.

Liza took over. "I think Nikki wrote the book out of desperation. She failed at many things in her life, then she had the attention of an infamous rock star, Gene Hayes. I know Nikki denies selling him information about me, but I am certain she did. Hayes told me that himself, and Nikki confirmed it to my best friend." Liza sat forward in her chair.

"Once Hayes did that, Nikki had no more value to him, and he cut her off. That's why she had to run to her to her dad—who by the way, she'd been estranged from. Her dad and stepmom had cut her off financially the year before that. I think this book is Nikki's sad, frantic, and very misguided attempt to get Hayes's attention again." Liza hoped that dug into Nikki.

"We have another question." Wayne handed the mic off to a viewer.

"Justice, after Gene Hayes's video accusing Liza of blackmailing World Rock Stage into pushing out Hayes and creating this contest to get your band in, how does your band feel about you and Liza getting back together? There's protests against you guys, and according to Nikki's book, your band banned her from your last tour. Do they still feel that way?"

"Why don't we ask them?" Justice suggested.

Since the guys weren't due out until after the next commercial break, Liza was surprised when Gray, Simon, River and Lynx all burst onto the stage in a whirlwind of energy. They fist-bumped the hosts, kissed Liza, and River jumped down into the audience to greet a few of them, then tugged a seventy-something woman into a dance. He helped her back to her seat and kissed her cheek, then leapt back up on the stage like a panther.

The stage crew scrambled to get stools for the guys.

Finally they all sat, and Lynx said, "How do I feel about Justice and Liza being back together? Relieved. Justice has been a bear to live with. Liza tames him."

River snorted. "Plus he kept wanting to sing sappy love songs."

Gray rolled his eyes and began singing, "My Heart Will Go On" by Celine Dion. He mimicked it dead-on.

Beth turned to Justice, happy to play along with the guys' teasing. "Sing it for me, please?"

He leaned in and lifted his mic to his mouth. "Sure thing, if you sing 'Oops!... I Did It Again' for me."

"Damn," Beth muttered. "You don't play fair, Rooster."

He laughed. "Nope, I play to win." He leaned in, and despite being on live TV, kissed her. "You're my prize."

"Aw, come on, Liza, you're cute when you go all Britney Spears," Simon said.

Liza leaned back to look past Justice. "I know where the clown is. Another crack like that, I'm going to go clown all over you. He'll show up when and where you least expect it."

Lynx busted out laughing, and Justice shook his head then grinned at the audience and cameras. "Simon has a well-known clown phobia. On our last tour, Gray pulled a clown prank on Simon, and after that, the clown kept turning up in different places for the remainder of the tour."

Wayne cut in, "Gotta comment here. Liza, did you call Justice *Rooster*?"

"I sure did, Wayne." She gave him a sweet smile. "It's my pet name for him. Because Justice loves nothing more than to strut."

"And, Justice, what's your pet name for Liza?"

Back to his easy charm, he answered, "Beth. Everyone else, except for her mom, calls her Liza, the girl that was invented after the rape, as if her aunt and Grandma could erase her life with her mom and the trauma Beth suffered at the hands of Gene Hayes. The woman I love? It's all of her, including the girl she was before the rape. She never has to hide any part of herself from me." He held Beth's free hand and added, "She's my Beth."

All the women in the audience sighed.

Wayne smiled. "Do you sing, Liza?"

"At home when I'm cleaning, or when I lose a bet, but I'm no rock star."

Justice smiled. "Beth can sing, but it's not her passion."

"What is?" Toby asked. "Nikki said in her book you like to write, although she claimed you wrote porn."

Pride mixed with the urge to bitch-slap Nikki. Staying focused, she answered, "Actually, I write women's fiction, and I've just sold my first book."

"In other words," Justice said, "Liza isn't like Nikki, who wrote trashy lies about us to get a fugitive rapist's attention. Liza has real talent. The book is amazing, so incredible it's killing me to wait for it to be published. I'm her biggest fan. My dad and her mom are fighting for the slot as her second-biggest fan."

"What can you tell us about this book, Liza?" Wayne asked.

"It's a story of how a woman discovers the power of love, survival and triumph in her child. Telling this character's story was a journey for me, a way to accept my own loss and tell my daughter that having had her in my life gave me a strength I didn't know I had. Filled me with more love than I believed myself capable of, and eventually, propelled me to choose to live and love again." When Justice squeezed her hand, she went on, "Justice is right, writing is my passion. It's my voice, my way of sharing my heart with the world through story." Liza made herself stop talking and quietly laughed in her head. Once she hid her writing, and now she couldn't shut herself up on national TV.

Toby asked, "Do you have a title?"

Liza turned to Justice and smiled. "I do." She'd

thought of it the night she talked to Justice in Savanna's room. Seeing how he'd kept her furniture, so she'd know she had a home anyway, and the utter devotion Justice had to those he loved. "*Savaged Devotion*. Because the character is savage about her devotion to her child, willing to kill or die to protect her baby."

They went to commercial.

Justice turned to her. "You didn't tell me that. You're...really?"

She smiled at her husband. "I would never have finished my book if you hadn't believed in me with your savage stubbornness. I wanted to honor that, so I titled it *Savaged Devotion*. The publisher may change it, but I wanted you know my reason for choosing it."

"Beth—"

"Dude, we have to move!" Simon demanded, and they rushed to take their places for the first song.

They came back from commercial, and the band launched into "Savaged Vows." Liza sat to the side with the two hosts, tapping her foot as Justice gave the performance from his soul. This was truly his passion, and she loved watching him sing.

The song ended on the death scream, and Liza jumped to her feet clapping like every member in the audience.

Wayne walked up. "Before you do the last song, we have another question. 'Savaged Vows' is still in the top five, along with Fury Run's 'Autopsy'—"

"We're two spots ahead of 'Autopsy,'" Simon put in.

Wayne nodded. "My question is, are you worried about Jagged Sin's new release? Their song, 'Witch Hunt,' featuring Gene Hayes, broke into the top one hundred in presales this morning. If they outdo you in sales, won't they win the owner's spot on World Rock Stage?"

Liza tensed, but Justice shrugged it off. "Nope, not worried, I'm pissed. First this was an underhanded, shady move by Jagged Sin. They always pull crap like this. They can't cut it on their own in this competition, and no one else will sing with him. No. One. Their only hope? A perverted rapist felon." Justice turned to the big screen behind them. Liza's picture at fourteen appeared there again. "Think rock fans are going to support a singer who drugs and rapes a child? No. They won't.

"In the end," Justice added. "It's going to come down to the two bands with real talent, us and Fury Run."

"On that note, what song are you going to sing to close the show?"

"Beth's favorite song. 'Reaper's Child' was originally by Screech Rizzo and the Hellblades, and this is our version. For you, Beth, and for our daughter, Savanna Rose."

Chills broke out on her arms and legs as Gray played the piano intro. The lights dimmed, bathing Justice in shadow as he began to sing.

Her heart ached with the words, the pain, as Justice leaned into the song, his voice rising in the battle to save his child from the reaper. During the chorus, Justice jogged over to her, grabbed her hand, and tugged her back to the stage.

Holding her hand, he sang the third stanza while locking eyes with her.

The screen behind him flashed on with the painting of her and Justice holding their baby, the beauty and pain as real and vivid as this song.

He finished, and unlike the night he'd ripped his shirt off to show his tattoo to the world, this time as the final notes faded, he dropped his forehead to hers.

While behind them the picture loomed a truth.

They both had loved their baby and fought for her in their own way. They'd survived and embraced their love. They'd shared their story and told their truth.

Would it be enough?

Chapter 23

LIZA HAD NO TROUBLE KEEPING up with Justice as they biked along the beautiful coastal trail in Alaska. They'd slept most of the seven-and-a-half hour flight from New York after the show, and once they landed, they hit their hotel, showered, changed, fueled and caffeinated up to hit the trail.

Liza inhaled the crisp air filled with sea and pine. She'd been worried about leaving her mom home and traveling so far from San Diego, but once she'd gotten on the plane with Justice, her doubts had vanished in the joy of being with her husband. Despite getting sketchy sleep on the plane, she felt great today. Energized.

Probably still riding high from their *Chatterbox* interview yesterday. By the time they'd landed this morning, the clip of Justice singing "Reaper's Child" to her, along with the picture of them holding Savanna in the background, had gone viral. The song spiked up the charts, breaking the top ten.

That hadn't been planned or even imagined. The goal had been to push "Savaged Vows" back up to number one.

Which it had. Now they had two top ten hits at the same time, and that was pretty damned fantastic.

She smiled, happy as they peddled the trail along the ocean. Close behind them was Ethan and one other bodyguard, Derek, but they tried to give her and Justice space to just be together. So far, no one paid any attention to them.

Justice stopped, leaned his bike against a railing, and climbed over to sit facing the ocean. After tugging off his backpack, he handed her a water and an energy bar filled with nuts, dried fruit and chocolate.

Sitting next to him, she asked, "Got any peanut butter cups in there?"

"Not with me, but I might have some in the room."

Liza loved the easy teasing in his voice. "I didn't see them when you unpacked."

"Because you'd have stolen them." A grin tugged up the corners of his mouth. "Since we have a bed and real privacy tonight, if you want some peanut butter cups, you're going to have to earn them."

"Are you seriously trying to bribe me, Rock Star?"

"Is it working?"

"Maybe? Are we talking full-sized or mini?"

He leaned in. "Every damn time I hear your voice or smell your scent or look into those bewitching eyes of yours, it's full-sized, baby. When I get you naked? We're talking super-sized."

Despite the warmth of riding for miles, a shiver of pleasure pierced right down her center. Capturing the moment, she kissed him. Tasted Justice and the freedom of being able to do that. "I'm not leaving for several more days, and I already hate it."

"Stay, Beth." He sighed and pulled back. "That's selfish. You love your job, you finally have your mom in your life, and all I want, all I fucking dream about, is having you with me every second."

"I do too."

"Any time you're ready, turn in your notice, and you can come with me full-time. We'll leave Whitney in San Diego to protect your mom and my dad. If she needs more help, we'll get it for her."

Every day it was more tempting, more compelling. She knew it wasn't forever, but living separate lives was wearing on her. "I can't. My job is helping me provide for my mom."

He stared at her for a beat. "So, you can help my dad, but I can't help your mom? Let's not forget that you're the one who supported us through my early days. Don't I get a turn?" He leaned closer. "I think your book is going to hit big and get a movie option, so then you'll support us."

Damn, how did he undo her so fast like this? She quickly tried to regroup. "I love your dad, I enjoy being with him. That doesn't count."

"I like your mom. Next."

Amused, she said, "Making it a challenge? Okay, you paid for my condo. Way more than I ever spent on our bills."

"That condo was so you had a safe, secure place to live. You're my wife, which means half of everything I have is yours. FYI, that condo didn't even come close to half my net worth."

She lowered her chin and glared at him. "Stop strutting your net worth, Rooster."

"Then don't insult me. You worked your ass off, took care of the house and my dad, all while carrying our baby. I value that more than a piece of real estate."

Well crap, how could she respond? "Yeah? Well, my mom killed my dad and went to prison to save me. I value that."

"So do I," he shot right back. "So much so, I'll give her anything she wants or needs because she did her best to get my wife out of an ugly situation. Amber has more than earned my undying respect, and I'll do whatever I can for her."

She pursed her lips and tried to find a reply, but there wasn't one. This was Justice. He was loyal to the bone. "You win this point. If my mom needs something—"

"We get it for her. No yours-or-mine."

He'd won, but she wasn't done messing with him. "Unless I get a movie deal. That's all mine." She jumped up and leapt over the fence, dashing for her bike. "I wrote the book. All mine!"

His arm snapped around her waist, lifting her off her feet and locking her back to his chest. "Not so fast, sweetheart. I saved your book for you, and I believed in you before you believed in yourself. Also...I recognized how fucking brilliant you are."

"Ha." She was struggling so hard not to laugh. "You're just after my money!"

"Nope." He set her down and turned her to face him. "I'm after something much more valuable, even priceless. Your heart."

"Sorry, but I gave my heart to my husband, and he's a possessive man. Trust me. Nothing I tried would make him give it back." Liza leaned up to take his mouth.

"Justice, Liza, this way!"

They both turned to find a man in a baseball cap wearing a hockey jersey. "What do you have to say to Gene Hayes's showing up to sing 'Witch Hunt' with Jagged Sin at their opening in Frankford, Germany tonight?"

Justice had started forward but froze at the words. "During their concert?"

Liza's heart dropped. Gene Hayes?

"Yep. Lights went down, smoke and shit, then the spotlight landed on Hayes. Tell my viewers, what do you think of that?" His turned to Liza. "Especially—"

Ethan rushed the guy, spun him around, and said, "Who are you?"

"Hey! I'm... You can't touch me! I'm an influencer! All my viewers will see you!" The man struggled in Ethan's iron grip, his camera facing the ground. "Derek, get the camera," Ethan ordered the other security guy.

"No! I'll have you arrested!" the influencer protested.

Justice walked up to the guy. "Gene Hayes sang and then what?"

"I want this on camera!"

"Tell me what I want to know, and I'll reserve a ticket for you and a backstage pass at the concert tonight. You'll get five minutes of Savaged Illusions appearing on your platform. But if you give me shit, I'll let my security erase your footage, and you'll get nothing."

"I'll sue."

Justice leaned in closer. "Go ahead. My sharks posing as lawyers are bored and need fresh meat."

The guy glared at him, struggled again in Ethan's firm hold, then sagged in defeat. "Fine. It was livestreamed on the Bring Gene Hayes Home website and Jagged Sin's social media sites, but no one expected Hayes to show up personally. Jagged Sin and Hayes had told everyone he'd be appearing on the jumbo screens, but then he was there in real life, taking the lead in the song."

A surge of hope bolted through her. "If he was there, the German police will arrest him. Right?"

The guy shook his head. "At the end of the song, the stage went dark, and he vanished. Maybe they'll catch him before he gets out of Germany, but the whole audience was screaming, *Run, Hayes, Run* and *End the witch hunt.* That's all I know. I saw the tweet that someone spotted you two out here, and I came to get your comment. I kept my part up. I want the ticket and backstage pass."

Justice got his information and texted Gavin, then strode to her, took her arm, and they hopped on their bikes. "Let's go."

An hour later, they were quickly ushered into the hotel and up to their suite, where the guys were all waiting.

"Was he arrested?" Liza asked.

Hank was on his cell phone but turned to look at her. "No."

"Not even close," Simon added. "Instead, he's got another video uploaded, this one bragging about evading the witch hunt. Jagged Sin put up their video about their interrogation but said they won't let Lyin' Liza the baby killer get away with this persecution."

Liza couldn't believe this bullshit. Sinking onto the couch, she ignored her phone screaming alerts.

"It gets worse." Gray sat next to Liza. "The video cut of Hayes performing with Jagged Sin is getting as many hits as 'Reaper's Child' did in those first hours. Their song is climbing. It broke the top fifty."

"Fuck me." Justice sat on the other side.

"Fuck us all," Lynx snarled.

Liza couldn't agree more.

A few days after returning from Alaska, Liza couldn't keep her mind on the staff meeting. The day had started off with aggressive protestors swarming SLAM. Jagged Sin, Hayes, and Nikki had fired them up into a frenzy, making Liza and her supporters the enemy.

So far, Gene Hayes hadn't appeared again in one of Jagged Sin's prescheduled concerts, but they had a new trick. They popped up at secret locations announced at the last second on their sites. Those were dominating all the music news and social media. Hayes and Jagged Sin would suddenly appear, sing, give a rousing little speech about being the victim of a witch hunt, and scurry off trailed by a camera crew.

The videos exploded. #EndtheWitchHunt, #RunHayesRun and #FreeHayes were trending all over.

"Liza."

Shit. Her mind had wandered again during the meeting with her staff. She directed her attention to Sophie. "Sorry, I was distracted." No point in lying. Her staff deserved better.

"We were discussing the Jeremy Carson of Carson Graphic Designs social media posts saying that he pulled out of the deal with SLAM to design the labels for SLAM Vodka, claiming he refused to work with you because of your questionable ethics. When he told you that, you threatened him with quote, 'I have destroyed more powerful men than you.'" Sophie walked over with her phone. "You can see it here."

Liza read it. Well, look at that, her heart rate zapped up, sending a nice, clarifying shot of adrenaline that got her focused on her job. What a worm, jumping on the bash-Liza bandwagon. "For now, we'll ignore it. Responding draws attention, but let's keep watch."

Sophie nodded. "I agree, but I did a little research this morning, and his company profits are declining. Yelp reviews suck. Two female employees sued him for harassment. I've got ammunition to destroy him if he goes any further. Instinct tells me he'll fade away. You stood up to his face, and bullies like him pick easy marks, like employees dependent on him for a paycheck."

Liza eyed her assistant director. She looked so pixie-like with her above-the-shoulder bouncy curls and cute face, but when it came to this job, she was ruthless. That cheered Liza right back up. "Agreed, excellent job."

"Then that's all for our agenda." Sophie closed her laptop.

"Okay, let's get to work," Liza said. Everyone started filing out.

One of the women stopped on her way out and touched Liza's shoulder. "I love the video of Justice singing 'Reaper's Child' to you. I hope it's okay to say this, because, well..."

Liza smiled. No matter what antics Hayes, Jagged Sin, or Nikki pulled, that video cut was the most-watched music video around the world. It didn't hurt her feelings that Nikki's book sales had begun dropping the night after *Chatterbox* aired either. She focused on the graphic designer with the twinkling nose piercing. "Go ahead, I'm okay."

"Your baby is, well, was..." Her rich mocha skin flamed, and she clearly got a hold of herself. "What I'm trying to say is that she's beautiful. Like an angel."

Liza stood and unprofessionally hugged her. "Thank you."

Sharing that picture had been a hard decision that had come down to the fact that she didn't want to hide her daughter. This moment? It was a rare glimmer of the pride a mother feels, and she embraced it.

Sophie grinned. "Told you! People are sharing the picture of you at fourteen too."

"Yeah, it's been a pretty good start."

"Did you see that Wendy of Fury Run retweeted not only the photo of you at fourteen, but the video of 'Reaper's Child'? How crazy is that? She's competing against Savaged Illusions!"

Liza couldn't help her smile. "She called me and said to tell the savages that was for me, not them."

Sophie closed her laptop. "Wendy and I would be like best friends. Introduce me, please. I want her to randomly call me too, so I can casually drop that bombshell into conversations."

Liza rolled her eyes. "I'll ask Sloane if we can use his plane to fly to South America...or is she in Argentina? Anyhow, we'll get a quick introduction and fly back to do our freaking jobs."

"Harsh, boss, real harsh."

Liza scooped up her phone to access her notes when she noticed a text from her agent. *Trouble. Nikki Poole is doing media interviews bashing your book and the publisher.* She listed a few spots.

"Something wrong?" Sophie asked.

"Turn on the TV, hurry."

Sophie got the remote and turned on the bank of screens.

Liza took the clicker and found a cable station with Nikki doing an interview. She wore another killer dress and heels and had that hated book propped up next to her.

"Liza wrote porn." Nikki answered whatever question the interviewer had asked. "I saw the scenes, they were vulgar. Always two guys from a band having

258

sex with one chick. Now she's thrown in a baby." Nikki looked stricken. "For profit. She's using her baby's suspicious death to profit. First they did *Chatterbox* and showed the picture, which I suspect is fake. It's a painting, people, not a real photograph. Now this book? A porn with a baby in it?"

"Some people might think you're profiting off Liza," the interviewer pointed out.

Nikki nodded. "That's fair. In fact, I encourage readers to be skeptical and think for themselves. I wrote an honest book, and I'm certain that will come through. Liza's book is pure fiction. Worse, I was told by a source in her publisher's office that Liza absolutely put the baby in the story to play on the public's sympathy. It's all part of some sick campaign to convince the world she's not a schemer like her parents, and that she didn't hurl herself down those stairs."

"You believe she did?"

"It's all in my book, *Friends to Enemies*. I take the reader through my journey as Liza's friend until the moment she turned on me."

"But what do you believe? You wrote this book about her, what is it you what the world to glean from the pages?"

Nikki lifted her chin. "That she lies and manipulates. Liza was never the victim she tries to portray. Anyone who writes a porn with a baby in it—well, that tells you all you need to know. It's all kinds of wrong, and I'm starting a grassroots fight against this travesty."

"How?"

"With an online petition demanding the publisher withdraw the publishing contract."

"What?" Liza surged up, grabbed her phone, and quickly searched online. "God, she did start a petition, and it's getting signatures. There are hundreds already." Hot rage swelled and she called her agent.

Natasha answered with, "Liza, I—"

"Nikki is claiming she talked to someone in the publisher's office," Liza snapped. "We were assured silence. Did that happen, or is she lying?"

"I don't know, but the damage is done. The petition is making the publisher nervous. They've had to pull several books in the past couple years. It just happened with an infamous child molester."

Fury overwhelmed her. "I'm not a child molester! In case the publisher has forgotten, I'm the woman who testified at fifteen against Gene Hayes, and he was convicted. He's the child rapist. I'm not the criminal."

"I know. This is a tricky situation. The publisher thinks maybe you should distance yourself a little from Justice and the band. You're suddenly back with him, and it's comes across as, well, convenient timing."

Liza stalked to the windows overlooking the city, while her mind raced.

Natasha continued. "There's so many rumors swirling, like that you threatened to sue World Rock Stage to get Savaged Illusions this chance, and now suddenly, after Nikki's book comes out supporting what Gene Hayes has been saying, the optics are a little damaging. The band's being labeled Savaged Cheaters, and you..."

When her agent trailed off, Liza filled in, "A baby killer."

Silence spread like a slow wince before her agent said, "Savaged Illusions is out of the country now, anyway. Your *Chatterbox* interview, while I personally thought it was awesome, some people are calling it contrived. Distasteful. A few people have even said it's in bad taste to show a picture of your baby. If you pull back, do something a bit more respectful, like start a charity in your daughter's name, then the publisher will be able to keep supporting your book."

There was a lot of twisted crap in there, but she honed in on, "They're actually telling me to not see my husband?"

"Liza, the book is about a girl who gets involved with a band. It's common knowledge that you and Justice were estranged because you refused to go back to him. He publicly begged you. You went back only when it appeared to benefit you."

"Choose between the book I ripped off chunks of my soul to write, or my marriage to the man who owns the very beat of my heart. Interesting dilemma, isn't it?" she mused while staring over the roofs of buildings to the ocean.

Justice had this same dilemma, choosing between love for her or the fame with his band. Except that Justice had had more pressure on him because dozens of people would have been financially ruined if he chose her.

All Liza would lose was her dream. Easy decision. "If that's how the publisher feels, pull the book."

"Liza, wait, don't get hasty here. You don't want to lose this deal. No one else is going to touch you while all this is going on. They just want to help you optimize your public image while reworking the book to smooth out some troublesome parts."

She fisted her fingers around her phone, the throb in her head ratcheting up to a gong. "Which troublesome parts?"

"The threesome."

Liza could actually feel her heart beating in her temples, *thump, thump, thump.* "No. I won't choose the publisher over my husband. No, I won't invent a fake charity for my daughter when her father and I honor her with every breath we take and every choice we make. No, I won't change the threesome because a lowlife opportunist hooked up with a fugitive rapist and wrote a book to target me. Tell the publisher to grow a backbone and look up the meaning of ethics, or I take my book and walk."

Liza cut the connection and slammed her hand on the table.

Nikki Poole and Gene Hayes should have stayed in their holes. Once they'd crawled out and threatened all that she loved?

She would—

The door to the conference room burst open, and Sloane loomed there. "Tess is hurt. Ambulance is taking her to the hospital."

Liza sat in the private waiting room, swallowing down another wave of thick nausea as John described what happened.

"Tess was on her way back to work from lunch when two of the protesters started hitting her car with their signs. One of them got the door open and yanked her out, and the other one hit her with their sign. I didn't see it, but our security did, and they got there quickly. Said she was covered in a lot of blood, was dazed, and her left wrist was swelling."

Don't throw up. Don't. Pull yourself together. Sloane sat so still next to her, she didn't know if he was breathing, but she could feel the heat of his pure, raw anger.

Liza was just as pissed and slammed with a brutal truth that she was putting people she deeply cared about at risk. Tess getting hurt made her want to vomit and cry at the same time, but she had to focus first on Tess. She had to be okay, she had two—"Oh, her kids! Are they at school?"

"Sherry's getting them from school." John sat on the other side of Liza. "She's going to tell them what happened and take them to our house. We'll bring them later to see her. Fuck. Sorry, but fuck. Not Tess, damn it."

Liza squeezed her eyes shut. "She'll recover. A week or two of rest, and she'll be back at her desk, running our lives."

Two men walked into the waiting room, both wearing scrubs. Liza recognized one of them and surged up. "Ben!"

"Hey, Em called me." He slung an arm around her shoulder and squeezed gently. "I tracked down our ER doctor. This is Dr. Newsom, and he's excellent. He agreed to let me come in here with him to talk to you. I've seen Tess, she's okay, that's the first thing. Now Dr. Newsom can tell you more."

The older man with the dark, gray-streaked hair pulled up a chair to face them. "She's a little banged up. She has a mild concussion, some cuts and bruises, left wrist is sprained but not fractured. I stitched a cut here." He touched the lower left side of his back. "We also x-rayed her ribs, no fractures, but she's pretty bruised and will be very sore. She can go home, but she requires someone to stay with her while she rests for a few days. She's insisting she can go home, and her kids will give her a hand, but—"

"She'll stay with me," Sloane announced. "I'll send someone by her house to pick up anything she needs, but she's going home with me."

The doctor cracked a grin. "You must be Sloane Michaels, as she said you'd say that." He shifted his gaze to Liza. "And you're Mrs. Cade. I recognize you. Tess said you're to stop blaming yourself or she'd hide the coffee and chocolate in the office kitchen."

Ben chuckled next to her. "Told you, she's going to be okay."

Relief sagged Liza. "We appreciate you taking care of Tess, Dr. Newsom." She looked up at Emily's boyfriend. "Thanks, Ben."

"Glad I could help."

The doctors left.

"Tess and her kids will stay with us until she feels better and things have calmed down," Sloane reiterated.

Now that she knew Tess would be okay, Liza tackled the reason this happened. "Things aren't going to calm down as long as I'm still working there." Liza walked to stand in front of Sloane and John. "I'm giving you my resignation, effective immediately. Before you argue, this isn't about guilt, it's about the safety of people I care about, and you don't get to put them at risk either. We'll make a public announcement that I've resigned. Behind the scenes, I'll continue to work remotely, if you're comfortable with that, and be available to answer questions as well."

Sloane ground his jaw.

Liza added, "It's the right thing to do, and the only thing."

He nodded once. "We'll work out a consulting agreement for the remote work and revisit this if things change and you want to come back."

She'd known he wouldn't like it but that he'd agree. Sloane cared too much about his employees.

"I suggest you consider making Sophie Acting Communications Director." That stung. She'd been enormously proud of that title, but she'd been dead honest about her motivations. No, she hadn't directly caused Tess's attack, but she was the reason the horrible protestors had been there.

The bigger blame? That lay right at the feet of Gene Hayes and Nikki Poole.

Chapter 24

THE LAST WEEK WAS A blur as Justice hit Russia, and now they were in China. Japan was next before a trip home. It'd been nonstop travel, singing, interviews, fans...and the endless shitstorm from Hayes and Jagged Sin with their insanely popular pop-up concerts that had become a reality show viewers couldn't get enough of.

Law enforcement around the world tried to nab Hayes, but fans created human shields and roadblocks. "Witch Hunt" was flirting with number ten on the charts.

Justice and his band were on fire as they fought to hold on to their lead, but he blocked all that out as the hot lights poured over him and the music pounded the final song of the concert. He powered into "Savaged Vows," right through to the soul-ripping death scream.

Thunderous applause and wild shrieking filled the venue as Justice and the guys said good night.

Dripping sweat as he left the stage, Justice hit the greenroom, with barely enough time to hydrate, down a handful of trail mix, change, and hit a meet-and-greet in the private suite. He chatted with fans, some who knew little English but loved their songs, and that made him summon more energy. Music crossed language and cultural barriers, and he fucking loved that.

They posed for pictures, signed autographs, even did a couple social media vlogs with influencers.

His phone buzzed a text from Wendy, lead singer of Fury Run. *"Witch Hunt" just cracked into the top ten. Shit's getting ugly. Some of our crew quit after being threatened. Watch your back, savages.*

How the hell was this happening? "Goddamn it."

His phone buzzed again, this time with a video call from Beth. He accepted it, and when her face appeared, he said, "Hey, can you hold a minute while I find a quiet place?"

"Sure."

He met Ethan's eyes over the heads of the others in the room.

The bodyguard strode to him. "Problem?"

"I need privacy to take a call."

Ethan quickly led him to a private bathroom. Once inside, Justice found a spot and sat. "Sorry, at a meet-and-greet. I can't wait to see you. Just, what, ten more days until I get a few days off?"

"Me too. You're coming home, right?"

"Yes." He noted the way she leaned toward the phone camera. "Everything all right?" He listened in frustrated fury as she summed up her publisher getting squirrelly and her decision to pull the book if the publisher didn't get their head out of their asses, then Tess being attacked and Beth turning in her notice. "Shit, Beth. I'm sorry. Tess is okay?"

"Yes, or she will be once she heals. She and her kids are at Sloane's."

"Where are you?"

"I'm with your dad in his room at the veteran's center." She paused, then said, "We need to stop Nikki, and your dad, my mom and I, along with Em's input, have come up with a plan."

He leaned his head back against the wall. Outside the door he heard Ethan telling someone the bathroom was occupied. As hard as things were on the road, Beth didn't have all these people taking care of her like he did.

He wanted to be there supporting and helping his wife. It hurt to be apart from her. "What idea?"

"Nikki's appearing on the *Court of Rock* finale in a week and a half. She's going to introduce a video performance of Jagged Sin and Hayes singing 'Witch Hunt,' as Jagged Sin's former intern, giving her a chance to mention her bestselling book."

Those last words were coated in bitterness. Justice grimaced. "Shit, I knew *Court of Rock* was showing the Jagged Sin and Hayes video, which is why we refused to appear, and so did Fury Run. I didn't know Nikki was getting her moment of glory." That really pissed him off.

"Any chance you'd reconsider performing there to help me push her into making a mistake?"

The hairs on the back of his neck sizzled. His first worry was always about Beth's safety. "How?"

"So, Nikki believes this will be her triumphant return to *Court of Rock*, not as some little intern, but as a bestselling author, right?"

"With you so far."

"Then we show her up. I introduce you as the surprise guest star band to close the show in a live performance, overshadowing her little taped one of Jagged Sin with Hayes. You can sing "Reaper's Child" to me again like you did on *Chatterbox*. It'll make her crazy that we upstage her big moment."

"That'll piss her off."

"Exactly, and it's the first time she'll see me in person since we left for Paris. It will throw her. Up till now, she's had the most control by springing her book on us, and obviously having a strategy worked out. We're going to throw her off her game."

Justice got it. "Like when Em and Ben confronted her the night we lost Savanna. She even called Hayes and found out where he was staying."

"She hadn't foreseen me losing Savanna, and that shocked and scared her, and she'd cracked. I can get her to cave again, and say something stupid. That will ruin her credibility, and hopefully show the world that she and Hayes are lying. I need you and your band's help to do it."

He understood the problem immediately. "You need me to make sure the suits on *Court of Rock* don't double-cross you and tell Nikki, allowing her to be prepared or pull out so she doesn't play second fiddle to you." It was devious and a great way to turn the tables on her after all she'd done to Beth.

"I need you, period. Yeah, if you could agree to appear as a surprise guest in exchange for letting me do what I want to, it would help."

"You'll be safer with all our security in case word leaks out," Justice added, thinking quickly. He could get the guys to agree, especially if Beth could pull this off. But it could go really bad and make Beth look worse too.

"Justice?"

The uncertainty in her voice tugged at him. "Okay. I'll talk to Gavin and the guys, and if it's possible, we'll do it."

"Thanks! I know it's a lot to ask, and I'm grateful."

"Grateful enough to come on the next leg of the tour with me? Costa Rica, Brazil, some of the islands like Barbados? That section of the tour is about a month."

She hesitated. "Maybe for part of it? I'll have to see how it goes. I'm helping Sophie behind the scenes, and there's my mom..."

"I'll be fine!" Amber shouted somewhere nearby Beth. "Go. God, I don't need a babysitter."

"Mom, don't start." Beth's voice brimmed with long-suffering patience. "I'm just watching out for you."

"Like a prison guard. Help, I'm under house arrest!"

Justice couldn't stop his laughter. Beth and her mom had been play bickering more and more.

"Not funny, Rooster. Yesterday, she was in the Jacuzzi and flashed some old man her boobs, who then called the cops insisting a naked woman was running around the pool."

"It was a wardrobe malfunction!" Amber insisted.

"You did it on purpose!" Beth yelled.

"Did not, but maybe he shouldn't have called me too old to wear a bikini."

Justice doubled over, striving like hell not to laugh out loud, but it was like being trapped underwater and trying not to breathe. His lungs burst with chuckles and, swear to God, he had to wipe tears from his eyes. Finally he managed to choke out, "What happened?"

"Two teenaged girls told the cops my mom hadn't meant to do it, and the old man was mean. Always walking by and making snide or creepy comments to all the young girls at the pool. Cops told the old guy to stay away from the pool and my mom to keep her clothes on. Then my mom and the girls ended up back here at the condo, eating cookie dough and laughing.

I was terrified what their parents might think of them hanging out with her."

"And?" Justice hadn't had this much fun in days. He wasn't worried, Amber had made a lot of new friends in the condo complex. People liked her there.

"Turns out they think their girls are safe with her, since she killed a man to rescue her own teenaged daughter."

He heard a rusty but familiar sound in the background of Beth's call. It took a second, then recognition hit. His dad's laughter. Noah'd heard this fight too.

Beth's dramatically pained sigh damn near set Justice off into another round of laughter. It wouldn't be funny if these spats upset Beth, but she laughed about them, admitting she was overprotective. At the same time, Beth was happy to see her mom hadn't been broken by prison. They both thrived on the squabbling. "So..." he drawled out. "Is it all you dreamed, having your mom back?"

"Keep laughing, Rock Star. I have video of you snoring, and I'm not afraid to use it."

Yeah, there was no heat in her threat. "Promise me you'll come with me on the next leg of the tour, even if you can only do part of the time, and I'll stop." At least until he hung up.

"A chance to escape the ex-con streaker trying to make me insane? Deal! Besides, I hear Costa Rica is beautiful. Can we swim with the turtles?"

"That's smokin'-hot streaker to you," Amber corrected.

Beth's nose crinkled in mock disgust. "Gross." Her eyes gleamed with amusement. "After a week or so of working from home with that crazy woman, I'll need a vacation. Dealing with rock stars will be more relaxing than running a reform school out of my condo."

His smile nearly cracked his face. "I'm planning a few days in San Diego after *Court of Rock*. Can you handle that? I can get us a suite at Opulence, and maybe we can look at some of the houses we've seen online."

She opened her mouth, then turned away as if listening to someone else. Before Justice could asked who, Beth handed off her phone.

His dad's face appeared.

Justice's mouth dried, and it took him a second to find any words. "Dad, you doing okay?"

"Yes." His gaze dropped.

Justice frowned, until his dad sat and Radar jumped into view with his mangled ear. The dog laid his head on Noah's shoulder.

"I'm in therapy," Noah announced. "Radar goes with me. I'm staying here at the center."

Stunned, Justice stumbled out, "That's great, Dad." His dad's counselor had predicted this, but Justice hadn't really believed...until now.

"House is empty. You can stay there." The picture of his dad blurred, and Beth came into view, then she moved outside to the small patio. He heard the door slide closed. She smiled into the phone. "He wanted to tell you himself."

Justice tried to speak, but all that came out was a croak.

"You okay?"

"Yeah, but...damn." His dad had even looked directly into the camera eye for a couple seconds.

She upped the wattage on that beautiful grin. "Your dad is working hard. He's even in a small group that trains their dogs together as PTSD emotional support animals. My mom helps with it."

Radar had changed his dad's life, but before he

could say anything, Beth went on. "Do you want to stay at the house? Is it secure enough? With me there too?"

He studied her face, and, God, he missed her. "Dad offered the house. I wouldn't pass this up."

"Perfect."

He shifted the subject back to her. "How are you really? You had a pretty shitty day."

"I'm off balance. Scared. Hurt. Pissed. Really pissed." Hot color flooded her face. "Who the hell is Nikki Poole to start an online petition to get my publisher to drop me? After she hid her book so I couldn't stop her. Who am I hurting with my book? No one! I wrote a damn good book, and that lowlife, double-crossing Judas is trying to take it from me." She sucked in more air. "It's not a porn! I don't write porn. Nor did I just throw a baby in there. Nikki is making me so mad, and you know what?"

"What?"

"She thinks she's smarter than me. I'm going to make her choke on that belief and show the whole world. I'm tired of this bullshit. I'll get her to reveal her connection to Hayes and whatever game she's playing now."

His grin spread so far, it made his cheeks ache. "There's my badass."

"Damn right. I'm fighting for us. We're going to destroy her, and Hayes won't be long behind her."

He'd wanted Beth to fight, and look at her now.

Jet lag was kicking Justice's ass with a headache, muscle fatigue, and a scratchy throat. He'd arrived in L.A. from Japan last night. They'd packed more concerts and appearances into their tight schedule through Russia, China, and Japan to combat Jagged

Sin and Hayes, which had strained his vocal cords.

Despite being with Beth, he'd spent the day mostly sleeping and downing the Throat Coat tea, while reassuring his wife he'd be fine. This wasn't his first dance with jet lag and exhaustion. Hell, the whole band and crew were wiped.

Now he, his band, and Gavin were all piled in the VIP greenroom of *Court of Rock* watching the show on the monitors.

The door opened, spilling in Beth and Emily, who'd arrived tonight to support her best friend. Ethan stood by silently doing his job as Beth's bodyguard for this trip since Beth left Whitney in San Diego to protect Amber and his dad.

Justice smiled at the sight of his gorgeous wife fresh from hair and makeup. She glowed, ready for battle in a shirt that dipped off one shoulder, skintight distressed jeans, and a pair of killer heels.

"You look like shit." Emily stood over him, studying his face.

He dragged his gaze to the annoying woman. "I didn't ask your—" A sudden spasm gripped his chest, and he coughed. Hard. Fuck, that wasn't good.

"And sound like a duck in a food processor," Em added.

Beth's soft, cool hand landed on his forehead. "Justice! You're running a fever."

Shit, shit, shit. "Dehydration probably." Or not. His head throbbed like a bitch. How long until he went on? Thirty minutes? He squinted at the clock, but doing the math was beyond him.

"What's wrong?"

Great, now his manager hovered over him.

"Nothing, just need Tylenol and—" His lungs tried to escape through his mouth on another coughing fit.

"Get cough syrup and Tylenol. ASAP."

Forcing his heavy eyelids open, he wondered how the hell Gavin had produced his cell phone and made a call that fast. And who was he talking to?

Beth leaned over him, her glasses magnifying the dangerous glint in her stare. "Why didn't you tell me you were sick?"

Hell, she was really pissed and worried. "Denial," he admitted. "Kept telling myself it was jet lag. Sorry, I'll perform. Just need—"

The door burst open again, and a show assistant rushed in. Liza whirled around, took the bag from her, and started issuing requests. "Water, please." She poured out two extra strength Tylenol. "Take these."

He obeyed.

"And this." She held out some syrup in a dosing cup.

He swallowed it.

"Drink." She handed him an open bottle of water. "We'll get a doctor. I don't think you should go on like this. Gavin, you'd better cancel."

That snapped him out of the fog. "No. If we pull out, and the suits won't let you have your moment." She wanted this, badly. Needed it. He started to add more, but his lungs twisted into pretzels in a bout of coughing.

"You could try lip-syncing," Gavin suggested.

"No," Simon snapped. "Fans are too sharp for that, plus someone here would rat us out. We'd be crucified. A stunt like that could tank 'Reaper's Child' off the top ten or even the top one hundred."

"He's right," Lynx agreed.

Justice took Beth's hand, but before he could answer, Em cut in.

"Nikki's on."

The all shifted their attention to the monitors.

Nikki walked out on the stage in a one-piece pantsuit and lethal-spiked heels. She waved and beamed. "Thank you! For those who may not know me, I'm Nikki Poole, the bestselling author of *Friends to Enemies*..."

They listened as she reeled off her spiel, including a story about meeting Liza here, and how Nikki had tried to help Liza before Liza turned on her. A total bullshit sob story about Nikki rising from the ruin laid at her feet by Liza.

When the segment ended, Em snorted in disgust. "This is supposed to be her big moment and half her lines were about Liza."

"Which is exactly why I'm not saying a word about her when I go on," Beth said. "Once the shock of seeing me dims, she'll realize that I don't consider her or her book worth mentioning."

Em nudged Beth with her elbow. "Subtle but evil. I like it."

His wife smiled, but her joy dulled to worry as she turned to him. "It doesn't have to be tonight. We can set her up another time if you're too sick to sing. Your health is more important."

She meant it, and her love pushed him to fight through. This was too important to Beth for him to back out because of a scratchy throat and cough. "It's just one song to close the show. Cakewalk."

He hoped.

Chapter 25

LIZA WALKED OUT ONTO THE stage, ignoring her image on the huge jumbo screen. A beat or two of silence accompanied her, then the murmurs rose like a wave.

"That's Liza Cade! Justice's wife!"

"Is Savaged Illusions the surprise guest?"

Excited applause mixed with a few nasty shouts as recognition of Liza spread.

"Baby killer! Lyin' Liza!" One person yelled.

"End the witch hunt!" Another screamed.

Focus and ignore the haters. It felt like a thousand spotlights burned through her skin, leaving her raw and exposed, but she kept walking until she reached the first of two mic stands set up for Justice and Simon. River's bass, Gray's piano, and Lynx's drums were set up behind her.

Once she stopped, she waved to the crowd. "Thank you!" She couldn't see much past all the stage lights, but she could hear the clapping and feel the support of the majority. "I'm Liza Cade and I'm honored to be here tonight! I have the privilege of introducing the surprise guest rock star band. Before I do that, I'd like to give a huge shoutout to *Court of Rock* for giving a young, ambitious and perpetually scared college girl a chance to intern on this show." She smiled and added in a conspiratorial tone, "That college girl was me, in case you're wondering."

A few laughed at her weak joke.

Liza relaxed a bit. "I'd like to wish luck and a future brimming with success to the two bands competing tonight for the big win."

More clapping rose, along with anticipated whispers.

"It's time to welcome a spectacularly talented group of friends—and one who happens to be my husband—to the stage. They are one of the greatest rock bands in the world with two songs on the top ten charts. Ladies and gentlemen, the guest stars of the night, Savaged Illusions!"

Shocked gasps dissolved into wild clapping and screams of excitement.

Gray ran out first, hugged her, and sat at his piano. Lynx slapped her a high-five before dropping behind his drum kit. River swooped her up and twirled her, making her laugh. Simon leaned in, kissed her cheek, grabbed his guitar, and slid into the strap.

"Justice! Justice!" the crowd thumped in time, demanding the frontman.

Justice strode out to screams and cheers. When he reached her, he leaned down for a soft kiss.

Shrieks resounded with more clapping. The energy ramped up. Justice took her hand while he faced the crowd and shouted over the shrieks, "Surprise, Los Angeles! We had to fly more than fourteen hours from Japan to get here, but you all made the trip worth it!" He turned, coughed slightly, and grabbed the water in the holder of his mic stand.

"Because we love L.A.!" Lynx shouted in agreement, covering for Justice.

"Hell yeah!" River added.

The crowd was still on their feet, clapping and whistling, but finally quieted.

Justice cleared his throat. "We want to sing a special song for you now, 'Reaper's Child.'"

More applause and yells.

Justice grinned. "To do this right, I need Beth to stay here with me. She's trying to slip off the stage, but this is her song."

She stiffened in surprise since the plan had been for him to sing to her onstage, so why was he—

"Can you all help me convince her to stay?" Justice asked.

Simon added, "Stay, Liza, stay!"

Lynx tapped a beat on his drums, and the audience joined in. "Stay, Liza, stay! Stay, Liza, stay!"

Oh, she got it. They were getting the audience involved. She glared at Justice for not warning her, and noticed his glassy eyes and slight sway. Damn, he was getting sicker, so sick he probably forgot to tell her. Squeezing his hand, she leaned into the mic. "I'm convinced. I'll stay."

The lights dimmed, and a spotlight snapped on Gray as he put his fingers to the keys. The haunting opening strains of the song began.

Justice pulled his mic off the stand, and his light snapped on, flooding them both in the circle of illumination.

She held her breath, both in anticipation for the song she loved and worry that he wouldn't make it through.

The words flowed out, his voice rougher than usual but somehow more beautiful.

Justice sang past the tickle in his throat and the building pressure in his lungs. The lights were too damned hot, making his head ache, and sweat began trickling down his back. Didn't matter, not when he looked into Beth's eyes. He would not fail her now. He used the music to tell the story of the fight with the reaper to yank back their child from death's hands. His love and passion for Savanna drove him to match his voice to the power of Gray's piano, all the way to the chorus, when the lights snapped on as Simon's guitar, River's bass, Lynx drums, and their voices helped mute his coughs and cover his vocal fumble.

The chorus ended, and he raised his hand to launch into the second verse, but the first word croaked like a frog. He tried to push into the next sound, but coughed. *Fuck, no. Sing, damn it.* The heat of flaming panic burned his skin when cool fingers wrapped around his, clamping the mic.

Beth leaned in, parted her lips, and sang the first line, her voice crackly and hesitant. He laid his hand over her death grip on the mic. Her shoulders rose as she hit the second line, and her chest opened up.

His wife who'd never had the dream of music, and once feared the spotlight, had stepped up to sing the second stanza to save his ass. Unbearable emotion welled up and filled his throat, but he couldn't tear his stare away even if the entire audience stripped naked and danced. In this moment, he could see traces of the girl she'd been when she and her mom danced around the house singing into hairbrushes. The more dominant part of her now was this grownup, strong, courageous woman who refused to silence her voice.

Even when it meant singing. Her pitch wasn't perfect, but her emotion was so damned real, he shivered as her voice climbed with the struggle and fear of fighting the enemy to save her child.

When she hit the chorus, Justice leaned into the mic, singing it with her. Everything else melted away but this moment on stage with Beth.

A magic fell over them, releasing more adrenaline into his bloodstream. At the third stanza, he couldn't hold back and merged his singing with Beth's as they soared into the final battle...only to fall into defeat as the reaper won.

Their child was lost.

The lights blinked off as the music faded away into one beat of emotional pause, then exploded into thunderous applause, every single person surging to their feet.

Justice's head screamed, chest burned, and his vision narrowed to one woman and a single thought.

He hadn't been able to sing, but Beth had carried them both. Just like he'd held on to her book for her, she'd held on to his song.

Liza walked off the stage holding Justice's hand torn between exhilaration and deep worry for her husband. His skin was hot, his face pale and sweaty. She spotted Gavin and Em waiting for them.

Em hugged her. "You were freaking awesome!"

"Thanks. That was crazy, but Justice is really sick, we need to get him to the hotel." She turned to Gavin. "Can you get a doctor to meet us?"

The manager pulled out his phone. "I know a few, hang on."

"I don't need a doc—" He broke off in a bone-rattling cough.

Liza rubbed his back, feeling so damned helpless.

When the spasms ended, he leaned against the wall. "Fuck."

Liza laid her hand on his cheek. "You're letting the doctor examine you. Don't argue."

"I'll agree if you and the guys go do the press thing. You need to follow through on your plan."

"He's right," Simon held up his phone. "It's all over social media about you singing with us. Thousands of comments, some loving, some raging, but you're the trending topic already and it's only been a couple minutes since we finished."

River touched her arm. "Your performance is going to make Nikki even more insane. You didn't just steal her thunder, you owned it and captured all the attention from her in the studio and on social media."

"Frank just came by." Em opened a bottle of water and handed it to Liza. "He took champagne to Nikki's dressing room, and she's furious. Said she downed a glass and a half while watching you guys on the monitor."

The producer had been instrumental in their whole plan, and the champagne was part of it. Nikki never could resist the high end bubbly. One thing Liza knew from growing up around her mom's drunken benders, alcohol fueled stupid mistakes and embarrassing revelations.

"Frank's expecting all of you in the media room," Gavin said. "But with the twist of Liza jumping in to help Justice sing because he's sick, it'll be okay if he doesn't go."

They'd convinced her. Liza faced her husband. "We'll do the backstage press junket if you get your butt to the greenroom and rest. You can watch from the monitors in there."

Justice nodded, and walked off with security, while they headed to the media room.

Court of Rock logos spread along the wall of the photo and interview area. Nikki was posing with the winning band, when Liza, Simon, Gray, Lynx and River walked in.

Everyone turned to them, and voices rose.

"Liza! Can we get a picture?"

"Simon, how does the band feel about Liza singing?"

They were herded over the wall, and Nikki ushered away. Nikki argued with security. "I'm a guest! A bestselling author! You can't push me out."

They piloted her toward the door, but couldn't get her to leave.

Liza heard the tinge of alcohol fueled belligerence in Nikki's rantings, but she refused to acknowledge her. Instead, Liza focused on posing with the winning band, then they graciously stepped away and cameras flashed to capture images and videos of her and the four members of Savaged Illusion. Reporters fired questions.

"Where's Justice?"

"He's resting in the greenroom. He must have picked up a bug and doesn't want to spread it around. But he should be fine in a day or two." Liza injected confidence into her voice, and hoped that was true.

"How did it feel to sing with the band? Do you want to be a singer?"

"Terrifying! I'm still shaking." She held her hands up, letting them tremble. "No, I don't want to be a singer, but I could feel Justice's frustration. He flew all the way here from Japan, getting in late last night because the fans of *Court of Rock* are important to him.

Many of them have supported Savaged Illusions through all their highs and lows, and Justice very much wanted to be here tonight to give a surprise thank you performance. It would have devastated him to let them down on stage, so I..." she shrugged sheepishly, "...jumped in to help."

"What about you guys?" Another reporter directed his question to River, Simon, Gray and Lynx. "How do you feel about her jumping in?"

"She saved our butts," Lynx said.

"And was cute doing it," River added.

Simon shifted next to her. "When she croaked out the first few words, I cringed, and was ready to take over the vocals."

Why hadn't she thought of that? Simon had a good voice and could have done it. Wait, was he annoyed at her?

Simon put an arm around her shoulder in reassurance. "Then she really sang. Not great, not like I would have."

Laughter filled the room, and Liza said, "Rock star egos, am I right?"

Simon grinned with a rare boyishness, then sobered. "Liza put her heart and soul into the song, and that beauty and passion shined through and more than compensated for any vocal mistakes. Liza and Justice sang that song with an authentic and fierce passion that resonated with the audience and with me. By the end, I was Liza's fan and proud to be a part of that special moment in Savaged Illusions and *Court of Rock*'s history."

Tears burned her eyes and she didn't care who saw them. "Thank you."

He didn't say anything, but Liza didn't need words to feel his acceptance and friendship. Tonight could have gone either way, Justice's bandmates could have been pissed that she'd overstepped by singing. Instead, they chose to support her panicked decision. She was Justice's wife, doing what she'd though the right thing in the moment.

Another reporter called out, "Why did you and Justice keep your appearance tonight a secret?"

Liza sobered. She was aware of Nikki by the door where security kept her but didn't show an interest in her direction. "My safety."

"From Nikki Poole?" the reporter prodded.

"That's a lie!" Nikki shouted. "I'm the one who's in danger from you. You ruined my life."

For the first time, Liza looked directly at her. "No, you did that when you chose to become a Judas friend for whatever coin Gene Hayes paid you. When that ran out, you wrote a book of lies about me. I don't care about your life, I'm too busy living mine, spending my time and energy on the people and projects I love. You just don't matter anymore."

Frank, the red-faced producer, rushed into the room with more security on his heels. All the cameras swung around to follow him. Anticipation crackled.

"Nikki, come with us, please." Frank tried to sooth her. "You can do more interviews later. Liza and Savaged Illusions have this time." He reached for her arm.

"What?" Nikki's face splotched and she jerked her arm away. "I'm supposed to be the guest star. Me. Not her."

"Nikki." Frank held his palm's up. "Or course you're a valued guest star. Didn't we send that bottle of premium champagne to your dressing room as a thank you? We had to guarantee Liza's security to get the live performance of Savaged Illusions. You understand she's more high-profile than you."

Nikki jerked her head back. "Do you know how hard I worked? What I had to do to get here? Liza had fame and all the attention she wanted, she's married to a freaking rock star. She did nothing for me, nothing. Got her other friend a cushy job at a luxury hotel while I had to work at a crappy adult diaper place and live in a hovel that stank." Her chin shot up as she glared at Liza. "So I made my own opportunities."

A ripple of shock sizzled over Liza's skin, making the hair on her arms stand up. *Hold it together. Egg her on.* "By selling me out to Hayes?"

"I wouldn't have been forced to do that if you'd helped me!"

The words hung there for a second before Nikki's eyes widened and she stepped back. Her arms came up as if fending off a blow. Her gaze darted around at all the cameras and faces locked onto her. "I mean that I wouldn't have been forced to sell my shoes, the designer shoes by father gave me. Not—"

"Is it true, Nikki? Did you sell Liza Cade out to Gene Hayes?" a reporter shouted.

"How did he pay you?" Another asked.

A wave of raw anger tinged with a streak of sadness filled Liza. Once, she'd truly believed Nikki was both her and Em's friend. They'd done things together, hung out, and she'd been fun. She and Em had seen her desperate needy side, but didn't everyone have faults?

Gray put his arm around Liza, while the other three closed in a protective circle that touched her heart.

"Liza!" Someone shouted. "Do you feel vindicated now that Nikki has admitted—"

"I didn't admit it! You're twisting my words!" Nikki shouted over the reporter.

Liza was finished with Nikki and settled her

attention on the man who'd asked the question. "I knew it was true, Gene Hayes told me himself, and Nikki had already confessed to my friend, Emily. It's just sad that people do things like that for money and attention."

With that, they finished up and left.

In the greenroom, Justice tugged her down into the chair with him, and held her. "I saw it on the monitors. You got the truth out there, Beth."

She pressed her face into his too hot chest, and let his love soothe the ache. Then she pulled herself together and rose. "Come on. We're getting you to the hotel, and into bed. Nikki's not important. You are, and all your bandmates who stood with me out there. And our friends." She took his hand. "But most of all, you."

Liza woke to an empty bed. She'd slept so hard it took her a second to remember she was in Justice's house in San Diego. What time was it? She rolled over and startled. After nine! Well, she'd been taking care of Justice for days after the *Court of Rock* show. Justice hadn't woken her coughing once last night.

Scooping up her glasses and phone, she glanced at her email to see if there was anything dire. Sophie was definitely rising to the challenge of Acting Director of Communications, but she called, texted or emailed when she needed help. Nope, nothing from her.

Her phone vibrated in her hand, and Liza's eyebrows shot up at the screen. Tantor Media? They were a sponsor for *Court of Rock*, and one of the biggest record labels. Fury Run was on their label.

Curious, she answered. "This is Liza."

"Liza, this is Jane from Tantor Media Foundation

of Hope department. I'm calling to inform you that you've been chosen to receive our Woman of the Year Award. If you accept, we'd like to arrange a gala dinner, where you'll be asked to give a speech and choose which charities you wish our donation to go to."

Stunned, she nearly pulled the phone from her ear to look at the caller ID again. She knew about the record label's charitable side, and their Woman of the Year Award. It was prestigious, but usually given to those in artistic fields making a difference in their communities or the world. "Me?"

"You," the woman said cheerfully. "You're using your position in the public eye to speak out against injustice. We really feel that you should be recognized, and ask that you talk about the heroes in your life who have motivated you to be a hero.

"A hero? I'm not." A hero was someone like Noah. Or Drake, the man who had changed so many boys' lives, including Justice's. Or her mom. Not her. "I'm flattered and grateful, truly, I'm just not sure I deserve this award."

"Speaking out against silence, against child rape, and against bullying. That's a hero. We're also aware that you started the SLAM Heroes program in San Diego, and many of those recipients, as well as your colleagues, have spoken highly of you. We hope you'll accept this award. It comes with a fifty-thousand-dollar donation to the charity or charities of your choice."

Liza sat up. Fifty thousand? She might be unsure of her worthiness, but she wasn't about to turn that down. "Thank you, I'm honored and will happily accept." She'd give a speech if it meant the charities she cared about would get donations.

"That's wonderful, Liza. I'll email you the information. You have a great day."

Liza lowered the phone, her mind spinning. That was...wow. Getting out of bed, she went to find Justice. She walked down the hallway and then stopped.

Justice lounged in the rocker in Savanna's room. He had coffee in one hand and his phone in the other, scrolling down. His finger froze. "No way."

"What?"

He lifted his head, and a slow smile spread over his face. "Nikki's father released a statement. *My wife and I are deeply disappointed with the path my daughter, Nikki Poole, has chosen. I never gave her designer shoes, and in fact, during the time she knew Liza Cade, we were estranged. She came to live with us after Liza lost her baby, and swore she had nothing to do with Gene Hayes. I wanted to believe my daughter despite her history of lying to me. We had no idea she was going to publish this book. That was our first shock.*

The second was seeing her admit on video that she had in fact sold out Liza Cade to the man who had raped her.

Words cannot express our regret. We send our deepest condolences to Justice and Liza Cade. This is our only statement.

He lifted his head. "You did it, Beth. You've exposed her."

"We did."

He set his cup on the side table. "Yeah, and it's not looking good for Jagged Sin and Hayes. While we sent 'Reaper's Child' to number one and 'Savaged Vows' is at three, 'Witch Hunt' has dropped all the way to midseventies and is still falling. Gavin said three venues he knows of have cancelled Jagged Sin's concerts and refunded tickets. The press and social media are hammering the *Gene Hayes and Nikki Poole Conspired to Destroy Liza Cade* story."

"In just a few days since the show." She walked to him, and Justice opened his arms. Liza settled on his lap.

"Yep. What do you want to bet her publisher pulls the book?"

"Sucker bet, not taking that one." This day just kept getting better and better, and it wasn't even ten a.m. She still had her conference meeting with the publisher and her agent, but Liza expected that to go well. She studied him. His color was good, and he hadn't had a fever since the night of the concert. His achiness and coughing had been steadily improving. "How are you feeling?"

"Good." He ran a hand over her unruly hair and wrapped a lock around his finger. "You feel okay? Not getting sick? You're a little flushed, like you just came in from a workout or something."

"I feel great. Slept like a rock." Unable to keep quiet any longer, she said, "Then I got a call from Tantor Media."

He tilted his head. "Well that's unexpected. What did they want?"

"To give me their Woman of the Year Award. Can you believe it?" She blurted the rest out, her excitement growing as she talked.

Justice beamed. "That's fucking awesome, Beth. Get the date, and I'll be there to escort you on stage. No way am I missing your big moment. You deserve to be recognized, and I'm so damned proud of you."

"Pretty good morning, huh? Nikki's ruined, I get an award, and best of all, we're home for a little longer." They'd delayed leaving for Costa Rica a couple days to let Justice fully recover from the respiratory virus. She settled against him. "I was surprised to find you in here."

He stroked her back. "I came in here a lot when I was home those first months. I liked to talk or sing to her. Like I would have sung her to sleep."

Liza snuggled closer. "You sang to her when I was pregnant. She would move around when she heard your voice."

"I remember."

The wistfulness in his tone matched her own heart. "She'd be a year and three months if she'd survived. Or if she'd been born on her due date, then a little over a year. Toddling around, babbling, getting into things." She lifted her head and smiled. "Twisting her daddy around her finger."

"Like her mom?"

"Me? You're the one who got sick to get me to sing on stage!"

He laughed. "Yeah, that was my evil plan. Let my wife show me up and steal all my glory."

"Please, Simon and the internet have gleefully pointed out that my voice shook in the beginning, and I sang off-key at a few points. Like I could worry about singing on-key when I was busy trying to save your career? And possibly your life since you had no business being on stage when you were so sick."

"Hmm, maybe you're right and I should be back in bed right now." Sliding his arms beneath her, he stood. "Naked for body heat, of course."

Liza wrapped her arms around his neck. "You think I'm going to let you get me naked when you didn't even defend my singing?" Liza marveled at how easily he strode down the hallway and into the bedroom while holding her. Clearly he was recovering well.

After laying her on the bed, he dropped his hands on either side of her face. "You sang with passion once you got past the first few words, stopped overthinking it, and embraced the music. True, you'll never sing like me, but it didn't matter. You didn't hold back and shared your heart with the world. I was so fucking proud, I somehow managed to finish that song as long as I was looking in your eyes. You're my song, Beth, and that night you showed the world why I will love you until forever."

She shivered at a flood of love for him, of trust. "We're a team." Always.

He lowered his head, melding his mouth to hers. Her heart swelled as he kissed and stroked her to a desperate need, then drove into her until she shattered into waves of please. All while safe in his arms.

Chapter 26

JUSTICE AND BETH SLIPPED AWAY from the house, and Hank drove them to the transitional center. It was a perfect San Diego day, in the upper seventies with lots of sunshine pouring over them accompanied by a breeze. Justice barely noticed as he leapt out of the car. "Hurry, I don't know how long he'll be out there."

She took his hand, and they started walking. "We're here on time. Relax."

"Can't. Dad actually invited me to watch him and Radar in the training group." He all but dragged her inside. After signing in, they rushed through the building toward the back.

"Do you think I need more exercise?"

Justice stopped. "What?"

"You're making me jog to keep up, so I assumed I need more exercise."

Well hell. He was keyed up and anxious not to screw this up. "Sorry, and for the record, I saw every inch of you this morning, and you're fucking perfect. You always were."

She smiled as they went out the doors and onto the covered patio with tables and chairs spread around.

To the right was a small playground for visiting kids. Straight ahead was an open field surrounded by a walking trail through some gardens, bordered with secured fencing and tall shrubs for privacy. The entire area had a security system to keep any intruders out.

Justice focused on the small group of people and dogs a few yards from the end of the patio. His dad stood among them. He wasn't the young, commanding Marine Justice remembered from his youth. Nor was he the ragged and defeated homeless man who had haunted him for over a decade. The long salt-and-pepper hair and ragged beard were trimmed, his thin shoulders prouder than the stooped and scarred man who'd lived in the shadows.

The bright sunshine showed the silvery web of burn scars on the left side of his cheek, temple and forearm. Noah had on a long-sleeved shirt pushed up to his elbows, camo pants, and black running shoes.

"Where's...?" Justice trailed off when he spotted Radar. He was in a down position in a row of six other dogs. Radar was the smallest of the dogs, but he held his head up proudly, good ear erect, and appeared to be staring at his dad as Noah walked with the other men around the dogs, while the instructor and Amber tossed a ball between them. Then Amber pulled a Frisbee out of the bag at her feet and sailed that right over the dog's heads.

Only one dog, the golden retriever, sat up, but a calm command from a youngish woman dropped the dog back to a down position.

The lean, dark-haired male instructor took something from Amber, walked up to the dogs, and snapped it open.

An umbrella.

Radar's ear twitched, and his nose moved, as if

trying to smell it, then he focused on Noah shuffling along with the group. Justice winced at his dad's limp. Walking in the thick grass had to be tough.

Amber tossed something else that clanged.

Noah froze, then whipped around, arms jerking up in front of him. His head swiveled.

Radar whined once, then broke command and trotted to Noah. He leaned into Noah's leg. His dad instantly dropped his hand to the dog's head and visibly relaxed.

No one else said a word until the instructor strolled at an easy pace, circling to get in front of Noah, then approached him. His voice was so low, Justice could only catch a few words and his dad's slow nod.

Noah spoke to Radar, gave him a treat, and the dog gulped it down while wagging his tail. His dad said something else, and Radar dropped down at his side.

Justice walked to the edge of the grass as the dogs went through more commands, some corrections, and more praise. Finally, they finished and headed to the patio.

It was all he could do to keep still as his dad slowly advanced. Beth's mom stayed behind, gathering supplies and putting them in the equipment bags.

When his dad got within a few feet, he stopped and Radar sat, although his tail thumped.

Noah released the dog, and he rushed to Beth. She dropped down, petting the dog and gushing over how smart he was, and the formerly proud dog rolled over on his back for belly rubs. "He loves Liza."

His dad's voice surprised him, but Justice kept his gaze fixed on Radar soaking up all the attention from Beth. "I see that." He gathered his courage and looked up at his dad. "I brought Radar a toy. Okay if I give it to him?"

Noah nodded.

Don't stare, move. He crouched next to Beth. "Hey, Radar."

The dog happily let Justice stroke his neck while Beth rubbed his belly. "Living the dream, aren't you, buddy?" He pulled out the soft stuffed toy from the pocket of his shorts and made it squeak.

Radar flipped over and sat up, good ear perked and front legs quivering. Justice couldn't stop the laugh that shot up his throat. He threw the toy. Radar shot after it, scooped it in his jaws, and squeaked in triumph. Trotting to Noah, he squeaked again.

"I see it," his dad said.

The dog ran to Justice, dropped it at his feet, and backed up, his big brown eyes full of anticipation.

How did anyone say no to that? Justice threw the toy. Radar darted after it. "His leg appears to have healed well."

"He never complains."

Neither did his dad. Noah never had, or at least Justice hadn't heard him if he had. Not even when he'd first come home after months in the hospital with burns and so many other injuries. He'd scream in his nightmares, and any sudden noise could throw him into a full-blown PTSD episode, but he never once said he was in pain.

Radar had zoomed back and dropped the toy, and when Justice didn't throw it quickly enough, Radar nosed the toy closer and danced impatiently.

Another laugh escaped him. "Yeah, yeah, I get it. Throw the damn toy." He tossed it again, and Radar ran in a joyful lope, so different than when he'd been working with Noah and the others a few minutes earlier.

When Justice looked back, Noah sat on a chair, and

Beth had filled a bowl of water, brought it over and set it on the ground, then headed back to a station set up with drinks.

"Radar, here," his dad called.

The dog turned his trot to head toward Noah, set the toy in his dad's lap, and sat.

"Get a drink and lay down."

Radar followed directions.

Beth returned, handing out bottles of water. Noah took his. "No chocolate shake?"

She dropped into the seat next to him. "Can't take Justice anywhere. Even the drive-through at McDonalds might start a riot."

Justice sat on the other side of Beth, and kept his dad in his peripheral vision.

Noah glanced at Beth. "I saw you on Court of Rock. I'm thinking you're as famous as Justice. The audience was screaming both your names."

Amber strode up. "My bossy controlling daughter was incredible on that show!"

Justice stood and hugged his mother-in-law. "Hey, Amber, good to see you." She had her hair in twin braids, and overall had a retro hippie rock vibe. These days, she volunteered at the center with her parole officer's approval.

"I'm not controlling," Beth responded to her mom's dig.

Amber leaned down, hugged her daughter, and flashed a grin at Justice. "I'm supposed to text her anytime I leave the house, even to get the mail. But she's not controlling."

"Have you forgotten the boiled egg incident?" Beth demanded.

Amber waved that off as she sat next to Noah. "I fell asleep by accident. Could have happened to anyone.

Besides, the smoke alarm woke me up. It's all good."

"Here's a thought, stop online shopping all night and go to sleep at a reasonable hour. Then you wouldn't be so tired and irresponsible in the days."

Amber turned to Justice. "She tried to insist I go to bed by eleven o'clock. Do you know how long I lived with lights out at a certain time? Now my daughter is trying to assume the role of prison guard."

Beth's smile turned wicked. "I prefer the term Warden. I was giving you structure as suggested by—"

Amber cut her off. "I'm paroled from your structure, Warden Bossy Pants."

A giggle burst through Beth's clamped lips. "She was so pissed at me last week, she told me to go to the infirmary to get the stick removed from my ass."

Justice busted up and the right side of his dad's face pulled up in amusement.

Amber sighed. "She told me to grow up. That was the best she could come up with. Sad. Good thing her characters fight with more creativity. Now, Molly can use words like a food processor on high speed. Obviously, Molly is based on me."

"Obviously," Beth said dryly. "Except she knows how to boil an egg without setting off the smoke alarm."

Justice asked his dad, "They like this all the time?"

"Half. Liza wins as much as she loses. Grow up is weak, though. Point to Amber on that."

Damn, what was that, nearly four sentences his dad had spoken to him? Noah'd kept his gaze averted, but he'd definitely answered him.

"It was on target," Beth muttered.

Justice snorted and took her hand. Interlacing his fingers with hers, he rubbed his thumb over the skin of her wrist.

She smiled at him.

"Did you see that Nikki's publisher announced they're pulling her book?" Amber asked. "After her dad released his statement, they appear done with her."

"About damned time." Noah turned to Beth. "What about your book?"

Justice flashed a proud grin. "Beth has news."

She rolled her eyes at him. "You want to tell them?"

"Yes."

She laughed. "Too bad, Rock Star. This is my news. I had a video conference with my agent, my editor, and the president of Mertz Publishing Group. They apologized, swear they'll support the book if I honor the contract, and will not try to take out the threesome or significantly change the story. They'll even go with the title Savaged Devotion, although they have suggested A Mother's Devotion."

"Are you happy with that?" Noah asked. "Seems like you could have gotten more. Maybe increased your advance or a bigger royalty."

Beth tilted her head. "You think so? Here all I asked for was a fifty-thousand-dollar donation to the charities of my choice to be added to the one Tantor Media is giving."

Noah's head jerked in surprise. "They agreed to that? Wait, Tantor Media is giving a donation in your name?"

"What's going on, Beth?" her mom demanded.

Justice couldn't hold back. "She's been selected as Tantor Media's Woman of the Year! They're doing a big gala in her honor in about six weeks. It's at a country club in Los Angeles and will be livestreamed."

Amber jumped up and hugged her. "That's my daughter." Pride rang in her voice.

"You stole my thunder," Beth accused him.

Justice took Beth's hand. "Would it help if I said sorry?"

"Are you?"

"Nope. Not a bit." He was too fucking proud to keep his mouth shut. "Bragging about you is a husband's privilege."

Sitting there in the sun with his wife, mother-in-law, dad and his dad's dog, Justice had it all, and that included bragging rights. Especially to the two people who loved her almost as much as he did.

Fame was fleeting, but love like this was forever.

Liza loved Costa Rica. She'd shopped tiny craft fairs and ate fresh seafood and exotic-to-her spices. For more adventure, she'd gone swimming with huge turtles, got to see sloths, and even went zip-lining. They were staying in an eight-bedroom luxury vacation rental with the rest of the band and their security.

Tonight, Lynx, River and Simon had gone out to a club. Gray stayed in, and the last she saw him, he was in the music room playing piano. She and Justice were piled in a huge bed, gauzy curtains floating from the breeze coming in off the sea, the two of them searching for houses in San Diego.

She wrinkled her nose at the sleek two-story. "That one is too modern. It looks like an office building."

Justice titled up one side of his mouth. "You're fixated on the Spanish-style one that has the kitchen the size of my dad's entire house."

"It's beautiful, and you liked it when we toured it before we left San Diego." She really wanted that house. "It's too expensive." Sighing, she leaned back against the pillows. "This isn't the time to buy anyway. You have more than half a year left on your tour."

"We need a home. Together."

Yep, they did, and she had the solution. "I agree, so what if we rented or leased through the end of your tour?"

"Leased?" He seemed to ponder it. "It won't really be ours."

"No, but it will give us our own space, and we'll have a better idea of what works for us after living in it and a clearer picture of our financial status."

He touched his index finger to the house Beth was obsessed with on the screen. "You love this house and it's for sale, not a lease or rental."

"It's been on the market for a while. We could ask if the seller is willing to do a lease with option to buy."

The corners of his eyes crinkled in amusement. "Are they?"

Liza held up a hand. "I didn't ask our real estate agent yet. I wanted to talk to you first. We do this together."

"Let's ask." He shut the laptop and put it on the floor. "We might have gotten ourselves a home."

Bubbles of excitement burst in her belly. She rolled over and straddled her husband's waist. "I love that house!"

He laughed a deep, rich rumble. "I know." He dragged his gaze down her throat, and over her naked breasts. Then lower to her belly and spread legs. "Now this is a billion-dollar view." His voice was low and bubbling with suggestion.

She returned the favor, taking a visual tour of his long nude body built of lean muscle, wicked drive and insane talent. Drawing a fingertip over her favorite tat, she grinned. "Think you can afford a private showing, Rock Star?"

"Greedy woman. You already have my heart, what else do you want?"

She leaned down, enjoying the way he fixated on her swaying breasts. "I want to feel and taste every inch of you, until I own you heart and soul."

His eyes flared hot. "Deal."

She leaned down and made good on the bargain. Teasing and tormenting him until his control snapped and filled her with joy. When he rolled her to her hands and knees, drove his cock into her with wild abandon, while telling her how fucking much he loved her...

That was priceless pleasure mixed with profound love.

A half hour later, she heaved herself out of bed and went to the bathroom. When she returned, she found Justice staring at his phone. Concern tightened her stomach. "Something wrong?"

"Not sure. My dad sent a link to a video. It's on a tabloid site. Dad said Nikki Poole was paid thousands for this."

Nikki? She'd been on TV a couple times for her crying apology tour, attempting to salvage something out of the ashes of her life.

"Paid her for what?" Liza'd heard she was trying to get a gig on some low-budget reality show, probably to pay for the lawyers she desperately needed.

"Let's find out."

She crawled back into bed and propped up against pillows. Justice pushed play.

"I'm Kurt Huff, and this is Afterburn! Tonight, we have a bombshell to drop on you. We've acquired the exclusive rights to an audio tape of Nikki Poole and Gene Hayes. We verified them with audio and voice recognition specialists. They're the real deal, and the documents authenticating that are on our website."

Liza's mouth dried. "Oh my God."

"The first male voice you will hear speaking is Gene Hayes, and the second voice is Nikki Poole." Kurt spent a few minutes detailing Gene and Nikki's histories and connection to Liza. Then he said, "Now let's listen to the tape."

The image of a voice spectrum analyzer appeared as the clip began. "Ace said you have something I want to hear about. Talk."

Liza instinctively drew back at that hated voice. "Hayes." He was talking about Ace, the lead singer of Jagged Sin.

Justice nodded his agreement.

"I did what you said. I wrote the book and I got the deal," Nikki said. "I want a guarantee, Gene. I've set up a whole publicity campaign for you and Jagged Sin. I want something in writing."

"Are you on crack, bitch?" Hayes shot back. "I'm risking enough talking to you. You'd better be damn sure no one ever finds that phone."

"They never found the last one, did they? I destroyed it and scattered the pieces in the ocean. I want a guarantee that when Jagged Sin wins and you replace Ace as the lead singer—"

Liza hissed at that revelation. She'd suspected that was his plan, but to hear it so plainly stated shocked her. "Ace has to be shitting himself."

Nikki's continued, "—I'll get the position of Director of Communications for World Rock Stage. Can't you do something like the nondisclosure agreements you did with the families of those girls you paid off?"

Justice whipped his head around. "He told her that?"

Liza couldn't believe it either. "Bragging maybe?"

Hayes said, "Do I need to send someone to check if you're screwing me over? Didn't you learn the lesson the first time you opened your big mouth? You told that interfering bitch where I was staying in Paris and called me on the phone in front of her! What if she'd been videoing or taping that? Dumb cunt." He paused, then added in a more menacing tone, "I did enjoy the pictures of you getting that beating. Your skin bruises nicely, although your voice is shrill when you beg."

"No! I..." Nikki's voice trembled, sending the analyzer into jagged spikes and dips.

Holy shit. Liza shivered, and Justice put an arm around her, tugging her close.

Nikki cleared her throat. "I'm not threatening you or doing anything like that. I was just trying to make sure I get the job."

"Do what you've been told, and you will."

The tape stopped, and Kurt reappeared on the screen. "Didn't I tell you? A huge bombshell! We're going to take callers and discuss. It appears from this tape that Nikki Poole wrote the tell-all book about Liza Cade at Gene Hayes's direction."

"Jesus Christ, she actually taped conversations with Hayes," Justice said.

"And sold them to a sleazy tabloid for a chunk of money rather than going to the authorities who might have been able to offer her some protection. Money and revenge meant more to her than doing the right thing. Sad, and very, very dangerous."

"She wanted your life, and risked taping Hayes, thinking she'd get the same title you had, Director of Communications." Justice pushed a lock of her hair back and studied her face. "You guessed she had a tape, didn't you?"

"I suspected she might. My goal was exactly what I did, getting her to admit on video she'd worked with Hayes, and that set the ball rolling to ruin both of them.

She'd gathered all those pics and videos of me. Hayes outed her once to me, and Nikki was left holding a bag of trouble, resulting in an investigation. I figured that if she was working with Hayes again, she was just cagey enough to believe she could gain enough leverage to make sure he kept his end of the deal by taping their conversations."

"Turning the tables on Nikki and Hayes. First he used Nikki to smear you, and now you're using Nikki to destroy him. Brilliantly ironic justice."

"Don't forget Ace. I had no idea Nikki and Hayes were going to announce their plan to shove him out of the group and Hayes take over. That was a hell of a bonus. Plus, it's going to cause huge problems when Ace hears that Hayes planned to get rid of him all along."

Justice laughed. "Think he'll be pissed?"

Her amusement spilled out in soft chuckles, yet in the back of her mind lurked the beat of danger. Hayes had sworn to find and kill her, and she just kept feeding his hatred.

Once she hadn't cared much if she survived as long as Gene Hayes was either captured or died.

But looking up into her husband's eyes, she now had every reason to live.

The next day, Justice held Beth's hand as they headed to the airport for the next leg of their tour. Even after two weeks together, he still relished every moment with her. It didn't matter that they both had work to do. She was helping SLAM, although less and less now, working on her speech for the Woman of the Year Award, and playing with ideas for her next book while waiting for revisions from her editor.

They were together, and that brought him peace. He was looking forward to the next couple weeks of island-hopping in the Caribbean.

Once they boarded the plane, he sank into a butter-soft captain's chair and tugged Beth down in the one next to him. She was teasing Lynx about something, and when she laughed, he couldn't help smiling in response.

Even Simon lounging on the couch smiled. Lynx threw a pillow at her, which bounced off her arm and River, walking through the cabin, caught it with his catlike reflexes. He lobbed it back at Lynx.

Gray brought up the rear and frowned. "When I saw pillow fight on the entertainment for this flight, I wasn't envisioning River and Lynx. I was thinking hot women."

"That's 'cause you're sexist." Lynx got up, went to the galley, got himself a beer and dropped back onto the couch and asked Liza, "Is it true you made Oprah's Most Anticipated Books list?"

"Hell yeah," Justice said.

Liza sighed. "You have to stop doing that, Rooster."

He shot her a grin. "You need your own public relations department these days." Ever since Tantor Media announced Beth as their Woman of the Year candidate, she'd shot to the top of trending lists. "Did she tell you that Rock Wives wants to do a special on her in conjunction with the Tantor Media Gala? They'll run it live on the Rock Wives special with cuts of interviews with her. They'll tape most of it when we get back to the States, but they're also sending a crew to get some footage of her on this next part of the tour with us. They've suggested we have her sing with us again."

"No!" Beth nearly shouted. "I'm not singing."

Lynx laughed. "Come on, you weren't that bad. I can drown out your pitchy parts with a drum solo."

"Don't mess with me, drummer boy, or I'll hide your sticks and tell the world you cry at chick flicks."

"That the best you got?" Lynx said.

"No, but I thought saying you sleep naked with a man-sized clown doll was going too far."

Gray burst out laughing. Lynx held up his beer bottle in a salute. "Now that's creative."

"And disturbing," Simon shuddered.

Justice grinned, grateful that Beth and his band were all comfortable with one another. He would get her onstage if he could, but ultimately it was her decision.

Gavin strode in, phone plastered to his ear. "Yeah, got it. Excellent. I'll tell them." He hung up, and a shit-eating grin spread over his face. "I have news."

Simon sat forward. "What?"

"Jagged Sin has been officially disqualified from the contest. World Rock Stage is announcing it today. They've been notified. Oh, and 'Witch Hunt' has fallen so far off the charts, it's invisible. Done."

"Whoop!" Lynx shouted.

"It gets better. The U.S. Attorney General declared that the capture of the fugitive Gene Hayes has become a priority. The public is demanding his apprehension."

They all erupted into cheers.

"Wait!" Laughing, Gavin held up a hand. "The members of Jagged Sin will be arrested if they return to the United States. I don't recall the exact charges, but they obviously helped Hayes."

Justice shot up and pulled Beth into his arms. "There's no chance Hayes can use them to get into World Rock Stage now."

"He's ruined, isn't he?"

"Definitely," Gavin broke in. "You didn't let me finish. Seven women have come forward claiming to be his victims, and three have produced nondisclosure agreements and some pictures that were used to blackmail families into signing. All the girls were underage at the time of the assault."

Beth released him to hug Gavin then threw herself back in Justice's arms. "It's over. Hayes is done."

Justice could feel her relief and vindication. "Oh yeah. His big comeback failed, he was exposed by the woman he used to hurt you, and everyone knows now what a slimeball he is."

Hayes was destroyed.

But he wasn't dead or caged, which meant he was still a threat to Beth.

Chapter 27

TWO WEEKS AFTER RETURNING FROM the Caribbean, Liza's big night had arrived. She was nervous as hell but trying to ignore the cameras following her and enjoy the whole experience of being Tantor Media's Woman of the Year. Liza and all the guests were having cocktails out on the patio of a country club located in the hills over L.A. with the stunning view of the city's bright lights spread out at her feet. The terrace was surrounded by gardens, and two lovely waterfalls added a soothing backdrop.

Keith from Indie Rock Broadcast which had the *Rock Wives* segment on its TV show, strode up to her, along with a cameraman. "Are you enjoying yourself?"

She nodded. Keith had always treated her fairly, and she'd liked working with him on taping the interview footage for the *Rock Wives* special this last week. "Very much, although I'm still awed by the honor tonight. It's pretty surreal to go from the most hated woman in rock to Woman of the Year."

His smile was genuine. "Did you ever imagine something like this?"

Liza looked around. Tantor execs, several musicians, rock stars, two of her favorite local authors, and most importantly were Justice and his bandmates, her mom, friends, and coworkers. Hank, Ethan, and several others from Savaged Illusions security team were here as well, mingling unobtrusively to provide protection for her and the band.

The only one missing was Noah, but he'd said he'd come later to her speech, even if he couldn't come inside. He was doing better, but sitting in a crowded ballroom wasn't his thing. Probably never would be, and that was okay. She loved him for trying to be here at all.

"No, I never imagined this," she answered honestly.

Justice materialized at her side and shook Keith's hand. "Hey, how's it going?"

Keith shifted his focus to Justice. "How does it feel to have a wife nearly as famous as you?"

"Like the world is finally discovering the heart of the woman I've fallen in love with." Justice added, "Did you know her book is optioned for a movie prepublication and will go into production soon?"

Keith opened his mouth to respond when a new voice interrupted.

"Liza Cade! There you are!"

Liza started to step back when she recognized the woman with the fuchsia-streaked hair rushing toward her.

"Wendy!" Liza hadn't seen the lead singer of Fury Run in person for more than a year.

"Move, Savage." The woman shouldered Justice out of her way and wrapped Liza in a fierce hug.

"I can't believe you're here!" Liza exclaimed.

Wendy let her go. "Flew in special for your big night. Congrats on being Woman of the Year, and a book deal, amazing! We women are kicking the boys' butts, yeah?"

Liza grinned. "Damn right." She took in Wendy's shiny gold bodysuit clinging to her generous curves, and thigh-high boots. Not many people could pull that off, but Wendy's huge personality and overflowing confidence made it work. "You look stunning. Are your label execs still trying to change you?" Liza loved the story when they'd tried to get her to slim down and revamp into a Disney pop star.

Wendy grabbed a champagne off a circulating tray. "They can dream. I'm not gonna do Britney. I'm all Wendy, all the time. No one's taking my chocolate cake away."

Liza raised her glass in a toast. "Amen." She took a sip. "So, was your new release 'Cradle to Grave' a plan all along? Or are you copying Justice and trying to get two songs in the top ten?" Their new release was damned good and shooting up the charts.

"It was a plan, unlike the savages stumbling into two top-ten hits because of you. Of all the sheer, dumb luck." She shook her head in bemusement. "Doesn't matter though, we're gonna make them cry big, fat, loser tears, and then do the loser dance on video." She looked over Liza's shoulder. "River's about to pee his pants trying to get your attention."

"Rude," River's voice floated behind her. "I was thinking of Liza. Surely she'd want to say hello to my date."

Date? She shifted her gaze to Justice. "River brought a date? Like..." Oops, had she said that out loud? With River and his date right behind her? Crap. She whirled around, wanting to see the woman who'd captured the infamous bassist playboy.

Liza stopped in surprise. Long dark hair and

familiar brown eyes... "Cassie!" She hadn't seen the girl in so long and hugged her, being careful not to pull her off balance from her prosthetic leg. "I can't believe you're here!"

"Justice and River wanted to keep it a surprise, is that okay?"

"More than!" She informed River, "I'm stealing your date. Em will be thrilled to see her, and I'll introduce her to my mom. Wendy, you too."

Liza took Cassie's arm and when they were far enough away, blurted out, "Are you really dating River?"

"Not yet, he thinks we're just friends," Cassie answered. "I'm working on changing that status."

Wendy's laughter rang out over the patio. "River's a goner." She glanced back. "He's staring at you right now."

Before Liza could ask anything else, Em, Sophie, Kat, Tess and her mom surrounded them. Wendy being Wendy announced Cassie's plan to snag the Playboy of Rock, and the women all piled on suggestions, some of them so outlandish, Liza feared she'd cry from laughter and ruin her makeup. Given all she'd lived through, that was a pretty damned good problem to have.

Jane Lewis, the director of Tantor Media's Charitable Foundation broke into their antics. "We're asking everyone to take their seats for dinner service. After that, we'll present the award."

Liza's nerves twanged. Oh God, was her speech good enough? What if she bombed? She'd begun edging into mild panic, when Justice took her arm. "Did I hear Cassie say she's trying to seduce River?"

He was distracting her, but it worked. "Does River like her?"

"He loves all women. But Cassie? Yeah, she's the one he thinks is too good for him. Dude has her on an imaginary pedestal."

Huh, that was interesting. Her thoughts scattered as they walked through the sliders into the huge room dominated by a stage at one end with an enormous picture of Liza on a big screen. Their table was front and center, adorned with fresh flowers, gleaming silver, and delicate china with a program atop the plate. Liza pushed her program aside, too nervous to see another picture of herself or read the inspiring quotes they'd asked for.

Dinner went quickly, with waiters serving soup and salad, fish or tri-tip, and finally dessert. She was sure it was delicious. Probably. She'd had a few bites while mentally reciting her speech.

The next thing she knew, Jane gathered her long skirt up and ascended the stage from the step by the doors to the patio. Cameras moved down the center, and Liza sipped her champagne, searching for anything resembling courage and trying not to think about this being livestreamed on *Rock Wives*. She was nervous enough.

"Ladies and gentlemen, welcome! I'm Jane Lewis, the Director of Tantor Media's Charitable Foundation of Hope. Every year, Tantor gives significant donations and grants to support the arts and causes that matter to our community. We reserve one very special award for a woman who makes a difference by speaking out against injustice and doing some form of activism to change our future. This year, the award ceremony is livestreamed by *Rock Wives*. I'd like to thank Indie Rock Broadcast, and *Rock Wives* for that, and for their generous donation. I'd also like to thank Mertz Publishing Group for their thoughtful donation, bringing the total of the prize money going to our Woman of the Year's charity of choice to one hundred and fifty thousand dollars."

Enthusiastic clapping rose then died off.

Jane smiled. "Please join me in welcoming Tantor Media's Woman of the Year, Liza Cade!"

Liza's mouth dried, and despite herself she turned to see Noah's empty chair at the table. She'd known he wouldn't come in, but she'd held a spot for him just in case. Was he here?

Justice stood and took her elbow to guide her to her feet. He leaned close for her to hear over the applause. "Dad's on the patio. He texted me."

As they walked toward the stage steps next to the sliders leading to the patio, she peered outside but didn't spot Noah.

Justice held her arm as she navigated the steps in heels, then stopped at the top, and kissed her. "This is your moment, Beth. Go."

She walked to the podium, where Jane held out a beautiful, foot-tall glass statue of a woman with her arms raised. The big stage lights trained on them glinted off the gleaming piece with the engraved plaque on the bottom.

Liza accepted the heavy award, her mouth desert dry and her heart banging around in her chest.

Jane hugged her and returned to her table, leaving Liza alone in the glare of the powerful lights, cameras, and a room full of people waiting for her to say something insightful and moving. Clutching the statue, Liza peered past the lights and went blank.

All her friends, Justice, her mom, everyone in the room was on their feet, clapping wildly.

Say something! Desperate to get control, she looked out the sliders to the patio and spotted a thin, older man with a dog sitting by his side. Noah. Wanting to make him proud, she leaned closer to the microphone. "Thank you! I'm so touched, seriously, thank you."

The clapping faded into a brief shuffling as they sat. "First, I'd like to extend my gratitude to Jane, who organized this entire event, and Tantor Media." She held up the statue. "This is lovely, and I'll cherish it." She took a second to find the shelf below the podium and set the statue next to a bottle of water. "I'm especially thankful to Tantor Media, to Mertz Publishing and to *Rock Wives* for their generous donations that will make a difference in young lives."

She went on. "Being chosen as Woman of the Year has deeply touched my heart and humbled my soul. I didn't know that so many people cared about one lone girl who many had characterized as nothing more than trash. Tonight, as I look out at all of you, I know that one lone girl did matter. We all matter. Each of you had a heroic moment in my life. Maybe it was something as simple as showing up to help me clean up a house after my father-in-law set a fire in an effort at matchmaking."

Shocked snorts erupted.

Liza raised her hand. "I swear, it's a true story." She looked at Sloane. "Or maybe it's when you offered me a job, and friendship." Her attention shifted to Sherry. "Or when you quite literally kicked my ass to teach me self-defense."

"Never let your guard down!" Sherry shouted.

Liza grinned. "There were days after a torturous workout that I called you a lot of things that didn't sound heroic, but you were always my hero, Sherry." She looked around the room. "All of you are because you took a moment to say a kind word, to share your stories of tragedies and triumphs, to care and make an effort. You see, my story begins not with crimes or terrible betrayals or even the rape of a fourteen-year-old girl. Those are the salacious details that the media and gossips love to pore over.

"Those are the things that made me a victim. I'm more interested in what makes us productive, successful and happy. What helps us find the strength in ourselves to heal, thrive and then reach out to help others. That's what brings me here tonight to share with you where I found heroes in my life.

"It begins with my mom, Amber Ranger. Mom, you were my hero when I couldn't fight for myself. Even when I had been drugged unconscious, I knew you were coming. I knew you'd save me. That was the night when I learned this lesson: Every child needs a hero to grow into their own power as a person."

She paused, looking into the camera and hoping that resonated.

"After my mom went to prison, my aunt stepped in, and she taught me structure and goals. She was hard on me, but reflecting back, I now see that my aunt believed in me." It was true, and she hoped Mari saw this. They might never heal their rift, but Liza wanted her to know that she appreciated the love and stability she'd provided when Liza had needed it.

"Later, my best friend Emily crashed into my life and refused to leave." Liza interjected some tales, making the audience laugh at Em's outrageously stubborn loyalty and her amazing bravery. "Emily taught me the priceless value of true friendship that supports you when you are in your most desperate moments, and calls you on your mistakes when you screw up. The kind that offers to fill your ex's car with opened cans of spoiled tuna." She grinned at Justice.

"Dude, you were so close to that fate."

Justice shot a glare at Em.

Her friend gave him a finger wave.

Liza went on, "Another hero came into my life." She turned her gaze to the man and his dog on the patio. "Noah Cade is the closest thing I have to a real father, and the strongest man I know. Noah hasn't let pulverized bones, burns or significant brain trauma or what we call PTSD—but is truly so much more complicated than a label—stop him from trying to be there for the son he loves. Noah saved my life once, but more than that, he's shown me how to survive even when we don't want to. Noah, I know I'm not your daughter, because, well, that would make Justice my brother."

More snickers.

"But you, Noah, made me feel loved like a daughter, and that's what counts."

Liza smiled at her husband. "When I met Justice, he burned with a ferocious and beautiful flame that I couldn't walk away from, and yet I was terrified if I stayed too close, I'd get singed. That fire called to me, intrigued me, and enticed me."

She paused, scanning her friends. "Yes, I got scorched, but I got so much more; a husband, friend and lover who has refused to let me stand in the warm shadow of his flame, but instead pushed me to let my own flame burn as bright and high as I can reach. Justice didn't know me as a child who needed a hero, but a woman who needed to learn how to be her own hero."

She took a sip of the water resting next to her statue. "I had a dream, a quiet, secret dream I told no one until the day I confided in Justice I wanted to write a book. From that moment, he encouraged me, cajoled me, and even bribed me with peanut butter cups to go for it. So I did, I loved it, writing every spare moment even through my pregnancy."

Liza paused again, letting the camera see her truth.

"Then we lost our child, snuffing out my flame, my passion and, I thought, my love for my husband. I retreated from the world, I refused to talk to Justice, and deleted all the copies of my book. I did two things: I survived and I worked.

"But like my mom, like my best friend and like his dad, Justice was my hero. He wouldn't let me slip away. When no one else, including him, could break through my pain, he did the one thing, the only thing I think, that could touch my heart.

"You see, through all this, through losing his daughter and his wife blaming and rejecting him, Justice kept my book. He guarded my dream when I no longer could. When he determined I was ready, he sent my book back to me. It didn't end there. He badgered me, challenged me, and countered every argument I gave him until I wrote the damned book just to make it stop."

The audience laughed, and Liza smiled at the memory.

"The truth is, that book was the only way I could express my feelings and cross the bridge from being trapped in grief to living again. Justice knew that. Justice has taught me that love is not just accepting who you are, but pushing you to shine your brightest in the good times, and being the keeper of your flame in the bad. Real love doesn't fear your partner's success, real love revels in it."

His smile was like a warm brush of love over her skin and against her heart.

"These heroes have shaped my life, given me the

hope to survive, the courage to fight back for as long and hard as it takes, and given me the push I needed to go after my goals and passions. So tonight, as Tantor Media Charitable Foundation of Hope, Mertz Publishing and *Rock Wives* are generously giving a hundred and fifty thousand dollars to the charities of my choice, I've chosen two that embrace that lesson my mom taught me all those years ago: Every child needs a hero.

"I'd like to give the first gift to The Drake Vaughn Center for Boys in honor of Drake Vaughn, who had a profound impact on my life and Justice's, and many others in this room tonight. And the second gift to SLAM Heroes in the name of our daughter, Savanna Rose Cade. She didn't get to take a single breath in this life, but we hope with this donation, she can be someone's hero too.

"Thank you all, and now, go out into the world and be someone's hero."

Applause exploded like fireworks, so loud she flinched and actually stumbled back. Wait, that boom was too loud for applause—

A hand grabbed her arm. Shocked, Liza spun. The face she saw gut punched her, ripping the air from her lungs. Dark malevolent eyes, black hair around a thin hawklike face.

Oh God.

It was Gene Hayes, and he was holding a gun.

Chapter 28

JUSTICE LEAPT TO HIS FEET, clapping and hooting. He was so damned proud of Beth. He turned to the left to meet her at the steps—

Boom!

Amber fell into him. People screamed. Ben scrambled over the table, leapt to the floor, pulled Amber down.

Something had splattered on his shirt. Blood. Not his. Amber's.

A split-second later, understanding dawned. Gunfire. Amber shot. Beth! He snapped his head up to the stage. Gene fucking Hayes loomed there with a gun to Beth's head.

He glared down at Justice. "You're all going to watch this fake Woman of the Year die."

Rage exploded. How the hell had Hayes gotten in here? Didn't matter now. *Move. Do something!* He took a couple steps when Hayes moved the gun and fired. Terrified shrieks. A loud voice called over the melee, "Shit, Derek's down!"

Justice processed that at light speed. Derek, one of their security team. Goddammit. Two people shot. He glared at Hayes, who'd jammed the barrel against Beth's temple again. She flinched. Justice growled low in his throat. The primal need to get to her nearly overpowered his rational brain.

Hayes curled his lip. "One more step and I blow her head off, Cade. Anyone moves, I'll splatter her damned brains all over this stage."

Justice forced his muscles to lock down until he could figure out how to save Beth. Had any of the security team gotten out of the room before Hayes saw them? Could they get to her from backstage? Trying to keep his head still, he glanced around. A shadow moving outside caught his attention. He risked turning enough to see his dad and Radar walking quiet and slow toward the door that led to a hallway and backstage.

Think. He returned his full focus to Hayes, not letting himself dwell on Amber or Derek getting shot. *Focus on keeping Beth alive and be ready.* His dad wasn't armed, but the band's security team was. All they needed was a distraction to move that gun far enough from Beth's head for one of the team to get a shot at Hayes. Justice had to trust Hank and Ethan, or the others would shoot if they got the opportunity.

Beth was so pale, he wasn't sure how she was staying upright. *Come on, baby. Don't panic now.*

Justice edged up another few inches, determined to keep Hayes's concentration on him. "How do you think this is going to end?"

Hayes smirked. "That stupid cunt Nikki Poole is dead. Cut her throat for being a rat. Amber Ranger is dying and on her way to hell where whores like her belong. This is going to end with all the goddamned bitches who fucked up my life getting what they have coming."

Beth gasped and tried to move.

Hayes smashed the barrel of the gun deeper into her temple. His fingers clawed into her biceps. "I had everything! I was a rock god, and I could screw any chick I chose. Especially the young ones." His eyes shone with sick glee as he shook Beth. "I had her first, you know. She loved it. Begged for it. Woman of the Year, ha!"

Justice's muscles twitched and jumped with the need to get up there and slam the bastard's face into the wall until he'd smashed the words from his throat. If he tried, the fucker would shoot Beth.

"She was a whore even then. Now she's a dead—"

A knee-high shadow shot out from one side of the stage, barking and growling.

Hayes whipped his head around.

Beth turned enough to swing her hands, which were clutching the glass statue, into Hayes's face. The force knocked Hayes's gun arm away. He yelped as his head snapped back. Blood spurted from his mouth and nose.

Before Hayes recovered, Justice's dad flew out onto the stage and crashed into Hayes. They hit the floor with a thud.

Justice leapt up on the platform as Hayes threw Noah off and rolled to his feet with blood pouring from his torn mouth and busted nose.

"You cunt!" He spat out a tooth and ran toward Beth.

Justice rammed into him, hurtling him to the floor and straddling his waist. Hayes swung his right arm. Justice caught his hand and twisted viciously.

Crack!

Hayes bowed beneath him, screaming in agony from his busted hand and wrist. Blood gushed from where Beth had smashed her trophy into his face, splitting open a gash from his lips up the side of his cheek to his eye.

"Justice, I've got him." Hank laid a hand on his shoulder. "Police are coming. Derek and Amber are stable. See to Liza."

Justice looked down one more time into the face of the man who'd raped and then tormented his wife for a decade afterward. A primal urge to kill him burned. When he took in the cocksucker's ruined face torn down to his cheekbone, deep satisfaction checked the urge to kill. Let him live in a cage and see the damage Beth had done for the rest of his miserable days.

He leaned closer and said, "That woman you called trash and a whore really fucked up your face with her Woman of the Year trophy. Guess she proved who the real winner is tonight, didn't she?" He smiled with pride in his wife's amazing resilience and rose.

Sirens wailed, and uniformed men and women poured into the building. His dad and Radar both stood in front of Beth as if guarding her from Hayes in case the bastard tried to get up. As soon as Justice started toward her, his dad moved aside.

Beth rushed into his arms, shaking uncontrollably. "My mom! Is she—?" Her voice broke.

He surveyed the room. "Your mom's alive, sitting up and looking this way. Em's with her, and Ben's taking care of Derek, who's swearing like a sailor. We're all alive." Thank fuck. He touched the red mark on her temple. Slightly burned and bruised from the gun barrel. He fingered the red marks on her upper arm from the bastard's grip.

"I'm okay."

He tugged her against him, holding her tight,

needing to feel her breathing, her heart beating against his chest. He could have lost her. This amazing woman who'd taught him what real love was and brought his dad back into his life. The thought was unbearable.

But his dad and Radar had come to the rescue, giving Beth the chance to fight back. Justice ignored Hayes on the floor, still screaming about his slashed-up face and busted hand.

He was done. They'd defeated the reaper.

Together.

With Justice's arms around her, her thumping heart and racing adrenaline calmed. It was over. Hayes had tried to kill her mom, shot one of Savaged Illusions' security team members, and fully intended to kill her.

Now he sobbed in a puddle of self-pity about his ruined face and smashed hand.

She clung to Justice, feeling his warmth and strength.

"Wait, Noah." She turned her head to search for him.

"He's down with your mom."

Liza spotted Noah on a chair, while Radar licked Amber's good arm and nuzzled her with extraordinary gentleness. "I need to go to her."

Together they walked down the steps, then Liza crouched. "How bad, Mom?"

"Hurts like fiery hell." She grimaced, her skin pale and lined with pain. "Ben said it's a deep flesh wound. Needs treatment, but I'll be okay. I was so scared for you. I couldn't do anything, couldn't save you."

Liza laid a hand on her mom's thigh, relieved to see the spark of fury in her eyes. "You already saved me the first time he attacked me when I was fourteen. You can't have all the glory."

Her mom's compressed lips twitched in a ghost of a smile. "You did good. I saw the way you hit him with—"

"This isn't over, bitch!" Hayes screamed as two cops dragged him down the stairs from the stage. "I killed Nikki. She couldn't hide from me, and neither will you. I'll kill you!"

Liza studied the swelling, bloody remnants of the face that had haunted her nightmares for far too long. She gave him her sweetest smile. "Have a nice life in a cage. I'm sure your cellmates will love your new facelift. Oh, and the fact that you raped children."

His eyes flared ugly. "You know how easy it was to get to you? I stole an ID and keys from a grounds-keeper. I'll do it again! No one's going to convict me, I'm famous! You're nobody!"

Wow, he'd really lost it. Prison was going to be a stark reality check. "You're boring me with your B-movie lunatic raving."

"You can't talk to me like that! I'm Gene Hayes! A rock star! You're nothing but trash! A whore..." His voice trailed off as the cops lugged him out to a cop car, or ambulance, or maybe even a garbage truck for all she cared. As long as he couldn't hurt the people she loved, or anyone else, she was satisfied.

Liza refocused on her mom. Hayes had taken too much, and she wasn't giving him another ounce of anything. Not her attention, anger, fear, or grief. He would rot in prison. Her mom was free, and once she healed, she'd have a full life.

Justice put a hand on her shoulder. "Ambulance crew coming in for Derek and your mom."

Liza nodded. "I love you, Mom."

With her good arm, she touched Liza's face. "I love

you, Beth. You are the one decision in my life I've never regretted."

Beth kissed her mom's cheek then moved aside for the paramedics to take care of her.

Once her mom was safely in the ambulance and they assured her they'd meet her at the emergency room when they could, Justice took Liza in his arms. "You okay?"

Ethan was arranging to drive them safely to the hospital after they talked to the cops, but right now, she leaned into Justice.

"No, but I will be." After a second, she added, "I believe him that he killed Nikki." She hated that it had come to that. She'd never really understood why Nikki made so many bad choices.

"Yeah."

Liza tilted her head back. "You didn't kill Hayes."

"Wanted to." He laid his hand on her cheek. "You told me how you felt about me killing him, and since he was no longer a threat, I honored that." He lifted one side of his mouth. "Using your Woman of the Year trophy to bash in his face proved what I've been saying all along."

"What's that?"

"You're a badass." He framed her face with his hands. "I love you, Beth. You're my song, the woman who owns my heart now and forever."

"I love you, Justice. The only place I want to be is with you. You're my home."

She'd finally found her home in the unlikeliest of places.

The heart of a rock star.

Epilogue

A YEAR LATER, LIZA LET Justice help her out of the car of the circular driveway of the home they'd closed on two months ago after Savaged Illusions won the World Rock Stage contest and became part owner in the group. By then, the contest was just for bragging rights, since the original group that had fought to bring Gene Hayes in agreed to be bought out, leaving two openings rather than one.

Savaged Illusions won their spot fairly. Fury Run bought in soon after, bringing some much-needed female influence.

Speaking of strong female influences, her mom rushed out to pull open the doors to the backseat, with Noah right behind her.

Radar, who evidently had more manners, came up to Liza, sat and waited.

Reaching down, she pet the dog. "Thank you, buddy. Glad someone cares about me. You know, the brand-new mom who just gave birth to twins a bare forty-eight hours ago."

Radar preened, his tail wagging in joy.

"Should I trust those two?" Justice said. "They won't drop our children, will they?"

Liza smiled up at him. "Not a chance. Did you see them practicing with the car seats?"

He grinned as he rolled up on the balls of his feet while his dad and her mom each eased a car seat from the back of the SUV.

"Relax," she told him.

"Are you laughing at me?"

She snorted. "Every chance I get, Rock Star."

"In the house," Amber ordered. "We don't want the babies to get cold."

"It's eighty degrees," Liza pointed out as Justice helped her up the three steps, through the atrium and into their Spanish-style home. The scent of fresh herbs and flowers surrounded her. She guessed something was cooking in the kitchen, while the source of the floral scents was from the bouquets all over the house from well-wishers.

Noah set the car seat he carried on the big coffee table and gently lifted out the pink bundle. "Addison Grace, my beautiful girl." Holding her in his stronger right arm, he softly touched the cheek of the sleeping child.

Liza got a lump in her throat. Noah may be scarred and still struggling with PTSD, but he'd shower these two children with love and teach them compassion and acceptance. He was doing even better since his hip replacement surgery had reduced some of his chronic pain.

Not to be outdone, Amber freed the blue bundle, lifting him easily and laying a kiss on his head. "Sebastian Noah, the sweetest boy ever."

"Ha, let's see how sweet you think he is when he gets hungry," Liza said. "That boy is demanding."

Her mom would teach these two how to live big, make mistakes and grow from them. Amber Ranger was a very different woman than she'd been the first years of Liza's life. She owned the transgressions of her past and embraced the life she had today. Watching her now, it was hard to believe she'd been shot in the shoulder a year ago.

Amber looked up. "I knew a girl like that. You insisted on eating every two hours."

"Oh man, feeding two babies every couple hours?" Liza mock-complained. So far, her son was the hungrier of the two. The longest he'd gone was three hours.

"We'll help." Noah sat on the couch and let Radar smell the baby's feet. Radar took a sniff, sat and laid his head on Noah's leg next to the child's foot.

Justice went to his dad. "Here, let me give her to Beth, and I'll take Sebastian. We need to show the babies their room."

Liza hid a smile and resisted the urge to tell him the babies weren't too interested in their surroundings yet. Or the wall she and Justice had spent months designing, then hired the best artist to render their concept. And okay, she wanted to show the babies too. She accepted Addy, and they walked their babies down a hallway, past Liza's light-filled office with its own little courtyard, the extra bedrooms that her mom, Noah and other guests used, into the nursery next to the master suite.

Despite having seen the mural for weeks now, it still took her breath away. In the center was the most exquisite soft yellow rose, and on two sides of the flower, baby-blue gossamer wings rose and curved in a perfect arc over each crib. Her heart swelled at the achingly sweet beauty of it and the symbolism.

She walked Addy to the wall, holding up the sleeping child.

Next to her Justice did the same with Sebastian.

There were no words; they didn't need them to talk to their firstborn daughter. Instead, they showed Savanna her brother and sister, and then laid each child in their crib beneath the wings of an angel.

Justice took Liza in his arms. "Any idea how we're going to manage twins, the careers of a rock star and a bestselling author while keeping our parents out of trouble?"

Liza grinned. "Nope, not a clue."

"Yeah, me either." He framed her face in his palms, his eyes boring into her. "But I want to find out." He kissed her and pressed his forehead to hers. "All in, baby."

Her chest swelled with love for this man, their children, and the chaotic and joyous life ahead of them. "All in, Rock Star."

Other Books by Jennifer Lyon

THE SAVAGED ILLUSIONS SERIES

Savaged Surrender, a novella

SAVAGED ILLUSIONS TRILOGY
Savaged Dreams (Book #1)
Savaged Vows (Book #2)
Savaged Devotion (Book #3)

THE PLUS ONE CHRONICLES TRILOGY

The Proposition (Book #1)
Possession (Book #2)
Obsession (Book #3)
The Plus One Chronicles Boxed Set

THE WING SLAYER HUNTER SERIES

Blood Magic (Book #1)
Soul Magic (Book #2)
Night Magic (Book #3)
Sinful Magic (Book #4)
Forbidden Magic (Book #4.5 a novella)
Caged Magic (Book #5)

Jennifer Lyon writing as Jennifer Apodaca

The Sex on the Beach Book Club
Good, Bad & Sexy, a novella

Writing as Jennifer Apodaca

ONCE A MARINE SERIES

The Baby Bargain (Book #1)
Her Temporary Hero (Book #2)
Exposing The Heiress (Book #3)

About the Author

Jennifer Lyon is the pseudonym for USA Today Bestselling Author Jennifer Apodaca. Jen lives in Southern California where she continually plots ways to convince her husband that they should get a dog. After all, they met at the dog pound, fell in love, married and had three wonderful sons. So far, however, she has failed in her doggy endeavor. She consoles herself by pouring her passion into writing books. To date, Jen has published more than twenty books and novellas, won numerous awards and had her books translated into multiple languages, but she still hasn't come up with a way to persuade her husband that they need a dog.

Jen loves connecting with fans. Visit her website at www.jenniferlyonbooks.com or follow her at https://www.facebook.com/jenniferlyonbooks.